A Frigh... ...ght

Katharine came instantly awake, ears straining. What had wakened her? Was there somebody in the house?

Nobody could get through the security system, she reminded herself as lightning lit up the storm-tossed yard. *Besides, anybody would be crazy to come out in this downpour to rob us.*

The wind flung handfuls of rain against her window. In flashes of light she saw maples and hickories flailing the air like demented creatures. She must have heard a branch falling, or a transformer blowing out. Still, she was not likely to sleep again. No matter how accustomed a person is to being alone, it is hard to recover from a fright in the night.

She heard a thump in Tom's library below. She snatched up her cell phone from under a pillow and leaped from her bed. She tiptoed to the door, opened it slowly, and peered into the hall. Everything was in utter darkness, but she heard little whispers of movement downstairs. For a joyful instant, she thought Tom had flown home to surprise her, and was getting a snack before coming upstairs. Then the narrow beam of a flashlight reflected on the staircase wall and somebody bumped into something and swore softly.

Tom knew his way around the house in the dark and swore more intelligently than that ...

By Patricia Sprinkle

PATRICIA SPRINKLE

A Family Tree Mystery

Death on the Family Tree

AVON BOOKS
An Imprint of HarperCollinsPublishers

AVON BOOKS
An Imprint of HarperCollins*Publishers*
10 East 53rd Street
New York, New York 10022–5299

Copyright © 2006 by Patricia Sprinkle
ISBN: 978-0-06-081968-2
ISBN-10: 0-06-081968-5
www.avonmystery.com

First Avon Books paperback printing: January 2007

Avon Trademark Reg. U.S. Pat. Off. and in Other Countries, Marca Registrada, Hecho en U.S.A.
HarperCollins® is a registered trademark of HarperCollins Publishers.

Printed in the U.S.A.

10 9 8 7 6 5 4 3

To Jim Huang,
who asked the inciting question

Primary Characters

Katharine Murray
Tom Murray, her husband
Dr. Florence Gadney, retired Spelman College professor
Dr. Hobart Hastings, Emory University history professor
Dutch Landrum, Katharine's father's best friend
Posey and Wrens Buiton, Tom Murray's sister and her husband
Hollis Buiton, their youngest daughter, a recent college graduate
Zachary Andrews, Hollis's high school classmate
Amy Slade, another high school classmate
Rowena Slade, Amy's mother
Brandon Ivorie, Amy's half brother
Napoleon Ivorie III, Amy's grandfather

Deceased but important:
Sara Claire Everanes, Katharine's mother's sister
Walter Everanes, her husband
Lucy Everanes, Walter's sister
Ludwig Ramsauer, Austrian exchange student
Georg Ramsauer, director of archaeological excavations for the Hallstatt Celtic site, Salzberg, Austria, in the mid-nineteenth century.

Acknowledgments

This book owes a major debt to *The Celts: Europe's People of Iron,* one of Time-Life Books' Lost Civilizations series (Alexandria, VA, 1994), in which I first encountered Hallstatt and the work of Georg Ramsauer. His story planted the seed from which this story grew.

I required the help of many experts to make the book as accurate as possible. Rebecca B. Moore, Curator of Decorative Arts at the Atlanta History Center, explained how Katharine might establish the identity of an archaeological artifact, unsnarled one major plot knot, and suggested the history professor. Mike Brubaker and his staff at the Kenan Research Center at the history center patiently introduced me to one method of tracking genealogy. Sarah Gay Edwards, Latin teacher and friend, reminded me that Julius Caesar wrote extensively about the ancient Celts and provided me with an English translation of his work. Judy Kash of InVestments explained the process of making hand-dyed silk scarves. Ann Bass, former 911 operator and mystery lover, helped me get that procedure right. Linda Bowers of Due West Security answered questions about home security systems. The Public Affairs department of the Atlanta Police Department provided information about home invasions. Any inaccuracies are not theirs but my own.

I owe special thanks to four special Sisters in Crime: Margaret Maron and Carolyn Hart, who listened to the concept for the series and urged me to write it; Edith Walter, from the Sisters in Crime Chapter in Munich, who offered her assistance with the German; and Joan Hess, who founded the Bi-Delt Sorority (for Dutiful Daughters caring for elderly relatives) and was my mentor when I joined.

And where would any of us be without friends and relations? Elfi and Bill Houck helped greatly with the German. Miriam Machida and Priscilla Apodaca reviewed the first draft and made it a better book, and Priscilla and Paul also provided a retreat as the deadline loomed.

Finally, I thank my agent, Nancy Yost, for believing in this series, my editor, Sarah Durand, for strengthening it and bringing it to life, and my husband, Bob, for supporting my life's mission as his own.

Gallia est omnis divisa in partes tres,
quarum unam incolunt Belgae,
aliam Aquitani,
tertiam ei qui ipsorum lingua Celtae,
nostra Galli appelantur.

Gaul, as a whole, is divided into three parts,
of which one the Belgians inhabit,
another the Aquitanians,
the third those who in their own language are called Celts,
in ours, Gauls.

JULIUS CAESAR

Death
on the
Family
Tree

Chapter 1

Wednesday, June 7

Katharine Murray woke on her forty-sixth birthday and real-ized that nobody needed her.

She got the message slowly, not being at her best early in the day. She was halfway through brushing her teeth before she even remembered it was her birthday, which was sur-prising, considering how much she loved any cause for cel-ebration. She spat, rinsed her mouth, smacked her lips to get full benefit from the peppermint flavor, then crooned, "Happy, happy birthday, baby," as she leaned closer to the mirror for the world's first glimpse of herself at forty-six.

She looked remarkably like she had at forty-five: same heart-shaped face with prominent cheekbones and a dusting of freckles, same long auburn hair in a practical blunt cut so she could wear it in several styles, same golden-brown eyes that Tom, her husband, used to call topaz back when he still said things like that. With one fingertip, she traced what she hoped people thought were smile lines around her mouth, not teeth-clenching lines from raising two children to adulthood.

"Same old same old," she murmured to her reflection and padded back to her bedroom.

She didn't bother to change out of the cotton knit shorts and

T-shirt she slept in when she was alone in the house, just stumbled downstairs barefoot to fix birthday breakfast for one.

At the kitchen door she was stopped in her tracks by her first clear thought of the day: *Why did I re-do this kitchen? I don't have a soul to cook for.*

Tom left Atlanta each Monday morning to keep Washington lawmakers aware of the needs of his corporation's far-reaching empire, then returned each Friday night to spend the weekend playing golf, puttering at their lake house, or watching televised sports.

Their daughter, Susan, was happily climbing the lowest rungs of the New York Stock Exchange with visions of her own trader's jacket one day.

Their son, Jonathan, had tossed his Emory mortarboard into the air three weeks before and caught a plane to China to teach English for two years.

And with the deaths of her mother and two elderly aunts in the past eighteen months, Katharine's membership in the Bi-Delts—that vast sorority of Dutiful Daughters—had expired.

Aunt Lucy had died five days before, and with her death, Katharine was well and truly orphaned. Her parents had married late and produced only one child. They hadn't even had the foresight to provide her with cousins, which in the family-conscious South made her impoverished indeed. She had never felt family-poor in the years when she was creating a home in Buckhead (still Atlanta's most desirable neighborhood) for Tom and the children, meeting the increasing needs of her mother as she battled breast cancer and Aunts Sara Claire and Lucy as they became frail and sank gently to sleep. But now—

She reached for the carton of orange juice and informed the refrigerator, "All the people in my life have gone away and left me like a useless piece of driftwood on the beach of life. Do you realize it is my birthday, and for the first time in my life, I don't have a soul to celebrate with?" As she turned for a glass, she added over one shoulder, "And don't you think it's pathetic that a woman has to have the first conversation of her birthday with a refrigerator?"

She tried a few bars of "Happy birthday to you" while she filled the glass, but it is not a song that sounds best when sung to oneself.

At the breakfast table she lifted her glass in a salute. "To us, kitchen. To the unneeded of the world."

If the room felt unneeded, it didn't show it. Its pale yellow walls were bright and cheerful, hung with blue-and-white plates she and Tom had been collecting for years from countries they visited. The plates echoed Delft tiles behind the stove and blue-and-white plaid cushions on the white chairs in the adjoining breakfast room. Katharine was particularly proud of the bay window they had added by the breakfast table. Sunlight spilled through it across African violets that sat like rich jewels on the deep sill, and ran in a broad stream across the white tile floor—a floor that was finally possible now that the children were grown and no longer tracking in red Georgia mud. Just looking at the kitchen lifted her spirits.

"It's not the end of the world to spend a birthday alone," she announced as she considered breakfast options. "Shall I make eggs Benedict, to prove I matter? No, I don't matter that much. An English muffin will do."

Until that moment, she had been clowning, for Katharine was not gloomy by nature. But then, as she turned toward the bread drawer, she caught sight of her reflection in one of the new glass-fronted upper cabinets and drew a startled breath. In that light, her face was a mere transparency through which she saw rows and rows of glasses. She had

the dizzying sensation that she would spend the next thirty
or forty years growing increasingly invisible until she disappeared.

Or had she already?

"Oh, God!" she cried, clutching the cold granite countertop and taking short, shallow breaths of terror. "What am I
going to do with the rest of my life?"

It was a purely rhetorical prayer.

She never expected FedEx to answer.

The doorbell rang while she sat waiting for the muffin to pop
up from the toaster and her tea water to boil, wondering
which appliance would win the breakfast derby and whether
her entire future would consist of such fascinating moments.

Two large boxes sat on the stone veranda and a FedEx
man was heading down the walk to his truck. The Murrays'
house was up a hill and far enough from the street that deliv-
ery trucks always came up the drive.

"Thank you," she called. The Birthday Angel had come
through after all, providing a day scented with roses, a
mockingbird cantata, and presents before breakfast.

"Just a minute," the deliveryman called over one shoulder.
"There's more."

Katharine watched mesmerized as he carried stack after
stack of boxes to her door. So many presents? From whom?
Tom had never been wildly romantic even in their dating
days. Jonathan was the dramatic one in the family, but surely
he wouldn't ship so many things from China. And when did
Susan have time to shop?

Maybe they had ordered all this on the Internet. What a
thoughtful family!

The man staggered up the steps and deposited two more

boxes with a grateful "Oooph!" He wiped his hands on his shorts and announced, "That's the lot." He couldn't have sounded more satisfied if he had just moved a new family into the governor's mansion a few blocks away. He thrust a small metal pad toward her. "Are you authorized to sign for the lady of the house?"

Katharine was already scribbling her signature.

He craned his neck to look up at the pale gray shingles, white trim, and slate roof with its many gables. "Nice house they got here."

"Thanks." Katharine would have liked to chat a while longer, maybe tell him how lucky they had felt to find the house, how much they had enjoyed living in it for twenty years. Anything, really. She hadn't spoken to a human soul for twenty-four hours and could have used the practice. But he was already headed to his truck.

As he climbed in, she recalled his first words. "Hey!" she yelled after him, "I *am* the lady of the house." He was already backing down the drive.

Not until then did it occur to Katharine that she would have to lug all those boxes inside.

He'd brought ten, four very large. But even the daunting task of getting them into the house couldn't dampen her excitement. She felt like she had on her fourth birthday when she had realized all the presents at the party were hers.

Until she bent to read the return address: AUTUMN VILLAGE. Her excitement whooshed down an invisible drain.

These weren't birthday presents. They were Aunt Lucy's personal effects, shipped from the retirement home. Katharine had told the manager on Monday to distribute Aunt Lucy's clothes, furniture, and knickknacks to anyone who wanted them, and to ship her only a mahogany secretary that had belonged to Lucy's grandmother. He had either misunderstood or hadn't listened. From previous experience, Katharine could guess which.

"Happy birthday to me," she muttered to a robin seeking worms in the dewy grass. He gave an unsympathetic hop and flew away.

For one long minute she considered hauling every dratted box to the garbage cans, to be carried away. However, it was faintly possibly that one of the boxes contained something somebody in the family might want. She'd carry them into the music room and go through them there.

She picked up the first box with no idea at all that it was about to change her life.

She had chosen the smallest box. It was so old that the cardboard felt like it could dissolve in her hands, and unlike its companions—which advertised products Autumn Village bought in bulk—this one was dusty and had no printing on its sides. Somebody had put tan tape over older tape that had yellowed and grown brittle with age, and Aunt Lucy had penciled on one side, in her round schoolteacher's hand, CARTER.

Katharine could not recall any Carters connected with the family.

When she had lugged nine boxes inside, they practically filled the music room floor. What did that matter? The house had twelve rooms, and that one to the left of the front hall was the least used. The decorator who had re-done the downstairs several years before had claimed, "We are aiming for intimacy in here." When he had finished, Katharine had wondered what his experience of intimacy had been. The only furniture he had allotted the room were the baby grand piano, a red wing chair that had belonged to Tom's father and that not even sentiment could make comfortable, and her mother's mahogany pie-crust table, which wobbled. Over the oak floor he had spread a Bokhara rug that Katharine disliked, but which Tom assured her was a good investment. On top of her mother's wobbly table the decorator had set a ceramic bust of Beethoven that Susan had won in a piano competition. The composer wore such a ferocious frown that Jon had dubbed him "the angry *artiste*."

The rest of the decor consisted of dark red floral drapery, taupe walls with creamy woodwork, and mahogany bookshelves from floor to ceiling on each side of the fireplace. The shelves were filled with decorator-selected bric-a-brac and coffee table books Tom planned to read someday. As far as Katharine knew, nobody had been intimate in that room since it was completed.

Beethoven glowered down at the new clutter on the rug. "You can jolly well tolerate these boxes until I get around to opening them," Katharine informed him, "if I ever do." She knew what she would find: lopsided straw baskets, poorly carved wooden animals, cheap souvenir mugs, plaques depicting badly colored replicas of well-known paintings, and coffee table books about every country in the world.

Lucy Everanes had been a small, plain woman with the heart of a romantic. Nine months of the year she taught world history at the same private high school she had attended as a girl. Each summer she set off on what she called "my little adventures." She brought back enormous quantities of souvenirs, most of them schlock, and snapshots of herself perched on various animals, staring up at the Himalayas, or squatting beside a half-naked child. As a little girl, Katharine had loved to visit Aunt Lucy. She would listen to Lucy's latest adventures and play with her collection of wooden animals from around the world. At seven, she had

fiercely defended Aunt Lucy when Aunt Sara Claire had said
with disdain, "For a woman of education, culture, and breed-
ing, Lucy has exquisitely bad taste." As an adult, however,
Katharine doubted there was a thing in those boxes she
would want to display in her home.

She was carrying in the final box when the telephone
rang.

She would have let the machine catch it, except it might be
Tom or Susan, so she dashed through the dining room and
the adjoining butler's pantry to her kitchen desk, thinking—
as she always did when she made that dash, "We really need
a telephone at the front of the house." Gasping for breath,
she dropped the heavy box on the desk and snatched up the
phone before the fourth ring. "Hello?"

"Miz Murray?" The voice was nasal, one she didn't recognize at first. "This is Leona, over to Autumn Village, about
Miss Lucy's thangs. We give away the furniture and her
clothes, like you said, and folks was real glad to get 'em, but
Mr. Billingslea said you hadn't said nothin' 'bout her books
and her purty little thangs, so he shipped 'em all to you yesterday, overnight. He'll send you the bill for the shipping
when it comes."

Katharine was so staggered by the thought of what FedEx
would charge to ship ten unwanted boxes across town overnight, she nearly missed what Leona added. "He said to tell
you if you're still wantin' that old desk with the glass front
doors, you hafta bring a truck on over sometime today or
tomorrow to fetch it, 'cause he's needin' her unit for somebody else."

The calendar above Katharine's kitchen desk showed the
ordered gardens of Versailles. Why wasn't she strolling
through their well-clipped shrubbery instead of standing in

that Atlanta kitchen dealing with yet another crisis on her own? The thing she most disliked about Tom's working out of town was having to make all the decisions.

"I don't have a truck," she pointed out. That wasn't strictly true. Tom kept a little truck at their house on Lake Rabun. He used it to pretend he was a good old country boy after wearing a suit in Washington all week. Katharine used it to haul plants. However, Lake Rabun was hours away and she didn't want to fetch the truck and find somebody to help her wrap and move a valuable secretary—if it would even fit the small truck bed and if they could load and unload the piece without scratching it. She would then have to return to the lake for her car.

That was the moment when Katharine realized what Jonathan's years in China were going to cost *her*: muscles. Even though he'd lived in a dorm and later in an apartment while attending Emory, he'd always been just across town with strong friends willing to work for occasional Mom-cooked meals.

What was she going to do without him?

"I'm jist tellin' you what Mr. Billingslea said." Leona sounded miffed. "Miz Diamond down the hall says she'll take that piece if you're not wantin' the trouble of moving it."

"I'll have somebody come and get it. Don't you all give it away."

Katharine hung up and picked up her mug. The tea was stone cold, as was the English muffin. She put them in the microwave and moved to the window to figure out how to deal with this new crisis. Instead, she found herself wondering: *What do women with husbands around to make some of the decisions do with all that free time?*

It was astonishing how many things she had learned to do in the past twenty-four years: put in doorknobs, replace the inner workings of toilets, spackle holes in walls, re-grout tile, even re-glaze a window after Jon and a friend got over-exuberant with a baseball. She could afford to pay a handyman, but could seldom wait for one to work his way down to such trivia.

She wondered how one learned to install a telephone. Perhaps the music room could become the telephone room, as well.

A butterfly distracted her, calling her attention to how spectacular the view was from her breakfast table that lovely June morning. Beneath the window, bright Oriental and Asiatic lilies, blue veronica, red impatiens, and Shasta daisies looked well against a deep purple butterfly bush. She was so glad she had decided to put a butterfly and hummingbird garden beneath the bay in that patch of sun. Beyond the flowers, the walk down to the pool was cool and inviting, shaded by tall trees and planted with white astilbe, Japanese painted fern, and wide hostas in many shades of green. The grounds were a living testimony to the faithful work of Anthony, who came every week to mow, weed, plant, and transplant. He often told Tom, "The missus never thinks a plant can grow 'less it's been moved twice," but he came reliably and worked without complaint. That was all she ever asked of him.

Except—

Anthony had a truck.

She abandoned the view and headed to the phone.

Anthony's wife, who took calls for his business, assured Katharine he could and would be glad to move a piece of furniture that evening. She offered the services of their son, Stanley, a junior at Georgia Tech, to help Anthony, and suggested using the lawn service trailer so they wouldn't have to lift the piece so high. She even had some old quilts they could wrap the piece up in, and cord to secure it. "They'll fetch it for you by eight, Miz Murray. You just be home around eight-thirty to show them where to put it."

Sending up a prayer of thanks for faithful friends, Katharine called Autumn Village to tell them to expect him. Another crisis averted, she took her lukewarm tea and rock-hard muffin back to the table.

As she sat down, she wondered, *If I could rub a magic lamp and be granted three birthday wishes, what would they be?*

Would she wish Tom had an ordinary job where he went to work each morning after a tête-à-tête breakfast and returned home every evening for dinner, instead of leaving early on Monday morning and coming back late on Friday night? Not any more. She had loved having him home before the children came and while they were small, but he had been doing this weekly commute for so long now that she was comfortable with the pattern. She looked forward to weekends and marvelous trips together, but during normal weeks she enjoyed eating what and when she liked, watching her own television shows with sole possession of the remote, and having time for clubs, volunteer activities, occasional trips, and spontaneous outings with friends. When he was unexpectedly home for a week, she seemed to spend inordinate amounts of time cooking and stocking the fridge, and she never knew whether to stay home from meetings or go as she had planned.

Would she wish for the children to be small again? No. As fleeting as those years now seemed, at the time they had felt like an interminable round of car pools, sports practice, dancing and piano lessons, parties, and orthodontist visits. Katharine loved having grown-up children with whom she could have intelligent conversations and eat sushi instead of noodle soup.

Would she wish for her mother, Aunt Sara Claire, or Aunt Lucy to still be alive? Not unless they could be healthy and vibrant. She had hated watching their health deteriorate, still flinched at the memory of her mother's final pain. And for the past four years she had devoted many hours to making their phone calls, running their errands, doing their shopping, handling their paperwork, and driving them to and from doctor and hairdresser appointments, bridge parties, luncheons, and what Aunt Lucy called "our little outings." Taking on parts of their lives had required giving up equal parts of her own.

Still, now that she had her own life back, what was she going to do with it?

She did not know. That, she felt, was her tragedy.

Since one of Aunt Lucy's boxes sat on the table, she thought she might as well open it and see what it contained. Her paring knife made short work of the tape. Peering inside, she discovered that Mr. Billingslea's packers had swept things off shelves helter-shelter and willy-nilly.

Nice words, those, she thought, helter-shelter and *willy-nilly*. Exactly how Aunt Lucy collected her artifacts. She lifted out a lamp made from an ox horn, its shade painted with a Highland scene, then an African letter opener with an ibex inexpertly carved for the handle. She grimaced at a long string of beads made from what looked like mildewed peach pits, and tossed several worn, obsolete maps into the trash. The bottom was filled with out-of-date coffee table books. Would the drama department at Lucy's old school like any of her things to use as props? Katharine crossed to the refrigerator message board and made herself a note to call them. Then she scooped the things back into the box and carried it to the music room. As she set it down, her toe nudged that small, old box. What could it contain? It looked like Lucy herself had fastened it years ago and never opened it since. All the packers had done, apparently, was retape it.

She knelt beside it and puzzled again over that one word written on one side in Aunt Lucy's neat script: CARTER. Then she fumbled in the open box for the ibex letter opener and carefully slit the tape.

Chapter 2

Before she could lift the fragile flaps, the phone rang again. Hoping it was Tom, she tucked the small box under one arm and dashed back to the kitchen. With a surge of anticipation, she lifted the phone from its charger.

"Hey, Doll Baby. I wanted to call and wish my favorite little girl a happy birthday."

Katharine concealed her disappointment with extra enthusiasm. "Uncle Dutch! How sweet of you to call." Dutch Landrum had been her daddy's best friend. His wife was gone, like both her parents, and Chapman, his only child, lived up in Schenectady, New York, and seldom bothered to come home to see his dad. A couple of months earlier Dutch had sold his big house and moved into Autumn Village, just down from Aunt Lucy, and the two old friends had enjoyed each other in the brief time they'd shared a hall.

"I figured you might be a little lonely today, with Lucy gone and all." Dutch's voice was wistful.

"I was just going through some of her things," Katharine told him. "Mr. Billingslea sent me boxes and boxes this morning. I thought for a minute I'd gotten heaps of birthday presents."

He laughed with her, a sound that was mostly wheeze made up of age, whiskey, and too many cigars. "Lucy would have gotten a kick out of that. She was a great old gal." They shared reminiscences for a minute or two, until Dutch said with obvious regret, "Well, I'd better go. They're fixing to take us on another outing. Some lecture, I think, with lunch to follow. I was never so busy in my life until I moved here. I think they try to kill us with activities so they can resell our units."

"Any luck getting them to call you 'Dutch'?"

"That's what they finally *call* me," he emphasized the verb, "but every blessed piece of paper I get from the administration comes to Lionel Landrum. Remember, Shug, I'm countin' on you and Tom to make sure they put 'Dutch Landrum' on my cemetery marker. I don't want Chap carving 'Lionel Deutsch Landrum' in stone."

"We've got you covered," she assured him. "If necessary, I can always knock him down." That earned her another wheezy chuckle. When she and Chap were little, Katharine had frequently been punished for knocking him down. Only Dutch had admitted he needed it.

"You're still keeping my cartons safe?" he asked with a trace of anxiety.

"Absolutely. They have a place of honor in my attic." Dutch had brought over three boxes of things he hadn't had room for in his new home but wasn't ready to discard.

"That's good. Nothin' in them except some old college yearbooks and a few mementoes, but I might want to look through them again sometime. Well, I better go. Still have to put on my tie. Happy birthday."

Katharine smiled. Dutch hated wearing ties as much as any six-year-old but kept one hanging on his doorknob for when he went out. She pictured him tying it and stepping into the hall looking so natty that half the widows in the building would be after him.

Not until a minute later did Katharine realize he might

remember a Carter connected with Aunt Lucy. Dutch had known Lucy since they were children. But before she could dial his number, the phone shrilled with another caller.

The voice that flowed over the line this time was thick as honey and almost as sweet. "Oh, Katharine, I am so glad I caught you. I was afraid you'd already gone out to some old meeting, and I am at my wits' end. I don't know what I'm gonna do."

"What's the matter?" Katharine didn't know why she bothered to ask. Posey Buiton, Tom's older sister, had been pouring her problems into Katharine's telephone for twenty years, and they all began with the same word.

"Holly, of course—or Hollis, as she now insists on being called. Neither of my other girls ever changed their names." Posey's voice dripped with indignation.

Katharine set the old box on the kitchen table and headed to the cabinet for a tall glass. She tucked the phone between her ear and her shoulder, fumbled in the freezer for ice cubes and silently slid them into the glass, filled the glass with sweet tea, squeezed in a slice of lemon, and stirred with one forefinger—remembering too late that she had carried those boxes and hadn't washed her hands. With a shrug to dismiss the germs, she carried the tea over to the breakfast table and settled in for the duration. All that time, Posey had burbled on about the ingratitude of children who change the names their parents bestow upon them.

Katharine raised her glass in a silent toast to Hollis for having the gumption to stand up for her name. Who but Posey would give three daughters sensible names like Laura, Mary, and Hollis, then call them Lolly, Molly, and Holly? After Holly's birth, Posey had even considered changing her own name to Polly until Wrens, her easygoing husband, said with a wave, "Go ahead, Sugah. Do whatever you like. But

Polly sounds like a damned parrot to me." Tom claimed that Wrens Buiton was the only man in the world who could live with Posey for thirty years and still adore her.

Katharine had always had a soft spot for Hollis. The child was dark, thin, and intense, unlike her sisters. They had been cheerful blond children who enthusiastically played soccer and tennis, won ribbons on swim teams, and served as secretary or treasurer of every service organization at Westminster School. They had grown into robust young women who efficiently organized their own households around their children's sports practices and their own aerobics classes, tennis matches, and Junior League events.

Holly had not arrived until Molly was six and Lolly eight. When taken to join a soccer team, she had gone onto the field, plopped down to the ground, and spent the next hour drawing designs in the dirt. When taken to the pool, she floated on her back watching clouds and refused to race. While her sisters were improving their tennis at the Cherokee Town Club, Holly was badgering the maid to teach her to sew. While her classmates were showing off the latest styles from Saks, Nordstrom, and Neiman Marcus, Holly was stitching up outlandish concoctions from scraps of silk, feathers, and beads. When other girls were getting blond highlights, Holly was streaking her dark hair purple, green, and blue. When her peers applied to Agnes Scott, Vassar, Sewanee, and the University of Georgia, Holly announced that if she couldn't go to the Savannah Campus of the Savannah College of Art and Design, she wouldn't go to college at all.

"I swan," Posey had wailed more than once, "if I hadn't been awake for that child's birth, with Wrens right there beside me, I'd swear they switched her at the hospital."

Back when Holly and Jon were both in seventh grade, he had summed up the struggles between his cousin and her mother in succinct terms: "Holly hates exercise and good works." Katharine had thought that perceptive for a thirteen-year-old.

She also identified with Holly, for even after twenty-five years, she still felt out of step in Buckhead. It was not because she had not been born and raised there. Unlike most Southern cities, where leadership and wealth are passed from one generation to the next and lifetime friendships are forged in the cradle, Atlanta has always been cosmopolitan. Buckhead, its most prestigious community, probably contains as many newcomers as longtime residents. However, Katharine had observed that women who moved to Buckhead, no matter where they were born, tended to quickly take on the persona of Southern aristocrat and to settle into a natural habitat of tennis matches, aerobics classes, elegant luncheons, gala balls, and the events and board meetings of civic and charitable organizations.

Katharine had grown up in Miami, where her mother taught fifth grade in an inner city school and her daddy was a professor at the University of Miami School of Law, and her parents were strong believers in the biblical injunctions to do justice and care for widows, orphans, the outcast, and strangers. Her father had helped draft civil rights legislation for the state and had worked in numerous ways to help the stream of immigrants that poured into Miami after the Cuban revolution. Her mother had taken Katharine from the time she was tiny to help in soup kitchens, homeless shelters, and tutoring programs. Their home was a gathering place for those who wanted to discuss books and politics, but it was not lavish. Neither parent valued a big house, new cars, or expensive clothes, preferring to channel their money to organizations that helped the poor. So Katharine had arrived in Buckhead a bookish woman who hated exercise for the sake of exercise and preferred hands-on work like tutoring, mentoring, and an occasional day with Habitat for Humanity to buying expensive tickets for fund-raising galas. She often thought it a miracle that she and Posey were as fond of each other as they were, and she loved Hollis for daring to be different.

Hollis had recently graduated from SCAD and come home—which brought Posey's lament up to the present. "I don't mind her getting a job with that dinky little theater sewing costumes, although lord knows she won't get paid enough to live on, but last night she asked Wrens if she can move into that filthy old apartment over our garage—the one the folks who built the house put in for their chauffeur. Her sisters lived in nice apartments with college friends until they got married. Why doesn't Hollis find a couple of friends to live with?"

Katharine sipped tea and didn't bother to reply. Posey was sure to answer her own question. Sure enough—"Although if they had purple hair and wore nothing but black, I wouldn't want her to live with them. But she wants to work up there as well as live there. Says she'll turn the extra bedroom into a workroom. What are folks going to think? Our daughter working at home and living in our servants' quarters! Besides, the place is poky and hot—not even air-conditioned— and we haven't used it for anything since the kids used to play up there. I doubt if the plumbing still works."

That indignant outburst was simply a precursor to Posey's real complaint. All over Buckhead, carriage house apartments were being rented out to singles and newly-weds, and the Buiton apartment couldn't be too small, built over a four-car garage. Paying somebody to clear it out, fix the plumbing, and install air-conditioning wouldn't strain their bank account, either, since Wrens had inherited a thriving business from his father and at least doubled his fortune.

"What does Wrens say?"

Katharine spoke automatically, because she could wait no longer to see what was in that old box. While Posey answered, she lifted the flap and peered inside. All she saw were a small book and something wrapped in what looked like a piece of old white sheet.

Posey gave a huff of disgust. "You know Wrens. Nothing ever fazes him. He told her, 'Do whatever you want to with the place, Shug. Fix it up however you like and put it on my card. Just make it pretty, so your mama and I can rent it out after you get married, to support ourselves in our old age.' I told him, 'Don't encourage her,' but—"

"He's got a point." Katharine lifted out the book and began to turn its pages. "Carriage house apartments are going for high rents these days."

"I know, but—" Posey started off again down the trail of why she didn't think Holly ought to be living alone instead of with other people.

Katharine let her rattle on without listening. She was turning the pages of what appeared to be a journal, its leather cover faded to a soft caramel and its pages covered with spidery German in black ink. German? She had taken two years of German at Agnes Scott, two grueling years that convinced her she would never be a linguist. Still, she ought to be able to read some of this. Where had she shelved her old German/English dictionary?

"Are you listening?" Posey demanded.

"Of course." Katharine grabbed the phone before it fell off her shoulder. "I was wondering what your real problem is with Hollis living in your carriage house."

Something fell from the journal and fluttered to the floor.

She bent and retrieved a newspaper clipping, also in German, with a small inset of a man's picture. She was gratified to find she could translate part of the headline: [*CHEMIKER*] DIES IN ACCIDENT. The man, identified as Ludwig Ramsauer, had a lean face and an attractive mouth bordered by a thick mustache and a pointed beard. In one margin of the article, someone had scrawled "November 1950?????"

Katharine stared at those five question marks while Posey insisted, "It's not that I mind her living in the carriage house, at least for a while. But do you know what happened this morning? At breakfast, trying to be nice, I offered to give up my whole day to go look at wallpaper and floorings. I knew she was going to be out most of the day at some birthday party, but I figured I could get some ideas for what might look pretty up there, you know? But guess what Holly said." Posey's voice trembled and Katharine knew her blue eyes were wide with indignation under her tousled blond curls.

She slid the clipping back into the book. She would try to read it when she found her dictionary. Right then it was a distraction she didn't need. Posey was reaching the climax of her latest Holly crisis.

"Hollis, not Holly," Katharine reminded her.

"Holly—Hollis—whatever. She said she already knows what she wants to do with it. You *know* what she's like, Katharine. If she's allowed to do anything she wants, we could get purple walls with orange carpet. I can't stand to have her ruin that charming little apartment!"

They had finally reached the place where the pecan met the brittle.

Katharine didn't mention the carriage house's rapid metamorphosis from a poky old place to a charming little apartment. It was time to take Hollis's side. Part of why Posey called was to be persuaded Hollis wasn't really odd or stark raving mad.

"Hollis has had four years of training since high school," Katharine pointed out, "and she won an award for that wallpaper she designed. Besides, she's now got a degree in—"

Like a bull seeing red, Posey charged in that direction. "Fabric! A perfectly useless degree. What does one do with a major in fabric?"

"It was fibers," Katharine corrected her. How did Posey think her other two daughters were using their degrees? Did she picture Lolly reading French novels to her seven-year-old twins, or Molly discussing economics with her five-year-old son and two-year-old daughter?

"Fibers, then," Posey conceded grudgingly. "What can she do with that?"

Having had a long conversation with Hollis about that very subject over Christmas, Katharine could answer. "She can design fabrics for home and commercial furnishings, textiles for clothing and accessories, wallpaper, or even stationery. She took a lot of art history courses, too, so she could go into museum work in areas like clothing, quilts, tapestries, or linens. Or," a concession to Posey's greatest goal for all her daughters, "she could get married and design fabrics and wallpapers for her own home."

Of course, considering the procession of weird young men Hollis had brought home, that idea might not comfort Posey much.

Sure enough, Hollis's mother made a rude sound. "I certainly hope she won't marry her latest. Do you remember Zach Andrews?"

"Oh, yes. He used to come play with Jon when he was little." Katharine conjured up a slender child with brown curls and an angelic face that completely belied the devil inside. She still had five small holes in her bedroom carpet to commemorate the day he had convinced Jon to light matches, drop them, and see whose could burn the longest. The boys were seven at the time, and that was one of several episodes that had led Katharine to tell Jon he could not invite Zach over any more. "Wasn't he in Jon and Hollis's class at Westminster School?"

"Only until he got kicked out his junior year," Posey corrected her. "Lord only knows where he went after that. Some folks said he was in juvenile detention. Then his parents sent him to an odd school out in California, one where they don't pay tuition, but work on a cattle farm." Posey sounded like Zach had been sent to outer Siberia to work the mines—which, if he hadn't improved, might have been a good idea. "Still, he finished at Emory, so maybe he's okay now," Posey conceded, "but do you know who he's gone to work for since he graduated? The Ivorie Foundation. And you know as well as I do that old Mr. Ivorie has practically turned the whole thing over to Brandon, who is downright tacky!"

The Ivories were a Buckhead family who had amassed a fortune three generations ago by dint of what some claimed were unsavory tactics, then had become so blatantly religious and radically conservative that moderate Christians and moderate conservatives alike considered them an embarrassment to their cause. The Ivories had no compunction about proclaiming that God blessed the wealthy with riches because they were more righteous and worked harder than anybody else—forgetting their own antecedents and that nobody amasses a fortune without somebody helping along the way and others going without so they can have what the Ivories considered their fair share of the national GNP. The Ivorie mantra was that the primary role of government was to make sure the wealthy retained their wealth and privilege so it would trickle down—although, as Katharine's father often pointed out, the only part that trickled down was what was left after they took what was required to maintain their own lavish lifestyle. The Ivories also claimed that the only way to keep the nation strong was to expel or forcibly restrain any persons whom they deemed undesirable. In the middle of the last century, Napoleon Ivorie III—the "old man" Posey referred to—had created the Ivorie Foundation to help finance the work of Senator Joe McCarthy. Since then, the foundation had channeled lavish grants to causes and think tanks perched on the far right wingtip of the political eagle.

What most galled Katharine was that while the Ivories regularly attended one of the biggest churches in town, they believed in and proclaimed not love, but hate. They owned a number of religious broadcasting stations that combined large doses of vituperation and a regular call for the faithful to separate themselves and their children from a contaminating world with sermons purporting to be about a God who loved the world so much, he sent his son to save it.

The Ivories practiced the separation they preached. They lived on the Hill, a gated Buckhead estate that most of their neighbors had never been inside. Napoleon Ivorie, who was surely over ninety and was a recluse, lived in the original mansion. He had built a second for his daughter, Rowena Slade, and a third for Rowena's son, Brandon.

Brandon was simultaneously the most conservative and the most radical twig that the family tree had produced. At twenty-eight, he was a fiery advocate of widespread and, if necessary, violent action against those he despised. Yet in clothing, style, and demeanor, he projected an image so stiff and proper that he made William F. Buckley Jr. look like a hippie.

"Brandon's never tacky, Posey," Katharine felt compelled

to protest. "I doubt if he has ever been tacky in his life." But she was as concerned as her sister-in-law that old Napoleon might be fixing to bypass Rowena and put Brandon at the helm, for Katharine liked Rowena. She was conservative but no bigot. In kindergarten terms, she respected and worked well with others.

Posey gave a little huff of disgust. "Well, he's dangerous. You know as well as I do that he's paying for those marches down at the capitol, with their cutesy little hats and lovely printed signs, even if the Ivorie name never appears."

"Speaking of appearing," Katharine interrupted, "did you notice old Mr. Ivorie and Rowena at Aunt Lucy's funeral? They slipped in a side door with two men I didn't recognize just before the service started, and left by the side door right after the benediction. I never heard Aunt Lucy mention him or Rowena."

"Lucy grew up in Buckhead, didn't she? And she was about Mr. Ivorie's age. Maybe they had a fling in their wild, misspent youths and he came to pay his last respects. Brandon wasn't with them?"

"No."

"It's a wonder. He seems to be everywhere else these days. How he manages to get himself in all the papers and on television and radio so much, I will never know. I saw him again last night on Fox, trying to scare folks to death about terrorists among us. I don't know how Zach can work for him, and I could not stand for a daughter of mine to get mixed up in all that."

Posey and Wrens, like many of their Buckhead neighbors, were genial, tolerant conservatives who kept friends in and contributed to candidates in both parties. What ultimately mattered in their world were not the vagaries of politics but the stability of their own wealth and the influence that wealth could buy, whichever party held office. No wonder Posey was chagrined that Hollis was dating anybody connected with the Ivorie Foundation.

Katharine disliked the Ivories' politics even more than Posey did. Whenever their bandwagon included a diatribe against "those godless liberals," she wanted to stand up and shout, "My parents were liberals and they were not godless!" (Not that she would, of course. She'd been raised by a Southern mother, and had better manners than that.) She was also surprised that Hollis would be dating someone connected with Brandon since during Hollis's years at SCAD, she had several times mentioned friends who were gay. In addition to terrorists, Brandon had targeted homosexuals as "a heinous threat to Georgia families."

"What is Zach doing for Brandon?" Katharine wondered aloud.

"Heaven only knows. Writing, Hollis says, and research, whatever that means."

Katharine suspected that Hollis saw Zach as nothing but a former acquaintance to hang out with to annoy her mother while she got her bearings after college. Time to get back to Posey's original lament. "My advice is, let her decorate the carriage house the way she wants and see how it looks. You may be surprised at what she does with it. And if you don't like it, you can always redecorate when she moves out."

It is so easy to be wise when it's someone else's daughter.

"Maybe so," Posey said dubiously. "Well, I better go. I've got a tennis match in fifteen minutes, and I'm running late. What do you have planned for today?"

"This and that," she said evasively. "Autumn Village sent me ten boxes of Aunt Lucy's stuff, so I thought I'd go through them and see if there's anything worth keeping."

"Poor Katharine. She wasn't really even kin to you, was she?"

"Not blood kin, but that never mattered. Mother and Sara Claire grew up with Walter and Lucy, so when Walter married Sara Claire, Lucy became part of our family. She always seemed as much my aunt as Sara Claire did, and she was a lot more fun. I don't mind winding up her last bits and pieces."

"Well, I think you're a saint. I don't imagine she left much of value."

"She had a nice secretary that belonged to her grandmother that she said I could have. Otherwise, I don't expect to find anything of value unless there's an unprecedented demand for small wooden animals and lamps made of Highland cattle horn."

"You're a dadgum saint," Posey repeated. "Well, gotta run. See you later."

Katharine hung up with a smile. In two or three days Posey would remember that it had been her birthday and would call full of apologies to invite her to a scrumptious lunch. Susan and Jon fondly called Posey "our great late aunt," for Posey Buiton was a lovable woman, but she had never been on time for anything in her life, including her own wedding and her father's funeral.

While Katharine had the phone in her hand, she called Dutch back and left a message on his machine asking him to call her when he returned.

She set the diary back in the box, thinking she might try to translate a bit of it later to test her college German, and reached for the thing swathed in cloth. It was metal, and felt like it had started as a long rod about as thick as her little finger and been bent into an almost circular shape, with knobs placed at regular intervals around three-quarters of its

perimeter. She pulled back the cloth and furrowed her brow.
What could it be? It was the soft green of old bronze. The
circle was not quite closed, but one end had been curved into
a hook and the other looped into an eye to fasten it. The
knobs were of the same metal, either shaped from the rod or
shaped and attached to the rod when the materials were hot
and pliable. If it were a necklace, it would not have been
comfortable to wear. Katharine lifted a yellowed tag, tied by
a cord through the eye at one end. On it was written, in faded
sepia ink, HALLSTATT 1850.

She carried it into the downstairs powder room and held it
up to her neck, afraid it would break if she stretched it and
put it on. It must have been lovely when it was new and pol-
ished. As she turned away from the mirror, her reflection
seemed to be that of a younger woman with a slim face and
long hair as black as a raven's wing. But when she looked
again, it was her own face she saw.

Knowing that most mysteries these days can be solved
with a few keystrokes, Katharine went upstairs to her bedroom, where her computer desk occupied one corner. On the
Internet, she searched for "Hallstatt" and found listings for
an Austrian village advertising the most beautiful lake in the
world. Had Aunt Lucy visited it and picked up the necklace
as a souvenir? It wasn't her usual trinket. Why had she kept
it in an old box with a German diary, marked CARTER?

Katharine read on and discovered that Hallstatt was also
a site where many objects from the early Iron Age had been
found—so many, in fact, that the term "Hallstatt" was
commonly used for artifacts from various cultures of the
late Bronze Age to the early Iron Age throughout Central
and Western Europe. She balanced the necklace on one
palm. Could it possibly be very, very old? She tried to push
her mind back past the Renaissance and the Dark Ages to

the early days of Rome, but her brain cells wouldn't stretch that far. Who was the woman for whom it was made? How valuable was it? What right did Lucy Everanes have to possess it?

"And most important," she murmured, perplexed, "what the dickens am I supposed to do with it now?"

Chapter 3

Katharine ripped open Aunt Lucy's other boxes and rummaged through letters and notebooks, searching for any mention of a Carter. By the time she found three photo albums, she was sneezing from dust. She decided to examine them outside.

She carried the albums out to the patio and stood with her hands full, looking around for some place to sit. She hadn't put cushions on the wicker chairs yet that summer, since none of the family had been around to sit outdoors.

She set the albums on the patio while she fetched cushions for one chair from the storage locker, then sat looking across her backyard. "Why don't I spend more time out here?" she asked aloud. "Why don't I eat out here?"

Because the only table was down near the pool, inconvenient to the house. "I am going to buy a small table to put up here," she announced to a passing butterfly, "and cushions I can leave out all summer. I'll come out every pleasant day." .

What was the matter with her? She didn't normally go around talking to refrigerators, robins, and butterflies. She turned her attention to Aunt Lucy's albums and found one that contained old sepia pictures with scalloped edges. Katharine chuckled at those labeled "Lucy (5) and her goat cart" and "Lucy (6) swimming with Walter (10)." Uncle Walter already had a pompous look, even in his underwear. "Going to Vassar" showed Lucy beside a train, trying hard to look sophisticated in a fur coat and hat. The other freshman with her had to be Sara Claire. Katharine recognized the tilt of that chin.

Several pictures showed Lucy and Sara Claire in London and Paris—surely before World War II. Finally Katharine found a slim young man dressed in the baggy pants, suspenders, and straw hat of the nineteen thirties, standing in front of a snow-capped mountain. Beneath, Lucy had written, "Carter, Austria, 1937." The next few pictures showed the same young man with Lucy holding his arm and smiling up at him. In another picture, Sara Claire stood clutching his arm like she would never let go. His face was never quite clear.

Katharine turned the page and found a professional picture of a wedding party labeled "Sara Claire and Walter, 1939." She pored over it, picking out faces she recognized. Her mother as maid of honor looked calm, poised, and pretty. Sara Claire was as haughty and aristocratic at twenty-two as she had been at eighty. Lucy, a bridesmaid, looked scrawny and miserable in a long straight dress that bared her bony shoulders. Among the groomsmen Katharine saw one man who looked a lot like her father, but it couldn't have been, since her parents hadn't met until they were forty. Next to him stood a tall handsome man with wide shoulders, a well-shaped nose, and—could that be Dutch's bullet head? He wore the same short crew cut, but Katharine would never have imagined he'd ever been that thin. As long as she had known him, Dutch had been what he called "portly."

Next to him stood a man who could be Carter. He had the same long, slender face, dark curling hair, and tall athletic body, but Lucy hadn't written names beneath the picture. In the whole album there was no clue as to who Carter was, what had become of him, or why Lucy had kept a journal and a necklace in a box with his name on it.

Katharine was still puzzling over those questions when the phone rang again. This time it was finally Tom. She felt her spirits rise at the sound of his voice.

"Happy birthday, sweetheart. Sorry I can't be there with you today, but I've got great seats for the symphony Friday night, and I'll fly in early enough so we can get dinner. Okay?"

"Okay." She pressed the phone hard to her ear. Even after all these years, she felt their separation most keenly when they spoke on the phone. She missed seeing his face and reading his body language while they talked.

It was his body language she had first noticed at a Christmas party in Buckhead during her freshman year at Agnes Scott. Her dad had retired and her parents had moved to Atlanta in December, to be nearer her mother's parents and Sara Claire. Through Sara Claire, Katharine had received invitations to several parties over the holidays. She was just recovering from a tempestuous high school romance and a broken heart and was not interested in men, but at one party, a young man near the fireplace intrigued her. He was medium in most respects—medium height, medium build, medium brown hair—but in that sparkly, frenetic setting he radiated calm. She had moved over nearer to see what he and an older man had found to talk about, and as she listened, she was amazed at both the breadth of what the young man seemed to know and at the courteous way he managed to disagree without being disagreeable.

When they were introduced, his face lit up and became quite attractive. "I've heard about you from Miss Lucy Everanes," he exclaimed. "I've been wanting to meet you." She suspected he said something similar to every girl he met, but she let him bring her a glass of punch. Soon they were deep in conversation about literature. He was a senior at Georgetown and the first man she had ever met who valued her for her opinions. Her roommates would later tease her that Tom Murray seduced her mind.

She found him fascinating, with many interests and a daunting intelligence. After he returned to Georgetown they wrote long letters. Katharine found herself looking up new words in the dictionary to be sure she used them correctly. She began to do what he liked to do and to read what he liked to read. She took up tennis, running, and biking, and saw all the movies he mentioned so they could discuss them.

When he came to Atlanta for spring vacation, they saw each other every day. She tried to go on four or five hours of sleep, as he did, until one night past midnight when he suggested they get up early and climb Stone Mountain the next morning to watch the sun rise. "I can't keep up with you!" she had cried in defeat,

"I don't want you to keep up," he had replied. "I love you for yourself." When he kissed her—a gentle, lingering kiss—she had gotten dizzy with joy.

They got married the summer after she graduated, and over the years of their marriage, she had watched with pride and amazement while his energy, courtesy, and ambition carried him up the corporate ladder. He continued to respect her opinions and to value her as a partner. She considered it a privilege to provide a calm, lovely home for him to return to. At almost fifty, he could still outride, outswim, outthink, and outread anybody she knew, and while he claimed to be looking forward to a day when he could retire and read all the books he had accumulated in his library, she couldn't picture him sitting still for more than one day at a stretch.

But she had learned to read his body language more carefully. Although his voice never showed it, she could tell when he was really interested in a conversation and when he was pretending to listen while his mind was miles away. She could tell when he was weary or bored and pumping himself up and when he was so genuinely excited about something that the energy generated itself. He often claimed, "You're the only person in the world I can't fool, Katharine. The only one I can really be myself with."

She often prided herself that they had built a better, more companionable marriage than most of their friends. They still loved to travel together or to sit by a fire and talk, and his absences lent a zest to the time he was around.

"What are your plans for today?" He sounded like he was settling in for a long chat, but she knew he must have a full schedule and couldn't talk long.

"Nothing much. Autumn Village sent Aunt Lucy's stuff— the things I told them to give away—so I've been going through it. They also want me to come get the secretary. Anthony's going to fetch it tonight," she added quickly, not wanting to burden him with domestic details.

"That's good. I'd guess the rest can pretty much be thrown out, right?"

"Most of it. But listen, did you ever buy any books about Celtic archaeology?" She needed to ask before he had to go.

"Celtic archaeology?" His mind, which catalogued and never forgot a fact, worked silently for a long minute. "One of that series of Time-Life books I ordered years ago was about the Celts, but I haven't gotten around to reading it yet."

"Did you know the Celts were all over Europe, not just in Ireland, Wales, and Scotland?"

"Sure. Didn't you take second year Latin?"

"Yes, but what does that have to do with it?"

"Remember the first sentence of Julius Caesar?"

"*Gallia in tres partes divasa est?*" she hazarded.

"*Gallia est omnis divisa in partes tres,*" he corrected her. "And what's the rest of that sentence?"

"There's more? I didn't remember that."

" 'Of which one is inhabited by the Belgians, another by the Aquitanians, the third by those who in their own language are called Celts, in ours, Gauls,' " he quoted.

She never could decide whether to be delighted or exasperated by his incredible memory. "You are amazing. Do you know where the book on Celts would be?"

"Try the bottom left shelf in my library. Gathering dust, like so many other books. When I retire, honey—"

"I know, you're going to read for five years straight, until you have read every book in the house. I hope you can do it on a freighter, because I want to see the world."

"You'll get seasick."

"I'll take pills."

She would have loved to talk longer, but somebody spoke behind him and he said, "Gotta run. We're due in a meeting in five minutes. Happy birthday, darling."

As she hung up it occurred to her that Tom hadn't shown the slightest curiosity about why she suddenly wanted to read about ancient Celts. Once again she had the feeling that she—her interests, crises, and little joys—were mere blips on the screens of other people's lives.

She located *The Celts: Europe's People of Iron* exactly where Tom had said it would be. She took it to the sofa in the den and in less than an hour had a few answers and more questions.

Hallstatt, she had learned, was the name given to a burial

ground and the remains of a Celtic village discovered in 1846 at Salzberg, an Austrian mountain with a core of hard rock salt (not to be confused with the Austrian city, Salzburg). Salzberg had been mined from 1000–400 B.C., and a thriving and prosperous community had grown up near the mine, because salt was a precious commodity for prehistoric people, so valuable it was sometimes called "white gold." They used it for preserving food and leather, for healing, and for trade. Mining the salt was extremely difficult with primitive equipment, but much wealth could be made from salt.

Katharine paused long enough to think about the woman for whom that necklace had been made. Had she been the wife of one who grew wealthy from the mine?

She returned to the book. A landslide shut down the mine around 400 B.C. and mining was not resumed until the middle of the nineteenth century. In 1846, Georg Ramsauer, the government-appointed director of the salt mines, was overseeing the excavation of gravel needed to pave a road when his men came across a human skull and a bronze earring in the earth. Ramsauer slowly excavated with a shovel and found an entire skeleton, then a second, wearing a bronze bracelet. He suspected he had found an ancient cemetery and tested his theory by staking an area and lifting away the topsoil. Sure enough, he unearthed seven skeletons laid in two rows, adorned with bronze jewelry.

Again Katharine put down the book. Had the woman who owned what she was coming to think of as "the necklace" died young and been buried with her jewelry? How young would she have been when she married? Was he kind to her, or brutal?

She sighed. It was that kind of unanswerable question that most interested her in history, not who fought whom when.

She learned that with the approach of winter, Georg

Ramsauer replaced the soil and put off further excavation until spring, and reported his finds to the Austrian government. The following spring he was given authority, funds, and detailed instructions for excavating the site. Ramsauer's team dug for the next seventeen years, turning up nearly a thousand graves and more than six hundred bronze, iron, and gold artifacts from the Celts, some dating as far back as 1000 B.C.

Ramsauer documented every stage of his excavations and kept a detailed diary and a running inventory of all recovered artifacts. He also hired artists to paint watercolors of some of the graves and of his best finds.

One sentence made Katharine catch her breath. Ramsauer's diary had disappeared, and had never been found. Could it possibly be—?

"Nonsense," she told herself aloud. "Where would Aunt Lucy get Ramsauer's diary?" But she felt her pulses quicken at a photograph of bronze necklaces very like the one in the box.

Katharine finished the article, closed the book and mulled over three facts:

1. Georg Ramsauer's diary disappeared.
2. He gave away many artifacts, with no record of who received them.
3. He was the father of twenty-four children.

Children? Wasn't the climber in the clipping a Ramsauer?

She returned to the music room, picked up the diary, and opened the cover, hoping for a name and date. The inside cover was bare and the first page simply dated 15/6—the European style for June 15—without a year. She read the first sentence and discovered that even without a dictionary, she could translate it.

Ein neuer Anfang ein neues Tagebuch verdient. "A new beginning deserves a new journal." Could that possibly refer to the beginnings of the official excavation?

She shook the book gently to locate the clipping. Sure enough, the dead man was Ludwig Ramsauer. Was he a descendant of Georg?

Katharine sank to the piano bench and held the book reverently. All her life she had marveled when a lost piece of music or work of art turned up in somebody's attic. She had never imagined it could happen to her. She wanted to sit down and translate the diary immediately, but feared she might damage it. She would make a copy. And first she'd try to find out if it was, indeed, Ramsauer's diary. Who would be likely to know?

She had volunteered at the Atlanta History Center for years and knew several curators. While they focused on Atlanta history, perhaps one of them could identify the necklace and diary or steer her to someone who could.

She could also use the Kenan Research Center to look up Aunt Sara Claire's wedding on microfilmed back issues of the old *Atlanta Constitution,* to verify that the man in the wedding picture was the elusive Mr. Carter. Aunt Sara Claire would have made sure her wedding was reported in the Sunday paper, with full names of all the attendants.

As she headed to shower and dress, Katharine sang, "It's my party, and I'll cry if I want to." Except she changed the words to "It's my birthday and I'll play if I want to."

She took special pains with her hair and makeup and squirted on perfume. Then she slipped on white pants, a soft yellow T-shirt, and her favorite big shirt, a fantasy in Southwest colors of dark brown, rust red, light orange, and turquoise. She added a silver and turquoise necklace and dangle earrings, and slipped her feet into soft brown huaraches she had bought in Mexico. As she passed the mirror, she told her reflection, "If only the FedEx man could see you now, baby. You clean up real good."

She wondered again about the heavy necklace downstairs, and the woman for whom it had been made. Was she dark or fair? Lovely or plain? Obviously she had once been the wife or daughter of an important man. Had she peered into a lake as Katharine peered into her mirror, examining her image, wondering if she was still attractive or if her beauty was beginning to fade? As Katharine turned from the mirror, for just an instant she again thought she saw the shadow of a dark-haired woman to one side, but when she stepped back to look, it was a trick of the light.

Katharine rewrapped the necklace and tucked it with the diary into a small cloth tote bag. As she picked up her purse, she noticed that she had left Aunt Lucy's peach-pit necklace on the kitchen counter. She scooped it up and dropped it into the bag with the necklace and diary, intending to stop just before she left her property and toss it into the bushes to decay. At least that way, it would be good for something.

But she forgot to toss it, because she got engrossed in her standard conversation with her father about her car. "A Cadillac is safer than a lot of other cars," she pointed out, "and an SUV is practical for hauling things around. Besides, Tom picked out this car and brought it home. I'd have bought a Saab, or maybe a Saturn."

Her father, as usual, did not reply—perhaps because he'd been dead fifteen years.

"What should I do with the rest of my life?" she asked the silence.

It must be break-time in heaven. She still got no reply.

*　　　*　　　*

She parked on the lower level of the parking deck and climbed the hill to the brick building that housed the history center's museum, gift shop, offices, and classrooms.

"I can't really tell you a thing about this," the Curator of Decorative Arts said regretfully a few minutes later. "As you know, we specialize in things connected to Atlanta history. I'd suggest you try Emory's Carlos Museum. But I'll tell you what—an Emory history professor is browsing the museum this morning and he said he'd be doing research in the Kenan Center later. He might be able to tell you more than I can. Ask the staff to tell him you want to talk to him when he arrives."

Katharine went up the hill to the building that housed the research center, produced her membership card, left everything in a locker except for a note pad and a pencil, pulled open the heavy glass doors, and stepped into another world.

Chapter 4

The history center library had always been one of her favorite places. In a bustling city, it was an oasis of calm with comfortable reading chairs and soft yellow walls interspersed with large windows looking out on restful green vistas of well-landscaped grounds. On other days she had sat for hours reading Atlanta history for pleasure, with no object in mind. Today she headed straight to the microfilm room, which was separated from the rest of the library by another wall of glass. An elderly woman was scanning one microfilm screen, but did not look up. She had a short silver Afro and skin the color of coffee with lots of milk, and she wore a red cotton top with a flowing cotton skirt in a swirling pattern of reds, blues, and yellows.

Katharine found the box for 1939, the year of Aunt Sara Claire's wedding, threaded the machine and moved the film forward to the second week of June. Sure enough, Aunt Sara Claire gloated on Sunday's bridal page. The article beneath included descriptions of her wedding dress and flowers and a complete list of attendants. One of the men was Carter Everanes.

Everanes? Was he a cousin of Lucy and Walter?

Katharine headed to the desk. "Is there a way to trace a man who might be related to the husband of my aunt? My aunt is dead, but I'd like to know if they were related and how."

She tensed, waiting for the librarian to ask what right she had to poke around in her aunt's husband's past. *Nosy* was a word that came to mind. But the librarian acted as if it were a normal request—and perhaps where she worked, it was. "You need to speak to our genealogy librarian." Her British accent hinted that her own genealogy wasn't catalogued in a Georgia library. "But he'll be in a meeting all morning. Perhaps—"

"I'll help her," rasped a gravelly voice at Katharine's elbow.

She turned to see a man not much taller than she, with a tanned face, a nose like a hawk's beak, and a gray ponytail pulled back at his neck. He wore black jeans, black boots, and a black T-shirt with GIVE ME LIBERTY OR ELSE on the front. When he smiled, his crooked teeth were stained and brown. "Lamar Franklin, ma'am, at your service. I do genealogy all the time." His accent was pure mountain Georgia. "What you wanna know? How your aunt's husband was related to this other guy?"

It took all her willpower not to step back from a gust of old cigarettes and coffee. "It's okay," she told him. "I can come back another day."

"It's no trouble." He waved a tanned arm bearing an anchor tattooed over ropy muscles. "Do you know when your aunt's husband was born? Roughly, at least?"

"Nineteen fifteen." She had filled out enough forms for Aunt Sara Claire to be able to figure that out.

"Two years older than my old man. He grow up around here?"

"Oh, yes. But I don't know where his—ah—relative grew up."

"Let's hope he came from Atlanta. What's his name?"

"Carter Everanes."

"Could you spell the last name?"

When she complied, he took her elbow and steered her away from the desk. "Let's start with your aunt's husband, then, and members of his family. We'll begin with the 1930 census. First, we'll need the Soundex code."

He went to a shelf near the microfilm room and pulled out a thick book. "This here's *The Soundex Daitch-Mokotoff Reference Guide.* Soundex is one of the finest systems ever invented." He led Katharine toward a table, still talking. "It's a method of indexing names phonetically rather than the way they're spelled, which makes it easier to find names which sound alike but are spelled entirely differently. This is very important in genealogical research, since a name may be spelled several ways by different generations. Even members of the same family may change the spelling of their name." The lecture went oddly with his appearance, for he reeled the long words off his tongue like he used them often. "Soundex groups consonants under six categories of key letters and equivalents and ignores vowels, so several names have the same code." He opened the guide. "What's the surname we're wantin' again?" He opened the book.

"Everanes. My uncle was Walter Everanes, and I'm looking for somebody named Carter Everanes." Katharine bent over the pages, fascinated. How could anybody make sense out of those consonant combinations?

He seemed to have no trouble at all. "Unusual name. I don't recall that I ever heard it." He ran his finger down the page. "Here it is. The code for Everanes is EVRN, E165. Now we need to look at the codes for the 1930 census, to find out where to look for them."

He took her back to the microfilm room, where the older

woman was still poring over something on her screen. Katharine paid the woman little attention, for her new companion was again explaining what he was doing. "The 1930 census is the most recent one that's been put on microfilm, and these drawers hold that census for Georgia." He gestured to the first row of a bank of small black file drawers. "And the Soundex Codes for Georgia are here. Three steps—see?"

He paused as if waiting for her to reply, so she nodded and remembered obediently, "First you find the code number for the name in the book out there, then you look up that number in one of these green boxes to see if that name appears in Georgia, and then—?" She stopped, for she didn't know what happened next.

"I'll show you." He opened a drawer from the second bank of drawers and brought out a green box from near the back. "Let's see what we can find."

"I really appreciate this." Katharine was grateful, but felt a bit overwhelmed by his determined kindness.

"It's no trouble a-tall," he assured her. "I have nothing pressing at the moment." He put the film in a machine and fast-forwarded to E165. "Here we are. Everanes. There's only one family, and they lived in Fulton County, like you thought." He pointed to the screen and read aloud. "Head of household, Clifford Charles Everanes. Other persons living in the house were Mildred Faire Everanes, wife, Walter Charles, son—well, looky here! Carter Simpson, son, and Emily Lucille, daughter. That help you any?"

Katharine stared at the gray screen, trying to absorb the information. Aunt Lucy and Uncle Walter had a brother she had never heard of? She was positive that not once in all her growing up years had she heard Walter and Lucy mention another brother.

"This what you wanted to know?" the man demanded.

"Oh, yes," she told him. "I'm surprised that he was a brother, that's all. I knew Walter and Lucy, but I never heard of Carter."

He gave a raspy laugh. "Mighta been the black sheep of the family. You wanta know more about him?" She nodded. He pointed to some words and numbers at the upper right of the screen. "Best place to start is the census. These numbers give us the volume of the census, the enumeration district, and the abode number." Again she was surprised with how easily he rolled off words like "enumeration" and "abode." She quickly jotted down the numbers he indicated, including the right frame of the microfilm, then followed him back to the drawers containing microfilms of the actual census records. He had already pulled out another green box.

"I can take it from here," she assured him. "Thanks so much."

"I'll stick around in case you get in any trouble." As Katharine headed back to the microfilm, he was so close behind that he trod on her heel.

She turned. "I'd really rather do this alone. I do appreciate your help, though."

He held up both hands and backed off. "Sorry, ma'am. No offence intended. You need any more help, you let me know." He swaggered back to the main library and she saw him pick up a periodical from a table and settle in as if to read. When she glanced that way in a few seconds, though, he was looking her way. He gave a grin and a wave. She waved back, and returned to the screen.

She inserted the film and started looking for the right frame. Impatient, she punched the fast-forward button and whizzed past the one she sought.

"Drat!" She spoke sharply before she remembered she was not alone. Her cheeks grew hot and she darted a glance at the woman on the other machine. What must she be thinking?

At the same moment she looked Katharine's way. "Why, Katharine Murray! You doing family research, too?"

Katharine's face broke into a smile. "Dr. Flo! I didn't recognize you."

A slim brown hand came up to pat the short shining curls. "It's my new look. I decided it was time to cut off that bun and get myself a new style and some bright, fun clothes."

For thirty years, until she'd retired a few years before, Dr. Florence Gadney had taught business at Spelman College. She always gave the impression that she meant business, too. Short and slender with an elegant carriage, she wore chic tailored suits, silk blouses, and a chignon that made her look as if she'd just stepped off a plane from Paris. In an evening gown, she resembled an Ethiopian queen, a fit consort for the handsome Maurice Gadney, M.D., in his tux. They used to make a striking couple when they attended art, musical, or theatrical openings in Atlanta, where their names generally appeared in the program as patrons, sponsors, or angels of the event. They had no children, but were often quoted as saying that the various organizations they supported served as their family.

Even after Dr. Flo retired and got more involved in community organizations, she remained chic and elegant. Katharine had often run into her at meetings of the Perennial Plants Association, at members-only events at the High Museum of Art and the Atlanta Botanical Gardens, at fund-raising galas for women's shelters, or at evening performances for adults at the Theater for Puppetry Arts. And while they weren't well acquainted, Katharine always enjoyed Dr. Flo. The woman's mind was sharp, her interests wide, and her conversation brilliant.

That morning, though, Katharine realized she had seldom seen the professor since her husband had died unexpectedly a year earlier. Dr. Flo hadn't seemed like a woman to hang up her socks after she was widowed. Maybe she had been traveling, picking up new clothes in street markets around the world.

"I like your hair," Katharine told her. "It's a softer look."

"I'm not feeling very soft right now." Dr. Flo gestured toward her microfilm. "I'm looking up some relatives of my husband's, trying to chase down one of Maurice's cousins. His people came from down in Butts County, and I always told him the lot of them were real good at butting heads in a butt-ugly manner. Maurice was the only decent one in the lot. Are you into genealogy?"

"A beginner," Katharine admitted.

"It's fascinating when you get into it." Dr. Flo's eyes danced. "You begin to feel like a detective or something, rooting around for clues. What are you looking for?"

"I'm trying to solve a puzzle I got handed this morning. My Aunt Lucy died last week—Lucille Everanes?"

Dr. Flo wrinkled her forehead. "I didn't know her, but the name sounds familiar. It's not a common one, so I wonder why. Was she on your mother's side of the family?"

Katharine shook her head with a rueful smile. "She wasn't on any side of my family. Her older brother married my mother's sister. But because they all grew up together and the Everaneses had no other family, Lucy got adopted into ours."

"An honorary auntie," Dr. Flo said with a nod. "I had several of those."

"I did, too, but I was in elementary school before I found out Aunt Lucy was one of them. I loved her like she was blood kin, and after listening to her stories all my life, I'd have sworn I knew everything there was to know about her past. Now, clearing out after her death, I'm discovering she had a brother Carter I never heard of."

"Carter Everanes. Now why does that sound familiar?" Dr. Flo cocked her head, wrinkled her forehead and pursed her lips, trying to come up with an answer. Reluctantly she shook her head. "Nothing comes immediately to mind, but my mind isn't what it used to be."

"Well, it's not like Carter has been mentioned very often in the past forty-five years. At least not in my presence." Katharine nodded toward the microfilm machine. "I hope to find out something about him in a minute."

"I hope you have better luck than I did. That no-good Drake doesn't appear in any of these records, but I know he existed, because Maurice talked about him all the time. He used to manage some property Maurice owned down near Jackson, and I want to find him to ask him about it. I guess I'll have to drive down there and see if I can locate him." Dr. Flo rolled back her chair and stood, shaking out her skirt, which fell almost to bright yellow flip-flops. Dr. Flo Gadney in flip-flops? What was the world coming to?

"Maybe he changed his name," Katharine suggested, calling on her recent lesson on genealogy research.

Dr. Flo let out a disgusted little huff. "Or maybe he skipped the country with Maurice's money. That's also possible." They chatted lightly while Dr. Flo gathered up a red canvas tote and a black shoulder bag. Finally she said, "Well, I'd better be getting home. Good luck with your search." As she walked from the room, her shoes made soft *slap-slaps* against the floor.

When Katharine found the Everanes census listing, she saw that family members in the household included Walter, fifteen, Carter, thirteen, and Lucille, eleven. All three were students. So by the time of Walter's wedding Carter would

have been—Katharine used her pencil to do the math—
twenty-two. What happened to him after that? Had he gone
to war and died a hero's death? Was it during the war that he
had gotten the diary and archaeological artifact? She shuddered to think she might be in possession of stolen war
gains.

But excitement rose like sap in her veins at the thought
that she might personally be able to solve this mystery.
Maybe she could trace Carter through the military, or perhaps there were ways to find out when a person died. She
wanted to talk to the Emory professor, too, and he hadn't
come to the library yet.

First, though, she needed sustenance. Her English muffin
and tea had long since departed, and her watch read ten past
one. She would lunch at the Swan Coach House up the hill
and return afterwards. The Coach House was one of her favorite restaurants, although she had never eaten there alone.
It was the sort of place one went with friends, or where
mothers and grandmothers took little girls in fancy dresses
for special birthday parties.

Today, she would give herself a birthday party. Treat herself to creamy chicken salad in crispy, heart-shaped timbales
with a generous slice of frozen salad on the side, rich with
whipped cream and slices of peaches and bing cherries. She
might even splurge for a meringue swan filled with chocolate mousse and covered in whipped cream.

She thanked the librarians, fetched her belongings from
their locker, and stopped by the ladies' room. As she came
out the door, she didn't notice the stranger in the hall until
he spoke. "You looking for me?"

Chapter 5

A lanky man detached himself from the wall. He wore crisp khaki slacks and a white Oxford-cloth shirt with green stripes, the sleeves rolled up to show muscular forearms. "The folks at the desk said a Mrs. Murray wants to ask me a question about something she's found." As he got closer, his jaw dropped. "Kate?"

Only one person had ever called her that.

"Hasty!" Katharine hadn't seen Hobart Hastings for nearly thirty years, but for the last three years of high school he had sat in front of her every day in homeroom and many classes, because "Hastings" came immediately before "Herndon" on the roster. In tenth grade they had been assigned as biology lab partners for the same reason and without him, she might never have passed. She had never been able to see a thing under a microscope. In exchange, she began to edit his papers for spelling and grammar. Studying—and frequently bickering—together, they became so inseparable that their friends began to refer to them in one run-on word: Kat-'n'-Hasty.

But Hasty had wanted Katharine to apply to Kenyon, where he was going, and she had chosen Agnes Scott instead. All summer after graduation he had griped about that and insisted she would never be able to survive without him.

She began to feel smothered, and insisted, "I have to do what's right for me." Then, the night before they were to leave for their separate colleges, he had drunk too much at a party and gotten himself entangled with a girl Katharine particularly disliked—one of the shapely, sun-streaked blondes in their class who seemed to stimulate raging hormones. When Hasty and the girl drove away together in the girl's red Mustang convertible, Katharine found herself another ride home. An hour later, Hasty had turned up on her front porch. Furious and hurt, she had refused to let him in. He had stood out in the yard under her bedroom window, yelling things like "Hey, it was just a little fun" and "If you won't go to college with me, you can't expect me to become a monk, you know. I have to do what's right for *me*," until her father had gone out and sent him home.

He hadn't called the next morning before she left for Agnes Scott, so they hadn't said goodbye. He had called her two nights later, after he got to college, but he had sounded more belligerent than contrite, so she'd hung up on him. Several times. After that, he didn't call again. She had nursed her anger until it subsided into a bruised and hurting heart. After a couple of months, she had permitted her roommate to fix her up, but the date was a disaster, so she didn't repeat the experience until Christmas, when she met Tom.

Looking at Hasty now, she wondered: if Agnes Scott had been closer to Kenyon, or if her father hadn't decided to move the family to Atlanta that same fall, would she and Hasty have eventually made up? Instead, they had never seen each other again.

Now he looked down at her with a surprised look that wasn't particularly flattering. "When did you get sophisticated and beautiful?"

"When did you get so tactful?" But he had improved, too.

She could see traces of the gangly boy he had been—the same square jaw, the same hazel eyes behind glasses that were now bifocals. However, he had filled out into an attractive bulk and the silver that threaded his black curls gave him a distinguished look. Unbidden, a memory of winding those curls through her fingers while she kissed him rose before her. She felt her fingers clench and heat rose in her cheeks. What on earth was the matter with her? She was a happily married woman.

"You're teaching history at Emory?" she asked to cover her confusion. "I had no idea you were in Atlanta. Besides, you hated history." His father had been an expert on the Age of Expansion and one of the shining lights of the new history department when Florida International University was founded in the seventies, but history used to be Hasty's worst subject.

His lopsided grin and loose shrug hadn't changed at all. "I discovered in college that it wasn't history I hated, it was Dad ramming it down my throat. I got hooked on the Vandals, Goths, and Celts. All that ravishing and rape." He wiggled his eyebrows.

"You never did master a leer," she informed him, "but if you know about Celts, you are just what I need."

"I can't remember anybody ever having that reaction to Celts. You intrigue me. Want to have lunch?"

She hesitated. "I was going up to the Coach House, and it's pretty much all women."

"I don't object to women." Seeing her look, he added, "But I have learned to respect them. Besides, isn't this your birthday?" Part of what used to astonish her about Hasty was his memory for trivia. She nodded. "Then you mustn't eat alone. Come on, my treat."

She wasn't in the habit of eating lunch with men, but she couldn't think of any reason to refuse, and after all, he was an old friend. So she fell into step beside him and hurried to keep up. He still had the quick nervous stride that had earned him his nickname.

He also still had a propensity to lecture. "Did you know that this restaurant and gift shop are housed in a garage the Inman family built on their estate to house a collection of racing cars? The mansion, completed in 1928, was left to the Atlanta Historical Society on Mrs. Inman's death in the nineteen sixties, and the society built the history center on the grounds. They opened the Swan House to the public, and created the restaurant in the garage to generate income."

Katharine had memorized all those facts back when she became a docent, but she had neither the breath nor the inclination to tell him. His long legs were taking the steep incline much faster than hers. When he saw she was falling behind, he put out a hand and she took it without thinking. Holding Hasty's hand felt so familiar that she didn't realize she hadn't let go until they started in the door and met two of her friends. She dropped his hand at once, but they gave Hasty a speculative look as he stepped back to let them out. Katharine's cheeks flamed. Why had Hasty turned out so handsome? They wouldn't have given her those looks if he'd been scrawny, ugly, and had a squint. Why hadn't she suggested somewhere else for lunch—preferably miles from Buckhead and everybody she knew?

However, they were there, so she might as well enjoy it. Tom probably had lunch with women all the time as part of his work. That's what they were going to have—a working lunch. Looked at that way, it was perfectly harmless. So why was she obsessing over this?

Because you have spent too much of your life with women and children, she told herself crossly, taking a seat on an old chest that doubled as a waiting bench.

"What have you been doing since high school?" she asked as Hasty returned from giving his name to the hostess. His story included graduation from Kenyon, a Ph.D. from Columbia, and positions at two colleges in the Midwest before coming to Atlanta to teach at Emory a year ago.

"Your turn," he finished.

Given her dreams in high school, her life sounded pretty lame. "Husband, two kids. Susan's working in New York and Jon just graduated from Emory last month. Now he's gone to China to teach for a couple of years. We hope to go see him at Christmas."

The ponytailed helper from the library came in just then and greeted her with a grin and a wave. "I see you had the same idea I did." He stuck out a hand to Hasty. "Hello, Dr. Hastings. Lamar Franklin. I caught one of your public lectures last winter on old burial customs. Fascinatin' stuff." He added in a lower tone, "The chow's pretty good here if you can remember not to eat with your fingers and to keep your napkin in your lap."

She feared Hasty would invite the man join them, but he was already crossing the foyer and greeting the hostess like an old friend. "Your usual table is ready, Mr. Franklin," she said, and took him right in.

Katharine felt a pang at the name, remembering Franklin Garrett, a great Atlanta historian who had died not too many years before and was still sorely missed.

She turned back to Hasty. "So, do you have a wife?"

A shadow crossed his face. "Yeah, but we're separated right now. When I came down here she and Kelly, who is fifteen, didn't want to move. What does your husband do?" His tone shut out sympathy or questions.

When she told him, he raised his brows. "A lobbyist?" It sounded like a disease.

"More of a consultant, making sure his company's interests are properly represented."

"Ooh—prickly, Kate," he chided her with a grin. "I'm sure he's a nice lobbyist."

"Very nice."

"So what are you going to do with yourself now that everybody's gone off and left you?"

He didn't have to put it so baldly. "I'm figuring that out." She hoped she sounded confident and enthusiastic. "I'm considering various options."

His grin widened. "From past experience, I'd suggest you not consider anything in the realm of biology."

She had forgotten how easy Hasty was to laugh with. They were still chuckling when the hostess came to tell them their table was ready.

He looked around at the white wallpaper with huge flowers, thick white tablecloths, dainty floral arrangement on each table, and the crowd of women and muttered, "So this is how the ladies eat."

Lamar looked up from his menu at the next table. "You just doubled the masculine population of the room. Thanks." He turned to give his order.

When they had ordered, Hasty leaned back in his chair and said, "Sounds like you've done well for yourself. Married a corporate executive, got a house in Buckhead, what more could a woman ask for? I'm happy for you. Now, what was it you wanted to ask me about?"

She reached down and brought out the book and the cloth-wrapped parcel. As she passed them across the table, she warned, "I can't guarantee they're sanitary."

He had already removed the cloth from the necklace and glanced at its tag. Then he took off his glasses, set them on the table, and held the circlet close to his eyes. His big hands turned it with a gentleness that surprised her. "It's bronze. Where on earth did you get this?"

Katharine told him about Aunt Lucy's box and about tracking down Carter Everanes in the history center library. "But I don't know where he got those things."

He didn't take his eyes from the circlet as he turned it again and again. "Hallstatt was a very important Celtic archaeological find. If this is genuine, it could be extremely valuable. But it shouldn't be in private hands. The person who can probably tell you for certain is at Emory's Carlos Museum, but he's in Europe for a couple of weeks."

Katharine was about to say that was what she had been told at the history center when Lamar leaned across the space between their tables. "That looks fascinating. Is it real old? Could I see it just a minute?"

Hasty didn't hand it over. "Sorry, but if this is as old as I think it is, it needs to be kept in a very safe place and not handled." He looked over at Katharine. "Why don't I take it—"

"Oh no, you don't." She grabbed it, surprising all three of them. But Katharine had recognized that look in Hasty's eye. He used to collect stamps and had founded a stamp club at high school to which she initially belonged. Unfortunately, whenever anybody brought in a stamp Hasty didn't own and wanted, he got a certain gleam in his eye. Then he badgered the owner until the poor soul would sell to him rather than put up with his persistent hounding. One student with a good collection had finally gotten so tired of losing stamps to Hasty that he had complained to the principal and the principal had shut down the club.

Katharine used the distraction of the waitress setting down iced tea and hot cheese drop biscuits to reach over and take back the diary, as well. It was admirable that Hasty had turned his passion for things of the past into gainful employment, but she felt better with Aunt Lucy's possessions on her side of the table.

"What was that?" he demanded, putting back on his glasses and peering across at her.

"A diary. It's in German, and I haven't tried to translate it yet."

He grew very still. "Was the diary with the necklace?"

"In the same box."

"What else do you have in that bag?"

"A piece of junk."

"Let me see." He held out his hand.

She handed over Aunt Lucy's peach pit necklace. He dropped it on the table after a quick look. "That's disgusting. It's even moldy."

"I told you it was junk." She put it back in the bag and was starting to rewrap the necklace in its cloth when she heard someone greet her from behind.

"Hello, Katharine." She looked up into the ice blue eyes of Rowena Ivorie Slade. Rowena was one of those women for whom wealth, brains, and grooming achieve what nature has not. Born a silver blonde, she still kept her hair "Ivorie" white and beautifully coiffed and was invariably so well dressed and confident that people spoke of her as attractive, forgetting that her eyes were too close together, her nose long and sharp, her chin insignificant. Today she wore a two-piece dress of navy linen with a gold necklace and earrings that probably could have bought all the lunches served at the Coach House that afternoon.

Aside from having sat on a few of the same committees, Rowena and Katharine had another thing in common: both were the only children of fathers who had been forty-five when they were born. With her father close to ninety, Rowena now reigned as queen in Atlanta's conservative political circles, chairing more committees than she had fingers and flying to Washington at least once a month to keep government on track.

Hasty stood. Katharine was about to introduce them when she met the startled dark eyes of her niece, who stood behind Rowena. Hollis gave Hasty an oblique look, then looked back at her aunt with a challenge in her eye. Katharine gave an inner sigh. Young adults could be so tedious about running into married relations eating lunch with somebody of the other sex.

She again started to introduce Hasty, but Rowena forestalled her by sticking out a hand. "How do you do? I am Rowena Slade."

Hasty shook the proffered hand. "Hobart Hastings, ma'am. I teach over at Emory and I heard you speak on a panel last year. A very impressive mustering of facts."

"Thank you." Rowena took it for praise.

Katharine looked down at her plate to hide her smile. Unless Hasty's politics had changed drastically since high school, he hadn't agreed with a word Rowena had said. Apparently, though, he had learned a little tact and diplomacy in the past thirty years.

Rowena turned and stepped aside slightly. "This is my daughter, Amy Faire Slade," she continued, "and her friend, Hollis Buiton, who also happens to be Katharine's niece."

Until Rowena mentioned her, Katharine hadn't noticed Amy standing beyond Hollis. Poor Amy was easy to overlook—a pale, drab child with her mother's sharp features and the hesitant look of a creature who fears the sun. Perhaps that was because she stood so consistently in the shadow of her mother and older brother. Even after four years of college, she seemed socially awkward, far younger than Hollis. Her summer dress was attractive and probably had cost as much as Katharine's whole outfit, but it hung on her skinny frame in a shade of pallid pink that was far too bland for her coloring.

"You've changed your hair," Katharine murmured to Hollis while Rowena and Hasty chatted. She was determined not to let the meeting become too important for either one of them. "It looks great. When did you get it cut?"

"We both got our hair done," Amy boasted with the pride of a ten-year-old. "Mama gave us makeovers for my birthday." Her limp brown hair cascaded in curls that would last until she slept on them, and her face had the disconcerting look of a child's made up for a beauty pageant.

Hollis's hair, however, was radically different. Instead of self-dyed black strings down her back or twisted sloppily on top of her head, it was beauty-shop mahogany with a burgundy stripe, and expertly cut to cup her chin in front but very short in the back. Her mother might have a fit, but the style suited her face. In an instant Hollis's expression went from stony disapproval to self-satisfaction. "This morning. Do you really like it?"

"Very much," Katharine assured her. Which was more than she could say about Hollis's vivid red lipstick, purple eye shadow, gold nose stud, and eyebrow ring. Worn with a black miniskirt and tank top, they made Hollis look like a vampire—or a New York model. Katharine wouldn't have chosen black rubber flip-flops for lunch with friends, either, but she loved Hollis for herself, not her clothes, and appreciated that her niece used clothing as both a fashion statement and a declaration of independence from her mother.

"It's quite the family day today, isn't it?" Now it was Rowena's curious gaze that roved from Katharine to Hasty. "We've been celebrating Amy's birthday. If I'd known you were coming here, Katharine, I'd have invited you to join us."

"We just arrived," Katharine replied. "We came up from the Kenan Research Center." She was speaking more to Hollis than Rowena, but Hollis was looking at the floor. Was she embarrassed because she had caught her aunt with another man, or because Katharine had caught her hobnobbing with the Ivories? Given Posey's opinions of the family, Katharine wondered whether Hollis had mentioned whose birthday she was celebrating.

Katharine hadn't realized Hollis and Amy were special friends. In fact, when they were all in high school, she remembered Jon saying that Amy was a "space cadet" who had no friends. If Hollis was dating Zach and he was working for the Ivorie Foundation, Katharine hoped she wasn't cultivating Amy for ulterior reasons.

Amy slid Hasty an admiring look and held out a clutch of bright gift bags with a giggle of delight. "Mama really went all out, didn't she? And Hollis gave me these great earrings she designed and made herself." She held back her hair and shook her head. Bright beads swung against her cheeks.

"It's Kate's birthday, too," Hasty informed them, "so we're celebrating."

"We were in the same class at Coral Gables High School years ago, and ran into each other over at the history center library. Isn't that amazing?" Katharine knew she was talking too fast. Were her cheeks as pink as they felt? She wished he hadn't called her Kate. Hollis had noticed, and was again looking at her with a speculative eye. "Hobart agreed to join me so I wouldn't have to celebrate alone." Maybe he'd get the hint if she used his full name.

Hollis looked down at the necklace lying by her plate. "Looks like you got a present, too. Did Uncle Tom send it?" She put a slight emphasis on his name.

"No." Katharine hoped she sounded cheerful and normal.

"He'll bring me something when he gets home Friday, then we're going to dinner and the symphony that night to celebrate."

"So what's that?" Hollis asked warily.

Katharine picked it up and held it out to her, ignoring Hasty's glare. "Something I found among Aunt Lucy's stuff. In fact, that's why a curator over at the history center suggested I talk to Hobart. He's a history prof at Emory."

Hollis eyed the necklace with the eye of an artist. "It looks real old. Is it?"

"Hobart thinks so. How old?" Katharine asked him.

He was watching the necklace like he wanted to snatch it and keep it safe. "If it's genuine, it could be twenty-five hundred, maybe even three thousand years old."

"Wow." Hollis had been lightly touching it, but jerked her hand away like the bronze was hot. Lamar Franklin was craning his neck to get a good look as well.

"The diary may be an important find, too," Katharine added. "It may be the detailed record of an important archaeological dig, lost for a hundred and fifty years." She gloated at the surprised look on Hasty's face. He hadn't been going to tell her about the missing diary.

Hollis looked from the necklace to the diary with a puzzled frown. "So how did Miss Lucy get them?"

"That's a mystery." Katharine stowed both artifacts in her tote bag. "I'm working on it as my birthday present to myself."

Amy giggled. "I hope you have as good a birthday as I am. I had lunch with Hollis and Mama, and Papa—my granddaddy—has promised to come with us to the club for dinner. That's really special, because he almost never leaves his house anymore."

Rowena turned to Katharine. "It was good to run into you.

Happy birthday." She ushered the girls ahead of her, checking her watch and picking up her pace as they reached the door.

"Probably running late for some important meeting," Hasty said as he resumed his seat.

"Don't knock it," Katharine told him. "Rowena's a competent woman. It makes me mad enough to spit that her daddy may skip over her and make her son head of the Ivorie Foundation."

"Brandon Ivorie is her son?" Hasty's brows rose in surprise. "I thought he was her younger brother."

"No, he was the product of a disastrous early decision, or so Rowena tells high school students when she preaches to them about the dangers of having sex before marriage. And to give her credit, she knows what she's talking about. Brandon was born when she was barely sixteen. The rumor is that her daddy held the proverbial shotgun to the young man's head and made him marry Rowena to legitimate the baby, but within weeks of Brandon's birth, Napoleon had paid the young man and sent him packing. Rowena got a divorce, took her baby to her parents, reclaimed her maiden name, and changed Brandon's last name to Ivorie."

"Bad precedent," said Lamar from the next table, lathering a biscuit with butter. "Shows young men that sex before marriage can pay off real good."

Katharine wished he'd stop eavesdropping and butting in uninvited. She lowered her voice as she continued. "After high school, Rowena went to Bryn Mawr, graduated summa cum laude, and came back to Atlanta. Her second husband was old and died not long after Amy was born. Since then, Rowena has devoted herself to politics and good works. And as much as I deplore what the Ivorie Foundation stands for, she would make an excellent director. She's more human than either her daddy or her son, and might moderate its politics a little—or its ferocious pursuit of them."

"Which may be why the old man is leaning toward Brandon," Hasty suggested. "We can't have women running things. You know that. You all aren't capable." He grinned, to show he was joking. "Did you ever forgive me for what I did back in Miami? I was a pig."

"You were," she agreed, "but I wasn't exactly a saint myself."

"All square?" When she nodded, he held out one hand and motioned with his fingers. "Then let me see that book. Please? I read German. Fluently."

"I read it, too." She put one protective hand over the tote bag, which was still in her lap. Hasty could probably read the diary in a day, but she wasn't about to let him take it away.

"You have no right to those things," he protested. "If that diary is what I think it is, it ought to be in a museum. So should that necklace. Heaven only knows how they got among your Aunt Lucy's things."

"Heaven only knows and I intend to find out." She stowed the bag under her chair. "Besides, Aunt Lucy was a history teacher. She'd have known if these things ought to be in a museum. The diary's probably unimportant and the necklace a copy or something."

His voice hardened. "Marked Hallstatt 1850? I don't think so. I know about these things. You don't."

"Aunt Lucy wouldn't have stuck them in a box if they were really valuable." It was amazingly easy to fall back into adolescent patterns with Hasty.

"Unless she was in the habit of pilfering." His expression was stony, and his eyes darted to the floor and back like he was measuring the distance to the tote bag and calculating whether he could grab it and run.

"Aunt Lucy was not a thief!" Katharine looped one of the handles over her right foot. She wouldn't let it go without a fight.

The waitress set food before them, but they didn't pay any attention.

"Come on, Kate. History teachers don't make enough to buy things like that. She had to have stolen it—or maybe her brother did. In either case, you don't have any right—"

"Neither do you!" She buttered a biscuit and reminded herself they were both past forty-five and ought to be able to conduct a civilized conversation, even a disagreement, without resorting to rudeness or raised voices. "I'll keep it safe," she promised, trying to mollify him. But his temper was up.

"You don't know the first thing about storing valuable artifacts. If anything happens to that necklace and that diary—"

She glared at him. "Are you threatening me?"

He pushed back his chair. "Not yet, but if anything happens to either one of them, I'll make sure somebody sues you for everything you've got." He flung his napkin onto the table and took out his wallet. He selected a fifty-dollar bill and dropped it beside the napkin. "Happy birthday. Keep the change." He strode from the restaurant, followed by the gaze of every woman in the room.

Katharine heard a low chuckle from the man at the next table.

Chapter 6

During the rest of her meal, Katharine felt other women's eyes sliding her way. Thankfully, the man at the next table ate quickly and left, but on his way out he called, "Be seein' you, Mrs. Murray," attracting more stares from other women.

She devoutly hoped she wouldn't be seeing him again. Or Hasty.

She forked in chicken salad and frozen salad without tasting a bite, mulling over the past hour. She knew she was reasonably attractive, but she had not consciously set out to attract either of those two. Was she sending out some subliminal chemical that announced, "I'm lonesome, pay me attention"? Was this the first sign of menopause?

She decided to pass up dessert. Before she went outside, she scanned people waiting for valets to bring their cars but saw neither Hasty nor Lamar Franklin. When she was halfway down the hill, though, Hasty rose from a bench just ahead. "Kate? Wait up!" He loped toward her.

Behind her, Lamar shouted, "Hey!" and she heard him jogging down the hill.

Being chased stimulates primeval fears. Katharine set off at a dead run—a mistake going downhill in huaraches with slick soles. She slipped, slid, and sprawled on the road.

"Watch that bag!" Hasty yelled.

His priorities were clear. As Katharine climbed awkwardly to her feet, she was glad she hadn't cherished any illusions that he was attracted by her charms. Still, his lack of concern for her turned her fear to fury. She clutched the bag under one arm and wiped her hands on her pants. "How dare you follow me?" she stormed. Her palms and knees were stinging, fueling her fury. "Scat! Both of you!" She shooed them away like two mangy cats.

Hasty turned to the other man and demanded, "What are you doing following this lady?"

"This lady obviously does not want your attentions, sir. Leave her be," the older man said in his gravelly voice.

"You leave her alone. She's a friend of mine," Hasty insisted. "Tell him, Kate."

"I never want to see either one of you again." She hobbled toward the garage with as much dignity as she could muster.

"You heard her," Lamar warned behind her. "Leave her be."

"You back out of this! I told you I'm—"

The next sound Katharine heard was a thud. She looked over one shoulder to see Hasty lying on the ground nursing his nose, with Lamar standing over him. "I told you, Dr. Hastings, leave her be. You go on, ma'am. I'll see he don't bother you none." He glared down at Hasty.

Two women stared from the sidewalk. Red-faced with embarrassment and fury, Katharine limped toward her car.

Before she got in, she looked around the covered parking garage—an automatic gesture after years of living and driving alone. As she unlocked her doors, Lamar was just coming inside, a black shadow against the light. She jumped in and locked the doors even before she stuck the key in the ignition, then she was immediately ashamed. Why should she feel so leery of him? He had been nothing but friendly and helpful. But his work-callused hands, mountain vowels, tattoos, and long, gray ponytail were so out of place in Buckhead, he could have come from another planet.

"Difference breeds distrust," her father used to say. "And we all have a tendency to be prejudiced against those who are different from us. Watch your reactions to people, Kat. You'll find it inside yourself."

"Okay, Daddy," she muttered to him, wherever he might be, "I'll admit it. I'm prejudiced toward outdated hippies who butt in where they aren't wanted and former classmates who want to get their hands on my possessions. I wish they'd leave me alone."

When she had started the car, she tucked her purse between her left side and the door, but dropped the tote bag down in front of the passenger seat. She doubted that any snatch-and-grab thief would be interested in an old canvas tote.

As she left the garage, she saw the hippie heading toward a red Jeep that sat beside a big black truck.

Going up the drive, she passed Hasty, who was stomping into the garage. He glared at her as she approached and tried to flag her down, but she didn't stop.

Traffic was heavy on Andrews Drive, so she had to wait to pull out of the parking lot. Before she could turn left, she saw the red Jeep zoom out of the garage just ahead of the big black truck. Reluctant to head home with those vehicles behind her, she decided to pick up Tom's shirts at the laundry while she was out. She turned right without changing her blinker. Both vehicles turned behind her. At West Paces Ferry Road, she turned right again. So did they.

Both also turned behind her onto Peachtree Street, but neither followed her into the laundry. Relieved, she left the drive-through window and headed back to Peachtree. She decided she might as well go somewhere and copy the diary. That way she could make notes in the margins.

As she stopped at the next light, she noticed a red Jeep a couple of cars behind her. Was it the same one from the parking garage? And was that the same black truck hugging its bumper?

Katharine had watched enough television to know how to figure out if somebody was following her. She switched lanes as soon as she could and watched her mirrors. Within a few seconds the Jeep also changed lanes, keeping two cars between them. The truck pulled in behind the Jeep.

Coincidence? She changed lanes again.

So did they.

By then she was pretty sure one of them was Hasty and the other Lamar. Two dogs after one bone, but which was which? Back in high school, Hasty had wished for a big black truck instead of the used Volvo his parents bought him. Had he finally gotten one as part of his recent midlife and marital crisis? Was he following Lamar, who was following her? Or was Lamar in the truck, following Hasty in the Jeep?

Her first inclination was to laugh. "This is so *silly*," she muttered. But when she turned right at the next intersection, the red Jeep turned a few seconds later with the black truck right behind. She put on another burst of speed and turned right again at the next intersection, planning to dash to the next corner and lose them. Instead, she got stuck behind somebody looking for an address. She was only halfway up the block when the Jeep turned the corner with the truck behind it.

Her arrogance turned to anger, tinged with anxiety. "It's just Hasty," she reminded herself. "He wouldn't hurt me." But what about the other? And how far would either go to get that bag?

"Get back on Peachtree," she told herself. "I'll be fine there." But when she wended her way back to Peachtree—

which wasn't as simple as it sounds, since no two streets in Atlanta run parallel or perpendicular—the red Jeep was not far behind and the black truck rode its bumper.

Some people complain about Atlanta traffic, but Katharine was grateful for every car. She felt safe surrounded by all those people. But what should she do? Going home was out, and she would feel silly calling 911 when one of her followers was an old friend. She peered into her mirror at the Jeep, which was now right behind her, but its visor was down and she could not see the driver.

In spite of her common sense, she was feeling menaced. She tried to think of a smart move, but her brain was sluggish. Articles about what do if you were being followed said, "Go to a police station," but she'd never needed one before, so had no idea where to find one. Why didn't police stations fly flags, like post offices? A special flag that could be seen blocks away?

But even if she found a police station, she couldn't drive straight through the door. What was to prevent whoever was in the Jeep from grabbing her as soon as she left her SUV?

She drove up Peachtree Street picturing a perfect world in which bright red flags flew over drive-in police stations.

When she saw an office supplies store ahead, she made a snap decision. Quickly she changed lanes and barreled through a cacophony of horns into a narrow strip of parking spaces that fronted on Peachtree Street. Then she remembered—the front of that store was at the back, down a narrow alley. Already the red Jeep was moving into the right lane.

She roared down the alley and swung into a parking place right in front, grabbed the tote bag and her purse, and leaped from her car. The blood on her knees, which had dried to her pants, tore loose, but she ignored the pain and dashed for the steps.

Yes, steps. Because of a hill, there was a flight of steps to the front door.

She was still sprinting up when the Jeep screeched to a stop beside her SUV and the big truck roared to a stop behind, blocking them both.

As the wide glass doors opened, spilling cold air onto the sidewalk, she heard doors slam behind her. Without looking back, she darted inside and yelled, "Restroom?" to the startled clerk at the counter. He pointed toward the copy center to the left. She ran in the direction he pointed, tote bag pounding against her thigh in time to the frantic beat of her heart.

The restrooms were tucked inside a large gloomy storeroom, down a hall that led past the break room. Inside, she leaned against the door, trembling. One part of her felt silly, the rest was downright scared. She hurried on rubber legs into the larger stall, locked the door, and leaned against it, gasping for air. How had she gotten into this mess?

She stood breathing hard for several minutes, wondering what to do next.

If she went outside, would one of them be waiting for her? Or both?

No. More likely, one was lying unconscious on the sidewalk right now, while the other prowled the store, hoping to get his hands on Aunt Lucy's antifacts.

What was to prevent him from coming into the ladies' room? Nobody would see him unless they happened to be taking a break. She thought of Edna Buchanan's *Miami It's Murder* and wished she hadn't. In that book, women were raped and murdered in locked restrooms. This one wasn't even locked. Did she hear somebody breathing outside her stall?

She held her own breath and listened, but heard nothing.

After what seemed like an eternity, common sense returned. She would be safer in the store than in an isolated restroom, so long as she was willing to scream if necessary. Gathering up her purse, her tote bag, and her courage, she crept from the stall into the empty bathroom and opened the door. She saw nobody in the storeroom but a clerk carrying a large cardboard box.

She walked cautiously into the store and still saw no sign of Hasty or Lamar.

She headed toward a copier, keeping a wary eye out for either man. All the clerks were bunched near the door, staring at something outside. Blue lights flashed in the parking lot.

"What's going on?" she asked a man in a store vest near the back of the huddle.

"Some woman came running in here yelling and two men started fighting in the parking lot. Probably drug-related or something. The manager called the cops."

She edged closer to the glass doors and saw Hasty and Lamar both wearing belligerent expressions while a serious young police officer talked to them. She considered going outside, but decided against it. She didn't know what either of those men was up to, but they had scared the living daylights out of her. They deserved whatever they got.

She headed back to the ladies' room, took off her bright outer shirt, and put it in her tote bag. She tugged her yellow T-shirt out of her slacks and let it hang loose. She dragged her hair back, and secured it with a rubber band. She put on a thick layer of lipstick and rubbed some into her cheeks. She perched her reading glasses on her nose. At the last minute she remembered Aunt Lucy's peach pits, so she stowed her silver-and-turquoise jewelry in her purse and slung the despicable pits around her neck. Tacky Kat, mistress of disguise, she headed for the copier.

One man in a store vest eyed her suspiciously. "Aren't you the woman who came running in here just before all hell broke loose outside?"

She frowned. "Didn't she have on a bright shirt?"

He thought that over. "Yeah, I guess she did."

She spent an hour copying the diary, careful of the pages and pleased to see that it became more legible if she heightened the contrast. Perhaps she would spend the afternoon trying to translate it.

The whole time, though, she kept checking to make sure Hasty or Lamar weren't lurking behind a display—and that nobody she knew was in sight. She didn't want somebody asking why she had left her house looking like that. When she left the building, she stopped at the top step and looked both ways.

She was so relieved to have run into nobody she knew that it took her a couple of seconds to register the fact that her car was gone.

She wanted to stomp her feet and scream, or sit down and bawl. Screams and tears, however, are only satisfying if there is somebody to calm or console you, so she hitched up her mental socks, headed around the corner, and pulled out her cell phone.

She wasn't about to return to the store and explain, so first she called information and got the number of the store against whose wall she was leaning. She told whoever answered that her car had broken down at their curb earlier that afternoon, and that while she was looking for help, it had disappeared.

"Oh! It was towed!" The clerk sounded horrified. "We'd had a bit of trouble in the parking lot, with the police here and everything, and one of our customers thought that car might be a car bomb. He called and had it towed."

"Don't you think terrorists would use something a little cheaper than a new Cadillac?" she asked. The clerk seemed so baffled by that question that Katharine didn't ask whether they hadn't been worried that the bomb might blow up the tow truck and driver en route. Instead, she ascertained that the number of the towing firm was on a sign in the parking lot and hung up.

While she waited for the towing firm to answer, she murmured to the sky, "Oh, Daddy, can you see the state we've worked ourselves into since you left? Terrorists behind every abandoned car."

The towing firm informed her that getting the car back was only going to involve showing up at their lot with identification and paying an arm and two legs. Katharine considered calling Posey or another friend to run her down, but she looked a fright and was in no mood to explain.

Some folks take a cruise on their birthday. Katharine took a cab.

It was nearly four before she got home, considerably poorer.

She was also jumpier than she could ever remember being. All the way back from the tow lot, she had watched her rear-view mirror. As soon as she got inside the house, she activated their alarm system—something she had gotten out of the habit of doing during the day when she was going in and out. Feeling like a prisoner and annoyed both at herself for being such a coward and at the two men who had made her that way, she dumped the tote bag beside the diary copy on the countertop, kicked off her shoes, and reached for the phone to retrieve messages.

The first was from Susan, bubbly as usual. "Hi, Mom! Just calling to wish you a happy birthday. The market's up and I actually made money! Did you get my package? They promised it would arrive today. Hope you like it. It reminded me of you."

Wondering what on earth might have reminded Susan of her, Katharine waited for her second message. It was from Dr. Flo Gadney and did nothing to calm her nerves.

"Katharine. I am heading down to Butts County for a day or two, trying to track down Maurice's no-count cousin Drake, but I will call you when I return. Driving home, I finally remembered why the name of Carter Everanes seemed familiar. I'll call and tell you all about it when I get back. He was murdered, back in the summer of fifty-one."

Chapter 7

When the doorbell rang, her legs began to tremble. Shakes moved up her whole body until she had to lean against the counter for support. She told herself she was being ridiculous, but the message didn't reach her extremities. Had one of the men followed her after all? What should she do?

She waited for the doorbell to ring again. It didn't. Had whoever it was concluded she wasn't home? Or did he know she was, and alone? Would he try to break in?

She couldn't stand the suspense. She tiptoed to the living room on spaghetti legs and peered through the arch to the front hall. Beyond the sidelight beside the front door sat a parcel. Down at the drive, a stocky woman in brown shorts and shirt was climbing into a UPS truck.

Katharine felt so foolish that she backed into the nearest chair and laughed until tears ran down her cheeks. Laughter provided catharsis and strength to get up and retrieve the parcel. She stood in the doorway for a few minutes vowing not to be so silly again. Still, she made sure the door was locked and the security system reactivated before she returned to the kitchen.

The box contained Susan's present: a perky blue kettle for her newly redecorated kitchen. "To cheer you up since we can't be there." Dear Susan. Tears stung Katharine's eyelids as she headed to the sink, washed out the kettle, and put it on to boil.

Out of the corner of her mind's eye she saw her daughter's dark head bent over the kitchen table, coloring. Jon's fiery mop caught the light as he played with trucks on the floor under her feet. Why hadn't she cherished every single minute she spent with those children? Whoever coined the term "empty nest" obviously never had one. Children may leave home, but they leave a houseful of ghosts behind.

A few minutes later she poured a mug of tea and sank into a chair, limp after the shocks she had sustained in the past few hours. As the tea began to revive her, she reviewed what she had learned.

Fact One: Lucy and Walter Everanes had a brother Carter, whom they never mentioned.

Fact Two: He was thirteen years old when the 1930 census was taken.

Fact Three: He was in Austria in 1937, at twenty.

Fact Four: By 1939 Carter was at home, in Sara Claire and Walter's wedding.

Fact Five: Carter somehow ended up with a necklace from Hallstatt, and a diary.

Fact Six: Carter was murdered in 1951.

Fact Seven: You got Carter's necklace and diary today, and two men chased you to get them. The words rose unbidden and hovered in the air.

None of the facts answered the questions of how Carter got the things or how Aunt Lucy wound up with them. Uncle Walter would have been more likely to be the executor of Carter's estate, and Uncle Walter would never have given them to Lucy. He'd have taken them straight to somebody to have them identified, then he'd have handed them over to any museum that would promise to put up a plaque stating that they were the gift of Walter Everanes. He'd also have had them evaluated so he could get a tax deduction. Walter Everanes had tight fists and a sense of his own importance—two reasons why he and Aunt Sara Claire got along so well.

The most logical conclusion, then, was that Carter gave the things to Lucy before he died. As gifts, or for safekeeping?

Speaking of safekeeping, what was Katharine to do with them until the curator of the Carlos Museum returned?

She considered the small safe behind books on Tom's library shelves, but it didn't feel secure enough. Finally she smiled. She knew exactly where no thief would find them.

She spent the rest of the afternoon going through Aunt Lucy's boxes. A call to Lucy's old school verified that the drama department would, indeed, like to look through whatever Katharine didn't want, so she sorted things into a pile the school might want, a very small pile for herself, and a minimountain of absolute junk—starting with the peach pits. After she took those off, she went straight upstairs to wash her neck.

Things Katharine decided to keep were a wall hanging from Colombia that Susan had always liked, a set of carved ivory (bone?) elephants Jon used to play with for hours, a rain stick from Chile for Tom's instrument collection, and a small, framed watercolor of the Alps for herself. The Alps looked like the ones behind Carter in his picture.

She shelved Lucy's books on the bottom shelf in the music room, to go through another day. Junk she put into large black garbage bags to be hauled away. Things she had set aside for the school she repacked into three of the boxes and carried out to her SUV to deliver the next time she was out. As she slammed the back door, she knew Aunt Lucy would have been pleased to think some of her things would remain at the school, whether anybody remembered her in ten years or not.

Katharine carried the empty boxes to the garage to be re-cycled, vacuumed up the debris, and sat on the piano bench taking a new look at the music room. It was a nice room, re-ally, with the fireplace and tall shelves—the perfect size for an office. She wondered why, since she had lived basically alone in the house for four years, she still had her computer and files in one corner of her bedroom. Last thing at night and first thing in the morning she saw a pile of things she ought to be dealing with. Surely that couldn't be good for her soul. Why shouldn't she work in the music room in-stead? She would just need to take out the piano.

Once she had mentally removed the piano, Katharine found herself stripping the room further. Those books weren't read. They could be packed away and her favorite books put on the shelves. The red floral drapery was heavy and dark, but if she replaced it with something lighter, the afternoon sun would stream through the double windows. Those dark oils had been chosen by the decorator. She would put up her favorite pictures, starting with Aunt Lucy's Alps. As soon as she had that thought, she took down a floral painting beside the arch to the hall and hung the Alps in its place. They looked splendid.

She would buy a new rug, she decided. Tom's investment could go to the attic or he could find another place for it. For her birthday, she would treat herself to what Virginia Woolf said every woman needs: a room of her own.

Katharine felt a small stirring within her that was not un-like the beginnings of pregnancy.

Posey called at five, bubbling over with indignation. "Why didn't you remind me it was your birthday? You know my girls start calling with countdowns before theirs—'Only five more shopping days before my birthday, Mama.' You need to do that next year, so I won't forget."

"Did Hollis rat on me? I saw her at the Swan Coach House with Rowena and Amy Slade, and she looks wonderful. Her new haircut suits her."

"It does, doesn't it?" Posey was always happy to accept compliments on behalf of her girls. "It's a bit odd, but not as bad as we've had before. The best part is, it probably cost the earth, but Rowena paid. She asked Holly if she'd come along with a group of girls to help celebrate Amy's birthday, and said she was treating them all to a makeover to celebrate their graduations. Holly wasn't too keen, but when she talked to some of the other girls and found out nobody else was going, she decided to go."

Katharine was touched, and embarrassed at her own suspicions. "In spite of her unorthodox exterior, Hollis has a very kind heart."

"She does," agreed Hollis's mama. "I am glad she went, too, because she found out it was your birthday. Listen, how about if we take you over to the club for dinner? Julia had a toothache today and didn't come, so we are going anyway."

Julia was Posey's cook, and "the club" in Buckhead meant the Cherokee Town Club, down on West Paces Ferry not far from the governor's mansion.

When Katharine hesitated, Posey begged, "Come on, you can't eat alone on your birthday."

Not until she hung up did Katharine realize that Posey hadn't mentioned Hasty. Did that mean Hollis hadn't mentioned him to her mother? Or that Posey was waiting to pounce?

She was choosing something to wear when Dutch returned her call. "Sorry for not calling sooner, Shug, but that little excursion plumb wore me out. I slept a couple of hours, then had to drive over to a meeting at the church. But hey, Doll Baby, are you having a good birthday even without old Tom?"

"An eventful one, anyway. And Tom will be here Friday to take me to dinner and the symphony. You'll never guess what I've been doing today."

Knowing how he loved a good story, she sat down on the bed in her underwear and gave him a colorful description of finding the artifacts among Aunt Lucy's boxes, going over to the history center, being helped by the aging hippie, running into Hasty, stopping to get the diary copied and having her car towed. She did not tell him about being chased. She didn't want to be responsible for his having another, possibly fatal, heart attack.

"I remember that long drink of water called Hasty," he rumbled. "Real sweet on you, wasn't he? Your daddy thought you all were far too serious for your age."

"He didn't need to have worried. It was just a high school thing."

His deep old chuckle rolled down the wires. "Maybe that's how you looked at it, but I knew the signs. That feller was real stuck on you back then, so you watch out. We don't want him gettin' ideas, with Tom away so much."

"I doubt if he'll ever speak to me again after I wouldn't let him take Aunt Lucy's things home with him to keep them safe."

"If they've been safe with Lucy all these years, they ought to be safe with you. But you say Hasty thinks they could be real old and valuable?"

"If they're as old as he says, they could be extremely so."

"Looks like Lucy would have sold them and taken a few more trips after she retired. She was pretty strapped in her later years. Walter put too much of her money in tech stocks. Where are you keeping the things?"

"In a safer place than she did. She just had them in an old cardboard box with Carter's name on it. You knew Carter, didn't you?" She held her breath, hoping he had.

"Sure. He and I were always in school together. We even both went to Sewanee."

She repressed a spurt of irritation that nobody had ever bothered to mention Carter in her presence, and asked, "Do you know how he might have gotten the things in the first place?" She again held her breath as she waited for his answer.

"No—" He drew out the word like he was thinking it over. "But you say they may have come from Austria? He studied in Vienna one year. Maybe he got them then. He went over the summer of 1937, planning to stay his whole junior year. I went to Oxford that same summer, but just for a six-weeks' course." His chuckle rumbled across the wire. "I don't remember doing much studying, either. Lucy and Sara Claire had just finished their first year at Vassar—Lucy was two years younger than Carter, but she had skipped first grade. Anyway, they came over with several of their Vassar classmates, and I met them in London and traveled with them nearly three weeks. I never was much for studying when there were girls around." His voice dropped to a confidential level. "And I was sweet on Sara Claire back then. Did you know that?"

"No, I never did." She had known these people all her life. Dutch and her daddy had always been best friends, and Dutch and his wife had a condo down on Key Biscayne in Miami, where they spent part of every winter. Summers, she and her mother always joined Sara Claire at their old family place in Cashiers, North Carolina. Aunt Lucy popped up for a few weeks, and Dutch's family had the house next door. Now, she was beginning to feel she hadn't known any of them at all.

"Well, I was," he said, "but she didn't give me the time of day when Carter was around. Carter was twice as handsome and a heck of a lot richer than me back then—my daddy kept me on a very tight allowance. Those things mattered to Sara Claire."

"I'm sure they did." Especially the richer, but Katharine didn't say that. Instead, she asked, "Did you all go to Austria while you were in Europe?"

"Eventually. I met the girls in London, like I said, and we went over to Paris. Carter came up to spend the weekend and we had a gay old time—not the way the word is used nowadays, of course, but a good time was had by all. The other girls stayed on in France, but Lucy and Sara Claire decided to go back to Austria with Carter, and since I'd never been to Austria, I went along. I hoped Carter would break Sara Claire's heart and I'd be around to pick up the pieces."

"Did he break her heart?"

"He certainly didn't pay her a speck of attention. Carter was bookish—he never paid girls much attention. But Sara Claire didn't look at me, either. She went moony over one of Carter's friends—an Austrian who had gone to Sewanee as a junior exchange student the year before. I can't remember his name right now, but he showed us a real good time. Lee and Donk Western were over there at the time, too. Did you ever know Donk? I guess not. He died in the war. Anyway, they had been in that Austrian fellah's class at Sewanee, a year ahead of us, and had gone over to visit him for the summer. Lee and Donk were both wild at college—both had just been kicked out, in fact. They were chemistry majors, and got caught giving girls some hundred-proof alcohol at a party. I think they stayed in Vienna that entire fall. Donk never did graduate from college, but Lee eventually came home and went—I don't remember where, but it doesn't matter."

It sure didn't. Katharine hadn't expected a novel when she'd asked a simple question, but Dutch had a lot of memories and few people to share them anymore. He was still rambling on. "We had great fun in Vienna, because that Austrian knew the best places to get good beer. We stayed and partied a week." He ran down and waited for her to speak.

"Lucy has some pictures of your visit, I think."

"She ought to. Every time I turned around she was sticking her camera in my hands and begging, 'Take another picture, Dutch.' But I never heard if any of them came out."

"She has three or four in her album. I'll show you next time you come over."

"I'd like that. We had a whale of a time. And don't worry that the Austrian broke Sara Claire's heart. Before I got home in August, she had already hooked up with Walter. He was heading up to Yale for his master's in bidness, and I guess they kept the roads hot the next two years, and got married when he finished."

All these revelations about her aunt's romantic life—or lack thereof—might have been interesting at another time, but right then Katharine had a one-track mind. "While you were in Austria, did you all visit a salt mine called Salzberg, where there's a Celtic archaeology site?"

"We were twenty years old, Shug. We weren't looking for archaeology sites, and salt mines would have reminded us of school. I don't think we left Vienna that whole week, then the girls and I went back to England."

"But Carter—he stayed in Austria after that?"

"Oh, yes. He meant to stay the whole school year, but he had to come back earlier than he planned. Hitler, you know. Snuck into Vienna early in 1938 and took over the place slick as a whistle, before anybody caught on to what he was up to, including most of the Austrians. Carter hightailed it home in March, scared the Nazis would conscript him." Dutch paused for a wheezing laugh. "As it turned out, he wound up in Europe with the American army. He was real worried he might have to shoot at some of his buddies from Vienna. He did all right, though. Got him a Purple Heart."

"Do you know that I never heard of Carter Everanes until today?" Katharine didn't try to keep the indignation out of her voice, although she knew it wasn't fair to dump it all on Dutch simply because he was the last of their circle alive. "Nobody told me that Aunt Lucy and Uncle Walter had another brother."

"They didn't talk about him." Dutch lowered his voice a notch. "You see, honey, there was a little unpleasantness."

"I heard he was murdered." Katharine had little patience with that generation's reluctance to talk "in front of the children"—especially now that she was forty-six.

"Yeah. It was made to look like a home invasion, but he was actually shot by his own yardman in his living room. Alfred Simms, the man's name was, and it shocked everybody. Alfred was a handsome-looking buck, well liked, good worker. We never knew how he came to do such a thing. Maybe looking for money. The police said all the drawers were emptied and closets torn apart, stuff strewn all over the rooms. A real mess. Alfred claimed he didn't do it, of course. Said he'd left right after six, when he finished cutting the grass, and that Carter was setting out glasses for a friend to come over for a preprandial drink. But Lucy and Walter asked everybody they knew, and they never found anybody who planned to visit Carter or go out with him that evening, and there was only one glass in the living room. Smashed. Then Alfred was seen wearing a valuable ring Carter brought back from Europe. When he claimed Carter gave it to him, the police arrested him, of course. That's where the unpleasantness began."

"Looks like that's where it would have ended. Was he convicted?"

"You'd better believe it, sweetie." Dutch's voice was rough with the same brutality she had heard in other Southern males when discussing punishment for folks of other races who, they felt, had gotten out of line. "But at his trial, Alfred said some very nasty things about Carter. Lying, of course, trying to save his own skin, and the jury sent him to the chair anyway, but the newspapers had a field day with Carter's reputation. Plumb ruined it. A lot of people believed what they read. Lucy and Walter never talked about Carter much after that. A sad bidness for everybody concerned." Dutch wheezed on the other end and grew silent.

Katharine was silent, too, trying to absorb the story.

"Did all that happen here—the murder and the trial?" she finally asked.

"No, it was down in Decatur." Dutch sounded like Decatur was south of Antarctica, not a few miles away and butted up so tight to Atlanta's eastern edge that nobody could tell where one stopped and the other began. "Why you want to know about all that, Shug?"

Katharine had no idea. She wasn't a morbid person. She never watched televised murder trials. She seldom even watched local eleven o'clock news, it was so blatantly a crime report. When you stay alone a lot, it makes no sense to fill your mind with scary things. Still, she knew she would be back at the Atlanta History Center as soon as possible, reading back issues of the *Atlanta Constitution* for information on Carter Everanes's murder.

She gave what she hoped was a careless laugh. "Just put it down to curiosity—or boredom. There's not much happening around here with Jon gone to China."

"How's he doing? Have you heard from him?"

When they had discussed Jon a few minutes, she asked, "Why was Carter living in Decatur?"

If Dutch thought it odd that she kept hopping back to Carter, he didn't say so. Many of his elderly friends hopped from one subject to the other other, so he probably thought it normal. "Carter *could* have lived with Lucy in their old home place. Neither of them was married, and their folks were dead. But Carter liked his privacy, so when he got back from the army and finished law school, he bought him a place with a little patch of yard around it and he hired Alfred to come help him out in the house and the yard. Alfred had a magic touch where flowers were concerned, and Carter was crazy about flowers. Between them, they created the prettiest yard in Decatur. But I never could forgive Alfred for the things he said about poor Carter. It nearly killed Lucy. She was crazy about Carter."

Heaviness for the honorary uncle she had never known and for Aunt Lucy's grief weighed Katharine down while she dressed. She considered calling Posey to say she had a headache and would prefer to eat alone, but if she did, Posey would bring take-out food to keep her from being alone on her birthday. Besides, Katharine reminded herself with a rueful smile born of experience, if she lied about having a headache, she would develop one out of guilt.

Chapter 8

Festive in a black silk dress and black sandal heels, Katharine was fastening a long gold chain around her neck when Posey and Wrens arrived. Hollis wasn't with them. "She's meeting us there," Posey explained. "She plans to go out afterwards, and will want her car. You know how kids are."

As soon as they were seated at the club, Posey handed Katharine a small white box. "I know my brother will bring you something, but I wanted you to have a present to open today."

A pair of delicate gold earrings shaped like dogwood blossoms glinted in the candlelight. Katharine gave Posey a wordless hug of thanks.

Hollis joined them before they had finished their first drinks and handed Katharine a package wrapped in tissue paper. Katharine exclaimed as she removed a square of colorful silk. "A scarf from the House of Buiton," Hollis said lightly, but her eyes were anxious as her aunt lifted up a stream of subdued shades of blue, green, and teal.

"You hemmed this?" Katharine exclaimed, amazed. The stitches were so small they were almost invisible.

"And designed and dyed it," Hollis admitted with pride.

"How?" When Katharine held up the scarf, it caught the light like jewels.

"It's an American variation of a Japanese process." Hollis's face grew animated and her slim hands flew as she began to describe a process that involved stretching the silk on a frame, painting long stripes of blue and green with a big mop brush, smudging the edges of the colors to soften them, drying it, and ultimately rolling it in newsprint, twisting it around itself and around PVC pipe, securing it at each end with rubber bands, and steaming it. "The steam sets the dye and blends it," she finished, stroking the silk.

Katharine immediately took off the necklace she had been wearing and draped the silk around her neck. "It feels more like satin than silk."

"That silk is called charmeuse." Hollis reached out and stroked it. "I thought those colors would look great on you, and they do."

"Well, none of us ever has to worry that you won't be able to earn a living. It's absolutely beautiful, and I love it." Katharine knew Hollis avoided hugs when possible, so she reached out and gave her niece's hand a squeeze. Hollis glowed with pleasure.

At dinner, Wrens was humorous and tolerant of his womenfolk and Posey managed to do no more than roll her eyes when Hollis started telling about her plans for the carriage house. "I want it to have a minimalist feel, you know?" She gestured with her expressive hands. "Furniture from Ikea, so it won't cost a bundle, and bare windows with blinds. The floors are oak, so I'd like to have them sanded, if Daddy doesn't mind." She gave him a hopeful look.

He waved away her concern. "Whatever you say, Shug, so long as it doesn't put me in the poorhouse."

"Sanding won't cost much more than carpet, I don't think, and will last a lot longer," she told him earnestly. "Zach knows somebody who will do it cheap, and Zach says he's good."

Seeing that Posey was about to say something—possibly uncomplimentary—about Zach, Katharine said quickly, "I understand you and Zach are seeing each other?" She hoped that was the right phrase. Language gets redesigned so quickly by the young.

Hollis fiddled with her fork. "Sort of." She looked at her plate.

Her daddy leaned over and put one of his hands over hers. "You know, Shug, Zach's a nice guy, but I don't like that outfit he works for, not by a long shot. You tell him for me not to go off the deep end."

One corner of Hollis's mouth lifted. "Like he'd listen to me." She turned and peered over her shoulder. "But don't talk too loud. He's right over there, with the Ivories." She gave a quick jerk of her head.

Katharine turned and saw him for the first time. Zach had been a pretty little boy. Now he was a handsome young man except for the discontented expression around his mouth.

The person who compelled her attention, though, was Napoleon Ivorie. Tall, slender, and extraordinarily handsome even past ninety, he had a shock of white hair and an aristocratic profile, and occupied his chair as if it were a throne. Posey leaned over and muttered, "Whatever the waiters think privately of his politics, they sure bow and scrape in his presence, don't they?"

Rowena sat to his right, Brandon at his left. Brandon was leaning toward his grandfather, talking earnestly. Amy sat next to Brandon with Zach between her and her mother. At a table for two just behind Napoleon sat the two men who had come with him to Aunt Lucy's funeral.

"Do you know who those two are behind Mr. Ivorie?" Katharine asked Hollis.

Hollis grimaced. "Bodyguards. They are with him all the time."

"They sure cast a pall over a party. The birthday girl isn't quite so radiant this evening."

Hollis looked over at Amy and scowled. "Maybe because she's getting ignored, as usual. Nobody else matters when Brandon's around. He's probably telling his granddaddy about his latest campaign."

"The gay threat?" Katharine hazarded.

"No, the terrorist threat. Zach says Brandon won't be happy until every person of Arab descent or the Islam religion is run out of the state."

Katharine looked back toward the Ivorie table just as Amy looked their way. Amy gave a little wave, so she waved back. To her surprise, in another minute Amy came prancing over to the Buitons' table and stood swinging clasped hands in front of her, like a little girl. "Would you come tell Papa about those things you found, Miss Katharine? He loves history and things like that." She wore a wide smile, but her eyes kept darting toward her family.

Katharine was figuring out how to excuse herself when Hollis said, "Go. It won't take but a minute."

Katharine had never spoken directly to Napoleon Ivorie, or been so close to the august presence. As they approached him, he was even more impressive close-up than he had been at a distance. His eyes were a unique shade of silver blue, and pierced her beneath frosty brows. His hands were large and looked remarkably strong.

The family genes had been diluted in each generation, for Rowena had inherited nothing from her stunning father except his fair coloring and his charisma while her two children hadn't even gotten that much. Amy and Brandon both had brown eyes, brown hair, and unmemorable faces. Amy

cloaked insignificance in shyness. Brandon cloaked ordi-
nariness in magnificence. Splendid in a tailored navy suit,
subdued tie, and gold cufflinks, and with every hair in place
and nails buffed to a shine, he could have gone on television
at a moment's notice.

"Papa, this is Mrs. Murray, who found the old necklace,"
Amy introduced them.

Brandon frowned up at them, obviously resenting this in-
terruption of their discussion. At a nod from his grandfather,
however, he rose from his chair and put out a hand to Katharine. His grip was firm but brief, as if he had more important
things to do with his time.

His grandfather half-rose from his chair and smiled. "Welcome." It was more courtesy than a man of his years owed any
woman, and as he lowered himself again, Katharine almost
found herself succumbing to his frosty charm, especially
when he put out a hand and held hers while he said, "Another
birthday lady, I am told. Many happy returns. But I don't see
your illustrious husband—" He dropped her hand and let the
sentence trail as he looked around the dining room.

"He's out of town." She was surprised Napoleon Ivorie
knew who her husband was. Tom was well known in corporate circles, but he didn't travel in the Ivories' league. "He'll
be home Friday."

Napoleon's eyes twinkled like sunlight on a frozen lake.
"And if I know anything about women, you will extend your
celebration until then."

Yes, he was charming, if you were partial to ice and snow.
Katharine found herself smiling back. "I certainly will. He's
promised to take me to dinner and the symphony. I'm sorry
to disturb you, but Amy asked me over here—" She hesitated.

"To tell me about something you found today. I understand it may be quite old. I find old things fascinating—perhaps because I am one." He gestured with his free hand. "Please sit down. Brandon will find himself another chair."

When she sat in the still-warm chair, she discovered Mr. Ivorie had still more surprises for her. "I knew your father," he murmured. "We didn't see eye to eye on things—" That was putting it mildly, and his lips curved as if he and Katharine shared a private joke. "—but he was a fine man."

Katharine found it a bit ominous when Brandon fetched himself a chair from the bodyguards' table and pulled it to block hers, but she told herself not to be silly and focused on what his grandfather was saying about her dad. "One of the most honest attorneys I ever knew. I have more admiration for a man of integrity with whom I disagree than for a hundred toadies who claim to think like I do."

"Daddy felt the same way," she murmured. Her father had claimed that most people are sheep, their political opinions largely shaped by their upbringing and friends. He used to say, "Honey, when you meet somebody you totally disagree with, keep reminding yourself, 'They probably can't help it.' Very few people take the time to think through opinions for themselves."

She wondered if Napoleon Ivorie was one who had made his own choices, or if he was merely the product of his upbringing. Holding the same political views for three generations doesn't necessarily make you right, just consistent.

He arranged his long fingers into an arch. "So tell me, what is it you have found that my granddaughter thinks I'd like to hear about?"

"I'm not certain exactly what they are," Katharine admitted. "One looks like a bronze necklace and has the word 'Hallstatt' written on a tag attached to it. The other is a diary, written in German."

He lifted one hand to his lips and she paused, thinking he was about to speak, but he only nodded. "Yes? Go on." He motioned with his other hand.

"It is possible they may have come from a site in Austria, which—"

"I am familiar with Hallstatt. Pardon my brusqueness, but at my age, you don't have time to waste on things you already know. A necklace from Hallstatt would be an intriguing find. How did you come upon it?"

Once again Katharine told the story of Aunt Lucy's possessions and the old box among them. He drew his brows together as if retrieving a memory. "Carter was at Sewanee while I was. He died violently back in the late forties, soon after the war."

"Nineteen fifty-one." She was sorry she had corrected him when a quick look of displeasure crossed his face. The year didn't matter and she suspected Napoleon Ivorie was not accustomed to being corrected.

"Possibly," he said shortly. He turned to Brandon. "That was quite a sensational case, at the time. Turned out his yardman had done it, for some jewelry. Went to the chair, of course."

"As he should have," Brandon snapped. "We are far too lax today."

Napoleon flicked the fingers of one hand. "No doubt, my boy, but we don't need to discuss it at dinner with ladies present. I thank you, Mrs. Murray, for your story. One has to wonder, of course, how Carter came into possession of these things. I presume you are intending to verify that the necklace is genuine and he had the right to have it?"

"I'm going to try, as soon as the curator of the Carlos Museum returns from a trip. The diary that was with the necklace may have come from Hallstatt, as well."

"I do not collect old books, but if the necklace is genuine and you can establish legal possession, I hope you will contact me should you want to sell it. As you may have heard, I have a small collection of antiquities." Again his lips curved at his own jest. The Ivorie collection was renowned, one of the largest in the Southeast. In addition, Napoleon Ivorie was rumored to have a private collection unrivaled in the United States.

He reached out and cupped Amy's chin with one hand. "Thank you, dear heart, for bringing Mrs. Murray over to us. You were right. I was delighted to hear about her finds."

Amy flushed and glowed at his praise.

His hand dropped. "Now I see that her dessert has arrived, so perhaps you would walk her back to her table? Brandon, let Mrs. Murray out." He picked up his fork and turned his attention to his cake.

Katharine walked behind Amy and Hollis with a stunned sense of unreality. Was that how it felt to be in the presence of royalty or the pope—a few minutes of intensely intimate conversation, then dismissal as if you had never existed?

"You didn't bow and scrape," Posey said when Amy was out of earshot. She stuck her fork into a luscious confection of chocolate. "I was watching the whole time, and you didn't scrape once. What was it he wanted you to tell him about?"

"Some old things I found in one of Aunt Lucy's boxes. It's hard to believe, but one of them may be a three-thousand-year-old necklace and the other an important diary that's been missing for a hundred and fifty years."

"In Miss Lucy's things?" Wrens shook his head in disbelief.

Katharine shrugged. "Like I said, it's hard to believe, and we won't know until I have them authenticated, but it's possible. Did you all ever hear of Carter Everanes, Aunt Lucy's brother?"

Posey showed surprise by widening her eyes without raising her eyebrows—a new skill she was practicing since her latest Botox treatment. "A brother besides Walter?"

Katharine told them what she knew about Carter, concluding, "So now I've got to find out where he got the things, apparently, before I can turn them over to somebody."

"I keep tellin' you that no good deed goes unpunished," Posey reminded her. "If you weren't such a saint— But what did Mr. Ivorie want?"

"To buy the things, I'd wager," Wrens suggested.

Katharine nodded. "Not the diary, but if the necklace turns out to be genuine and Lucy had a legitimate claim to it, he has asked me to let him know if we want to sell it."

Posey chewed and swallowed a big bite with a thoughtful expression. "You'll be able to retire to your own Caribbean island on the proceeds from that. And you said Miss Lucy didn't leave you a thing of value." She viewed Katharine with delight in her possible good fortune. There wasn't a jealous bone in Posey's body. "But Mr. Ivorie didn't cut you dead with those icy eyes? I guess your politics don't matter if he wants something from you."

"He was charming," Katharine murmured, digging into her own dessert. "Not at all what I expected. The whole time we were talking, I had his undivided attention."

"Snakes give you undivided attention, too," Hollis muttered. "Most of the time he doesn't know Amy exists, and he and Brandon both treat Zach like a slave."

"They do pay his wages," Posey pointed out.

"That still doesn't excuse—never mind." Hollis stood abruptly. "I'm supposed to meet somebody, so I'd better be going."

"Oh, no!" Katharine looked at her watch in dismay. It was eight-twenty. "I forgot that Anthony is coming to my house at eight-thirty to bring Aunt Lucy's secretary. Will you all forgive me if I thank you for a delicious dinner and beautiful presents, but take my dessert home in a box? And can you drop me off, Hollis? I don't have my car."

She gave Posey and Wrens both a quick kiss and hurried out after her niece.

Zach and Amy joined them while Hollis was opening the driver's door of her little black-and-white Mini. "It was easier than I expected," Zach murmured to Hollis.

"They hardly ever notice me if Brandon is talking," Amy said as she climbed into the back seat.

Zach followed her in, saying to Katharine, "You ride up front with Hollis, okay?"

Katharine had feared she would have to fold herself double to get into the tiny car. Instead, there was plenty of room for four. Hollis noticed her astonishment and grinned in the dimness. "Fooled you, didn't it?" She patted the dashboard fondly. "It's a great little car—in spite of people saying rude things about it." She had raised her voice on the last phrase and spoken toward the rear seat.

"I didn't say anything rude," Zach protested. "I just said it looks like a toy box on wheels."

"If you aren't nice, you will have to walk."

"We'll be nice," Amy assured her. "Won't we, Zach?" A satisfied purr in her voice bothered Katharine, but Hollis didn't seem to notice.

Anthony's truck was pulling up to the front walk when they screeched to a stop behind him. He climbed out and gave Hollis the frown of a man who had known her since she was in diapers. "Mighty good of you to stop before you hit my trailer," he said mildly.

"I thought so," she agreed. Then she saw the tall young man getting out of the other side of the truck. "Stanley! Is that you?" She jumped out and ran to throw her arms around his ebony frame. "I haven't seen you for a hundred years. Look how big you've gotten!" Oblivious to his embarrassment, she turned back to the car and informed Zach and Amy, "Stanley and I used to play together when we were little. Now he plays football for Georgia Tech. What are you doing here?" she asked him.

Stanley gestured to the back of the lawn service trailer, which contained a tall item wrapped in old quilts. "Helping Daddy move some furniture for your aunt." Like most African Americans, he used the British "ahnt" rather than the white folks' "ant."

"Do you need any help?" Hollis put her hand on his shoulder and peered around him into the back of the trailer. "What is it?"

Katharine climbed out to join them. As she did, she glanced in the back again. Amy and Zach sat so close they could have added another person, but watching Hollis and Stanley, they wore identical expressions of disgust.

Katharine answered Hollis's question herself. "Aunt Lucy's secretary. It used to be her grandmother's, and I thought it would be nice to keep as a memento of her and Uncle Walter." *And now of Carter*, she added silently, not particularly happy with that.

Zach stayed in the car with Amy and made no offer to help Anthony and Stanley as they let down the back of the trailer and maneuvered the secretary to the ground. "Where you want it?" Anthony asked.

Katharine knew in an instant. "In the front room to the left of the hall. I'm going to fix that room up as a study, and this will be lovely in there." She ran to unlock the front door and disarm the security system.

"No room in here," Anthony objected when they got to the music room.

"Then leave it in the hall. I'm going to move the piano somewhere else. I'll place the secretary then."

"Might as well shift the piano while we're here." He spoke in the matter-of-fact tone he used when he pointed out that if she planned to put in another rosebush, he'd better start by moving the daylilies that were in the way. He and Stanley set the quilt-wrapped secretary carefully in the hall and went to the piano. "Where will you be wantin' this?" he asked.

She hesitated. She hadn't gotten that far in her planning.

"Over there." Hollis pointed to the back corner of the living room. "And we'll put the chair that's there now over here by the fireplace." She bent and gave the chair a shove. Katharine watched, speechless, while Hollis rearranged her whole living room. Not one chair, sofa, or table remained in its original location. When they were finished, Hollis looked around with satisfaction. "That's a lot better. Now people can talk to each other and you have a great place to read near the fire."

Katharine shook her head in amazement. "Why didn't I rearrange it that way years ago?"

"Looks wonderful," Stanley agreed. "You've got a real knack, Hollyhock." A dull flush rose in his cheeks. "Sorry. That slipped out."

Hollis grinned. "It's okay, Stan-the-man." She turned to Katharine with a pucker of worry between her eyes. "If you don't like it, Aunt Kat—"

"I love it," Katharine assured her. "Want to help me fix up my new study?"

Hollis wandered over to the arch and considered the room. "What do you have in mind?"

"I don't know yet. I just know I hate the rug, I hate those pictures, and I hate the drapery."

"Good." Hollis's voice carried a trace of relief. "Why don't you pick out a rug you like and we can decorate around it? Or buy a picture—something you love. Then we'll figure out what else to do."

Katharine wandered into the almost-empty room to get a feel for it without the piano. As she passed Aunt Lucy's secretary—which looked very at home on the back wall—she saw in its glass-fronted door a thin, dark face with an unreadable expression. She was bending to have a better look when Hollis exclaimed, "I'd better be going. Zach will be wondering what's happened to me. Good to see you, Stanley. You, too, Anthony."

"It's always a pleasure," Anthony told her, "so long as you don't run over my truck."

Hollis's laugh lingered in the room as she ran out the door.

When everyone had gone, Katharine felt like she had been taken from a place of laughter and light and thrust into a place of shadows and silence. Worse, the silence tonight seemed menacing. She returned to the music room to look in the secretary glass, but saw only her own reflection.

"Of course, silly," she told herself as she armed the security system. "There are no ghosts in this house." Nevertheless, she turned on lights in every room downstairs, put on the television in the den and the radio in the kitchen, and checked all the doors and windows to be sure they were locked—even though the alarm would let her know if they weren't. She was tempted to open the front door and leave it open long enough to test how fast it took a knight in police armor to come roaring up the drive.

"Get a grip," she said aloud. "Check your messages, eat your dessert, and go to bed. And stop talking to yourself. That's the first sign of senility."

She had one message, a gravelly voice that sent shivers up her spine. "Mrs. Murray, this is Lamar Franklin. I was calling to see if you got home safely. Call me back when you get this message so I'll know you are okay."

She considered not complying, but he would probably call again. He answered on the first ring, the sound of televised sports in the background. "This is Katharine Murray," she said, keeping her voice carefully neutral. "I am fine, thank you. But how did you get my number?"

"That's easy for an old researcher like me. I just Googled you." His raspy laugh came over the wire. "You watch out for that other fellah, you hear me? I was sitting in my truck after you left this afternoon, having a smoke before going back to the library, and he jumped in his Jeep and started following you. I don't know if you noticed us or not, but we were both right behind you for quite a while."

"I noticed," she assured him.

"Well, I hope you'll put that necklace in a safe place. You never can tell who might be after it. Good night."

She hung up and cast a look at the darkness outside her breakfast room window. Why hadn't she put blinds on that window? She felt very exposed. She checked the alarm system again, to make sure it was armed.

While she was eating her cake with a big glass of milk, the doorbell rang. She almost didn't answer, but it rang again and she figured it might be Anthony, who had forgotten to take his wife's quilts. She switched on the porch light and peered out the sidelight to see Hasty standing there, a bouquet of daisies in one hand. Daisies had been her favorite flower since she was a little girl and picked them with Aunt Lucy.

"What do you want?" she called through the door.

"To apologize," he called back. "I won't come in, but I wanted to tell you I'm sorry. See? I have learned a few things since our high school days." He held up the flowers. "These are a peace offering—and a belated birthday present."

She opened the door, turned and quickly punched the buttons to disarm the alarm. She turned back to see he was wearing a lopsided grin. "Forgive me?" he asked.

In spite of herself she felt the old tingle she used to get at that grin. To make sure her voice wouldn't quaver, she gave a huff of surrender. "Sure. And thanks." As she stepped forward to take the flowers, she exclaimed, "You've got a black eye."

He touched it gingerly. "And a red nose, not to mention damage to my pride, but I'm sorry I let my temper get away with me at lunch. I didn't mean to spoil your birthday."

She considered inviting him in, but it didn't feel like a good idea. For one thing, she was lonely and, in spite of herself, feeling some of the old pull toward Hasty. For another thing, he *had* followed her that afternoon. She stood in the doorway with the bouquet between them. Since he was a step down, their eyes were nearly level. "Why were you following me?" she asked.

"I didn't like the looks of that character at the next table— and rightly so. When I picked myself up off the sidewalk and got to the garage, he was sitting in a big black truck, ready to go after you." He stepped back and leaned against a small column that held up the veranda roof, crossing his arms on his chest. He used to lean against the supports to her parents' porch like that. Her mother often joked that their porch would fall down if Hasty stopped holding it up.

The night was warm and sultry, with lightning bugs dancing on the dark lawn. Without conscious thought, she stepped down and leaned against the doorjamb across from him. They used to stand like that on evenings after he'd brought her home, when neither of them wanted to say goodnight.

"Maybe he was having a smoke," she suggested.

"Not a chance. As soon as I got in my Jeep, he started his engine. I didn't have your cell phone number, so I couldn't warn you, but I managed to get between you and him. I could tell you had noticed me, but I wasn't sure you had noticed him, and he stayed right behind me the whole time. I decided to follow you long enough to make sure you didn't do something stupid, like go home and show him where you live. That was a smart move, by the way, running into the store like that."

"What happened afterwards? I didn't stick around to see." She propped herself more comfortably and prepared to listen. Hasty always could tell a good story.

"Yeah, so I noticed. I'd barely gotten out of my car when he jumped down from his truck, shouted something, and came at me like a crazy man. Ripped off my glasses, knocked me down, and blacked my eye before I saw him coming. Lordy, he like to scared me to death. Fortunately, somebody called the cops. I was bleeding all over the sidewalk, woozy as all get-out, not your typical knight in shining armor but willing to get up and defend you again—"

She chuckled in spite of herself. "So what happened when the police arrived?"

"I can tell you what *didn't* happen. You didn't come out to vouch for my good character. I tried to explain to the cop—who didn't look much older than my daughter—that I was protecting you from the other man, but then *he* jumps in and starts claiming he was protecting you from *me*. I pointed out that you and I have been friends since Moses came down off the mountain and that the other fellow had been awfully familiar at lunch, but he said—oh, never mind. Anyway, the cop gave us each a warning and let us go."

"Well, after that, some customer in the store decided my car might belong to a terrorist who was going to blow them all up, so he called and had it towed."

Hasty's laugh was pleased. "Served you right."

As they laughed together, Katharine again considered inviting him in—nothing serious, she told herself, just a cup of coffee between friends. But before she spoke, he spoiled the mood.

"You watch out for that hippie, you hear me? He had his ears cocked to every word we said about the necklace and that diary, and I wouldn't put it past him to try and track you down to get them. Where are they, by the way?" As he waited for her answer, she had the feeling he was holding his breath.

She felt like he had dowsed her with cold water. He wasn't there to apologize. He wasn't even there to rekindle old feelings. He was a man on a mission to find out where she had put the necklace and diary.

"In a safe place," she replied coolly. She stepped up into the house. "Goodnight. Thanks for the flowers. It was nice of you to bring them."

He gave her a little salute. "Goodnight. Sleep well. And happy birthday."

When he'd gone, she rearmed the alarm, and put the daisies in a vase. They looked so fresh and pretty, she decided to carry them up and put them on her dresser.

Her sense of humor kicked in halfway up the stairs. "Nobody was pursuing you," she said aloud. "Both guys were protecting you. Doesn't that make you feel a hundred and three?"

Chapter 9

Thursday, June 8

The phone shrilled in the darkness.

Katharine came instantly awake and snatched the receiver with a trembling hand. Which of those she loved was in danger? Her "Hello!" was a demand for instant information.

Instead, slightly off-key, she heard, "Happy birthday to you—"

She pried her eyes open wide enough to see the clock. Only six? No wonder she was still asleep. "Jonathan Herndon Murray, do you have any idea what time it is?"

"Six? It's almost dinnertime over here and I wouldn't have called you so early, but I just finished teaching my first day of classes and was fixing to grab a bite with some guys before we go watch a swordfighting demonstration, so I wanted to call now in case I forgot when we got back." With that kind of run-on sentence, heaven only knew what kind of English the Chinese were learning from him.

She didn't have the heart to tell him he was a day late. A dollar short, too, apparently, since he hadn't mentioned sending even a card. "Daddy's taking me to dinner and the symphony tomorrow night. You're sweet to call, honey." She propped her pillow behind her back and inched up on it. Then she shoved hair out of her eyes and willed her brain to function. "How's everything over there?"

"Okay, I guess. I don't know if anybody's going to learn anything, and I don't know if I'm a very good teacher, but I've met some really great people. Speaking of which, I have to be going. We're going to dinner and a swordfighting demonstration."

"You told me that. Don't get cut or anything." She wanted to keep him on the line all morning, it was so good to hear his voice. She missed him terribly.

"I'll stay out of their way," he promised. "You have a happy birthday, you hear me?"

"I will. Thanks for calling—" She was talking to air. He had already gone.

Katharine got up and headed to the shower. While the hot water ran down her back, she began to think about Carter Everanes again. "Why do I care?" she asked the steam. "It all happened a long time ago, and it had nothing to do with me."

But it did. As she shampooed her hair and washed away the last remnants of sleep, she dredged up several good reasons for learning all she could about Carter. First, even though she hadn't known him, he had been part of her family's story until a few years before her own birth. Like Walter and Lucy, Carter had grown up with her mother and Sara Claire, and once Walter became family, so did Carter, in a Southern manner of reckoning. Carter's unknown story was like a black hole in the jigsaw puzzle of her life. A family as small as hers couldn't afford to have missing pieces. So while she had no idea what she would find when she read the newspaper accounts, she suspected they might clarify some of her childhood memories.

For instance, she remembered how Lucy and Sara Claire would never let yardmen inside their houses. Katharine used to sneak them glasses of ice water, but when her aunts found out, they cautioned, "Keep away from them. You can't trust them. They can be violent men." Was that because of Carter's murder? Had Katharine herself been wary of Anthony at first because somebody named Alfred killed a man named Carter before she was born?

Katharine also remembered how Aunt Lucy had given her a new Teddy Bear and she had wanted to name him "Alfred," but Aunt Lucy had cried, "No!" And her daddy had said, "He looks like a Thomas Bear to me." When Katharine was introduced to Tom Murray, one of her first thoughts was that he looked a lot like Thomas Bear—a square, comforting figure with soft dark hair and intelligent dark eyes.

She remembered that when she went to Vienna for spring break during college, Aunt Lucy had mentioned, "I was in Austria once. It is very beautiful," but she had looked sad and had not spouted reminiscences as she usually did. Katharine had been relieved at the time. Now she understood.

As she shut off the water and ran a squeegee down the shower walls, she named another reason for learning about Carter. Her mother firmly believed in "things we are given"—certain people and situations that God gives somebody to deal with at a particular time. Katharine had been given that necklace, diary, and Carter himself. She had no idea why, but she would do her best with what she had been given. And she would not let Carter's things fall into Hasty's acquisitive hands.

Still, the thought of Hasty made her smile again. She hummed as she wrapped herself in a towel and wound another in a turban around her head. Imagine him being right there in Atlanta without her knowing it! As she fixed her face, though, she turned her thoughts to Carter again and admitted her strongest reasons for reading newspaper accounts of his death: "I'll always wonder, if I don't. And what better do I have to do?"

She dried her hair and dressed in white cotton slacks, an emerald top, and white sandals. With a white blazer over one arm, she headed downstairs, carrying her birthday daisies. When she reached the kitchen, she was astonished to find it was still not yet seven.

Her stomach wasn't ready for breakfast, so she took her secateurs and headed into the yard to deadhead some flowers. The day was still cool enough to be pleasant, the grass dewy enough to exchange her sandals for green rubber clogs. When she had cut off old blooms, she cut a small bouquet of sunny yarrow and spiky blue veronica to add to Hasty's daisies on the kitchen table. She snipped one perfect yellow rosebud as well.

As she set the rosebud over the sink, she thought with a pang, *this is the first time I ever cut flowers just for myself.* Usually she was taking them to friends or preparing the house for the arrival of Tom, the children, or a guest.

That morning, she prepared breakfast as if for a special guest—a slice of cantaloupe, a sunny-side-up egg, hot buttered toast with strawberry jam—thinking about what she would like instead of reaching for whatever was handiest. Then she sat at the table and ate slowly, savoring each bite. As she looked out at the patio and how pleasant it was out there, she firmed up her resolve to buy a little table and chairs so she could eat out there whenever she liked.

"I'll do it today," she announced to the dishwasher as she put her dishes in. "I'm going to clear off my desk and get ready to move it downstairs. I'm going to box up the books from the music room shelves and roll up that ugly rug. And I'm going out to buy me a new rug!"

When the maid arrived and saw the changes to the living room and music room, she placed both hands on her ample hips and demanded, "What fer you want to go changing all the furniture around? Nobody plays that piano, so why put it in your living room, takin' up all that space?" Rosa might only stand five feet tall in her new running shoes, but she could swell like Mighty Mouse with indignation.

"Because nobody goes in the living room except for parties, when somebody might want to play it, and I plan to make the other room my office."

Why did she feel forced to explain? Katharine wondered. Posey, for whom Rosa's sister Julia worked, never had to justify the many changes she made in her house.

That, Katharine told herself ruefully, *is one of the big differences between us.*

Rosa galloped on to another topic. "What you needin' an office fer? You ain't workin', and you got a perfectly good computer desk in your bedroom fer your little bits and pieces. Nobody can see it up there, which is a good thing, as messy as you keeps it. You put it down here, you gonna have to learn to tidy it up and keep it that way. And you gonna have ridges in the bedroom rug, too, where the computer desk usta be. Just leave it where it is and get on with things. That's what I say."

"Well, I say I want an office," Katharine retorted in exasperation. "I'm the only person in this house most of the time, yet I do all my work scrunched up in one corner of my bedroom."

"You just restless, is what it is," Rosa muttered, heading down the hall to fetch her supplies. She called back over one shoulder, "Jon and Miss Lucy leavin' so close together has discombobulated you, that's what. Or maybe you're goin' through the change of life. Why don't you go up to the lake for a little spell? Or throw a party? Miz Buiton's havin' a party in a coupla weeks. I'm gonna help Julia in the kitchen."

"I know all about Posey's party," Katharine told her, "But today I'm not planning a party. After you vacuum the rug in the front room, I want us to roll it up and I want you to clean that floor real good. I'm heading out to buy a new rug."

"What you wantin' a new rug fer?" Rosa objected. "They's years of wear in that rug yet."

"Probably so," Katharine agreed, "but I hate it and don't want to look at it any more. Tom can figure out something to do with it. I'll bring some boxes back, too, so we can pack up the books and clean the shelves real good. When Tom comes, he can help me move my desk."

"You'll mess up your back," Rosa warned. "Better call some of Jon's friends to help, or Hollis's new boyfriend. He's sturdy-looking." She sidled to the door of the music room and peered in at the new secretary. "Where'd you get that piece in there now?" Her tone implied that Katharine had picked it up on the black market.

"It was Aunt Lucy's. She left it to me." Their conversation could go on forever unless she left. Rosa would far rather talk than work. "Well, I'm off now, to buy a new rug and a surprise for the patio. I don't know if I'll be back before lunch, so don't count on me."

She picked up her purse and the second volume of the Atlanta Yellow Pages and headed to the garage with the strange feeling that she was going on vacation. She waited until she was in her car before she opened the phone book and ran her finger down the list of Oriental rug dealers, feeling the same anticipation she felt picking out a cruise itinerary.

On the way, she tried to analyze her delight. With Tom gone so much, she chose most things for the house—everything from new carpet for the den after the dishwasher overflowed to a new digital camera to record Jon's college graduation. But she always made the choice wracked by indecision. Would Tom like it? Was this the very best price she could find for the quality? She also braced herself to answer his invariable questions about why she had chosen that color over another, or why she hadn't chosen another (possibly superior) model over the one she had bought. He didn't mean to criticize—just wanted to understand the process by which she had made her choice. But it wore her out having to consider his opinion of every decision.

Exhilaration bubbled up in her as she turned onto West Paces Ferry Road. For the first time in her life, she was going to make a major purchase to please no one but herself.

First, she stopped by Aunt Lucy's school and dropped off the boxes. On the way to the first carpet dealer she spied a lawn furniture place. They had exactly what she wanted for the patio: a round metal table for two with matching chairs that didn't need cushions. They also had some cushions that could be left on the wicker furniture even when it rained. Posey and Tom might think them tacky, but Posey and Tom didn't have to live with them.

"Your husband will have to assemble the table," the clerk warned as he put the big flat box in the back of her SUV with two chairs on top of it.

"I can manage," she informed him in a tone worthy of Aunt Sara Claire. "Any woman worth her salt knows how to use a screwdriver."

Worth her salt? Now she knew where that old saying came from.

Having conquered the patio, she set out to capture a rug. She found an antique Aubusson in shades of cream, green, and peach with occasional accents of deep cherry red and felt she could gaze at that rug forever and never tire of it.

"I'll take it with me," she announced.

With the rug fitted around her new chairs, she stopped at a phone store and bought herself a dark green phone to complement the rug. She also bought supplies to install a new line and a book on how to do it. "How hard can it be?" she asked herself as she headed back to the car. "The folks who do it every day aren't rocket scientists." That was her mantra whenever she had to master a new skill.

Euphoric from all she had accomplished, she stopped by a couple of dumpsters and fitted cardboard boxes around the rug, table, chairs, and cushions. Feeling like the Joads in *The Grapes of Wrath*, she headed home. Only as she drove up the hill toward her garage did she begin to have qualms. Nothing in the house was in those colors. Except for the kitchen, which Katharine had dreamed of for years, the house was decorated in taupe and cream accented with red, hunter green, or brown. That was what Tom preferred and was what she had preferred, too—until she saw the rug. Now, she wondered, "Do I even know who I am and what I like?"

As usual, Rosa's growl had been a sham. She had vacuumed and rolled the old rug and dragged it into Tom's study, where it lay against the far wall. Aunt Lucy's secretary glowed from a brisk polishing. Rosa had even taken all the books down and dusted the shelves.

Katharine eyed the piles of books on the floor and followed the sound of the vacuum to the upstairs bedrooms.

"I've asked you not to climb ladders when nobody is here," she said without preamble.

Rosa shrugged. "I didn't climb no ladders. I pulled in a straight chair. You get you a rug?" She didn't wait for an answer. "The way you look, it must be something really special."

"It is," Katharine promised. "I'm going to love it."

"You get us some boxes?" Before Katharine finished nodding, Rosa had abandoned her vacuum cleaner and headed for the stairs. "Might as well get them books out of the way, then. What you gonna do with 'em?"

"Take them to the public library for their book sale." Katharine had the heady feeling that she was making a lot of spur-of-the-moment decisions all of a sudden. "Except for those from the bottom shelf. We'll put them back. They were Aunt Lucy's and I need to go through them."

She lost her nerve, though, about getting rid of the books without asking Tom. As she and Posey often joked, he might be a businessman by profession, but he was a pilot at heart: pile-it here, pile-it there. And she had promised years ago not to throw out anything of his without asking him first. If those books suddenly disappeared, he would remember them fondly and forever as his favorites.

Rosa and Katharine staggered down the hall with the boxed books and stacked them in the library beside the rug. Heaven only knew when Tom would get around to doing anything with either the books or the rug, but that was his concern.

"What you gonna put in place of the books?" Rosa asked.

"My own books and favorite things," Katharine told her. "That can wait."

Rosa headed toward the door to the garage. "I guess we might as well fetch that rug in, then. I sure hope you hasn't wasted your money."

The rug would have to be rolled up again when the room was painted, but Katharine was as eager to see it in place as Rosa. They could scarcely lift it, and by the time they had dragged it from the back of the SUV and carried it through the house, both were panting. Katharine fetched scissors from the kitchen junk drawer to cut the twine and they carefully unrolled it. It lay like muted jewels on the music room floor.

Rosa stared down at it, hands on her hips. "That's the prettiest rug I ever did see," she admitted. "but it don't match your walls or drapes."

"I'm going to paint the walls," Katharine explained, "and I'm changing the window treatment, too. Hollis is coming over to help me choose fabrics and colors."

"You'd better hang on to your seat," Rosa advised. "Hollis has some pretty wild ideas. Good ones, mind—she's fixed up her own room real strikin' lookin', but Miss Posey is worryin' herself sick about what she's fixin' to do to their carriage house."

"I'm not worried." Katharine spoke absently, looking at the window and wondering if she ought to go ahead and take down the heavy drapery while she was in the mood. "She rearranged my living room last night. Don't you like it a whole lot better?"

Rosa wasn't committing herself quite that far. "All I'm sayin' is, you better make sure you got veto power." She turned back toward the stairs. "Hollis is mighty arty. And strong willed? Next thing you know, she'll have painted three of your walls black and the other one purple."

"Over my dead body," Katharine vowed, but Rosa was already gone. She liked having the last word.

Chapter 10

Katharine assembled her new table and carried their lunch out there. Rosa grumbled at the heat, but grudgingly agreed the table was "right nice." Afterwards, Katharine went to the history center to read newspaper archives for the summer of 1951. She didn't know the date of Carter's murder, but it had to have been front-page news. He had been a war hero and a member of a Buckhead family. *And white*, she mentally added.

She found the story in the third week of June. PROMINENT ATTORNEY GUNNED DOWN AT HOME, screamed Thursday's headline over a picture taken at a formal function some time before. Carter stood with a glass in his hand talking to someone who had been cut from the picture. He was stunning in a tux. It was no wonder the paper described him as "one of Atlanta's most eligible bachelors." Katharine did the math. He was thirty-four at the time. She stared at his picture and felt tears sting her eyes. What a waste!

She printed out the story when she had read it, then printed follow-up stories for the next few days without reading them. She was wondering how to find the trial for his killer when she smelled stale coffee and cigarettes over her shoulder. "You back researching your family?" Lamar Franklin asked.

Katharine greeted him with mixed emotions. He had nearly scared her to death the last time she saw him, but maybe he'd been telling the truth and was only trying to protect her from Hasty. And she respected his skill at digging into the past. "I'm still checking out Carter Everanes," she told him. "The man I was looking for last time."

He bent and peered at the screen, where the headline read NEW LEADS IN EVERANES MURDER. "He got murdered?" She didn't bother to reply, since that was self-evident. Besides, he was already demanding, "You doin' this for somebody else or for yourself?"

"Just for myself. Why?"

"Because you'll need to be certified if you're goin' into the business."

"Business?" Did people look up old murders for pay?

"Genealogy research. They's people make a living doing family research for other people. For me, now, it's a hobby, but my daughters say I might as well get paid, 'cause I might-near do it full-time. But I don't take money for it, exceptin' for lectures and classes."

If he lectured and taught, that might explain his familiarity with all the big words associated with genealogical research.

"It does kind of grab you," Katharine admitted. "It's like a real-life detective story."

He gave her a wide grin that showed two gold-crowned molars. "It sure is. You done any research into your own family?"

She shook her head. "I don't think I have very interesting ancestors."

"Heck, everybody's got interesting ancestors. They were people just like us—some of 'em good and some as ornery as all get-out. But you find out all kinds of things that help you make sense of who you are. For instance, take my family, now. Every one of us loves to play cards. One night I went home from doin' research and found my daughters and their husbands all at my house, drinking my whisky and playing canasta. And you know what I told them? That very day I had found records of a church trial where my great-granddaddy was accused of visiting a lady for immoral purposes. You know what he said?"

"What?" Katharine was interested in spite of herself. She rested her chin on one palm while she listened.

"He told 'em he hadn't done what they accused him of, but he had two sins on his conscience. He had traveled on a Sunday and he had a habit of playing cards. What you think of that? Card playin' has come down in our family for at least five generations." He chuckled softly. "Talk about the sins of the fathers bein' visited on their children—You never know what you might find if you start diggin' into your family. Could be horse thieves or could be kings."

"Farmers and merchants, more likely." But his enthusiasm was contagious. Maybe she would check out her family one day.

However, his blend of stale cigarettes and coffee was almost overpowering. She gathered up her papers and prepared to leave. She wanted to read the stories about Carter, but not with him breathing fumes down her neck.

"Did you find out anymore about that necklace?" he asked as she picked up her pocketbook and stood.

"Not yet. But this was the man who apparently owned it before my friend got it, so maybe I'll find out something if I learn more about him."

"Well, you keep it safe, now."

"I will," she promised—not that it was any business of his.

She drove to a nearby Starbucks and perused the clippings over a cold frappuccino.

A neighbor had found Carter Everanes late Wednesday evening. "I figured something was wrong," he had said, "because the dog kept howling. Then, when I got over there, the front door was standing wide open and all his lights were on. He's usually in bed by ten-thirty, and his dog wasn't the noisy kind. So I called through the screened door, and that's when I saw him, sprawled on the living room floor. I ran right home and called the cops."

According to the police, Carter had been killed by a shot through his brain, probably sometime between seven and nine p.m. It had been a warm evening, so doors and windows stood open, but all his immediate neighbors had been at church for Wednesday night suppers and prayer meetings. The perfect time to commit murder in the Bible Belt.

Robbery was believed to be the motive, for the house had been torn apart. Walter Everanes had declared, "Whoever did this was after my brother's money and valuables. Several pairs of jeweled cuff links are missing and a set of diamond studs, along with a gold and ruby ring he was particularly fond of and a fine set of silver he inherited from our parents." Walter also claimed that his brother was accustomed to carrying several hundred dollars for day-to-day expenses and emergencies, but no money was found in the house.

Saturday's paper carried an article that filled more than half of page two, and contained pictures of Carter in his army uniform, Carter with his law partners, and Nappy, Carter's pet schnauzer, sitting woebegone on the front veranda of a one-storied house with a graceful mock-Tudor roof rising to a point, then swooping down to one corner. The grounds, according to the article, included a second lot which was shaded by mature trees and beautifully landscaped, "with a small fountain splashing merrily, oblivious to tragedy, surrounded by early summer flowers and a freshly mown lawn."

Sunday's paper announced that two boys playing ball had found Carter's silver, money, and all his jewelry except the ruby ring late Saturday afternoon. The valuables were in a large grocery bag that had been shoved inside a stand of tall Formosa azaleas circling a tree two blocks down the street. The boys were pictured receiving a quarter each from Walter Everanes for their honesty in returning the valuables.

"Good old Uncle Walter," Katharine murmured. "Generous to a fault."

Tuesday's paper reported that Alfred Simms, Negro, Carter Everanes's yard man, had been seen wearing his employer's ruby ring and was being questioned in the case. Alfred's high school picture was included. He had been a sweet-faced young man with a shy grin.

EVERANES MURDER SOLVED! screamed Thursday's headline. A picture showed Alfred hiding his face behind handcuffed wrists as he was led to a police cruiser. The story said that the ring "and other evidence" linked Simms to the murder.

Katharine found herself wanting to see the house where it had happened.

She checked the address and found it on a street map she always carried, Atlanta's metro area not being the easiest in the world to get around in. Streets are apt to change names once or twice and may cross each other a couple of times under various pseudonyms.

Thirty minutes and only two wrong turns later, she pulled up to the curb. The house hadn't changed much in fifty years, but the side yard had been replaced by a long narrow house that looked like it had been added in the midfifties. Knowing

Walter Everanes, Katharine figured he had built that one. Uncle Walter had had no use for any unproductive land except the spacious acres around his own home.

She sat in air-conditioned comfort trying to picture herself in a simpler but less comfortable era when doors and windows were left wide open at night to catch a breeze. She imagined a shadowy figure creeping up the front walk at twilight, pulling open the screen, entering the house carrying a sack. Saw him pull a gun, saw Carter turn in surprise and crumple as the bullet struck him. Saw the man frantically rifling the dim house, stuffing the silver service, jewelry, and money into a sack, hurrying down the sidewalk. Was he surprised into dropping the sack? No, he had shoved it far under the bush. Had he hidden there, hearing something? The paper did not say. Why had he left his loot behind?

A young woman pulling weeds near the front steps had begun to watch the big SUV out of the corner of her eye. A toddler plied his shovel in a nearby sandbox. Katharine wondered if the woman suspected she wanted to snatch the child, or whether she knew her house's history.

When the woman glanced her way again, Katharine had seen enough. No point in distressing the natives.

She drove back to Buckhead trying to square her imagination with reality.

The fact was, Carter's front walk was open to the street, not hidden by bushes, and the windows were double at the front. So how had someone crept up the walk and into the house without Carter seeing him? Atlanta is less than fifty miles from the western edge of the eastern time zone, and that was the week of the longest days of the year, so twilight wouldn't have fallen until nine or so. Surely Carter would have shouted and even run if a stranger had entered. Why didn't he run? Or fight back? And how could the murderer be certain of not being seen?

She still wanted to read the story of Alfred's arrest and trial. After she talked with Dr. Flo again, she would return to the history center. She might even read up a bit on her mother's family.

She smiled as she thought of how engrossed Dutch had been in recent years in putting together the history of his family, with papers and books spilling off his desk. If she got that engrossed in it, she would have a real reason for claiming the music room as her own.

Katharine spent the rest of the afternoon working on the room. She took down the red floral drapery and stuffed it into a black plastic bag to haul to the cleaners. She browsed all the shelves in the house for books she particularly liked and arranged them on the deep music room shelves by category and alphabetically by author. She left lots of space for more books she might want to buy. She chose favorite pieces of porcelain, mementoes, family snapshots, and a couple of her childhood dolls to set in front of the books. Since the shelves were built-in, they could be covered while painting was in progress.

Rosa stopped by on her way out to give one last opinion. "You ain't gonna want to bring down that tacky old computer table from your room. You better use that pretty piece of Miss Lucy's for writing on, then you can close it up and hide your mess. And get you a real pretty computer table and a coupla good chairs. Something snazzy, to match the rug."

"I didn't know you were a decorator," Katharine joked. "You ought to go in business with Hollis." But Rosa was right. Even without its new paint job or anything at the window, the room glowed like a foster child that has finally been adopted. It deserved to be beautifully furnished.

After Rosa left, Katharine decided to take a stab at translating the diary. She took the copy to Tom's desk, which was pristine except for a blotter, a penholder, and a jade paperweight. It also had good light. She added a desk lamp to her mental list of things to get for her study.

She fetched her German/English dictionary, a legal pad and a pencil, and set to work. Since she had inadvertently cut off the edge of the first page before she had figured out how to place the diary on the copier, she retrieved the original from its hiding place and carefully printed in the end of each line on the copy.

Translating was harder than she had expected. Languages had always been her weak subject, and very few of these sentences used the German vocabulary she had struggled to memorize: "Where is the post office?" "When is the next train?" "Do you have any rooms?" "I would like Wiener schnitzel with strudel to follow." The last had always been her best sentence. The professor had joked at one point, "If Katharine ever goes to Germany, she may have to sleep on a sidewalk, but at least she won't starve."

Determined to redeem those two difficult years, Katharine struggled on. Finally she stopped to read the fruit of her labor.

A new beginning deserves a new journal. That this will actually happen after months of planning and hoping, I still cannot believe, but L² assures me it is "set in concrete"—an amusing phrase. L² is far more sanguine than I. I fear that something will happen to crush my hopes. Until everyone is here, I will not permit myself to feel secure. Even then, the endeavor may fail.

No, I will not think that way. I must not. So much

depends on me, and if I think negative thoughts, it could affect us all. I must begin to plan now, so that all will be perfect from the very beginning.

Katharine was surprised when her stomach growled. She glanced down at her watch and saw it was past seven. At seven-thirty she was due downtown for a meeting to evaluate a tutoring project she participated in during the school year.

She stacked the copy, her legal pad, and the dictionary neatly on one side of the desk and set the diary next to the jade paperweight.

She had been working for hours and completed only two paragraphs. At that rate, she wouldn't live long enough to finish it.

Later, she would wonder if that had been a premonition.

Chapter 11

Friday, June 9

The morning was bright and fresh. Katharine stood in the breakfast room looking at the pool sparkling in the middle of her lawn and wondered how long it had been since she swam in it. As a child and teenager in Miami, she had practically lived at Coral Gables's Venetian pool. When she and Tom found their house, they had immediately put in the pool and she had swum with the children every summer day until they got old enough to prefer the company of peers. "I might as well fill it in and plant a flowerbed," she muttered. "Nobody is around to use it anymore."

Almost as soon as she finished that thought she marched upstairs and put on a bathing suit. As she padded down through the shade garden to the pool, she heard a voice she had long ago identified as Sara Claire's inside her head: *Never swim alone, dear. It can be fatal.* She dove cleanly off the side, swam the length of the pool, and turned over to float on her back. As she watched birds swoop high across the sky, she murmured, "If I drown, at least I'll die happy."

She floated, swam laps, sent up silent prayers of thanksgiving for such a marvelous day. But one minute she was reveling in beauty and the next she was asking aloud,

"What's the matter with you? You're acting like you're on vacation. You have to write up minutes from two clubs, you need to make calls for the cancer society, you've got a hair appointment in two hours and a cake to bake, Tom will be home by five, and here you are lying on your back in a swimming pool watching birds."

She turned over and started for the ladder at a resolute crawl, fully intending to climb out and get on with what she had to do. But the sky was so blue and the water so lovely, even the threat of being thrown out of the Protestant Ethic Society couldn't get her out of the pool for another half hour.

As if that weren't hedonistic enough, after lunch she sat in the salon chair, looked in the mirror at the hairstyle she had worn for twenty years, and said, "Do something different."

Michael considered her with his head tilted to one side and his scissors poised above her right shoulder. "Layers would be brilliant."

Katharine suspected his British accent and British adjectives both came from watching Brit coms on TV, but his sense of style made him one of the most sought-after hairstylists in Buckhead. "Do it," she said. Then she sat in fear and trembling while he wielded the scissors. Afterwards, her hair fluffed in layers from eye-level to just above her shoulders.

"This style brings out your eyes," Michael announced proudly. "They are your best feature—truly unusual. You should always wear your hair like this."

She knew that was hyperbole to get him a bigger tip, but she headed for her car feeling as gorgeous as Lady Godiva when she flung off her clothes and climbed up on her horse. All the way home she kept shaking her head to feel the soft layers swirl around her. Wasn't Tom going to be surprised?

But she was surprised first. A BMW sat in her drive and

Hollis and Amy Ivorie sat at her new patio table, drinking Cokes.

"Hi!" Hollis greeted Katharine when she joined them. "I don't have to go to work until four, because we have a performance tonight, so we thought we'd come over here so I could talk to you about your room. Since you weren't here, I let us in and got Cokes."

"That's fine." Katharine had given Hollis a key and the security code back when she was in high school, so she could feed Jon's fish and Susan's dog when the family went out of town. Katharine had never asked her niece to return the key because she had always suspected that on some weekends when they were up at the lake, Hollis needed a place to retreat from her family.

Amy sat hunched in the second chair, her eyes darting to Katharine in short nervous spans, as if she expected to be evicted momentarily. "Your hair looks real nice," she said shyly.

Hollis finally noticed. "That's a fantastic cut! Did you just get it done?"

Katharine whirled and preened. "Sure did. You think Tom will like it?"

"I guess so. When did you get this table?" She ran her hands down one leg. "It's perfect for out here."

Katharine had known Hollis all her life. It wasn't hard to interpret that abrupt change of subject. She leaned down, rested her hands on the table, and looked her niece straight in the eye. "I got the table yesterday. And I got this haircut today for Tom. And for me. Nobody else. The man I had lunch with Wednesday was somebody I knew in high school. I hadn't seen him since then, nor do I expect to ever see him again. We got together at the history center because he was already there and the librarian thought he might be able to tell me about Aunt Lucy's necklace. Not long after you left, he stomped out mad because I wouldn't let him take it home with him. He isn't interested in me, he is hot for Aunt Lucy's necklace. Got that?"

Hollis looked at Katharine with a flicker of uncertainty in her eyes, but Katharine stared her down until Hollis shrugged. "Okay."

Katharine grinned. "I'm flattered you think I've still got what it takes. Now come on, let's go look at that room. I've got things to do before Tom gets home. Coming, Amy?"

Amy looked around uncertainly. "Zach's here somewhere. Zach?" Katharine wondered whether Amy was slightly simple or just very sheltered. She seemed more rabbit than human, too naive to someday inherit and manage millions.

"He said he was going to admire the azaleas," Hollis reminded her. "Zach? Zach! We're going inside."

He came around the corner almost immediately. "Hey, Mrs. Murray. You've got some great azaleas."

As far as Katharine knew, her azaleas were no better nor worse than anybody else's. Azaleas are—well—azaleas. She murmured noncommittal thanks.

"What did you ever do with that necklace and book you found?" He came to the table, reached for Amy's Coke, and took a sip.

Katharine managed not to wince and swallowed the word "germs," but she couldn't repress a little shudder. "I put them in a safe place," she answered. Actually, the diary wasn't safe, it was still lying on Tom's desk where she'd been working on the translation the afternoon before. She would show it to Tom when he got home, then return it to its hiding place.

Hollis's smirk implied that she guessed the hiding place, but she didn't say a word.

Amy asked in a worried voice, "Shouldn't they be in a bank safe-deposit box? That's what Zach says. Did finding them like that give you goose bumps?"

She so obviously wanted goose bumps that Katharine obliged. "Absolutely."

"Did that Emory professor tell you all about them?" Hollis asked. "What was his name, again?"

"Hobart Hastings."

"Dr. Hastings in the history department?" Zach exclaimed. "He was my advisor."

"Did you like him?" Amy asked.

"Not much." Zach bent and brushed some mulch debris from his pants. "We disagreed about a number of things, and I wasn't sorry to see the last of him. Still, he knew a lot about ancient tribes of Europe."

Hollis headed for the door, then turned and gave her two companions a careless wave. "You all can wait out here while Aunt Kat and I check out her room."

As they reached the front hall, Katharine said softly at Hollis's back, "Aren't you worried Amy might snag your boyfriend?"

Hollis shrugged. "Naanh. Is this your rug? Not what I would have chosen, but we can work with it. Paint three walls green, maybe, and one in that deep red."

"Paint the walls cream," Katharine said firmly. "To match the rug."

Hollis blinked. "Cream is *so* out. And with all that cream in the rug, it would look insipid. How about painting the whole room peach?"

Katharine considered. Peach would brighten the room and set off the mahogany shelves. And she'd look good in there, too. Peach was one of her better colors. She nodded. "Agreed."

"I have three friends who could paint it for you, if you like," Hollis offered. "They do real good work, and could use the money. They haven't found jobs yet."

"That would be great. The folks I usually use would tell me they could come sometime around October." Posey might find Hollis difficult, but Katharine found her resourceful.

Hollis peered around. "What else were you thinking of putting in here?"

"I may use that secretary as a desk, but I'll need my computer table and something for files."

"Don't bring your ratty stuff from upstairs." Hollis was as fierce as Rosa. "You'll want things in here you enjoy being around. Speaking of which, the first thing we need to do is get rid of that chair. Why you ever bought it in the first place—"

"It was your Grandfather Murray's." Katharine's voice was sharper than she had intended, but she had always hated that chair and resented that she had been stuck with it. "Your mother wouldn't have it in her house, but neither she nor Tom could bear to part with it."

"Give it to Goodwill and don't tell them," Hollis suggested. "They'll never notice. If they do, ask forgiveness, not permission."

"That is not kind," Katharine objected. "I can't throw it out without asking. Besides, one of you grandchildren might want it one day."

"Not this grandchild. At least put it in the attic for now." Never one to waste time, Hollis went to the kitchen and called, "Zach? Amy? Come help me carry a chair up to the attic."

She came back and said, "I'll get samples of paint colors, call the painters, and look for drapery fabric. You concentrate on finding some pictures you like, a computer desk, and a nice-looking filing cabinet—a lateral file so it's not as noticeable, preferably in wood. Get furniture that looks good with the secretary," she added. "We ought to be able to knock out the whole project in a couple of weeks." She crossed the hall and stood in the living room arch. "I like this room a whole lot better now, don't you?"

"I do. So does Rosa, although she wouldn't admit it."

Hollis grinned. "I'll bet she had a fit if you told her I was helping fix up your new study."

"She did mention purple and black walls," Katharine said with an answering grin.

Hollis gave a snort of disgust tinged with hurt. "I haven't painted anything black and purple since I was in tenth grade, but they'll never let me forget."

Katharine went over and gave her a hug that surprised them both. "Don't worry about what they think, honey," she murmured. "You're going to do just fine."

"You wanted us?" Zach demanded. Amy was pinker than the heat would account for and he looked smug. Katharine threw him a look of disapproval, but he ignored her and moseyed over to the foyer table. "Nice jade." He picked up several pieces and inspected them. "Don't I remember you have more in the library?" He headed that way without an invitation, and stood looking into the curio cabinet. "I remember that jade from when I was a kid. I've always liked jade."

"Come help me move this chair," Hollis commanded.

As he turned, he spied the papers on the desk. "Hey, is that the famous diary?" He ambled over and picked it up. "Hell, it's not in English."

"Which makes sense, if it was written by an Austrian," Katharine pointed out, hoping he wouldn't damage it.

"I guess so." He dropped it back on the desk and went to help Hollis maneuver the chair awkwardly up the stairs.

Amy trailed behind them offering helpful advice like, "Don't hit the banisters. Careful! Don't fall!"

Katharine watched their progress as far as the landing, then went to look at her new room with misgivings. She had always used a professional decorator in the past. What if she and Hollis had bad taste—or no taste? What if they finished the room and she hated it? What if she tried to install her telephone and failed?

She was considering calling the whole project off when the phone rang. She dashed to the kitchen.

"Katharine? This is Flo Gadney. I told you I'd call—"

"I'm glad you did. Did you ever find that cousin of your husband's?"

"No, but I found his mother. She says he's moved to California. She also claims Maurice gave him that property and he sold it. I know Maurice never gave it to him—Maurice couldn't stand him—but the question will be how to prove it. I didn't call about that, though. I called to tell you what I know about Carter Everanes. He was a lawyer, and he got murdered—"

"I found that out." Katharine interrupted because she didn't want to waste Dr. Flo's time. "His yard man shot him and stole some things."

"No, he didn't." Dr. Flo sounded as severe as if Katharine had given the wrong answer in class. "Alfred was a second cousin of my mother's, and a sweeter man never lived. Coming up, I used to talk to Alfred at a lot of family gatherings. He was ten years older than me, but he never talked down to me like some people. By the time I was fourteen, I thought he was the cutest thing in pants, but he was never interested in me that way. Still, when I heard he'd been arrested, I cried for days. And when he was executed? I thought my world had come to an end."

"But you never thought Alfred killed Carter?" Katharine could understand. It is always hard for a family to admit that one of their own has committed a horrendous crime.

"Anybody who knew Alfred knew he wouldn't kill Mr. Everanes. He admired him tremendously. Besides, he had an alibi. He said he left Mr. Everanes mixing drinks in the living room a little past six and went home to bathe and dress before going to his auntie's house for supper. He arrived at her place before seven and didn't leave until after ten. His lawyer proved that Mr. Everanes talked to his sister on the phone around seven, and Mr. Everanes's next door neighbors got home from church at nine and sat on their porch until ten-thirty, when they were ready for bed. But Mr. Everanes's dog was howling, and since his lights were still on, the neighbor went over to ask him to quiet it down. He found Mr. Everanes, dead."

Katharine was half listening to Dr. Flo and half listening to creaks overhead. Somebody was walking around in Jon's bedroom. Hollis must be showing Amy the house. She realized Dr. Flo had stopped. "But the jury—" she murmured.

"Pshaw! Alfred was convicted by an all-white jury who didn't pay one speck of attention to a single witness Alfred's lawyer produced, including Alfred's auntie, a god-fearing woman who taught Sunday school at Daddy King's church."

"Couldn't he have appealed?"

"It wouldn't have done him any good. That was 1951 and he was black. What good lawyer would take his case? And he'd been arrested because he was wearing a ring that had belonged to Carter Everanes. I guess they thought he'd stolen it or something. Maybe he did. In those days a lot of Negroes—that's what we were, back then, Negroes—and a lot of Negroes who worked in white houses figured they had what was called 'toting rights,' the right to carry home food and little things left lying around from time to time, to supplement the pitiful wages they were paid. I'm not condoning stealing, mind, but it's the way things were. So Alfred may have taken that ring, as much as I hate to think he would."

Katharine's mother's maid used to carry a full bag of food home almost every week. When Katharine was eight, she had hotly accused the maid of stealing, but her mother had shushed her and whispered, "It's all right, honey. Just ignore it."

"Did he say how he got it?" she asked Dr. Flo.

"I don't know. Soon after the trial began, Mama shipped me off to a cousin out in Memphis. I didn't get to come home until the trial was over. I remember the night Alfred was executed, though. Our whole church got together to pray and cry. Alfred was very loved in that church."

Katharine felt physically ill. "How awful for you all!"

"That's not the only awful story I could tell you, but I won't waste your time. Things are somewhat better now, and our task is to make sure they get even better than this before our time on earth is done. I just wanted to let you know why the name Carter Everanes was familiar to me. I can't believe I forgot at the time why that was. You reckon I'm getting old and forgetful?"

Katharine laughed. "I reckon your mind is so full, it just can't hold everything up front where you can get to it right away. That's what my Aunt Lucy claimed, anyway. She's the one who started me poking into this, since she was Carter Everanes's sister and left me his things mixed in with hers when she died."

Dr. Flo sounded a bit discomposed. "I don't mean to ruin your memories of your Aunt Lucy. She didn't have a thing to do with this."

"Of course not. But if Alfred didn't, either, I wonder who did kill Carter?"

"I guess we'll never know that, after all this time." Dr. Flo's voice was matter-of-fact. "The best we can do is trust that God punished whoever it was, in His own good time and way."

"God can do the punishing, but I still want to learn all I can about this. Family history has grabbed me in a big way. Do you have any elderly relatives who might know more about the case?"

Dr. Flo considered. "Alfred's sister Cleetie is still alive, but I don't know if she'd talk to you. She's a bit shy around strangers. I'll call and ask her, though, and let you know."

"Thanks, Dr. Flo. I really appreciate this."

Dr. Flo sighed. "You cannot believe what a relief it is to me to find somebody who cares what happened to Alfred after all these years. I've been a little down after failing to find Maurice's cousin, but you are likely to restore my faith in humanity."

Chapter 12

By four-thirty Katharine had laid out the green silk dress Tom had bought her on their last trip to Paris and sexy gold sandals with four-inch heels. She had baked his favorite chocolate cake ("my birthday cake," she reminded herself, although she preferred caramel), and while it cooled, she went out and cut armfuls of hydrangeas to decorate the house. She was bringing them in when she heard the telephone.

"Katharine?" It was Tom. When she heard the hesitancy in his voice, she went limp as an earthworm. Scarcely able to breathe, she sank into a chair before her legs collapsed under her.

"Did you have a wreck on your way from the airport?"

"No, hon, I'm still in D.C. We just learned today that an important meeting will be held Monday morning to draft some legislation that could be detrimental to us. That's got everybody hopping, as you can imagine, because we have to come up with our own recommendations and figures to back them up. I've been running to catch my tail all day, or I'd have called sooner. But obviously I'm not going to make it home this weekend, so we'll have to celebrate next weekend, okay?"

Her relief that he wasn't hurt was followed by anger so

intense, it scared her. Her whole body shook, and it took all her willpower not to hurl the phone through the window.

Tom went right on. "But listen, the symphony tickets are at Will Call. Find somebody to go with you, will you? And dinner is on me."

So what's new? she thought through a red haze of rage. *My whole life is on you.*

She had never worked, because Tom and she both felt she should be home with the children. Besides, in all those years while he was battling his way up the corporate ladder, she often had to attend business functions with him or host them. Even in these pseudoenlightened times, few men climb high in corporate structures without a supportive, stay-at-home wife.

She knew that wives' birthdays weren't high on the corporate priority list, but Tom and the company owed her something. She had raised the children almost single-handedly. She had attended hundreds of boring functions on Tom's arm. Had sat through interminable dinner parties, picked up his dry cleaning so he could be presentable on the job, kept the house going so he'd have a home to come back to, and dealt with all the chores and emergencies he wasn't there to handle. Even a servant deserved to be treated better than that late, offhand call.

The lightning flashed, white hot as her resentment. When a sudden gust of rain sprayed the glass, she felt the sting in her soul. She still hadn't said a word.

"Honey?" Tom sounded puzzled. No wonder. She had always understood before when his plans had abruptly changed. Or had she? Was she being swept out to sea on twenty years of pent-up rage?

She wasn't sure what had changed, why this time was different, but she knew it was.

She couldn't trust her voice, so she said nothing. Tom grew defensive. "I'm sorry, honey, but you know how it goes. We could be in for a real big fight. If I can change their minds, I'll get a great bonus."

"That's all that matters to you men, isn't it?" she snapped. "Your battles and your bonuses. Not wives' birthdays, children's piano recitals, family vacations. It's nice if they fit into your schedule, but what really matters is duking it out and collecting the Almighty Dollar."

"Katharine!" Now he was shocked. "I do all this for you, hon—so you and the kids can have nice things."

She wasn't ready to canonize him yet. Sure, she and the kids had reaped benefits from his job, but Tom reserved for himself the exhilaration of the fight and the right to control everybody's schedule.

The rain came down in a rush, drumming on the patio and muffling his voice. Katharine held herself very still. If she moved, she would gush tears from every pore. "I'll miss you," was all she could manage when Tom finally stopped talking.

When she didn't say the rest of the things he was accustomed to hearing her say on similar occasions—"It's all right, honey. I completely understand"—he muttered, "Yeah, well, I'll miss you, too. We'll do it next weekend, okay? Or something."

"Or something," she echoed and hung up.

Her anger drained, leaving her limp with self-pity. Hot tears trickled down her cheeks, mirroring the drops slowly gliding down the window. "It's not fair!" she cried in a sharp whisper. She pounded her fists on the tabletop until she felt pain, then she pressed them against her cheeks and let sobs overwhelm her. She cried for herself and for all women who celebrate birthdays alone. She cried for all the good times she and Tom had missed because he was out of town. She cried for what she and Hasty had had and had thrown away. She cried for the absence of Susan, and of Jon. She cried for her mother and father, and for Aunt Lucy.

One by one all the losses in her life rose up and towered over her, until she cowered against the tabletop, oppressed by their weight. Finally, when there were no more tears in her, she slumped exhausted in the chair with her cheek on the table, watching the rain.

Gradually she could think again. The depth of her misery surprised her. "I ought to be used to this," she told herself. "It happens often enough. And I don't really mind missing the symphony or the dinner. I would rather have cooked him a special meal for two. It's just ..."

She came to a dead halt. What *was* it that held her like a lead weight in her chair?

It was this new feeling since her birthday that she was slowly fading away. The sense that everybody else was real and she was a reflection in their windows. She remembered Hasty across the table: "It sounds like you've done real well for yourself, Kate. Married a corporate executive, got a house in Buckhead, what more could a woman ask for? I'm happy for you." Was this all she could ask for—a big house and a wedding ring?

She held out her left hand and considered her rings. The diamond was a large emerald cut, the wedding ring a band of diamonds that had belonged to Tom's grandmother. The stones were large, but dim. When had she stopped cleaning them every week?

She reached out and traced a raindrop as it trickled down the pane. "I've got all the restrictions of marriage and none of the privileges," she whispered. She stared across the rain-soaked yard and down a tunnel of years and years of disappointing phone calls. Tom would retire in fifteen years or so, but then what? If he came home to stay, would she know him? Every Saturday when he was home, they ate waffles and read the paper together. On Sundays, they ate French toast and went to church. What did he eat for breakfast on Tuesdays? What television did he watch on Wednesday nights? What book was he reading that week? He was always reading something. They used to read the same books and have animated discussions about them. When had that stopped? If she were on a quiz show and in order to get a prize, had to name his favorite color, current favorite author, and favorite food, could she win?

She felt drained and a little nauseated after her personal storm. She certainly had no inclination to call friends hoping somebody could take her up on a late invitation to dinner and the symphony. Not only was it pouring rain, but she could not face making the explanations, getting dressed, driving through slick streets to pick somebody up, making brittle conversation when she felt like lead. Maybe Hollis and Zach would like to go. She was about to call when she remembered that Hollis was working that night.

She felt one last spurt of anger. Why was she trying to save Tom's tickets? She would call Symphony Hall and release them. If nobody needed them and Tom had to eat them, he could pay for them out of his precious bonus.

That energized her. She made the call, slammed the phone down in its charger, and made thick gooey chocolate icing for the cake. She took a Stouffer's tuna casserole for one from the freezer—comfort food—and while it microwaved, she made a salad and poured herself a tall glass of Pinot Grigio. She cut herself a sinfully wide slab of cake, noting that the storm was growing worse. Rain pounded the patio like snare drums. It was just as well she hadn't gone out in her gold sandals.

As lightning flashed and thunder crashed, she assembled candles and a flashlight in case the power went out, then carried her dinner upstairs on a tray. She put on the pretty nightgown she had planned to wear for Tom, fetched a P. G. Wodehouse collection from the hall bookshelf, and chuckled her way through the adventures of Jeeves and Bertie while she ate. Rain lashed her windows and wind assaulted the house, but her room felt like a safe cocoon.

When she finished one story, she remembered that Dutch was nervous about storms. She reached for the phone and gave him a call, but though his phone rang seven times, he did not answer. Probably downstairs watching a movie, she figured.

When the power went out a little after nine, she pulled the covers up to her chin and went fast to sleep.

She came instantly awake, ears straining. What had wakened her? Was there somebody in the house?

Nobody could get through the security system, she reminded herself as lightning lit up the storm-tossed yard. *Besides, anybody would be crazy to come out in this downpour to rob us.*

The wind flung handfuls of rain against her window. In flashes of light she saw maples and hickories flailing the air like demented creatures. She must have heard a branch falling, or a transformer blowing out. Still, she knew from years of experience that once she woke up nervous, she was not likely to sleep again. No matter how accustomed a person is to being alone, it is hard to recover from fright in the night.

She peered at the clock to see what time it was, how much

more time she would have to sweat it out before dawn, but the clock was black. The power must still be out. Was it out all over the neighborhood, or had somebody cut her wires? Had she reset the alarm after she went into the yard for the hydrangeas? Had she locked the French doors to the patio? She had been intent on getting to the phone, and afterwards, she had been so angry. Had she forgotten to reset the alarm? Those questions would plague her as long as it stayed dark.

She fumbled under her pillow for her cell phone to check the time, to see how many more hours she would have to endure before dawn. But before she could turn on the phone, she heard a thump in Tom's library below. It sounded like books falling from a shelf.

Katharine snatched up the phone and leaped from her bed. She tiptoed to the door, opened it slowly, and peered into the hall. Everything was in utter darkness, but she heard little whispers of movement downstairs near the kitchen.

For one joyful instant she thought Tom had flown home to surprise her, was getting a snack before coming upstairs. Then the narrow beam of a flashlight reflected on the staircase wall, and somebody bumped into something and swore softly. Tom knew his way around the house in the dark and swore more intelligently than that.

She caught her breath—a sharp sound in the silence. That galvanized her into action. She darted on tiptoe across the hall and into Jon's room, a rapid shadow, willing the old wood floors not to creak. She wended her way through the darkness to the closet and pulled its door shut behind her. As silently as she could, she pushed her way past clothes and sports paraphernalia Jon had left behind. His down sleeping bag draped over a hanger in the far corner, for Jon was more careful of his sleeping bag than of his clothes. She felt behind it for the almost invisible handle of a little door in the wall. The opening was sized for children, not women, but she forced her limbs through, feeling the satin of her gown snag on a rough place. She jerked it loose, pulled the door shut behind her and rammed a sturdy bolt in place.

She flipped the light switch before she remembered that the power was out. Then she stood in silence, her pounding heart the only sound. The little space was hot and dark and might house unknown creatures, but at least she was hidden and safe. That was far better than being in the rest of the house with an unknown human.

She felt for the button to turn on her cell phone and winced at the musical chime that announced it was powering up. While it sought a signal, she pressed her ear to the door, straining to hear any noise beyond the closet. When she still heard only silence, she held up the phone monitor and saw with relief that she was reconnected to the world. She also saw it was just past ten o'clock.

"There is somebody in my home," she whispered to the 911 operator.

"I'm sorry, I can't hear you. Where is your emergency?"

Katharine gave her address then froze. The door to the closet beyond the wall had opened. Somebody was moving around inside.

"Hello? What is the nature of your emergency?"

She did not speak.

"I cannot hear you." The operator's tinny voice sounded loud as cymbals.

"Help me," Katharine whispered, then closed the phone to break the connection.

She did not dare breathe.

Beyond the wall, somebody was shoving aside clothing, moving soccer shoes and tennis rackets—almost as if the intruder knew there was a door, but didn't know where to find it. In another minute he or she would reach the back of the closet, shift the sleeping bag, and see it.

Exactly how sturdy was that bolt?

Her heart thundered, keeping time to a desperate prayer: *Oh, God, oh, God, oh, God!*

Then, over her heartbeats and his fumbling, Katharine heard a blessed sound. A siren wailed somewhere in the neighborhood, coming closer.

The other person heard it, too, for everything grew silent. Then she heard another oath and feet hurrying from the closet.

But the sirens did not come to her house after all. They whined off into the distance.

Chapter 13

Katharine's legs refused to hold her any longer. She slid down, felt for a thick cushion she knew was there, and sat with arms clutched around her knees and her back against a prickly stud. She had no idea how long she trembled once the sirens died away. Finally, hearing no sign of anyone returning, she opened the phone, rejoiced to see the small square of green light, and punched 911 again.

"I called a few minutes ago, but we got cut off," she told the operator in a shaky voice. "There was a man in my house. He may be gone by now, but I'm not sure of that."

"What is the location of your emergency?" It was a different voice, but equally calm. Katharine pictured the woman sitting in a place of safety, a Coke on the console, reaching out with a lifeline. That image did a lot to steady her nerves. Her voice did not tremble as she gave her address and name.

"We have already dispatched units to that location," the operator said. "They are on their way."

Relief was followed by panic. "How will I know it's them? I can't go out into the house until I'm sure it's safe."

"Where are you?"

"Locked in a small room behind a closet in an upstairs bedroom—the one to the right of the stairs. I should be safe here, but—"

"Stay there. I'll give them your location and they will call out to you, using your name. Would you like for me to stay on the line until they come?"

Katharine would have liked that very much, but the operator might be needed for other emergencies. "No, I'm okay for now. Just tell them to hurry, please." She slumped against the stud and told herself it was silly to feel abandoned when she had access to immediate comfort in her hand. She checked her phone again to see what time it was, and was astonished that it was still just a few minutes past ten. She considered calling Posey, who was probably piled up on her bed with Wrens watching some old movie, but there was no point in scaring them into getting dressed and coming over when there wasn't a thing they could do that the police couldn't do better. Besides, if the intruder was still on the grounds and had a gun—

Katharine refused to dwell on Posey and Wrens getting ambushed in her yard. Instead, she finally asked herself why she had instinctively hurried to that hiding place instead of shoving a chair under her bedroom door and calling 911 from there.

She smiled in the darkness. Jon would be so proud.

His third grade teacher had taught a Safety First at Home course, which involved the entire family. She had arranged for each child to be fingerprinted and photographed for identification, and then she had given each family three assignments.

First, they had to choose a family code word that children would ask for if somebody besides parents or grandparents approached them and said, "Your parents sent me to pick you up."

Second, they had to designate a place at some distance from the house where they would all gather in case of a fire or tornado. The family had to practice meeting there, to be sure all family members knew exactly where it was, and parents were asked to instruct children to remain there until everybody was accounted for.

Finally, they had to do one project to make their family safer in the home. Parents had to sign a statement that their family had established a confidential code word and a gathering place, and each student had to give an oral report on the family's project.

According to Jon, most families labeled poisons, changed batteries in smoke detectors, or put medicines out of reach. He revealed more about his family than he knew, for he had decided, "We need a plan for what to do in case somebody breaks into the house when Daddy isn't here." He had chosen his own hideout as the place they would go, and he made Susan and Katharine practice climbing in and out of the little door quickly and quietly until they were both sick of it.

Katharine felt her breath grow ragged as she remembered one night when Jon had waked her and said urgently, "Mama, there's somebody in the house! Come on." Terrified, she had wanted to pick him up and run for the front door, but he had grabbed her hand and dragged her unerringly through the dark to his room, into his closet, and through the door to the hideout. She found Susan already there, cowering in fear.

Only when the bolt was shot did Jon turn on the light and announce, "Okay, that wasn't real, but you all did good."

Now it *was* real. Katharine thanked God for that teacher as she sat in the darkness of the small space that cradled her safely.

She also felt kind thoughts toward Tom. This room was one of the things he had done right in raising the children. At six, Jon had asked for a secret place. Tom had calculated the slant of the roof behind Jon's closet and figured they could put a hideout there. He and Jon had cut a hole in the closet wall for the door, carried narrow sheets of plywood inside, and pounded down a floor. They had worked together all weekend, lit by a trouble light on a long cord. The next weekend Tom had let Jon help him wire a bulb and a switch. The third weekend they had constructed the door behind Jon's clothes and installed a sturdy bolt that could be locked from the inside. "Nobody can go in there without your permission," Tom had told Jon, "but if your parents tell you to open this door, you must obey. You are not to use this as a place to go and defy us. If you do, I will nail it shut. Is that understood?"

Jon had agreed and he had kept his promise. But he had spent many happy hours in the hideout, with friends and alone. It had been a space ship, with an old computer monitor and spools nailed to studs for controls and old sofa pillows for seats. It had been a fortress against various Bad Guys. During one period, Jon had decided he'd rather *be* a Bad Guy, so it had become his pirates' den. In high school years, it was the refuge to which he fled when he wanted to be alone. But he had never changed it much. The space ship controls were intact. Comics and dog-eared Three Investigators and Encyclopedia Brown mysteries overflowed a rudimentary bookshelf in one corner. Water pistols and other plastic weapons were stashed in an old milk crate. And a crayoned Jolly Roger still dangled from the rafters.

She slid over toward the shelf and felt underneath a stack of comics, expelled a breath of satisfaction when her fingers found the necklace concealed between the soft pages. Then she gasped. The diary still lay on Tom's desk, where she had been working on it.

Nobody would steal a diary, she consoled herself silently. She hoped that was true. But when she recalled Hasty's threat, she shivered in the hot darkness. To distract herself from thinking about the diary, she named and mourned what was likely to be missing: the televisions, her small CD player, her computer, their silver. Insurance would replace it all, but the hassle that would entail infuriated her. What made anybody think they had the right to inflict that much chaos on somebody else?

Then she had a heartening thought. Maybe the burglar had noticed that ugly rug in Tom's office, rolled and ready for stealing. Maybe she could get enough insurance money for it to refurnish her study.

Sirens screamed so near she knew they must be in her own driveway. Katharine held her breath and heard doors slam, voices call, the doorbell ring. She climbed to her feet and flexed her muscles, then stood rigid with hope until she heard a shout, feet pounding up the stairs, and a friendly call. "Mrs. Murray? Police. The house is secure."

She climbed awkwardly through the small door and limped into the glare of a bright flashlight that went right through her gown.

As she clutched arms across her chest, the officer courteously tilted the light to show his face. "I'm Officer Williams, ma'am. Your power seems to be out. Do you need me to help you walk?" With the light at that angle he looked like a jack-o'-lantern, all head and no body, but he sounded kind.

"No," she told him. "I'm just a bit stiff. Did you catch him?" She grabbed Jon's old blue terrycloth robe from a hook and pulled it on.

"No, ma'am, but we found your front door wide open and your security system disarmed." That was the second officer, standing in the shadows. His tone was disapproving, as if she had left her door open and invited burglars in. His partner turned toward him to light up his face and badge, which read HOWARD. He didn't look a day older than Jon and stood ramrod straight, like he had a poker up his backside.

"The alarm system must have gone off with the power," she concluded.

"They have backup batteries," he said curtly. "You're sure you heard a prowler?" Skepticism oozed out of every word. "It couldn't have been the door blowing open?"

She might be standing there barefoot in nothing but a flimsy gown and tatty bathrobe with blood trickling down her leg from one of the scabs that had torn open coming through the child-sized door, but not for nothing was she the niece of Sara Claire Everanes. She tilted her chin and said with hauteur in her voice, "Absolutely not. I heard him moving around, saw his flashlight, even heard him swear. After I was hidden, he came up into this very closet, but a siren scared him off and he ran out. That must be when he left the front door open."

"But why wasn't the alarm on?" Officer Howard demanded.

Katharine hesitated with a furrowed brow. Had she rearmed the system after she went for the hydrangeas? Had she even locked the doors? Everything seemed hazy.

"Let's walk through the house to see if anything is missing," Officer Williams suggested. He shone the light so she could lead the way.

She saw nothing missing upstairs. As they headed downstairs, the grandfather clock in the hall chimed ten-thirty. To make conversation, Katharine said, "My husband was supposed to come home this afternoon. If he had, we'd have been at the symphony tonight and whoever it was would have had time to empty the house."

"Thank God for small favors," Office Williams responded.

But Katharine wasn't feeling too thankful just then. They had reached the foyer. "Tom's jade!" she cried. The entire collection was gone.

"Isn't it insured?" Office Howard asked when she had told them what was missing. He didn't sound too sympathetic. Katharine supposed on a scale that included rape and murder, a missing jade collection was pretty small potatoes. Still, it mattered greatly to Tom.

"The silver's still here," Officer Williams called from the dining room. He shone his light across the buffet, and even from the hall Katharine could see the glint of her grandmother's tea service, which she had inherited on the death of Sara Claire. She checked the drawer where they kept their flatware and it was all there, as well.

The police moved toward Tom's library. When Officer Williams's light roamed the room, she gasped. The stack of dictionary, legal pad, and copy of the diary were still there, but the diary and the jade paperweight were gone.

"Something else missing?" Officer Williams swept the desk again with his light.

"Another piece of jade and an old diary. I had it there, working on it."

"A book," muttered Officer Howard from the shadows.

"Maybe you can get some fingerprints," she suggested. The desk kept a bright polish, thanks to Rosa.

"Doubtful," said the surly Howard.

"There were none on the front door, either," Officer Williams told her. "Looks like whoever it was, he was savvy enough to wear gloves."

Her conscience was asking unanswerable questions. *How much was that diary worth? Why didn't I put it back in the hideout when I wasn't using it?*

Was it really her conscience, or Hasty's voice?

The rolled rug still lay on the library floor, but as wedges of light circled the room, she saw that the rest of the jade was gone from Tom's curio cabinet. At that point she felt like sitting down in the leather desk chair and bawling, but the two officers were already taking themselves—and their lights—to the den and she was too leery of shadows to let the lights get away.

"He didn't come for electronics," Officer Howard pointed out, shining his light on the entertainment unit where the television's big blank eye gleamed back. "If you don't see anything missing but the jade and the book, shall we wrap it up?"

Katharine was beginning to dislike that young man intensely. "You aren't planning to do much investigating, are you?" She didn't bother to keep the irritation out of her voice.

"Ma'am, it's Friday night. By morning we may have a dozen homicides, gunshot wounds, and drive-by shootings. So far all you're missing are some pieces of insured jade and an old book. There's no sign of a forced entry, your alarm was turned off—" His tone was familiar. Her father used to have the same impatience with rich people who thought their sufferings and losses equaled those of the hungry poor. But dammit, she *was* suffering. Wealth doesn't provide armor against pain.

Office Williams interrupted. "Anybody else have a key to your place?"

"My husband and children," she told him, "but none of them are in town. And my sister-in-law, Mrs. Wrens Buiton." She mentioned Posey instead of Hollis because Wrens's name was familiar to anybody who knew Atlanta. It worked its magic with the older officer.

"Calm down," he told his colleague. "As much as I hate to say it, ma'am, there's not much we can do tonight except file a report. We can come back out tomorrow for a good look around outside and a detailed list of the pieces that are missing—"

"We have a list with pictures in our safe-deposit box," she told him. "I can get that for you Monday morning."

"Good. Now do you happen to have any suspects in mind?"

"I do, actually." She hesitated, for words spoken cannot be taken back. "Zachary Andrews was over here this afternoon with my niece, and he spent part of the time prowling in my bushes. He said he was admiring the azaleas, but what's to admire? Maybe he was doing something to the alarm system. He's very bright. Maybe he's clever with electronics." (She thought, "Or maybe my niece gave him my security code," but she didn't say it.) "He also picked up a couple of pieces of jade and looked them over. And he played in this house as a little boy with my son, Jon, and I swear that whoever it was who broke in was coming directly for the hideout when he was frightened away. Zach played in that hideout many times."

Office Howard was writing in a notebook. "Do you know where we can get in touch with Zachary Andrews?"

"I don't know his address, but he works for the Ivorie Foundation."

Officer Williams whistled. "That makes it touchy."

"I realize that, but maybe they could give you a home address."

"We'll check him out," Officer Williams promised. "We'll also put a description of the jade out on the wire in case it turns up. But there's not much more we can do here. We can't look for evidence outside in this gully-washer, and you'll need to go over the house again when it's daylight. I suggest you go to a hotel or a friend's house for the night."

"I'll go to my sister-in-law's," she decided. "Will you wait until I pack a few things?"

"Sure." He handed her his light. "Would you like me to come up with you?"

"Maybe to wait in the hall." Her imagination pictured a hidden intruder stepping from her bedroom closet and creeping up behind her in the dark.

"I'll wait here." Howard lounged against the kitchen cabinets. Those two probably had no trouble whatsoever playing good cop, bad cop, Katharine reflected as she led the way upstairs. It seemed to come naturally.

Officer Williams waited in the hall outside her door while she pulled on some clothes and slid her feet into shoes. She didn't want to waste time going to the attic for a suitcase, so she dumped what she would need for the night into an old Bloomingdale's carrier. "One more thing," she told him when she rejoined him. "I left something where I was hiding." She climbed back through the door and retrieved the necklace. As she shoved it down in the carrier under her clothes, her fingers tingled as if a current ran through them. As she passed the upstairs hall mirror, she saw again the reflection of a dark-haired woman with a worried face. Or was that her own face in the odd light? She shivered and ran down the stairs.

As she got downstairs, she decided to take the copy of the diary and her German/English dictionary to Posey's, as well. At least she could salvage that much for the historians.

The officers had come in two cruisers. They waited until she headed down the drive, then drove out behind her. One turned off in the other direction, one followed her. She wondered which one was on her tail.

Wind and lightning had abated, but rain still poured down

and the hilly streets were slick in her headlights, littered with small branches and clumps of leaves. The familiar route to Posey's seemed eerie and unfamiliar with no streetlights, no gate lights in estate walls along the way, no brightness in any of the windows. Her vision was blurred, too. Not from rain, but from tears. How could she have lost that diary?

She was halfway there before she remembered she had not called Posey to say she was coming. Was the cruiser still following? She peered in her mirror and saw a car not far behind. Was that a bar of blue lights on top? She couldn't tell. She also couldn't recall whether the city had passed a proposed law against talking on cell phones while driving inside the city limits. Since she seldom did, she hadn't paid any attention. But she didn't want to show up at Posey's without calling first. She pulled the cell phone from her purse and set it in her lap, ready to call at the next stoplight.

There weren't any stoplights. All the power was out. Katharine crept through streaming intersections wondering if she could place a quick call without being seen from behind.

At a four-way stop she opened the phone and punched in "8." *I really ought to delete Mama, Aunt Lucy, and Aunt Sara Claire*, she told herself. *I'd be mortified if Posey found out she was that far down on my auto-dial.*

"Yes? Who is it?" Wrens answered, gruff and drowsy. They were probably watching the late-night news.

Katharine glanced behind her. Was the cruiser near enough to see her? Getting arrested by Officer Howard was not how she wanted to end the day.

"It's me, Wrens. Katharine." Intent on avoiding discovery, she spoke softly.

"Speak up," Wrens barked. "I can't hear you."

"Sorry. It's Katharine. I've had an intruder, and am coming over to spend the night in one of your guest rooms. Tell Posey to unlock the back door, please, and lay out the sheets. I'll make the bed when I get there."

"You will not!" That was Posey, indignant. "I'll have you know there's always a bed made in this house for guests. We never know when one of the girls or the grandchildren will sleep over. But what happened? Wrens just handed me the phone, and all I heard was that you need a bed. Did you and Tom have a fight?"

"No, he's still in Washington and I had an intruder," Katharine repeated. "Do you have power? It's out in our block."

"Ours went out for a few minutes, but it's fine now." Posey and Wrens lived near the governor's mansion. If any part of the neighborhood had power, it would be theirs. "But what do you mean you had an intruder? And what's Tom doing in Washington? He's supposed to be—"

"I can't talk any longer. I'll be there in a—"

Blue lights flashed behind her.

"Gotta go. Bye." She punched the off button and pulled over at the next driveway. How mortifying, to get a ticket from the policeman you summoned with 911.

The cruiser behind her executed a U-turn in the middle of the street, turned on its siren, and disappeared in the other direction.

Chapter 14

Posey's kitchen was a happy place, decorated in red, white, and black with roosters everywhere. Even the teapot was a rooster, for roosters were one of Posey's passions. But Katharine stood in that happy kitchen, took one look at Posey, and burst into tears.

"Oh, honey!" Posey was beside her in an instant, cradling Katharine's wet cheek against her soft one. "Cry it out. It was a terrible thing to happen. Go ahead. Cry it out. What did you do to your hair? It looks fantastic!"

Once Katharine had permission to cry, she lost the urge. But her knees felt weak. She took the tissue Posey handed her and stumbled over to a kitchen chair. Dane, the Buiton's Weimaraner, padded over and lay down with his soft taupe nose on her shoe. As Katharine blew her own nose, Posey propped against the counter and demanded again, "What do you *mean*, Tom's in Washington? Did he forget your birthday?"

Facing Tom's irate big sister, Katharine tried to soften his crime. "Some meeting got scheduled for Monday, and he has to prepare. We'll go out next weekend."

"But I can't believe you actually had a burglar inside the house. Were you there?"

Katharine nodded. She couldn't trust herself to speak.

Posey clutched her throat. "What did you do? I'd have died on the spot."

Speaking of dying, Katharine wished Posey would make hot tea. Their air conditioner must be set low, for she was shivering like a naked Eskimo. Posey must have heard her teeth chattering, for she went to fill the kettle while Katharine told her story. "I followed the drill Jon had us practice years ago for his home-safety class. Remember? I ran across to his hideout, behind his closet—almost without thinking. And I felt pretty safe, with the bolt on the inside."

"You weren't scared?" Posey turned from fetching mugs with a skeptical look.

"Terrified," Katharine admitted, bending to fondle Dane's velvet ears. "Especially when he came into Jon's closet." She clenched her hands together, trying to keep them from shaking.

Posey had been putting tea bags in the mugs, but she stopped with one dangling from her hand. "He actually came into the closet?"

"Yeah, but then a siren started down our street, so he panicked, I guess. Anyway, he left."

"And you climbed out and called the police, cool as a cucumber." Posey clearly didn't believe a word of it.

"No, I called on my cell phone from inside the hideout and I didn't stir until the police came and assured me that's who they were." Katharine was glad to hear the kettle beginning to crinkle and sputter on the ceramic cooktop. The water might boil in a century or two. She wrapped her arms around her chest and held tight.

"That could have been the burglar, coming back," Posey pointed out.

"It could have been," Katharine agreed, "but they came

upstairs calling my name. A burglar would have to have a colossal nerve to do that. Besides, the 911 operator had said she'd tell them exactly where to find me."

"I swan." Neither spoke again until the kettle boiled. Posey poured hot water over each tea bag and carried the mugs over to the table. Then she fetched milk and sugar and shoved one mug Katharine's way.

Finally she sat down heavily across the table and stared morosely into her mug. "What is this world coming to? People coming into other people's houses when they are there? It didn't used to be this way."

Katharine pulled her mug toward her and cupped her hands around it, bent low to inhale the steam. "Sure it did. Carter Everanes was shot by somebody who came into his house when he was there."

"Who?"

"Aunt Lucy's younger brother. He was killed in 1951 by somebody who came into his house looking for money. I've been reading about it in the paper."

Posey was seldom interested in anything other people were reading. "It still seems incredible in this neighborhood. Why didn't your security system go off?"

"I don't know." Katharine sloshed her tea bag up and down in the dark brew and wound the string around it on the spoon. "I may not have re-armed it. I was out cutting hydrangeas when Tom called, and ran to get the phone. I may even have left the back door unlocked." But as she added milk and sugar to her tea, she could see herself holding a large bunch of hydrangeas and reaching awkwardly to punch the re-arm button and twist the deadbolt on the French doors before she dashed to the phone. Had she really done that? Or was she merely wishing she had?

"Lucky burglar," Posey pointed out, "picking the one house on your street with the alarm off and the door unlocked. It's hard to believe, don't you think?"

Katharine almost voiced her suspicions about Zach, but Posey was already worried enough about Hollis. She didn't need to think her daughter's boyfriend was breaking into houses. Time enough for her to find out if he was arrested.

Posey sipped her own tea. "Don't you always set the alarm and check the doors before you go to bed?"

"Yes, but after Tom called I threw something in the microwave—"

Posey gave her a penetrating look. "Frozen tuna casserole?"

She nodded. Posey reached over and covered one of her hands with her own. "I could cheerfully throttle my brother."

"It's okay." But her throat was clogged with tears again, and her eyes burned. She lifted her cup to her lips and felt the rich warmth filter all the way down to her stomach.

Posey gave her a few minutes then asked, "What did he take? The burglar, I mean."

"That diary I found in Aunt Lucy's things. And Tom's jade."

Posey's eyes widened. "*All* the jade? Even the Chinese seal Granddaddy gave him when he turned twelve?"

Katharine nodded, miserable. "He was using it as a paperweight on his desk. The guy got everything, both from the hall and from the library. And the diary—" She couldn't go on. Every time she thought about that diary, she wanted to howl.

Posey was far more prosaic. "Who'd steal a diary?"

"Anybody who thought it might be valuable." Hasty's face rose before her, but she shoved it away. He wouldn't. He just *wouldn't*. At least she hoped that was true.

"Thanks for letting me come over," she added. "I couldn't bear to stay there."

"Of course not, honey. Stay 'til Tom gets home, if you like."

"No, I'll be fine once it's daylight and I can see." She hoped that was true, too. At the moment the thought of her house—big, dark, empty, and possibly haunted—made her tremble.

She couldn't possibly go to sleep yet and Posey was a night owl, so they turned on the tail end of the news.

"Look," Posey exclaimed, "here's our favorite media personality." Brandon Ivorie spoke behind a podium, then handed a check to somebody in law enforcement. "To help in the war against terror," he said with a confident smile.

Posey shuddered. "I wonder if he'd give me a check to combat terror? *He* terrifies me."

Katharine brushed her hair from her face. "But doesn't he seems a bit off his stroke tonight? He stumbled twice in one sentence, and now he's repeating himself." The audio cut quickly and the newscaster came on, smoothly completing the story.

They were on their second mugs of tea when Dane gave a soft "woof!" and padded to the back door. Hollis came in from the garage two seconds later, looking like a witch who had flown in through the rain. Her black T-shirt and jeans clung to her skin and her new hairstyle lay in bedraggled tails on her cheeks. "It's raining bats and salamanders out there," she announced before she was in the door, "and I had to park all the way across the lot from the stage door. I am soaked to the bone." As she bent to fondle Dane's head, she did a double take and demanded, "What are you doing here, Aunt Kat? I thought you all were going to the symphony."

Katharine shrugged. "Uncle Tom couldn't come home. We'll celebrate next weekend."

"But she had a burglar," Posey announced. "Somebody broke into the house. While she was there!"

Hollis skipped a beat, then her eyes widened. "Really? Who?"

"We don't know," Katharine told her. "He ran away."

"You're dripping all over the floor," Posey chided. "Here." She handed Hollis a towel. While Hollis toweled her face, shoulders, and hair, Katharine repeated her story about waiting out the intruder in Jon's hideout, because Hollis had spent hours up there and would appreciate the fact that it had saved her aunt's life.

Hollis had the towel over her whole head, so her voice was muffled. "Did he take anything?"

"The only things I know about so far are Tom's jade and Aunt Lucy's diary—the one I found in her things with the necklace. But the power was still out, so I couldn't take a thorough inventory before I left."

Hollis dropped the towel onto the countertop and went to the fridge to pour a glass of milk. Her hand shook as she raised the glass to her lips. She must have felt as cold as Katharine, soaked and in the air conditioning.

"Why would anybody steal a diary?" Posey demanded. Her forehead creased in thought until she remembered the cost of removing wrinkles. Then she smoothed it instantly. "Do you think it was somebody who heard you talking about the stuff you found, thought it might be valuable, and expected you to be out tonight? Who all knew you were going to the symphony?"

Katharine ran down a mental list and sighed. "Practically the whole city. Somebody could have overheard me telling you all or Napoleon Ivorie at the club, I told Dr. Flo Gadney and Dutch—"

"Dutch wouldn't rob your house! How can you even suggest such a thing?"

"You didn't ask who would rob me, you asked who knew I was going to be out."

She didn't add that she had also mentioned the symphony to Hasty. He might have memorized her disarming code the previous night, she realized with a jolt. He had a good head for things like that. Dutch might remember the code, as well, because over New Year's, when she and Jon had joined Tom in Washington, Dutch had stayed in their house because his was being painted before he put it on the market. But Posey was right—Dutch wouldn't rob her house. He could have told somebody else the code, though.

Hollis could have told somebody, too—specifically Zach. Katharine gave her niece a speculative look, but Hollis's face was buried in her glass of milk.

"Maybe he took the diary to blackmail you or something," Posey suggested, stirring her tea with as thoughtful an expression as she could muster after her surgery.

That finally made Katharine laugh. "For what? My indiscretions aren't that big. Besides, I never write them down in a diary."

When Hollis's dark eyes turned on her with a brooding expression, Katharine felt a flush rising up her neck. She was glad to hear the phone ring.

Posey's eyes darted to the clock. "Who on earth could that be this late?" Katharine knew exactly what she was thinking. *Which of my girls or their children is in trouble?*

"It's probably for me." Hollis went to answer. "Oh, hey," they heard her say. She listened, then turned her back and dropped her voice to a low murmur. She listened again, darted an anxious look toward the adults, and swore softly. "Okay. I'll be right there. Just let me put on something dry." She set the phone on its charger and headed for the stairs.

"Who was that at this hour?" Posey asked sharply.

Hollis paused on the bottom step, but she didn't answer.

"It was Zach, wasn't it?" Posey set her mug down with a sharp click. "You're not going out this late, are you?"

"Just for a little while." Hollis took a couple of steps up.

"Don't you all go to those clubs up on Peachtree, the ones where the shootings take place. You hear me?" Posey's voice was edged with fear.

"We'll be fine." Hollis may have intended to comfort her mother, but the sentence came out in the exasperated tone young adults use with parents of diminished intelligence. She still hadn't turned around, and her slim back was stiff and unyielding.

"You won't be fine if somebody does a drive-by shooting," Posey warned. "And don't tell me you won't get shot. Nobody sets out planning to get shot. That's why they are called 'accidental shootings.'" Her fingers sketched quotes Hollis couldn't see.

Hollis heaved an enormous sigh. "I am twenty-two years old, Mama. I know how to take care of myself. Besides, we may not even go to a club. I'm going to Amy's first, and you know good and well that nothing bad could possibly happen up on the Hill."

Her voice oozed scorn and contempt.

"Not unless their politics rub off on you," Posey replied. But her voice was lighter. Posey would love to drop "when Hollis was up on the Hill Saturday evening" into conversations.

When Hollis came back downstairs, she had put on dry

black jeans and a black tank top, but had merely pulled a comb through her wet hair. She looked anxious to get on the road.

"Can't you find Amy a boyfriend?" Posey asked as Hollis reached for cookies from the jar. "It wouldn't have to be serious or anything, just somebody to—"

"That's none of your business!" Hollis stomped out the door and slammed it behind her. In another minute they heard her car roar down the drive.

Posey stared at the back door like she had been struck, and Katharine was as surprised as she. Hollis didn't always do what her parents wanted, but she never raged. Her weapons were icy, supercilious silence or ignoring what her mother said.

"If I'd ever spoken to my mama like that—" Posey carried their mugs to the sink and sighed. "Another happy evening in the Buiton household. Come on, Katharine, you look ready to drop. Let's get you up to bed."

Posey's guest room had a nineteenth-century canopy bed so high it had its own set of steps, and a wide chaise over by one window with cushions of down. Too restless to sleep, Katharine put on her gown and robe and stood by the window, watching rain fall in sheets. She wondered idly about the call Hollis had gotten. It hadn't sounded like an invitation to party. Katharine had gotten the impression that something was wrong. What might Jon know about his three classmates?

It was the thinnest imaginable excuse for calling halfway around the world, but for a mother, any pretext will do. She fetched her cell phone and punched "3." While she waited for the phone to ring in China, she gave thanks for Tom's gift of cell phones the whole family could use for international calls. Katharine had considered it an extravagance when he got them. Now she counted it a blessing.

Jon answered almost immediately. "Hey, Mom, what's up? Isn't it nearly midnight there? You ought to be getting your beauty sleep. I was fixing to head out and find a bowl of noodles."

"I'm about to go to bed, but I wanted to ask you something and tell you something. Do you remember Zachary Andrews?" She had to move away from the window a little to hear him, the rain was drumming so loud on the slate roof.

"Zach? Yeah. Why?" His voice was guarded.

"Tell me a little about him."

"You remember him. He used to come over and play."

"And took apart the chain on our cuckoo clock, as I remember, and burned holes in my new bedroom carpet."

"Not two of his finest moments, huh?" Jon's gurgle of laughter sounded as if he were just across town and made Katharine clutch the phone, she wanted so badly to have him near.

"What was he like in high school?" she asked.

"He didn't improve much. He was both a genius and a wild man. He got straight A's when he bothered to crack a book, but he got into trouble a lot."

Katharine jumped to the immediate parental conclusion. "Drugs?"

"Among other things. He took his daddy's new BMW without asking one weekend and wrecked it drag racing. He drank a lot, too, and threw parties when his parents were out of town. The neighbors called the police a couple of times. I wasn't ever there," Jon hastened to add, "but I heard about it. He was kicked out junior year because he threatened a teacher who was fixing to give him a C. I don't think I've seen him since. Why do you want to know?"

She answered his question with one of her own. "Do you know how long Hollis has been dating him?"

He laughed. "Hollis? No way. I mean, she knows him and all—"

"Posey says she's been dating him at least since Christmas, and I've seen her with him a couple of times this week. Both Hollis and Amy Slade."

"Oh, really?"

Something about the way he said that made her press him. "What about Amy?"

"Nothing." He was obviously considering what to tell the grownup. "In high school, she was a space cadet."

"She must be brighter than she seems. She got into college and managed to graduate."

Jon gave a cynical laugh. "Her granddaddy's contributions may have helped. I used to wonder if Amy had dropped in from another planet. Really. She's always been weird. But maybe she's improved since high school. Zach has, from what I've heard. He's still a bit intense, but people say he's a lot calmer and straighter than he used to be."

"Straighter than an arrow," Katharine agreed. "He's working for Brandon Ivorie."

Jon whistled. "Are you serious?"

"Yes, and as you can imagine, the idea that Hollis is dating Zach and hanging out with Amy has your Aunt Posey in conniptions."

Jon laughed. "Tell her to be careful, or she'll wrinkle her face. And tell her not to worry. You know Hollis—champion of lame ducks and lost causes. But underneath the black clothes and vampire lipstick, she's solid." He changed the subject abruptly. "Did you and Dad finally celebrate your birthday?"

"No, he couldn't get home. We'll celebrate next weekend.

But I did want to tell you something else. Remember that escape plan you made up years ago, in case we had a burglar when Dad wasn't there? It works. I had a burglar tonight and came out unscathed."

"While you were home?" His voice rose so high it nearly cracked. Katharine could picture his green eyes wide, red eyebrows almost meeting his hairline, freckles standing out across his nose.

"Yeah, but I ran to the hideout and was able to call 911 on my cell phone."

"I didn't put cell phones in the plan."

"A definite improvement on the original. Everything is fine, now, and I'm over at Posey's for the night. There's a big storm going on and all the power is off at our place."

"Did he steal anything?"

"I'm afraid so. He got your Daddy's jade."

"Dad's gonna die!"

"Let's hope not. But it seems incredible to me that anybody would come out in a storm like this to rob a house."

Jon was silent for an expensive half-minute, then quipped, "And I'll bet it happened too late for you to make the eleven o' clock news, huh? There went your ten seconds of fame."

She was glad she had called. Jon could always make her smile. But the lightness was gone from his voice when he added, "You didn't get hurt or anything, did you?"

"Not at all. I wouldn't have told you, but I didn't want to tell your Dad yet, and I needed to tell somebody. You came to mind because your hideout may have saved my life."

"Cool. I wonder if it's too late to get extra credit from my third grade teacher. But why not tell Dad yet?"

"Because he's got an important meeting Monday morning, and I don't want to bother him until it's over."

"So what's new?" On that note their signal either got dropped or he hung up.

What's new? Jon's question hung in the silent room.

She stared into the darkness beyond the window and silently totted up what was new. This restlessness was new. Anger with Tom and his job was new. That crying jag after his call was certainly new—Katharine never cried, she coped. She prided herself on that. Having her house broken into and her privacy violated was new. Seeing Hasty again was new—and had dredged up emotions she had all but forgotten. And this sense that she was useless and slipping away, and nobody was noticing—that was definitely new.

Perhaps it was a reaction to so much newness, but she felt a need to touch something old. She fetched the bag with the necklace and the copy of the diary, wrapped herself in a soft afghan Posey had draped over a small side chair (the air-conditioning was definitely too cold in their house) and stretched out on the chaise. Perhaps she would translate a few pages of the diary to help her sleep, but first she felt a strong need to hold the necklace. She would turn it over to someone else soon enough, but for tonight, it was hers.

She laid her head back against the soft down cushions and closed her eyes. While the rain drummed on the patio below her window, she stroked the circlet of bronze.

A sound startled her. She opened her eyes and saw that the lights had gone out, but in the dimness, she could make out the shape of a man coming through the door. "Wrens?" she tried to ask, but could not speak. She tried to sit up, but could not move. She watched, terrified, as he closed the door behind him and felt his way through the darkness. Then she heard a voice. A woman's voice, drowsy and soft. "It is finished, then?"

The words were in a harsh, unfamiliar language, but Katharine understood them. She also understood the man when he growled. "It is complete." She could tell that he was pleased with his work, whatever it had been. She heard the soft whisper of covers drawn back, although the bed was not where it should have been. She sat paralyzed, wondering what she should do. Slowly she reached for her cell phone, which she had left on a table by the chaise. The table was no longer there.

The man began to snore.

With heroic effort Katharine willed her muscles to move. She slipped silently from the chaise and tiptoed toward the door. The other woman was there before her, opening it without a sound. Katharine crept out behind her and found herself not in Posey's upstairs hall with a nightlight burning, but in a dim room lit only by a banked fire on a hearth. The light was sufficient to see that the ceiling was low, the room without windows. The air was thick with the smells of hot metal and damp earth, and the floor rustled underfoot. Katharine knew, without knowing how she knew, that she walked on rushes and straw.

She could hear the other woman ahead of her, but when she tried to speak, she still had no voice. The woman bent over the fire and rose with a small taper of light. She held one hand in front of the light as she crossed back to the door and closed it, then she went to the middle of the room and lit a wick. The flame flared in a small pottery lamp and leaped in the darkness to reveal the woman herself. She was tall and dark, her hair black as a crow's wing and hanging loose to her waist, her face long and thin with eyes as dark as night—a face Katharine felt sure she had seen before. The woman wore a shapeless gown tied at her waist. Its sleeves fell back on her bare wrists as she fumbled in a nest of cloth and lifted something up to her face.

Katharine gasped. It was the necklace! But it was no longer green. It gleamed in the dim light from the lamp. She had not imagined it had ever been so beautiful.

"You are not complete." The woman's voice was little more than a whisper. "Your metal has been fired, but it is not inspirited."

Her fingers moved around the circlet of bronze. "You have been shaped to the neck of the overseer's bride, but you will give more pleasure to the one who made you and the one who gives you than to she who wears you. Those knobs will lie heavy on her slender chest—as heavy as this marriage will lie on her body and soul." Her fingers touched each knob in turn. "Poor child, do you know what a brute you will wed? He whips men to death who bring out too little salt. You will need strong protection from him—and from his relations, should he die before you. If they believe, with or without cause, that you had any part in his death, they will consign you to fire." The woman turned in one sharp movement. "But I must turn my thoughts away from such darkness. My mind must be clear and pure for what I would do."

She carried the circlet and glided on silent feet toward a door in the far wall.

Katharine knew she ought to try and find the stairs. Posey's stairs must be there somewhere. Instead, she followed the woman.

The carefully opened door swung without a sound on leather hinges. The woman murmured, "Thank you, blessed spirits," as she hurried out. Katharine hurried after her.

Stars glittered overhead. Katharine recognized Orion the Hunter and was comforted to meet a friend in that strange place. The Great Salt Mountain—she knew it at once—loomed black against the fainter gray of the sky. She shivered, for the air was cold and damp and she was glad for Posey's afghan as she followed the woman up a steep track. The woman did not seem to mind the cold, or the breeze that whipped her hair around her shoulders and across her face as they climbed. She held the circlet aloft to the wind, bent to dip it in icy dewdrops that dotted tall grass along the bare path, and touched it gently to the earth. "Bless it, Oh Wind, Water, and Earth, but you alone are not strong enough for what I desire. That requires the Fire."

Her foot encountered an obstacle in the path and she bent and pried out a large stone. "A sign!" she exclaimed, her voice stronger. "You were not there the last time I ascended the mountain. But it is your nature, Oh Earth, to throw up things that have long lain hidden, the nature of all the blessed spirits to uncover, scour, reveal, and refine. Nothing can stay hid forever. Nothing!" Her voice was fierce, and she turned and looked straight into Katharine's eyes. But she said nothing more, just turned and began the steepest part of the climb.

Katharine was gasping by the time they reached a broad flat rock. She hung back as the woman climbed onto it, sat down, and waited.

Katharine knew the woman was praying, for she felt her own spirit joined to the prayer, groping wordlessly toward that which is too mighty and holy for words. At last a rim of gold edged distant mountains and began to spread upward. The woman rose and held the circlet up to the faint light. The bronze gleamed with light of its own, as perfectly shaped as the day.

She intoned softly:

I call upon thee, Fire of heaven,
brighter than any forge.

*Purge this circlet of any impurity in which it was
   created.*
Shield her to whom it is given
*from the evil of him who forged it and of him who
   bestows it.*
Protect her from darts of hatred and vice
*and those who would commit violence against her
   life.*
*Guide the woman who possesses it through strange
   and fearful places,*
grant her blessing and brightness, wisdom and joy
now and forever.
And through the refining of your mighty flames,
Bring her enemies to judgment.

As she finished, the first cock crowed to herald the dawn. She held the circlet aloft until the sun was full over the shoulder of the mountain, until gleam of metal and gleam of sun mingled into one flash of light. "Now you are complete!" she cried.

Trembling, she turned and began her descent.

Katharine moved aside to let her pass and saw a girl step from behind a boulder down the hill. Little more than a child, perhaps twelve, she had pale gold hair and eyes like a mountain pool. "What were you doing?" she asked in a high childish voice.

The woman stopped, as if uncertain what to say. Finally she held out the necklace. "I was blessing this."

The girl drew a breath of delight. "Is it for me?" She took the necklace and clasped it around her neck. "It fits perfectly! Your man is so clever with his hands!" She reached up and touched each of the knobs.

"Of course," the woman agreed with a haughty lift of her chin. "His rings, bracelets, and circlets are prized by princes. Fortunate is the mere man of wealth for whom he consents to make a circlet such as that."

"His works are also considered amulets against ill fortune. Some are credited with saving lives." The girl's face had grown anxious. "Is that true?" She clutched the necklace as if aware for the first time how dear life is.

"Some have that power," the woman acknowledged. Her gaze wandered to the top of the mountain and the rock now bathed with sunlight. "Not all."

"I pray this may be one of them." The girl took it off reluctantly and handed it back.

"Pretend to be surprised when you receive it," the woman cautioned. "My man would beat me if he knew I had taken it from his forge."

"I will. Good morrow!" The girl skipped down the hill as lightly as a gazelle.

The woman watched her go, then turned and looked back up the hill. "Protect her and all to whom it belongs," she said softly. Then she turned, looked again at Katharine, and dissolved like mist.

Katharine lay on Posey's chaise wrapped in the afghan. Rain tapped the pane, and the sky was dark. She felt disoriented and muzzy-headed. Had she dreamed? Or had she slipped through a crack in time? Whichever, she was holding on to the necklace as if for her own dear life.

It tingled in her hands as if a current ran through it. Her fingers were stiff as she unclenched them and laid it on her lap. She closed her eyes and saw again the wide blue eyes of the child for whom it had been made, and the dark eyes of the woman who had blessed it. "I will be faithful," she vowed in the empty room. "I will take care of it while it is mine."

By now she was wideawake. She stroked the circlet once more, then wrapped it in the cloth and returned it to the bag. Now she would tackle that diary. Reports from an archaeological dig ought to put her to sleep fast enough.

She started by looking up the German words for "archaeology" and "archaeologist," to be sure she would recognize them. As in English, they were taken straight from the Greek: *Archäologie* and *Archäologe*.

The sheets of the copy had gotten mixed up when she thrust the first ones back into the envelope, and it took her a while to reorder them by date. The second entry was written over a week after the first, and as she thumbed her dictionary for unfamiliar vocabulary words, she discovered that it did not deal with picks and shovels.

> *When will we finally come together? Can you care for me as I care for you? Will you ever come to me of your own free will? I do not deserve that you even look my way, but I shall die if I do not possess you—no, never possess, but rather discover together what love can be. I nearly despair when I think that may never be. But L² assures me it will, that I must only be patient until you are ready. And because L² knows you so much better than I, I will be patient.*

Surrounded by the music of rain on the roof and hitting the patio below, Katharine let the sheet fall to her lap and sat staring into the darkness beyond her window. This was such a letdown. Either Georg Ramsauer had fooled his fellow archaeologists into thinking he was keeping a detailed account of their work while he was actually conducting an affair, or the diary belonged to someone else—probably Carter. Georg Ramsauer had twenty-four children and a

full-time job. When would he have had time for a passionate affair?

Still, a man with twenty-four children must have an enormous sex drive.

And why should Carter keep his diary in German? To
practice the language while he was in Vienna? Why would
Lucy have kept it all these years?

One thing made it likely that this was Carter's diary: the
name L^2 scattered throughout. Katharine thumbed through
several more pages and saw it on almost every one. That was
probably his code name for Lucy, something they had
dreamed up when they were children. Was Sara Claire his
intended love? Was he far more involved with her than Dutch
had known or been willing to accept?

Katharine had a hard time picturing her aunt ever inspir-
ing that kind of passion. Sara Claire had about as much
warmth and sex appeal as a Canadian lake in February, and
her nose was so permanently tilted up in scorn that Susan
and Jon used to giggle when it rained and say, "Call Aunt
Sara Claire and warn her not to go out. She could drown."
Yet she must have had something in her college days, if
Dutch had been, in his own words, "sweet on her."

Katharine rested her head against the chaise and watched
drops slide down the window. Their journey was erratic and
unpredictable, without pattern. She had grown up believing
that human lives have a pattern, that there is purpose in everything. Now she was losing the pattern of her life—and realized she had never known that of her parents and their friends.
Had Dutch looked at Sara Claire over the years and regretted
he had lost her to Walter? Had she, in fact, become the person
she did because she married Walter? It was all so long ago.

"Why didn't I ask more questions when they were all still
alive?" Katharine murmured.

Because you cannot ask what you do not know needs asking.

She used to be pleased that none of her elderly relatives ever got to the stage where they lived in the past instead of the present. Now she thought with regret, *If they had babbled about their youth and childhood, I might have some answers.*

For the third time that day, tears coursed down her cheeks, but this time they were neither tears of anger nor of fear, but gentle tears of sadness, weariness, and release. She relaxed and let them flow.

She must have dozed, because when she next glanced out the window the rain had stopped, the sky had cleared, and her face was reflected against darkness silvered with the light of a bright half-moon. Or was it hers? The face was long and thin, the hair dark, the eyes watchful. But when she bent closer, it was definitely her own face she saw, as transparent and no more substantial than it had appeared in her kitchen two days before.

Chapter 15

Saturday, June 10

Katharine didn't wake until nearly ten and she had a crick in her neck. Posey's fat guest pillows were chosen for decorative appeal rather than comfort. Or was it because she had slept with the necklace under her pillow?

After stowing it at the bottom of her Bloomingdale's bag, she headed down to breakfast.

The Buiton cook prepared most of the family's meals, but on Saturdays, Wrens fixed country ham, eggs, grits, and his famous cheese biscuits. That morning, however, Katharine went downstairs to find Wrens gloomily reading the paper at the breakfast room table with half a muffin still on his plate.

Posey slid a plate of suspiciously yellow eggs, flat bacon, and muffins in front of Katharine and handed her a glass of juice that was a peculiar shade of orange. "At our age, we need to watch our calories and cholesterol, so today we are having carrot-apple juice, turkey bacon, egg whites, and banana bran fat-free muffins. They taste almost like the real thing."

"And make you wish you had a real meal," Wrens added gloomily. "Would you like some artificial butter for your sawdust muffin?" He passed the spread. "Did you sleep all right?"

"Not entirely," she admitted. "I kept wishing I had put that diary and necklace in our safe-deposit box yesterday afternoon. My bank's not open on Saturdays."

Posey poured coffee that tasted suspiciously like decaf. "If that diary's been gone a hundred and fifty years, nobody is missing it now."

"That's not the point." Katharine stirred in lots of milk and sugar. "It might shed light on some valuable history. And the thing that makes me most miserable is that whoever's got it may not know what it is and throw it out."

"It's done, Katharine," Wrens said firmly. "Always look forward, not back."

Posey leaned over and murmured in his ear, "I'm going to remind you of that when you lose your next golf match."

Katharine was determined to go home and check out the damage in the daylight, but Posey insisted she come back to spend one more night and take Dane over to keep her company that day. Katharine didn't object. She also left the necklace in the bottom of her Bloomingdale's carrier, which she hid under an afghan on the shelf of Posey's guest room closet.

Her own house looked remarkably normal in the sunlight. The shrubs stood tall and perky after their soaking the night before. The flowers had been beaten down but were beginning to lift their heads. Robins explored the grass for unwary worms washed out of their holes by the storm. Katharine expected to feel a foreboding as she drove into the garage, but all she felt was relief to be home. With Dane padding beside her, she roamed the downstairs looking for signs of the intruder, but except for the bare table in the foyer and

Tom's empty curio cabinet, everything looked fine. Nor did she see any broken windows.

With a curious sense that she must have imagined the whole thing, she left Dane in the kitchen and started upstairs. That's when she noticed how big and hushed the house was. It took all her willpower to mount the first step and as she lifted her foot for the second, a wave of unease swept down the staircase and pressed her back. "Dane, come!" she called. Tom would have a conniption if he knew the dog had been in the house, but she was unable to go upstairs without him.

With Dane beside her, she had no problem checking the house from top to bottom. He was perfectly willing to sniff his way in and out of every room. In the basement he had such a fine old time snuffling the dark corners that Katharine began to wonder what small creatures they harbored.

Back in the kitchen, the big dog stretched out on the cool tile floor and chewed a treat while Katharine called the police for a status report on her break-in. They assured her that the officers who came the night before had filed a crime report and would call her that afternoon.

Frustrated that nothing was being done at the moment, she decided to make a list of all the people who knew she'd be out and who had access to her key and her security code, then do a little checking on her own. The police would check out Zach, but what if it hadn't been Zach? She didn't want to send them to her friends and family until she had eliminated the innocent.

She fetched a pen and paper and quickly wrote "Hasty, Dutch, Zach." It took longer to add Hollis to the list, but she told herself, "You can't leave anybody off until you are sure."

She also added Lamar Franklin from the history center. He'd heard her telling Rowena that Tom was coming home Friday and they'd be going out, and a man with his research abilities probably could find information on the Internet about breaking into houses.

She called Dutch first, because she knew his number by heart.

He sounded delighted to hear her voice. When she brought up the storm, he said, "Oh, this place lost power soon after dinner, but fortunately I had already gone up to my room. I'd had a touch of indigestion after dinner, and wanted to lie down. But some folks were stranded downstairs without their medications until somebody figured out how to get the generator up and running. What's the point of having a generator if they don't train anybody on the nightshift how to use it? One of the residents had to show them how to turn it on." He wheezed. "If they'd let us, us geezers could run this place a heck of a lot better than they do."

"But you were in your room? I tried calling you, and didn't get an answer."

Several seconds of silence filled the line. "You musta dialed the wrong number, Shug. I was right here."

"I called your number," she insisted.

Silence fell between them, then he admitted with embarrassment she could hear over the line, "I stepped into the facility for a minute and couldn't make it to the phone."

She didn't mention her intruder. If his touch of indigestion had been a mild heart attack, she didn't want to bring on another. But she hoped he hadn't faked the indigestion—and lied about being in his room—to cover up the fact that he had gone out in the storm to rob her. He had always admired Tom's jade.

Before she could look up Hasty's number on her caller ID, the phone rang. She was startled to hear a familiar mountain twang. "Hey, Miz Murray. Lamar Franklin here. Just wanted to be sure you and those things you found are still safe."

Was he putting out feelers to see if she had missed the diary yet?

"Everything is fine," she said. "Did you all lose power in that big storm last night?"

"I don't know. I'm over in South Carolina this weekend making two speeches on genealogical research. Spoke in Greenville last night and I'll be over in Columbia this evening. But I just wanted to check and make sure you are okay."

Katharine assured him she was, and scratched his name off her list. She just wished she could scratch her name off his.

Which brought her to Hasty, the prime suspect after Zach. He wanted the necklace and the diary, he had possibly memorized her alarm code, and he'd always been good with mechanical things, so he could probably break into a house. On the other hand, he was Hasty, once her dearest friend. She felt guilty for suspecting him. On the third hand, as the father in *Fiddler on the Roof* would say, she could either check him out herself or turn his name over to the police. That was enough to make her find his number and call it.

She had planned to chat casually and ask where he'd been the night before, but once she heard his voice on the other end she felt sixteen, not forty-six, and blurted out her troubles like she used to. "I got robbed last night. Somebody took the diary."

Silence filled the line. Finally he said, "I thought you were going to put those things in a safe place." From his tone, he was clenching his teeth and trying not to swear.

"I did. But I was translating the diary Thursday, and left it on Tom's desk. Somebody came in last night and took it."

"Came in? You mean a burglar?"

"Yeah. But all he took was the diary and Tom's jade collection. Every piece of it."

"I guess Tom was pretty furious, huh?" Hasty didn't sound particularly upset by that.

"Tom doesn't get furious, but he'll be upset when he hears about it."

"When?"

"He didn't get home. And he has an important meeting Monday that he's preparing for, so I don't want to bother him yet."

"You came back alone to an empty house and found it had been robbed?"

"I didn't go out, with the rain and all. I was here the whole time."

Hasty swore long and fluently. Was that because he was worried about her or because he was furious she'd been in the house while he was robbing it? It was some comfort that he swore better than the intruder. His next words, however, were not comforting. "So now that priceless diary is gone. Who knows what it might have told us? I warned you—"

"Don't, Hasty. I already feel terrible. Besides, I did make a copy."

"You did?"

She reminded herself that the relief in his voice could be faked, that he could have the diary right there beside him. "Sure. While you and Lamar were talking to the policeman."

"Well, that's something. At least the data isn't lost. How about the necklace?"

"It's safe."

"Let me keep it until—"

"It's safe," she repeated.

"That's what you said about the diary." With that, he was gone.

Why should she feel bereft?

* * *

She roamed the downstairs, uneasy and uncertain what to do next. She took out the booklet she had bought on how to install a phone line, but didn't feel like learning anything new at that moment. Finally she went into Tom's library and made another copy of the diary so she would have one to write on. His copier wouldn't do books, but it made excellent copies of flat sheets. While she waited for it to finish, she realized that the diary might tell her when the necklace was found, and where. With a new sense of excitement, she read a page at random. It described an evening in a *Biergarten* with friends. L^2 had taken the others away and left the lovers alone.

She was trying to make out the next bit when the telephone rang. A clipped voice started speaking as soon as she answered. "Katharine, this is Rowena Slade."

"Ohhh—" Katharine drew the word out, trying to figure out how to ask when the Ivories' dinner meeting had ended and whether Zach could have been burglarizing her house by nine-thirty. Nothing tactful came to mind.

That didn't matter, because Rowena didn't pause long enough for her to speak.

"Brandon had a great idea about that necklace you found. Daddy's ninetieth birthday is next month, and we'd like to give it to him, if it turns out to be authentic. I know he told you to call him once you have established its authenticity, but I want you to call me instead. Would you do that, please?"

"The diary—"

"We aren't interested in the diary." Katharine could almost see Rowena brushing it away. "Daddy has never collected books. But if the necklace turns out to be genuine—"

A man spoke in the background. "Excuse me," Rowena said to Katharine, then spoke in a lower voice to somebody else. "I don't know if she even knows him."

"Her son went to school with him, and Hollis is her niece."
It was Brandon, and he sounded real put out about something. "Here, I'll ask her."

His voice came on the line, formal but irritated. "Mrs. Murray, do you know how to reach Zachary Andrews? He was supposed to bring my speech to a dinner last evening, and he never arrived. I had to wing the whole thing. He hasn't showed up today, either, and he's supposed to be helping me with logistics for an important march down at the capitol on Monday. Do you have any idea where he might be? We're getting rather p—ah—perturbed. "

Katharine got the impression "perturbed" wasn't his first choice of word.

"Sorry," she told him. "I have no idea." *Unless he has hightailed it with my husband's jade,* she wanted to add. But her father had drilled into her all her life that a man is innocent until proven guilty. She added, instead, "I don't really know Zach. I hadn't seen him for years until Wednesday night, with you all."

Rowena came back on the phone. "So you will call us as soon as you have a price for the necklace?"

Katharine wasn't certain she could ever part with the necklace now, but what could she say? Had anybody ever said a successful "no" to Rowena?

Katharine sat at Tom's desk and set to work on the diary again. The third entry, dated two days after the former one, was not at all like the ones she had already read. Instead, it was brisk and businesslike:

> *Everyone is here. We had our first meeting this evening. All are agreed on what we must do, although some protested the method. L^2 stressed that unanimity*

is essential for success, and was able to persuade
them all. L² also reported that all supplies have been
purchased and stored in safety. D has acquired the
necessary skills. I have the maps and schedules. One
week from today, we begin.

Katharine reread what she had written with rising excitement. Perhaps this was Ramsauer's diary after all, and he had interspersed personal remarks into the report on the dig. Why hadn't she studied harder, so she could read these pages with ease?

Dane got up and padded to the door, needing to go out. She left the diary and took him into the front yard where he could chase butterflies for an hour while she did some weeding. They had been there scarcely thirty minutes when she heard a car in the drive and Dane sent up a volley of barks.

Chapter 16

Hasty rolled down his window and asked in a mock British accent, "Does your dug bite?"

Katharine immediately responded with another line from *The Pink Panther*. "That is not my dug. He's my brother-in-law's dug. And if you are nice, he won't bite."

Hasty eyed the taupe snout and sharp teeth warily. "How will he know I'm being nice?"

"Good point. Come, Dane." She bent to grab his collar, glad of a reason to duck her head. She didn't want Hasty to see how glad she was he had come. She told herself she wanted to observe him at close range, to figure out whether he seemed familiar with her house, but because she was generally honest with herself, she also admitted she had gotten tired of her own company that morning.

He reached into the back seat and brought out two Publix bags. "Lunch," he announced, holding them aloft.

As they went inside, she had little luck figuring out whether he seemed familiar with her house, for his whole attention was focused on Dane. "Stay," she commanded when they reached the kitchen. Dane sat on his haunches like a great taupe god, watching Hasty as though he might be the next sacrifice.

Hasty started taking food out of the bag and setting it on

the counter. "Roast chicken, potato salad, coleslaw, and mixed fruit. Good eating where I come from."

"Where I come from, too," she agreed.

He looked at her with an unreadable expression. "Nice haircut, Katie-bell. Really dynamite."

She flushed at the old pet name and the praise. "Thanks." She touched it self-consciously.

Hasty looked around. "Where did the burglar get in? Did he break a window?"

"Not that the police or I have found. The police said the front door was open when they arrived, but I didn't leave that door unlocked. He must have gone out that way."

"Well, you sure have come up in the world." He looked around her kitchen, then peered into the backyard with admiration. "This place is elegant and enviable."

It was only the truth, so why should she feel defensive? "It's also empty, now that the kids have gone," she said sharply.

He grinned. "So how did your folks like it?"

She grimaced. "What do you think? Mama's first comment when she saw it was, 'Do you plan to open up an orphanage?' and Daddy's was, 'Can you get your money back and support half the homeless in Atlanta?' But it grew on them. They used to love to come over and swim with their grandchildren."

"Do you think you'll move into something smaller now?"

She could not imagine Tom ever moving unless he was elderly, decrepit, and too poor to afford a maid, a cook, and a lawn service. He'd been born and bred in Buckhead, and took its amenities for granted. She didn't say that to Hasty, however. Instead she shrugged. "Maybe, eventually. Jon only graduated last month, so we haven't talked about it. Have you bought a house in Atlanta?"

"Not until my wife decides what she's going to do. For now, I'm in a little apartment about as big as this kitchen." Still eyeing Dane, he began to roam.

Dane gave a low growl, but Katharine said, "It's okay, boy." They followed Hasty through the dining room, den, and the sunroom. He moseyed, picking up small knick-knacks and putting them down. When they reached Tom's library, he whistled in admiration. "This is one terrific room. Is this where you work?"

"No, it's where Tom plans to work when he stops traveling so much. His intention is to read every book on the shelves."

"I could go for that, with breaks to swim in that pool out yonder. Man, you folks have got it all, haven't you?" Before she could reply, he spotted the pages she had left on the desk and hurried to bend over them. "Is this the diary?"

"Yeah. I was working on it—" She trailed off, because he had picked up the sheet she had just worked on for an hour and scanned it in seconds. His hands trembled.

"I can't believe you let it get stolen." He flung the page back on the desk and stomped across the hall to the music room. He held on to the doorjamb. "What's this room for?"

"Nothing much at the moment. We used to have the piano in here, but now I'm fixing the room up for myself."

He looked around. "So where's the piano?"

"I moved it to the living room."

He stepped across the hall and gave the room a long, con-sidering look. "The living room where nobody lives, appar-ently." He slid onto the piano bench and lifted the cover from the keyboard. A rippling arpeggio filled the air. "Nice tone."

She had forgotten that he played. She had also forgotten how much at home he had always been in her house. He played a thunderous Chopin prelude then stood. "How about lunch?"

She was ready. It had occurred to her, a bit late, that he was managing to leave fingerprints in every room.

"How about eating on the patio?" She preferred to have him outside the house. Dane would be happier, too, out where he could roam.

"Or down by the pool? It's shadier." He started putting food back in the bag. "Have you got paper plates in this swanky place, or do we have to use china?"

"Don't be ridiculous." She filled a small cooler with ice, then collected paper plates and napkins and plastic cups and utensils. At the last minute she grabbed up a damp sponge and a couple of placemats. "The table may be filthy. It hasn't been used all spring."

He carried the bags of food and jug of iced tea. "What's the point of having a place like this if you don't enjoy it?"

"Don't be rude." She refused to admit she had been asking herself the same question that past week.

Hasty set out the food while she returned for the telephone and turned on the outside ringer. "In case the police call," she explained. "They promised to give me a report."

Dane explored the yard briefly, then lay with his nose on her toe. Hasty sprawled in a chair across from her and shook his head. "Seriously, Katie-bell, all this for you? Doesn't it make you feel decadent? When did you last swim in that pool?"

She tilted her chin. "Yesterday morning. I haven't had time today. Did you bring a suit?"

"No, we'll have to swim another time. But I can't dive any more. I've developed real bad sinuses, so I don't put my head under water."

He had some nerve presuming there would be another time. But that was Hasty all over—give him an inch and he'd take over your whole life. She reached for the carrier and began to spread food on the table.

He speared a grape from the fruit salad and chewed it thoughtfully. "So who do you think robbed your house? I'd vote for that old hippie, myself. If he's any good at research, he could find out where you lived and how to break in, and he was mighty interested in the necklace. Seriously, let me put it in a safe place."

"It's in a safe place," she said hotly. "Besides, Lamar Franklin has an alibi and isn't the only person interested in the necklace. What about you? Where were you last night?"

His mouth dropped open. "You think I'd break in your house to get it? I would just come to the front door and ask nicely, 'Would you hand it over, Kate?' You'd do it at once."

Was he playing a game? He seemed to be joking, but he had been president of the high school thespians. During a performance of *Guys and Dolls,* he had brought the house down with his performance of a stooped elderly man sweeping the street in the opening scene. Later the principal had run into him in costume in the hall and asked, "May I help you, sir?" before he realized who it was. Katharine's suspicions sharpened when he leaned back in his chair and asked, "So where are you keeping it?"

"You haven't answered *my* question," she pointed out. "Where were you last night?"

He frowned. "Mostly on the telephone with my daughter, Kelly. She and her mother were having one of their eternal quarrels, and she had to give me a blow-by-blow description." He gave an exasperated huff. "I guess it's her being fifteen, but I don't remember them fighting so much before. Now, they're at each other's throats half the time, and I get caught in the middle. You've raised teenagers. What am I supposed to do?"

"Be there," she said promptly. "Be there to back up your wife when she has to be the heavy and to take your daughter out when she's feeling moody."

"Your husband wasn't here," he reminded her.

"He was here almost every weekend, and I had Jon. A third person in the house is a lot of help. Why don't you go back up there and persuade them to come down here with you? Does your wife hate Georgia so much?"

"No, she likes living near her mama so much."

"Is her mother ill?"

"No, demanding. Things were fine all those years we lived away, but once we'd been in the same town for three years, Melissa got convinced her mother needs her."

"Persuade her you need her more. Have her come down to visit. Look at houses. Bring her and Kelly over here to swim. She might be just waiting for you to beg her to come."

"I don't beg."

"You could."

"That's my business. Now where is the necklace?"

"That's my business," she parroted him. "But would you like to look at the diary? I tried translating more of it, but I'm very slow. I made a second copy to make notes on."

He started clearing the table. "Let's get it, then."

He took in the scraps and dishes while she fetched the copy and a couple of pencils. She also brought her dictionary, in case his German wasn't as perfect as he had bragged.

They laid the pages on the table between them and weighted them down with stones from her flowerbed. Katharine knew she was taking a risk. Would Hasty eventually try to overpower her and make her tell him where the necklace was? Would Dane attack him if he tried?

The man didn't look dangerous as he picked up a handful of pages and started riffling through them, scanning lines here and there. He looked like a handsome college professor going gray around the temples, with bifocals.

The telephone rang. "Good afternoon," Officer Williams said, "I wanted to check back and see if you have discovered anything else missing, ma'am."

She got up and moved away from the table, out of earshot. "Nothing except the jade collection and that diary. And you might be interested to know that Zachary Andrews has disappeared. His employers called here this morning wondering if I knew where he was."

"They called us, too. We're checking him out. Now, if you can get those pictures and the list for us Monday, we'll pick them up."

She got back to the table to find Hasty muttering while he read. As soon as she sat down, he slammed the pages on the table and exploded. "This isn't Ramsauer's diary! It's tripe— some woman prattling about her boyfriend. Listen to this." He snatched up the top page. " 'As we stood watching the sun set over the Alps, did I feel you beginning to care for me as I care for you, my little love?' Drivel!" He flung the pages back on the table. "You told me this was from Hallstatt."

"I never did," she protested. "I said the diary was with the necklace, and they were the only two things in an old box. I have no idea what it is. The most logical explanation is that it belonged to Aunt Lucy's brother, Carter."

"The phrase 'my little love' is masculine. It was probably your Aunt Lucy's diary."

"I can't imagine her keeping a diary in German. Besides, she wasn't in Austria very long, and she certainly wasn't holding meetings and making plans. Here, read the first three entries." She found them and slung them toward him.

He read swiftly what had taken her hours to translate. "It's a seduction," he concluded. "A deliberate plan to meet somebody in Vienna and seduce him. But I don't understand about these meetings. The whole thing is ambiguous enough that if that's all you had read when you first saw me, no wonder you said it was Ramsauer's diary." It was a grudging admission, but as close to an apology as she was likely to get.

Katharine's temper rose. "I hadn't read any of it yet, and I didn't say it was Ramsauer's diary. I said it might be. Later that afternoon, when I read the first page, I still thought it might be. Now I don't know what to think."

"Think it's some love-crazed woman plotting to get her man. I can't think of any other explanation, can you?"

He picked up another couple of pages and skimmed them. "It's twentieth century, too. Here the writer talks about going to the movies." He dropped the page to the table and scanned another. His lip curled. "Well, here it is. 'Drove to a rustic inn in the mountains to spend the weekend, and I have achieved my desire. Oh, ecstasy! L^2 was right—the right setting, good wine, plus gentleness and tenderness won in the end. Afterwards, my little love wept in my arms with remorse, but I overcame all his qualms and we have pledged our love forever.' "

Hasty read to the bottom of the page then gave a grunt of disgust. "The writer of this diary was not a nice person, Katie-bell. After the seduction, she shared all the juicy details with the one referred to as L-squared, and boasts, 'How jealous he was.' Not a nice person at all."

"I thought L-squared might be Aunt Lucy," Katharine said hesitantly.

"No, he's a man. Besides, L-squared implies somebody whose first and last names both begin with '*L*.' Maybe Aunt Lucy was the seducer, and used unorthodox methods of inducing jealousy in multiple lovers."

"It was more likely Sara Claire." Had Sara Claire been fluent in German? How little she knew about her relatives!

"The Acid Aunt? Not likely." Hasty's laugh was rude. He had met Sara Claire when she visited Miami and had dubbed her that immediately.

"She might have been different in college," Katharine argued. "More—you know—loose."

"This woman was loose all right. A vamp."

"Dutch was saying this week that he liked Aunt Sara Claire back then," Katharine protested. "He wouldn't like a tramp."

"I said vamp, not tramp," he corrected her. "Is Dutch still around? I always liked him."

"He's very much around. Lives over at Autumn Village, where Aunt Lucy and Aunt Sara Claire used to be. And he was telling me just this week about how he, Lucy, Sara Claire, and Carter were all in Europe the summer of 1937, and how much fun they had."

Hasty wiggled his eyebrows at her. "I'll bet he didn't tell you *all* about how much fun they had. Not if he was part of this."

She scarcely heard. She had just remembered Dutch's real name: Lionel. Lionel Landrum. L-squared. And he had once been crazy about Sara Claire.

The thought of Dutch listening to a blow-by-blow description of the seduction of another man was repugnant, but so was the notion that either Lucy or Sara Claire had deliberately set out to seduce a man sensitive enough to cry with remorse.

Hasty perused another page. "You may be glad to know that the seduction was not in vain. Three weeks later, the seduced seems to be enjoying himself, from the amount of time they spend in the hay. Torrid descriptions abound—

considerably stretching my vocabulary. I never needed these words to get a Ph.D."

Katharine was trying to translate a description of a party when Hasty dropped another bombshell. "I think the writer is Austrian. Here she says they spent the weekend at a house up in the mountains 'which has been in our family for four generations.' And here," his long finger jabbed the page, "she talks of the joy of showing off her beloved Vienna."

"So it wasn't Lucy or Sara Claire." Katharine was astonished at the relief she felt. "Carter must have had an Austrian girlfriend. Maybe she gave him the diary when he came home, as a memento of their time together. He left right after Hitler took over Austria, so she may have realized they might never see each other again."

"That's an awful feeling." Hasty glared at her over the rim of his bifocals and Katharine felt her cheeks grow pink. She bent to the cooler to replenish the ice in their glasses so he couldn't see her face. But when she refilled both glasses with iced tea and handed him one, he said sourly, "You don't have to start blushing. Reading this diary is enough to turn anybody off sex for life. Listen to this. 'A rainy afternoon between the sheets. Delirium. Ecstasy. Well worth the long wait and all the planning.'"

Katharine laughed. "'Lacks literary style and merit of content.' Remember Miss Cole in eleventh grade?"

Hasty snorted. "Don't I, though. She wrote that on most of my papers."

"All the ones I didn't write for you." Katharine ducked to avoid an ice cube he tossed at her. "I wish we could find out for sure whose diary it was, and why Aunt Lucy had it. I wonder if Dutch would tell me, if he knows."

"Do you see him regularly?"

"Not regularly enough, but we talk on the phone pretty often." She hesitated, then admitted, "His real name is Lionel. He could have been L-squared."

Hasty laced his fingers behind his head and leaned back in his chair. "Old Dutch and Sara Claire? I can't picture it."

"You don't have to picture it," she retorted. "Not if the woman was Austrian. I just wonder who she was. Dutch said they were all over there that summer. He was studying at Oxford and Lucy and Sara Claire were touring with some friends from Vassar. Meanwhile, Carter and some of his Sewanee friends were in Vienna. But Dutch didn't mention any Austrian girls."

Hasty gave a gusty sigh and leaned back farther, still cradling the back of his head in his hands. "Ah, the carefree lives of the rich and to-be famous. Austrian vacations, Baltic cruises, Parisian nightclubs. I spent my college summers stacking concrete blocks."

"I spent mine filing for an insurance company. But didn't that diary start in June? Carter and his girlfriend seem to have been carrying on before Lucy, Sara Claire, and Dutch arrived. That wipes Dutch out as L^2."

"If it was Carter doing the carrying on," he reminded her. He brought his chair back to earth with a thump that made her fear for its legs.

"Who else?" She drained her glass and reached for the jug. "The personality fits. Dutch said Carter was more interested in books than in Sara Claire, but if he was involved with an Austrian girl by the time Sara Claire arrived, that could explain why. She'd have looked like chopped meat next to that sizzling romance. I'll talk to Dutch again and see what he remembers. His memory is still pretty good."

"I wonder if he remembers me," Hasty murmured.

"Oh, yes," she replied without thinking.

"Confess," he ordered. "You are blushing again. What did you tell him?"

"I mentioned to him that I ran into you at the history center the other day."

"And?"

"That's all. I wasn't about to tell him how you scared the living daylights out of me, following me all over Buckhead. The man has a bad heart. But he remembered you."

"That doesn't sound like enough to make you color up like you did."

She pursed her lips and turned to look over the pool, hoping he wouldn't notice she was coloring up again. "He remembered that you were 'sweet on me,' to use his very words."

"He got that right." Hasty glowered at her over the top of his glasses. "You damned near broke my heart, woman. It's no thanks to you I'm not a confirmed misogynist."

Chapter 17

"So how did you finally get rid of him?" Posey's penciled brows rose, and then dropped faster than an amusement-park high drop. She must have remembered wrinkles.

Katharine wished she hadn't mentioned Hasty. She wished she had kept Dane and slept at her own house. But Posey had been so solicitous, calling to insist that she come to dinner and reminding her she had promised to spend one more night with them. So at dusk she had put Dane in the car along with her pajamas and her own pillow, and driven back to the Buitons' house like a teenager come for a slumber party. On the way, though, she had vowed, "This is the last night. Tomorrow I will sleep in my own bed and face the rest of my life."

She just wished it didn't seem so empty.

"Well?" Posey asked. Katharine realized she was still waiting for an answer.

She shrugged. "I just told him I had things to do, and we could read more of the diary later. That was why he came, you know." Why had she mentioned to Tom's sister that another man had come for lunch? Maybe the wine Posey had plied her with at dinner had something to do with it.

"I thought the diary got stolen." Posey tapped one nail on the glass top of her wicker table. Stories she couldn't follow always made her irritable.

They were sitting out on her sunroom, a place of white wicker, colorful cushions, and a red tile floor. Outside, the light was beginning to fade and lightning bugs danced across the lawn. A breeze wafted through the open windows, heavy with the scent of night-blooming jasmine. Katharine rubbed her bare feet across the cool tiles under the table and wished all of life could be so pleasant and simple.

"It did get stolen," she explained, "but I made copies we can work with. Hasty thinks it's probably contemporary, though, and not very important." She wasn't about to mention how torrid it was. Posey would insist that they translate it themselves, and her German wasn't any better than Katharine's. They'd be up all night.

"*We* can work with? *Hasty* thinks?" Posey parroted what Katharine had said last, with emphasis, and gave her a shrewd look. "So you're planning on seeing him again?"

Katharine wished she didn't blush so easily. "Heavens, no, unless it's to translate more of the diary. He's good at German. And he's a friend, that's all. "

The trouble with protests is, they sound like protests. Posey's mouth puckered like a drawstring bag. "Sounds like my little brother better get his behind on a plane and head back to Georgia if he knows what's good for him. Whose diary does this guy Hasty think it is?"

Katharine shrugged again. "We haven't figured that out yet. At first, I thought it might be Aunt Sara Claire's."

Posey snorted. "Was it written in vinegar?"

"Maybe she changed as she got older," Katharine tested the theory. "Maybe she had a wild, misspent youth."

"Yeah, right. And I'm the Little Mermaid. You want some more wine?" Posey heaved herself to her feet and trotted barefoot to the kitchen. She appeared a minute later with a bottle of Pinot Grigio and two iced-tea tumblers.

"Those aren't wine glasses," Katharine pointed out.

"No, but they hold about half what I need right now, hon, after putting up with Holly all day. I swear—" Katharine braced herself for the old story about Hollis being switched at birth, but Posey surprised her. "—the way she's been moping around here all day, I wonder if she's going into a depression or gotten bipolar or something. One minute she's snapping off my head, the next she's bawling in her room, and the next she's mooning out the window like the world has come to an end and she's waiting for the messenger. You think I ought to call a psychiatrist?" She poured both glasses full to the brim. "Or maybe she has broken up with Zach. If that's the case, I'm gonna have a hard time pretending to be sympathetic."

Katharine hesitated, but surely it couldn't hurt anything for Posey to know as much as she knew. "Zach seems to have disappeared. Rowena Slade called me this morning and Brandon got on the phone asking if I knew where Zach could be. Remember how Brandon messed up his speech last night? He claims that was because Zach was supposed to bring him a speech and he never showed."

"I hope he's gone to Outer Mongolia." Posey sank into her chair and shoved one tumbler across the table, then lowered her voice to a conspiratorial level. "I went to aerobics to-day—a makeup for missing a class this week—and ran into Millie Meister, whose daughter was in Holly's class at Westminster. I asked—casually, mind you—if she remembered Zach Andrews, and the stories she told me curled my toenails. I nearly had a hissy fit right then and there thinking about Holly dating him. Did you know he stole his mother's BMW and wrapped it around a telephone pole? Or that he stole tests from a teacher's desk and sold copies to other kids? Or that he actually told one teacher her life wouldn't be worth mud if she flunked him?" She didn't wait for an answer. "But don't breathe a word of this to Holly. If she thought I didn't like Zach, she'd run off and marry him—if she could find him."

"Hollis has better sense than that." Katharine had been comparing Millie's stories with Jon's, and thinking how stories got changed as they progressed up the grapevine, and had forgotten to keep her voice down.

Hollis spoke from the doorway. "Better sense than what?" She looked like an escapee from Halloween in a long black skirt, black tank top, black beads around her throat, and chunky black heels. Her lipstick and nail polish were such a dark red that they looked black, too. But what startled Katharine most were the smudges under her eyes and the pallor of her skin.

The two women exchanged guilty looks. "Better sense than to make a mess decorating the carriage house," Posey improvised with the agility of one who has raised three girls. "Katharine thinks you're going to make a good job of it."

"I am. What are you all drinking?"

Posey held up her glass in a salute. "Wine."

Her jaw dropped. "In those glasses? You'll both be drunk as skunks." She took a vacant chair and set a carton of blueberry yogurt on the table, although a vial of blood would have seemed more appropriate.

Posey heaved a martyred-mother sigh. "What do you care? You're driving me to drink, moping around here all day. Weren't you supposed to go to work?"

"No, I went last night to get a feel for the theater. Now I'm going to be working at home, making costumes for the next play. I'll have to go in for fittings and stuff, and to make sure that what I'm doing matches the sets, but I'll do the cutting and sewing here. Can I use the dining room table until my own place is ready?"

"Lord help us," Posey muttered. "Whatever happened to the empty nest?"

"I've got an empty nest you can have," Katharine offered.

Hollis shifted her chair and turned one shoulder toward her mother. "Are you lonesome at your place, Aunt Kat? I could come over and stay until we finish the carriage house here, if you'll let me sew in your dining room. I won't scratch your table. I have a pad to put over it when I'm cutting. And as you can see, I am not welcome *here*." She shot her mother an angry look.

"You're welcome, honey," Posey assured her. "I'd just prefer a bit of sweetness and light." She got up. "I ought to go ask Wrens if he wants a snack."

"Sorry," Hollis muttered after Posey had gone, "but I don't feel sweet or light at the moment."

Katharine pretended to be fascinated with the wine in her tumbler. "What's going on?" Young people were more likely to talk if they thought you weren't seriously interested.

Hollis heaved a sigh that took five seconds to exhale. "Nothing." She ripped the top off her yogurt as if she'd like to be removing somebody's body parts, and stirred savagely.

Katharine hazarded a guess. "I understand Zach has disappeared."

Hollis lifted an overloaded spoon to her mouth with what would have looked like indifference to anybody who hadn't known her all her life, and didn't say a word.

"I had a call from Rowena this morning," Katharine continued. "She was wanting me to sell her the necklace as a present for her father. Then Brandon got on the phone, asking if I knew where Zach was. Apparently he was supposed to take a speech to Brandon last night at some dinner, but he never made it."

Hollis swallowed the yogurt and wiped her mouth with a cloth napkin she'd found on the table—possibly her own. "Yeah. I heard about that. Rowena came home from the banquet mad enough to chew nails and spit them out."

"What time did she get there?" Katharine tried not to sound too eager.

"She'd been home long enough to put on a robe before I got there."

That wasn't much help, considering that Hollis hadn't left home until nearly midnight. Katharine was more interested in Zach, anyway. He had shown an inordinate amount of interest in the jade. "So you don't have any idea where he might be?"

Hollis frowned. "No, and Amy must have called a hundred times asking the same question. He was supposed to help Brandon get ready for a march Monday down at the capitol, and Brandon was hopping mad. I kept telling her I'd call if he showed up, but fifteen minutes later she'd be back on the phone with the same question." Hollis sighed. "She can be so dense. Just like the rest of her family." She dipped up another large spoonful of yogurt, and then muttered so low that Katharine almost didn't hear, "It would never occur to them that maybe Zach has finally decided he doesn't want to promote hatred any longer."

"I beg your pardon?"

At the rate she was going, Hollis would soon be queen of sighs. "That march on Monday? It's part of Brandon's big campaign to get gays out of Georgia. Hasn't he ever read European history? He sounds like Hitler when he talks about 'those people.'" Hollis sketched quotes with sarcastic fingers. "And that's the only thing he does talk about these days—except terrorists, and how none of us will be safe unless we all carry photo IDs and guns and ship all foreign-born people back to the countries where they came from. To hear him talk, you'd think he was a pureblood American Indian. I don't know how Zach can stand working for him. Of course, Zach is pretty mixed-up himself." She stared morosely into her yogurt.

Posey ought to be upstairs dancing a jig. This conversation did not bode well for a long-term relationship. "So have you and Zach broken up?" Katharine inquired.

Hollis shook her head. "Uh, no. We haven't broken up. I just don't know where he is."

Katharine hoped he wasn't out of town somewhere trying to sell Tom's jade. Maybe she ought to at least mention that possibility. She listened to be sure Posey wasn't coming back, then asked urgently, "When you all came over the other day, did Zach watch you disarm our security system? And is there any way he could have gotten your key?"

Hollis's head came up like a deer's, alert to danger. "Why?"

"Because I've been wondering if it was Zach who came into my house last night. I am almost positive I locked the doors and put on the alarm. I can picture myself doing it. And there was no sign of a break-in. So whoever came in may have had a key and known our code, may have even been in the house before. He knew where to find the safe, knew about Tom's jade, and actually came into Jon's closet, as if he knew the hideout was there. Zach used to come play with Jon sometimes, and I'm sure Jon would have bragged about the wall safe and his daddy's jade. He and Zach played in the hideout a lot, too. So that leaves me wondering—"

"I wouldn't give him your key!" Hollis shoved back her

chair and jumped to her feet, knocking over her carton and sending yogurt flying all over the table. She ignored it, whirled, and dashed into the kitchen. The back door slammed.

When Hollis neither returned to the house nor drove away in her Mini, Katharine became alarmed. She went to the garage and heard the sound of stormy weeping above.

She climbed the stairs to the carriage house and found the door open. In the dimness—for the only light came from a halogen light on the parking apron—Hollis sat on a lumpy couch, shoulders shaking, dabbing her eyes with the remnants of a sodden tissue.

It was not an ideal place to sit and cry. The air was thick and close. In the scant light, Katharine saw that cobwebs festooned the windows and dust lay like white powder on an old coffee table, the only other furniture. The linoleum was cracked. The sofa sagged with age. Through an arch at the left side of the far end, a small kitchen alcove was bare except for a wide shallow sink, supported by two unpainted pipes that dubbed for front legs. Katharine couldn't suppress a groan of dismay at the thought of how much work would be needed to turn the place into something habitable.

Hollis jumped, and her head swiveled toward the door. Tears sparkled on her lashes.

"I'm sorry I upset you." Katharine walked in and pretended to examine the angles of the ceiling and the dimensions of the room.

Hollis sniffed. "It's okay. But I did not give Zach your key. Or your code." She sniffed again and tossed the soggy tissue into a pile of debris on the floor. "There's so much dust up here, it gives me allergies." She got up with an unconvincing little laugh. "I know it doesn't look like much yet, but this place has great potential." She walked around waving her arms. "With a little paint and some paper, and the floors refinished, plus some cleaning—it's a bit dirty."

A bit dirty? An army of cleaners would need a week to make a dent in the filth. But Katharine wasn't half as concerned about the apartment as she was about Hollis. Years of living with teens had taught her that while some of their tragedies seem minor to adults, few are to them. Hollis's expression just then reminded her of Anna Karenina's before she leaped in front of the train.

Katharine strolled over to peer out the grimy front windows. Because the garage faced the backyard, the carriage-house views were reversed. Its front windows overlooked the acres of woodland that covered the back of the Buitons's lot while its back windows looked out onto their large front lawn and flowerbeds. Just then the woodlands were so dark, Katharine felt like she perched at the edge of the world. "You'll have a good view." She adjusted a crooked blind and it fell with a clatter. She jumped back. "Sorry!"

"It doesn't matter. I'll need new ones." Hollis moseyed to the kitchen and turned the water tap on and off several times. "The guys said they can come paint your room Tuesday morning. Will that be okay?"

"Fine with me. I never imagined they could come so quick."

"I told you, they need the work." Hollis was silent for another minute or two. "Are you positive you locked your door and turned on the alarm?"

"Not positive, no. I was waiting for Tom, you see, and went out to cut some flowers. Then, after he called to say he wasn't coming, I decided to take my supper upstairs and read in bed. I may have forgotten to lock up and put on the alarm, but I think I remember doing both. I'm just not sure."

Again she saw herself standing with an armful of hydrangeas, awkwardly punching in the numbers.

"Oh." It was a small chilled word. "Do you still have the necklace at your house?"

"Not any more. I had hidden it under Jon's comic books in the hideout—"

Hollis made a small, barely perceptible sound, then grew still again.

"—but whoever broke in last night seemed to suspect the hideout was there, so I had to find a better hiding place."

"Take it to a bank!" Hollis said fiercely. "Anything else is dumb!"

"I know. Now, tell me why you want to live up here instead of getting a place of your own." Katharine didn't want to think about burglars any more. Her courage was beginning to fray at the edges.

Hollis came back to the living room and flipped on the light, revealing more dirt. But she held out her arms and twirled as if she stood in a palace. "Because this is a *great* place. I always loved coming up here as a kid. Of course, it wasn't so dusty then. Julia used to clean it when we played up here. " With one toe she nudged a ball that looked like a dead mouse.

"Don't!" Katharine didn't mean to squeal, but it came out that way.

Hollis laughed, sounding like herself again. "It's just a dust bunny. I know the place is filthy. Julia won't come up anymore. She claims it's too hard to drag the vacuum cleaner and supplies up the stairs, but she's really scared of ghosts. Molly and Lolly told her the place is haunted by a woman who was murdered up here fifty years ago."

"Really? Your mother never mentioned a murder or a

ghost." It was the kind of story Posey normally would bring up at every opportunity.

Hollis grimaced at her aunt's gullibility. "There weren't any. Molly and Lolly told Julia that because they were smoking up here and didn't want her telling Mom. But once it's cleaned out, this will be a perfect place to work. I can put my stretching frames over there—" she waved toward the back, "and the steamer in the kitchen, and a big cutting table under the front windows. This room gets lots of light during the day."

Maybe it did. It extended across the entire depth of the garage, which meant it had windows both on the front and the back.

"The windows will need to be washed, of course." Hollis added in the offhand tone of one who wouldn't do the washing. "Come see the rest."

She led the way like a realtor showing off a prize property. "That's the bath, and here are the two bedrooms." Bedrooms, bath, and hall would fit into Hollis's room inside her parents' house, but she boasted, "I'll sleep in the little bedroom—" she waved toward the back room as if that part of her life was inconsequential "—and sew in the big one." She strode into the front bedroom, which had a double window looking out into the forest and a single side window overlooking the pool. Katharine wondered how the former owner's chauffeur had enjoyed living up there looking out at a pool he wasn't allowed to use.

She tuned in as Hollis was saying, "And my sewing machine under the big window." As she pointed, Katharine could see, dimly, the ghost of her dream, and she felt an unexpected twinge of envy. Hollis was right. It would be fun to have a little place like this, all of one's own. And Hollis knew what she wanted to do with her life.

"Don't you love the way the roof slants at the front?" Hollis touched the slanted ceiling with a loving hand. "I'm going to paint that wall dark green, so it will blend with the trees and grass outdoors, and I'll feel like a saint living out in a wooded hermitage or something."

Anybody less like a saint than the thin dark girl in front of her—or less likely to tolerate living her life totally isolated from other human beings—Katharine could not imagine, but Hollis did burn with some of the same intensity saints are made of. That evening she was talking so feverishly that Katharine wondered if she was on some kind of drug.

"It could be charming," she said with reservations.

"It will!" Hollis insisted. "It's going to be perfect. *Everything* is going to be perfect!"

Then she burst into tears, dashed toward the living room, and clattered down the stairs. In a minute Katharine heard the Mini engine rev and Hollis roar down the drive.

Chapter 18

After church and dinner with Posey and Wrens, Katharine insisted on returning home Sunday afternoon. She couldn't live in fear all her life. But what was she to do with the necklace until she could get it to the bank?

She set the Bloomingdale's bag on the kitchen counter and reached down inside to touch the circle of bronze, considering her options. Where could she keep it until the bank opened? No place in the house felt secure. Should she hide it among the garden tools in the shed? Under the cushions in the patio locker? Bury it? She opened the cloth and peered inside, trying to remember exactly how wide it was. It glowed a soft green. That's when she got her inspiration. The color should be perfect.

But first she carried it into her downstairs powder room and switched on the light. The soft taupe wallpaper flamed with red-orange poppies, Katharine's one flamboyant choice when the downstairs was being redecorated. Her hair gleamed in the mirror lights and her skin was softly tanned above her creamy dress. "Not bad-looking for an old lady, eh?" she asked her reflection, pleased with the way her hair seemed to float around her head. She held the necklace to her throat and waited. Sure enough, as she looked at its soft green gleam in the mirror, she seemed to see, dimly, the woman with dark hair and proud dark eyes. That day the sun seemed to shine fully on her long, thin face, which was also tanned by the sun. Her lips moved as if in supplication, and her eyes were anxious.

"I'm doing my best to protect it," Katharine whispered. She held the circlet reverently and carried it back to the kitchen, where she put it inside a one-gallon Ziploc bag, pressed out the air, and closed it tight. She put the first bag inside a second and again pressed out the air. Then she went outside.

In the yard, she tossed a stick to send Dane off in another direction and strolled down to the pool. After a quick look around, she knelt and dropped the treasure into a corner near the diving board, where the water was ten feet deep.

The necklace drifted slowly and settled on the bottom, so close to the color of the pool that it looked like twigs or a clump of leaves. She gave a satisfied nod. The pool man wasn't due until Tuesday. Nobody else was likely to be near it until then. While Dane nosed around in the bushes, she sat beside the pool and took stock of her afternoon.

Katharine's parents had considered that the commandment to remember the Sabbath and keep it holy was God's way of telling people they needed one day for worship, rest, and recreation after a week's hard work. Neither went to their desk on Sunday afternoons nor did Katharine do homework. Instead, their family snorkeled or rode bikes together, lazed around with the Sunday papers, or visited with friends. When Katharine and Tom married, he had insisted that he had too much work to do getting established in business to take a whole day off every week, but when the children came—and especially after he started traveling—he had capitulated and they began to set aside Sundays for church and family fun. When the children grew older and wanted to go out with friends, Tom and Katharine relaxed together. In the past year, if she knew he would be gone on a Sunday, Katharine had either invited Jon and his friends for lunch or planned a special outing for herself and Aunt Lucy.

That particular Sunday afternoon stretched ahead like a mini version of the rest of her life: a big void. She was too restless to read, too lazy to call a friend, too apathetic to swim.

She decided to do some family research. She took Dane inside and left him in the kitchen while she pulled out every old family album and box of letters she could find and pored over them for any hint that either of her aunts had a wild and lurid youth. The closest she came was up in the attic, where she found a stack of letters Sara Claire and Walter had exchanged between Vassar and Yale. She sat down in Tom's daddy's uncomfortable old chair and spent an hour reading the record of what was surely the most boring and circumspect courtship in American history. Only when the air grew hot and stuffy did she re-tie the letters with the blue satin ribbon Sara Claire had used to keep them together and drop them back in the dusty box. Feeling grimy and sticky with heat, she headed toward the kitchen for a glass of tea.

She paused in the front hall, surprised. Through the sidelight of her front door she saw Hasty's Jeep in her drive. She opened the door and peered out, but he wasn't in the Jeep, nor was he in the front yard. Puzzled, she went to the kitchen, where she found Dane perched in the bay window emitting low growls in his throat. When he heard her enter, he began to bark.

Across the lawn, Hasty swam lazily, turning after completing a lap. Any minute now he would peer down through the water and spot the necklace.

She left Dane in the kitchen (she drew the line at dogs in the pool) and dashed outside. "How did you get in the yard?" she demanded, breathless from running. "Wasn't the back gate locked?" What she wanted to ask was "How dare you come swim in my pool without a specific invitation?" and "Have you spotted the necklace yet?"

He pulled himself up to rest his arms on the side. She couldn't help appreciating that he really did look magnificent in a bathing suit. "Yeah, but when you didn't answer your doorbell, I climbed over. I figured you wouldn't mind. This feels great. Come on in."

If he'd climbed over today, he could have climbed over Friday night.

She eyed him warily. "Do you make a habit of climbing over people's walls?"

He grinned. "Only when the walls are low, the pool inviting, and there's the potential for good company. Come on, Katie-bell. The water is great."

He must not have found the necklace yet, but she moseyed down to the deep end and took a surreptitious look. When she had verified that it still lay on the bottom, she went over and kicked the diving board. "Don't dive," she warned. "We haven't had this checked lately."

"I told you, I can't put my head under water anymore. I get sinus infections."

"Good!" She spoke before she thought. "Good idea to swim, I mean."

"So are you coming in?" He reached out as if he would drag her in fully dressed, which he had been known to do.

Katharine stepped back and considered. She hadn't intended to swim, but the pool did look inviting and she'd rather talk and swim with Hasty than spend the rest of the afternoon alone. Besides, she couldn't think of any better way to keep an eye on the necklace. In the water, perhaps she could distract him. "Sure. I'll be right back." She turned toward the house.

And how do you plan to distract him? inquired Sara Claire's disapproving voice in her head.

She felt her cheeks grow hot. "He's a *friend*," she insisted, lifting her chin defiantly.

Whom are you trying to convince?

Flustered, she was glad to hear the phone ringing as she entered the house. "Maybe it's Tom," she told Dane. He gave a woof without lifting his head from his big paws.

Instead it was Dr. Flo. "Katharine? I am sorry to bother you on Sunday, but I have spoken with Cleetie, and she'll be glad to talk to you. She said she has always wanted—"

Cleetie? Katharine remembered with difficulty that she was the sister of Alfred Simms, the man convicted of killing Carter Everanes. She tuned back in as Dr. Flo was saying, "—can meet with us Thursday morning. Would that suit you?"

Katharine cast a quick glance at the calendar over the kitchen desk. "Sure. What time?"

"About eleven. She's elderly, so it takes her a while to get going in the morning."

As she went up to put on her bathing suit, Katharine wondered what Alfred's sister could tell her, beyond declaring her brother's innocence. Could she possibly have any idea who else might have killed Carter? Not that it would matter to anybody, after all these years, but Katharine wanted an answer to that, as well as to the question of who wrote the diary. She had never had a real-life mystery in the family before.

She had never swum alone with a man since she got married, either. He's a friend, she repeated to herself as she debated between her three bathing suits. Finally she chose the green—the one Jon said she looked too good in to be any-body's mother—telling herself she wanted Hasty looking at her instead of the bottom of the pool. It wasn't until she got back to the pool and saw his glasses lying on the table beside his towel that she realized he probably couldn't see the bottom of the pool. Unfortunately, he could see her. When she saw the appreciative gleam in his eyes, she knew she should have worn her old black suit, the one Tom swore she had bought in a thrift store where nuns dropped off their used clothing.

Feeling unusually shy, she made a surface dive and swam to the far side. "Feels good, doesn't it?" she called to him. When he started her way, she swam underwater to the deep end to make sure the necklace was still safely in place, then turned and did a lap toward the shallow end. He joined her before she got there.

"Race?" he challenged when they reached the wall. He flipped and was off before she had a chance to reply.

For the next half hour they raced, swam laps, lazed on foam noodles, and talked about friends neither of them had seen for years. Swimming with Hasty had been a big part of Katharine's high school years. Except for making sure to keep herself between him and the necklace, she gave herself up to the pleasure of the silky water.

Then Hasty pointed to a puffy cloud overhead, a brilliant white against the deep blue sky. "I'd give that cloud an A-plus. What would you give it?"

When she opened her mouth to reply, he splashed her playfully in the face.

"I'll give you a drowning," she retorted and heaved water with both hands.

He swung an arm around, sent a wave over her, and the

battle was on. Like two teenagers they dowsed one another again and again, laughing and shouting.

Suddenly he pinned her between his outstretched arms against one side of the pool. His lips were smiling, but his eyes weren't.

"Get away." She playfully pushed against him with both hands.

He grabbed her wrists. She had opened her mouth to protest when he bent and kissed her, hard. Kissing Hasty felt so natural that she found herself kissing back. All the loneliness and frustration of the past week welled up in her, and she pressed herself to him as closely as he pressed to her. She had no idea how long they stood there, reliving the past. He broke the spell when he gently lowered one strap and murmured, his lips close to hers, "How about once, between old friends?"

That reminded her how many years had passed since Hasty was part of her daily life. Annoyed with them both, she twisted her face away. "Stop it! This isn't what I want. It's not what either one of us wants."

He grabbed her wrists again. "It's what I want. And you were acting like it what's you want."

"It isn't. Not really." She edged around in small baby steps, turning them both so her back was no longer against the side of the pool. "Let me go, Hasty."

He tugged her wrists, drawing her gently toward him. "Make me." His voice was husky.

She edged around a little more, to give herself space, then hooked one leg around his knees and pulled while shoving his chest with her hands. It was a trick Jon had taught her. Hasty sank in a cloud of bubbles.

She swam to the side of the pool and climbed out while he surfaced, gasping. Then she picked up her towel and spoke as if nothing had happened between them. "Time to get out. I have things to do this afternoon." She tried to think of just one so it wouldn't be a lie, but her mind was strangely disordered. Kissing Hasty had brought back all sorts of feelings and memories she had thought she had given a decent burial.

Toweling her hair, she turned her back on his admirable physique as he climbed out, streaming water and furious. "I've got enough water up my nose to give me the grand-daddy of all sinus infections," he grumbled. "That was a dirty trick, Katie-bell. I wouldn't have expected it of you."

She gave him her sweetest smile and moved farther away from him. "Raising kids taught me skills I didn't used to have—or need. Now it's time for you to leave."

He reached for his own towel. "Can I at least go inside to change my clothes? And I had hoped we could translate some more of your pornographic diary." He put on his glasses and reached for a bag of clothes he'd left on a chair. "And that you'd let me see that necklace again. Where is it, by the way?"

"Safe. But not where I can get to it real easy. I'll let you change clothes, though, if you leave right after that. Deal?"

"Deal." But the next minute her heart leaped into her throat as he turned toward the deep end of the pool.

"Where are you going?" Her voice squeaked.

"To fetch the noodles."

"Leave them. I—I may come back out later tonight."

"You aren't going to swim alone, are you? At night? You never used to like swimming at night." He knelt beside the pool and reached for the purple noodle.

"Oooh! Snake!" Katharine jumped up and down and pointed to a spot in the grass in the other direction. "I think it's a copperhead!"

Hasty leaped to his feet and hurried toward her. "Where?"

He grabbed up the long-handled net used to scoop leaves from the pool.

"Heading toward that tree. That one!" Her finger jabbed the air toward a magnolia covered with wide creamy blossoms.

He started across the lawn, mincing on bare feet. "How far out?"

"A little farther." She sidled over and retrieved the noodles. "A little bit farther. Right about there."

He peered around. "I don't see anything." He bent and examined the grass, then turned and looked at the distance between them. "How could you see it from way over there?"

"It was closer at first and I was over by the table. But it was moving pretty fast. It's probably in the bushes by now. Let's go inside and get something to drink. I'll tell my yardman to keep a look out for him." She slung her towel around her like a sarong and led the way.

"Watch out for Dane," she warned as she stepped inside.

The dog was stretched out on the kitchen floor taking a Sunday afternoon snooze. He gave one "woof" when they came in but seemed accustomed to Hasty. Katharine didn't find that reassuring. If Hasty returned later to look for the necklace—or to pick up where they'd left off—she didn't want him greeted with licks and slobber.

She pointed him toward the downstairs bathroom and took Dane upstairs with her while she changed. "You are here to protect me," she reminded the dog. But she locked her door before she stripped.

She slipped on a white shirt and some comfortable striped sand pants, then took a few minutes to blow-dry her new hairstyle into fluffy waves. When she finally ran barefoot down the stairs, Hasty sat at the breakfast room table drinking iced tea.

"Well, make yourself at home," she said sarcastically.

"I did," he said with perfect equanimity. "You saving that cake for something special?"

She sighed, thinking of her ruined birthday celebration. "I was, but we might as well eat it."

Katharine could see why scientists claimed chocolate was good for women. After a big slice of chocolate cake with sticky fudge icing, they were both so mellow they chatted idly about this and that. She even dared to ask, "Did you think about what I said, about calling Melissa and Kelly to come down for a visit?"

"I'm thinking about it. I don't have a place for them to stay, though. When I got down here, I was so mad at Melissa and in such a hurry to start the semester, I took the first place I found. It's tiny. But my lease is up in August. I thought I'd look for something bigger and maybe invite them down then."

If he thought she'd invite them to stay with her, he had another think coming. "Atlanta has a hotel or two," she pointed out. "Or you could find a bigger place and sublet the little one."

"Maybe." She could still read his face. He didn't want to talk about it.

The doorbell rang. "Grand Central Station," Kate muttered, heading to the hall. And to think, three hours earlier she had thought that day was boring.

Hollis stood on the veranda with Amy behind her. Both looked strained and Amy had tear-stained cheeks and damp lashes. Her birthday hairdo was a thing of the past. Long straight hair hung limp and lifeless on both sides of her pallid face and she clutched one hand to her throat, as if afraid Katharine might throttle her instead of inviting her in. The sophisticated young woman of Wednesday had become a child with woebegone brown eyes and a clownish red nose.

Make that a child dressed in what Katharine knew for a fact was a five hundred dollar powder-blue cotton sundress with a matching sweater and three hundred dollar powder-blue sandals. It had been years since she had catalogued things by their price. Was Hasty making her look at her world through new eyes? Or was she getting back her old ones?

Hollis was wearing a red-and-black long skirt, a black T-shirt, and her black flip-flops.

Katharine stood back to let them in. "Come on back to the breakfast room. I'm eating cake." Not until they got to the kitchen did she remember Hasty.

When Hollis saw him at the table, she turned back toward the door. "I didn't know you had company."

"I don't." Katharine took her arm and dragged her back. "This is Hobart Hastings, the Emory history professor. You all met Wednesday, remember? We've been talking about the diary. Sit down and let me get you a piece of cake and a glass of tea. Or would you rather have hot tea?" Amy's teeth were chattering and she was shaking like she was naked on an ice floe.

Hollis, on the other hand, looked flushed and warm. Katharine hoped that wasn't because of Hasty. She also hoped Hollis didn't notice that she and Hasty were both barefoot and his hair damp, or that his bathing suit lay wrapped in a towel on the countertop. She shielded it with her body and carried it into the laundry room. He watched with a smug grin.

"Hot tea, please." Hollis collapsed into the chair beside Hasty and smoothed back her hair with both hands, an unexpectedly sensual gesture. As Katharine filled the kettle, she noticed that Hollis had cheered up enough that day to paint her nails bright red.

"So what do you teach?" Hollis asked, leaning on her elbows and leaning toward Hasty in what Katharine could only call a seductive pose.

"European history," he told her.

Amy sat down across from him. "You were Zach's advisor. Zach Andrews? He graduated last month. Do you remember?"

Hasty grimaced. "My memory may be slipping, but it stretches back that far. Zach would make a fine historian, if he applied himself. Tended to be a bit lazy, though. What's he doing now?"

"Working for the Ivorie Foundation. You know, my brother, Brandon." Amy took it for granted that everybody knew her brother, Brandon.

Hollis turned to Katharine, "I hope you don't mind us just showing up, but we're worried, and we can't talk at my house or Amy's." She bent to stroke Dane, who was leaning against her leg.

"Of course." Katharine fetched mugs and two tea bags. When the kettle boiled, she poured steaming water into Hollis's mug and held the kettle aloft. "Do you want hot tea, too, Amy?"

Amy brushed away her tears. "Do you have herbal tea? Caffeine is so bad for you."

"Somewhere." Katharine rummaged in the pantry and found an assortment of herbal teas Susan had bought last time she was home. She poured water into a mug for Amy, fetched sugar and milk and spoons, and added a dish for their used bags. Then she cut two slices of cake and found forks and napkins. Neither girl made a move to help. If she ever needed to go to work, Katharine reflected, maybe she could get taken on at a Waffle House.

She had just sat down beside Hasty when Amy asked, "Do you have honey?" Katharine returned to the pantry for a clear plastic bear with a yellow hat that doubled as a spout. She set it before Amy, who was staring at her tea bag, but making no move to open it or put it in the water. She seemed to take seriously the concept of being waited on hand and foot. However, Katharine had done all the waiting she intended to do. She slid into the seat across from Hollis. "So, what's happened?"

Hollis looked at Amy. "Zach has disappeared!" Amy declared. "He—he's not anywhere," she added, in case there was something about the word "disappeared" the grown-ups didn't grasp. Tears filled her eyes. "Papa and Brandon have had the police looking for him since yesterday, but nobody can find him."

"Maybe he's with his parents," Katharine suggested.

The tears spilled out onto her cheeks. "No, ma'am. They're on a Baltic cruise."

Katharine didn't trust herself to look at Hasty. She looked at Hollis instead. Hollis's eyes were surprisingly dry. Maybe she was too worried to cry?

Hasty reached over, unwrapped Amy's tea bag and dipped it in and out of the water, then wrung it out efficiently with a spoon and laid it in the bowl. He squeezed in some honey and pushed Amy's tea toward her hand. "Here, drink this. It will make you feel better."

"Nothing will make me feel better except finding Zach," Amy declared. But she obediently sipped the tea, alternating sips with heavy sniffles through her nose.

Katharine looked from one girl to the other. Hollis

shrugged. "Maybe you've already figured it out, but I'm not dating Zach, Amy is. Her family would freak out if they knew, though, so we've been pretending."

"I'm not just dating him," Amy corrected her, chin in the air. "I am going to marry him. Just as soon as Mama has time to go see the lawyer."

"Amy came into a trust fund from her father on her birthday," Hollis explained, "but her mother has been too busy to take her down to the lawyer to sign all the papers."

"Then we are going to get married." Amy gave a watery smile, her cheeks pink.

It seemed to Katharine that a woman old enough to inherit a trust fund and get married ought to be mature enough to take herself down to the lawyer's to sign her own papers, but she didn't mention that. She also feared that Zach wasn't marrying Amy for her watery charms. Was he working for the Ivories in order to worm his way into their graces, so they wouldn't object to the marriage? After all, what Amy got from her father would be peanuts compared to what she would inherit from her mother's side of the family one day.

So why had Zach disappeared?

Hasty reached for a box of tissues and handed it to Amy. "Blow your nose and let's think where he might have gone."

Fathering a daughter had apparently taught him some skills, for Amy sat up at once, blew her nose, and obediently began to speak. "He's not at his apartment, because the police went over there, and he's not at work, because Brandon is furious, and he's not at his parents' because the police looked there, too. Besides, they are on—"

"A Baltic cruise," Hasty finished for her, looking at Katharine.

She concealed her snort of laughter with a cough.

"Couldn't he be at a friend's house?" she asked. "Or visiting grandparents? Or maybe he's out of town on private business."

"What kind of business?" Hollis narrowed her eyes as she looked at her aunt.

"Selling your Uncle Tom's jade," Katharine felt like saying. Hollis must know that was what she suspected. Instead she shrugged. "You all would know better than we would."

Amy swabbed her eyes and shook her head. "He doesn't have any business except Brandon's, and I don't know about his friends or relatives. He never mentioned any. You don't know who they are do you?" she asked Hasty.

He shook his head. "Sorry. That never came up in conferences."

She sat up straighter in her chair and said with pathetic dignity, "I'm sorry, Mrs. Murray, for falling apart like this. You are very nice to let us come over."

As if Katharine had had any say in the matter.

"Would you all like to talk privately?" she suggested to Hollis.

Hollis's gaze flitted from her to Hasty and back. Did she think Katharine was asking for private time with him?

"Hobart was about to leave," Katharine said firmly.

Hollis stood. "Then come on, Amy, let's go to the library." She pushed back her chair.

"I need to use the powder room first," Amy said primly.

Hollis waited until she was gone, then leaned forward and asked, "Are you staying here tonight? Mama said you are."

Katharine was touched by the worry in her eyes, but was there a bit of fear, as well? What did Hollis know? And how could she encourage her to tell it?

"I can't go on staying with your folks forever." She tried for a light tone.

"But if somebody came in—" Hollis broke off, her voice strained.

"—if he came for the necklace and didn't get it, he may come back," Hasty added.

"I've got Dane." Katharine bent and stroked the soft ears. He gave a low "woof."

"I'm staying over." Hollis's expression was belligerent. Katharine suspected she thought Hasty was fixing to offer the same service.

"Or I could take the necklace and keep it safe," he suggested with a sideways glance at Katharine.

"The necklace is safe and I have Dane," she told them both with more confidence than she felt—and, she suspected, a whole lot more than she would feel around eleven that night. As much to convince herself as them, she said firmly, "He's not going to let anybody in the house. Now you need to leave," she told Hasty, "and you need to talk to Amy," she reminded Hollis. "I'm sorry about Zach," she added, "but he'll probably turn up in a day or two."

"I hope so," Hollis said soberly. "Otherwise, I don't know what Amy might do."

Chapter 19

After the girls went to the den, Katharine expected Hasty to leave. Instead, as he carried his dishes to the sink, he noticed the bag she had gotten from the telephone store. "Are you swapping out a telephone?"

"No, I plan to install one, if I can figure out how. I want one in my new study."

"Show me where, ma'am. I'll have it done in a jiffy."

Hasty always had been handy, and she did want the phone installed, so Katharine led him to the music room. While he was working, Hollis and Amy came out and Hollis decided that was as good a time as any to get the room ready for the painters. Katharine suspected that had something to do with not leaving her alone with Hasty. By the time he had the phone installed, Hollis and Katharine—supervised by Amy—had rolled the rug and moved it and the secretary into the front hall and had taped old sheets over the bookshelves.

After that, it would have been churlish to send them home unfed. Katharine ordered pizza and they ate out by the pool. Amy had a few qualms about eating pizza made by human hands she was not absolutely certain had been thoroughly washed, but once they got past that objection, supper was a lighthearted meal. Katharine was almost sorry when it was over. As they rose to carry things back in, the telephone rang. She ran in to answer, leaving the others to clear up.

"Katharine?" It was Tom, his voice concerned. "Are you all right? Posey called this afternoon and said you had a break-in. I'd have called earlier, but things are real hairy up here, getting ready for the meeting, and I just listened to my messages."

"I'm fine," she assured him. "Somebody broke in Friday night while I was asleep, but I heard him downstairs, so I went to Jon's hideout and locked the bolt. Then I called the police on my cell phone. I really am fine." She noticed she was reassuring him as she always did that she was perfectly able to cope while he was away, so she added, "But it was terrifying at the time—one of the scariest experiences of my life. I sure wished you were here."

"I'm sorry I wasn't." The words were the right ones, but he sounded as if his attention had drifted away. Then she heard voices in the background and knew he was still at the office, making final preparations for their big meeting. "Did they take anything?" he asked. When she hesitated, he added, "Posey said you'd have to tell me about that."

Bother Posey. Why couldn't she have let Katharine tell Tom in her own time and her own way?

She sighed. "I didn't plan to tell you until after your meeting, but whoever it was got your jade."

"All of it?" He sounded like somebody was choking him.

"Every last piece. I'm real sorry, honey."

He was silent for a long minute. "Nothing you could have done, I suppose." She got the impression he himself would have managed to think of something. "Did he get anything else?"

"Nothing I've missed yet, except a diary I found among Aunt Lucy's things."

She realized with a shock that while the necklace and diary had occupied most of her thoughts and time for the past four days, Tom didn't even know they existed. Nor was he interested in a diary right that minute.

"Have they caught whoever it was?" When she admitted they hadn't, he said, "Call the police tomorrow and tell them to get a jump on it. And take them the pictures from the safe-deposit box. Maybe they can trace at least some of the jade. And you need to—"

"I'm dealing with it," she said sharply, "just like I always deal with emergencies when you aren't here. Don't hassle me, Tom, when you aren't around to pick up some of the load."

Silence flowed from D.C. to Atlanta. Finally he asked, "You aren't staying at the house until they catch him, are you?"

"I stayed with Posey for two nights. Now I've borrowed Dane. He'll protect me."

His voice grew sharp. "You aren't letting that dog in the house, are you?"

"Well, yes. He wouldn't be much protection in the backyard."

"He'll pee on the rugs. Keep him out of the music room."

"I've moved the music room rug. It's rolled up in your office for you to decide what to do with when you get home."

"Why on earth—" His voice was baffled.

He probably didn't want to discuss rugs at the moment, but she told him anyway. "I'm turning the music room into my study, so I've bought a new rug I like better."

"Will I like it?"

"I have no idea. It's not your study."

She missed his reply, because the girls and Hasty came into the kitchen just then, laughing and talking loudly. "Who's that?" Tom asked.

She was tempted to retort, "I don't ask who is talking in your background." Instead she lowered her voice, hoping the others couldn't hear. "Hollis, a friend of hers, and a history prof I ran into at the history center last week. They came over for a while and stayed for pizza. He installed a new phone in my new study."

"You'd better have somebody check it out. I doubt a history professor knows much about installing phones. Well, I need to go. I'm sorry about the jade, but I'm glad you're okay. Listen, why don't you fly up here for a few days? You can visit museums or something while I'm at work, and I'll feel a lot better without you in the house by yourself until they catch that guy. See what time you can get a flight and let my office know when you'll be coming in."

Katharine almost said yes, but then she remembered that she needed to talk to Dutch Monday and wanted to take the necklace to their safe-deposit box. Hollis's painters were coming Tuesday and would need at least two days, and she had to meet with Dr. Flo's cousin on Thursday. "I'm sorry, hon, but I'm tied up until Thursday afternoon. Could you come home early? Or could I fly up Thursday and we could go somewhere for a long weekend?"

If he had begged her to come, she would have canceled everything in a heartbeat. Instead, he said in a surprised tone, "What's so all-fired important?"

"My life," she said before she thought. "Everything is not about you, Tom."

Hasty spoke right over her shoulder, and she wondered how long he'd been there. "We're going, Kate. Will you be all right?"

"Who's that?" Tom demanded.

She gestured for Hasty to move away. "The history prof."

She ignored Hasty's snort and said quickly, "Listen, I need to go. Can I call you back later?"

"No, a bunch of us are heading out to eat, then we want to wind up loose ends for tomorrow's meeting. I'll call you tomorrow night and tell you how it went. We can make plans then. Goodnight."

It was not a satisfactory call, but she'd gotten used to that, being apart so much. Some calls were good, some were so-so, and some were the pits. That one hovered on the brink of the pits.

Katharine and her guests moved to the front hall. "You'll be all right?" Hasty asked again at the front door.

"I'll be fine. Thanks."

"Shall I come back tomorrow to work on the diary? I could even take one of the copies with me and get a head start."

"You made copies?" Hollis asked from behind Kate. "So it's not a total loss?"

"I made copies," Katharine told her, "but it may be a total loss. Hasty thinks it's not very old and certainly not valuable."

"So why are you translating it?" Her eyes roved speculatively from one to the other.

"Because it's still a historical document," Katharine said.

"Because it's there," Hasty added with a grin. "You'll talk to Dutch, Kate?"

"Tomorrow at the latest," she promised. "Good night."

"What could Uncle Dutch know?" Hollis demanded as Hasty headed down the steps.

Katharine shrugged. "Probably nothing, but he knew Aunt Lucy and her friends."

Amy stepped from behind Hollis and held out her hand.

"Thank you so much, Katharine. I had a really good time."

Katharine couldn't remember the last time somebody Amy's age had shaken her hand as they left a casual event— probably when Jon was about twelve.

"I wasn't real good company," Amy continued, "since Zach—" She blinked away tears "—you know. But you all helped me forget for a little while. He'll probably be back tomorrow."

When Hollis stayed behind, Katharine asked, "Didn't you all come together?"

"Yeah." Hollis fondled Dane's ears. "But I'm staying. I don't want you here by yourself."

Did she think Hasty was coming back? Or was she worried that Zach might return for the necklace?

"I don't need you," Katharine said firmly. "I have to start staying by myself again some time, so I might as well start now. I've got Dane. Amy," she called loudly so the girl could hear. "Wait a minute. Hollis needs a ride."

As she closed the door and locked it, Katharine reflected that if she didn't take control of her own life, there were a lot of people willing to run it for her.

She considered watching TV, but in spite of her brave words, she didn't feel like sitting in a big empty house for two or three hours waiting for bedtime. She'd go see Dutch. It wasn't yet nine, and that old night owl wouldn't go to bed for ages.

"I'll be back soon," she promised Dane as she went for her keys. She took Lucy's oldest album and one copy of the diary along.

Dutch greeted her in a faded bathrobe, blue striped pajamas, and slippers so old and tatty that the Salvation Army would have turned them down. When he saw who it was, he took her arm and dragged her into the room, looking both ways to make sure nobody was watching. "Don't want the hall biddies getting the wrong idea," he said gruffly. "They talk enough as it is. To what do I owe the pleasure of this late-night visit?"

"I was a little lonesome, to tell the truth. Tom didn't get home—remember? And you're one of the few people I know whom I can visit this late."

"Well, sit down and make yourself comfortable."

"Which isn't exactly easy, is it?" she teased, heading for a scruffy old sofa that she knew had spent years down in his basement.

In contrast to the elegance of Autumn Village and the comfortable living quarters of most of its residents, Dutch's living room was Spartan. With his usual stubbornness, he had brought only his favorite things to his new home: the scruffy sofa, a massive walnut desk, his computer and printer, a gray metal filing cabinet, several mismatched bookshelves, a small kitchen table and two chairs that had also been relegated to the basement years before, and a wide-screen TV. Not one picture hung on the walls. He had placed the desk in the best spot in the room, over by the window where the light was strong, and had filled the shelves with books and untidy stacks of papers. Books and papers also overflowed the desk and sat in piles on the floor, for Dutch spent most of his time working on genealogy or minutes for various committees.

"That was the most comfortable couch we ever owned, I'll have you know," Dutch insisted, waving her toward the sagging cushions. "Would you like some sherry or a Coke?"

Katharine accepted the sherry. Dutch always bought the

best. Besides, maybe it would loosen him up so he'd reveal more than he might otherwise.

He brought the drinks in Waterford crystal. "See? I still retain a remnant of culture." He sat down at the other end of the couch. "What you been up to?" She told him about translating the diary, but didn't mention Hasty's contributions.

"I've been wondering who wrote it," she concluded. "It seems to be an Austrian. Do you remember any Austrian woman Carter was involved with while he was over there?"

He pursed his lips and made a soft "pooh, pooh, pooh," bobbing his head while he thought. "No," he said finally. "There were a bunch of fellahs who went around together: Carter, Lee and Donk Western, and that Austrian fellah who went to Sewanee—I still can't remember his name. There were a few girls around, as well, but I can't think of anybody special. Besides, Carter never paid women much attention. He was always bookish. Lucy used to tease him that if a man could marry a library, he'd be first in line."

"Well, let me ask you another question. Did you have a nickname back in college?"

"Dutch. Mama called me Lionel, but nobody else did after first grade. My teacher read out my name as 'Lionel' and the kid behind me started whispering 'Choo-choo, choo-choo, choo-choo.' That made me so mad, I told her I was called by my second name. She pronounced it Dutch instead of Deutsch, and I've been Dutch ever since." He chuckled. "I bloodied the nose of that other kid at recess, too."

"Were you never called 'L-squared,' for L. L.?"

"Not to my face. Why?"

"Because somebody in the diary was, and I thought it might be you." She didn't add how relieved she was that he wasn't the one who had arranged a seduction.

"I can't recall anybody called L-squared, but it seems

ut had thought that was for a year or two between growing p in New York and moving to Miami. By the time she was orn, all his New York relatives were dead, so it had seemed atural that all their family vacations should be spent in Buckhead or Cashiers, North Carolina, with her mother's riends and relatives. She had never imagined that they were is long-time friends, as well.

"Did Mary Frances have family here?" she asked, wondering if she wanted the answer.

Dutch chuckled. "Why, sure. Remember Ouida? She was Mary Frances's little sister."

"Aunt Ouida?" She had been another honorary aunt, a friend her parents always spent an afternoon with when they were in town. Aunt Ouida never forgot Katharine's birthday, sending small but delightful presents until the year she died. Now, Katharine was startled to realize that if the kaleidoscope had tuned another way, Ouida would have been her blood aunt.

Or she could have grown up in Cuba or something.

"Why did they keep all that a secret?" Katharine demanded, her voice harsh to her own ears. "Didn't they think I had a right to know?"

"I don't think they intended to keep secrets, honey. Everybody knew."

"Everybody but me."

She wondered what other secrets her family had kept, and vowed that as soon as she had solved the mystery of Carter Everanes, she would start researching her own family—if she dared. Who knew what she might find? "If I wanted to search my own genealogy, what books would I need to read?" she asked, hoping she sounded casual.

"Start on the Internet with www.ancestry.com," he advised. "That makes things so much simpler. Here let me show you."

like—" He paused. Finally he said with regret in his voice, "Nope. I thought I had an idea, but it took a hike. Happens more and more these days. If you ask me, we've got too much to remember."

It was his favorite complaint, so Katharine sipped her sherry and let him rumble on. Finally he demanded, "What happened to plain 'off' and 'on' switches? If I was younger, you know what I'd do? I'd start a company making a line of simple products that just do what most people need them to. I don't need ten temperatures on my microwave or a television and alarm clock I can program. So long as the microwave heats coffee and makes popcorn, the TV changes channels and has a volume control, and the alarm clock wakes me up, that's all I need. If I was a little younger—"

"If you were younger, you'd still be running your brokerage firm," she reminded him. "Why don't you and some of your poker buddies go ahead and start that company?"

"Don't be silly. We've been put out to pasture." But his eyes were thoughtful behind his trifocals.

"Tell me about Carter," she ordered. "This is his picture, right?" She handed him the album.

Dutch fetched a magnifying glass from his desk and peered at the pictures. Then he chuckled. "Yep, that's him all right. The short girl is Lucy and the one hanging on to him for dear life is Sara Claire." He scrutinized the pictures again. "Can't blame her, really. Carter was a handsome devil, wasn't he? Of course, she switched to that other feller—the Austrian whose name I can't remember—when Carter wasn't interested."

Katharine turned the page to the wedding pictures and put a finger on one face. "Is that you? You weren't too bad-looking yourself back then."

His face grew pink with pleasure. "I wasn't, was I?" He

bent to the picture again, and picked out two faces with a gnarled finger. "Your mama and daddy met at that wedding. Did you know that?"

Katharine was startled. "No. I thought they met nearly twenty years later."

"Nope, they met right there at Sara Claire and Walter's wedding. He was a classmate of Walter's from Yale. I wouldn't have called him a friend, exactly—Walter didn't make friends, even then, but he knew your daddy as well as anybody, so he invited him down to be a groomsman. That's where I met him, and we hit it off right away. He liked Atlanta, so he decided to come down and teach at Emory when he finished school. Taught there for years, until he moved down to Miami."

"But Sara Claire's wedding was 1939," she protested. "My folks got married in 1958."

"That's right." He nodded his big head and sipped his sherry. "They met again at Emory around 1952 and got married a couple of years after your daddy was widowed."

She sat up so quickly the springs creaked. "My daddy was widowed?"

"He sure was. He and—let me see—" He placed his thick finger beside a dark laughing girl. "—Mary Frances Wilson met at the wedding and got married the June before Pearl Harbor. She was a real sweetie. Pretty too, if you like brunettes. I dated her a few times myself." He stopped and looked wistfully at all those lovely young people who had not yet tasted war or death. "Funny," he added, "that your daddy would meet both his wives at the same wedding."

"What happened to Mary Frances?" Katharine felt like she was looking at her life through a kaleidoscope and Dutch had just turned the dial. Did she have a—what would Mary Frances be? A retroactive stepmother?—living somewhere in Buckhead?

Dutch's voice dropped. "Died of lung cancer. She [smoked] like a chimney. We all did, back then, but Mary Fran[ces was] the only one who got the Big C. She died in fifty-si[x]."

Katharine was still trying to get her head around [that] when Dutch rocked her on her heels. "Your mama ha[d come] back from Washington and gotten her divorce a fe[w years] before, and gone to work at Emory, too—"

"My mother got a divorce?" Her voice came out [a stran]gled protest.

"Had to. She was married to a fellah named Fran[k, one] who was a card-carrying Communist. Your mama [, she] was a bit of a radical—maybe to balance out Sara [Claire.] She and Frank were real good friends of Carter's back [then."] Dutch stopped, and added as one both apologizing a[nd ex]plaining, "A lot of guys played around with Comm[unism] back before the war. Most gave it up afterwards, of c[ourse.] But Frank never did. He went to Washington and ed[ited a] Communist rag up there until McCarthy started m[aking] things hot, then Frank decided to move to Latin Am[erica.] Your mama had given up a lot for him, but she woul[dn't go] to Latin America, so she came back to Atlanta, d[ivorced] him, and got a job as a secretary at Emory Law Scho[ol. Your] daddy was teaching there and we all ran around toge[ther. He] was the one who encouraged her to get her teachin[g certifi]cate. After Mary Frances died, they started dating, a[nd when] he landed that job in Miami, they decided to get ma[rried and] go down together. You were born a year later." H[e reached] over and patted her hand. "You were the best thin[g that ever] happened to either of them, Shug. Don't you eve[r forget it."]

Katharine clutched her glass. The kaleidoscope [was whirl]ing. She had always pictured her parents as g[rowing up] each waiting for the perfect mate until they'd [found each] other. She had known that her daddy once taug[ht at Emory]

Before she could protest that he didn't need to bother himself that evening, he had headed to his desk and was typing in commands. She went to stand behind him and watched, fascinated, as he pulled up the same census she had found at the history center. In just a minute he had located her grandparents' records, showing that her mother and Sarah Claire were both teenagers living in the house at the time. After her experience with Aunt Lucy's family, Katharine half-expected to find unexpected names listed there, but all she discovered was that her grandmother was two years older than her grandfather. She pointed to the figures.

"I never knew that, either."

Dutch chuckled. "You'll find all sorts of secrets in here. But don't hold it against them for not telling you everything, sweetie. You know that old saw—the best kept secret is something everybody knows."

Katharine headed back to the couch. "I guess everybody knew Aunt Lucy and Uncle Walter had a brother named Carter and that he got murdered. They just never saw fit to mention it." If she sounded like a ten-year-old working up to a tantrum, that's exactly how she felt.

"Now, that was different." Dutch held up a hand to still her temper. "The murder and the trial—well, they upset Walter and Lucy real bad. They never wanted to discuss Carter after that."

"But why?"

He sighed. "Some things are best left alone, Shug. No point stirring old pots."

"This from a man dedicated to family histories?"

"This isn't my family history and it isn't yours, either." She could tell that he wouldn't discuss it any further that evening. She'd have to try again later.

She reached over and picked up her glass, finished her

sherry, and took the glass to the sink to rinse. "I'd better be going. Listen, why don't you have lunch at my house tomorrow?"

He pursed his lips to consider the invitation. "What were you thinking of having?"

"What would you like?" She'd been thinking along the lines of soup and sandwiches.

"Corn on the cob," he said promptly. "They never give it to us here. Probably think we can't chew it. And see if you can't get us some home-grown tomatoes—the red kind. Haven't seen anything but a pallid pink tomato this whole blessed summer."

The meal was turning into an old-fashioned midday dinner, but Autumn Village served its main meal at noon. She took a mental inventory of her fridge. She'd have to shop, anyway. "Do you want fried chicken? Oh—I forgot. You aren't allowed fried foods. How about baked fish?"

"Fry that chicken, Shug. If it kills me, I'll die smiling."

"You want mashed potatoes and gravy with that?"

"Spoil me that much and I'll be moving in with you. Don't worry about how much fat and salt I'll be eating. If I'd known I was eating right all these years so I could wind up sitting on my duff in a retirement home wondering what to do with myself all day, I'd have eaten what I wanted to. Then I'd be up in heaven with all my friends about to play a perfect round of golf with your daddy. Imagine, no balls in the water, none in the sand traps—"

"Don't talk like that," she said crossly.

He chuckled. "'Have I softened you up enough to invite me to move in? Actually, I like it here. I've got that bunch of guys I play poker with every morning, the place shows good movies several nights a week, and I get plenty of exercise running from the widows. If I get bored, why, I get in my car and drive up to Phipps Plaza and ogle pretty girls. But I still appreciate good home cooking. I'll be delighted to come. Make me a pecan pie from your mama's recipe, and I'll be your slave forever."

As she started to gather up her albums and papers, the copied pages of the diary fell from her hand and scattered on the carpet. Picking them up, she came across the copy of the clipping of Ludwig Ramsauer's death. "Does the name Ludwig Ramsauer mean anything to you?"

Dutch beamed and snapped his fingers. "That was the Austrian fellah whose name I was trying to remember, the one Sara Claire was crazy about. He knew Carter and the others at Sewanee, and showed us all over Vienna. Does Lucy have a picture of him, too?"

"No, but this clipping was in the diary." She carried it across to him at his desk.

He took it eagerly then echoed Zach. "Hell, it's in German." He peered at the margin. "Why did Carter write '1950' and all these question marks?"

Katharine took the page with excitement. "Carter wrote that? Are you sure?"

"Looks like his writing. Do you know any German? Can you tell what happened to Ludwig?"

"It says he died in a climbing accident. He was climbing alone and fell." Katharine was still looking at the margin note. It made Carter seem more real, somehow.

"That doesn't sound right." Dutch furrowed his brow. "Ludwig was always telling us not to climb alone, that the mountains could be treacherous and you never knew when an accident might happen. I went for a little walk alone once and he had a hissy fit."

"An accident seems to have happened to him. What else do you remember about him?"

"Not much. I didn't know him well. He was a year ahead of me at Sewanee and hung around with chemistry majors—that wild bunch I was telling you about. Lee and Donk Western spearheaded the group. Did you know Donk? No, he died in the war."

He had said the exact same thing before, with exactly the same intonations. Some of his memory tapes were probably automatic by then, replaying at the push of a particular button.

"So I guess you don't know whether Ludwig Ramsauer was related to a man named Georg Ramsauer who excavated a Celtic cemetery in the eighteen hundreds." She made it a statement, but hoped he'd correct her.

"Nope. Don't know a thing about his family. I'll tell you what I'll do, though, if it matters. I'll call the Sewanee alumni office and see what they know about Ramsauer. It's amazing how alumni offices keep up with folks. Looking for money, of course. But would that help?"

She doubted it, but it was worth a try. "Ask them something else, please," she added as he showed her out. "Ask if there was an Austrian girl in the class, as well."

Dutch guffawed as he held the door for her. "If so, she'd have been kept well hidden, sweetie pie. In those days, Sewanee was a college for men."

Chapter 20

Monday, June 12

Monday was hot and muggy from the start. Instead of dragging the necklace up with the pool net, Katharine decided to dive for it, and the water was so tempting, she stayed in longer than she should have. By the time she threw on some clothes and wrapped the necklace in its original cloth to take to the bank, she was running late. She'd barely have time to take Dane home, go by the bank and the grocery store, and cook a midday dinner before Dutch arrived at noon. And while she wouldn't mind if the meal was late, she knew he liked to nap at two.

Just before she left, she snatched up both copies of the diary and took them with her. She would put one with the necklace and keep the other with her at all times.

She dropped Dane off, arranged to pick him up that afternoon, and turned down Posey's invitation that she have one cup of coffee. "Dutch is coming for lunch, and he's expecting a feast. It's been so long since I cooked a chicken dinner, I may have forgotten how."

The bank was crowded, so she had to wait to get into her safe-deposit box. She dashed out of the bank lighter by one piece of jewelry, one copy of the manuscript, and a load of anxiety she didn't realize she had been carrying. She carried out a copy of the list of Tom's jade and all the pictures, for the police. She'd photocopy the pictures and drop them off that afternoon.

At Publix, she hurried through the produce department trying to pick the tenderest white corn, the reddest tomatoes, the creamiest potatoes. She added a big slice of a watermelon that looked particularly sweet and headed to the meat counter. Checkout lines were longer than usual, and the clerk in her line was a new trainee who took forever to ring her up. "Help!" she winged a prayer as she wheeled her cart to the parking lot. "I'll never get dinner ready on time at this rate." She wanted to fix a dinner that Dutch's own mama would have been proud of.

As she slowed to pull into her drive, a dark blue truck roared out. It was the size of a large U-Haul and its cab windows were tinted so she could not see inside. It had no company name on its side, either. Had Hollis's painters come a day early and found her out? Puzzled, she parked in the garage, collected her groceries, and headed to the kitchen with five plastic bags dangling from her hands.

In the doorway, she froze.

Every drawer had been dumped. Pantry containers had been emptied and tossed. Cereal, corn meal, sugar, coffee, and flour mingled in a filthy mess on the floor. The seats to her new chairs had been slit, their stuffing yanked out and left in piles like snow.

Katharine knew she needed to leave, but her feet wouldn't move. Finally she took a deep breath and plunged back into the garage. In the car, she locked the doors and tried to get the key in the ignition, but her hands trembled too badly. Once she got the SUV started, she nearly forgot to raise the garage door in her frantic haste to depart. She hurtled down and drive up to Phipps Plaza and ogle pretty girls. But I still appreciate good home cooking. I'll be delighted to come. Make me a pecan pie from your mama's recipe, and I'll be your slave forever."

As she started to gather up her albums and papers, the copied pages of the diary fell from her hand and scattered on the carpet. Picking them up, she came across the copy of the clipping of Ludwig Ramsauer's death. "Does the name Ludwig Ramsauer mean anything to you?"

Dutch beamed and snapped his fingers. "That was the Austrian fellah whose name I was trying to remember, the one Sara Claire was crazy about. He knew Carter and the others at Sewanee, and showed us all over Vienna. Does Lucy have a picture of him, too?"

"No, but this clipping was in the diary." She carried it across to him at his desk.

He took it eagerly then echoed Zach. "Hell, it's in German." He peered at the margin. "Why did Carter write '1950' and all these question marks?"

Katharine took the page with excitement. "Carter wrote that? Are you sure?"

"Looks like his writing. Do you know any German? Can you tell what happened to Ludwig?"

"It says he died in a climbing accident. He was climbing alone and fell." Katharine was still looking at the margin note. It made Carter seem more real, somehow.

"That doesn't sound right." Dutch furrowed his brow. "Ludwig was always telling us not to climb alone, that the mountains could be treacherous and you never knew when an accident might happen. I went for a little walk alone once and he had a hissy fit."

"An accident seems to have happened to him. What else do you remember about him?"

"Not much. I didn't know him well. He was a year ahead of me at Sewanee and hung around with chemistry majors— that wild bunch I was telling you about. Lee and Donk Western spearheaded the group. Did you know Donk? No, he died in the war."

He had said the exact same thing before, with exactly the same intonations. Some of his memory tapes were probably automatic by then, replaying at the push of a particular button.

"So I guess you don't know whether Ludwig Ramsauer was related to a man named Georg Ramsauer who excavated a Celtic cemetery in the eighteen hundreds." She made it a statement, but hoped he'd correct her.

"Nope. Don't know a thing about his family. I'll tell you what I'll do, though, if it matters. I'll call the Sewanee alumni office and see what they know about Ramsauer. It's amazing how alumni offices keep up with folks. Looking for money, of course. But would that help?"

She doubted it, but it was worth a try. "Ask them something else, please," she added as he showed her out. "Ask if there was an Austrian girl in the class, as well."

Dutch guffawed as he held the door for her. "If so, she'd have been kept well hidden, sweetie pie. In those days, Sewanee was a college for men."

like—" He paused. Finally he said with regret in his voice, "Nope. I thought I had an idea, but it took a hike. Happens more and more these days. If you ask me, we've got too much to remember."

It was his favorite complaint, so Katharine sipped her sherry and let him rumble on. Finally he demanded, "What happened to plain 'off' and 'on' switches? If I was younger, you know what I'd do? I'd start a company making a line of simple products that just do what most people need them to. I don't need ten temperatures on my microwave or a television and alarm clock I can program. So long as the microwave heats coffee and makes popcorn, the TV changes channels and has a volume control, and the alarm clock wakes me up, that's all I need. If I was a little younger—"

"If you were younger, you'd still be running your brokerage firm," she reminded him. "Why don't you and some of your poker buddies go ahead and start that company?"

"Don't be silly. We've been put out to pasture." But his eyes were thoughtful behind his trifocals.

"Tell me about Carter," she ordered. "This is his picture, right?" She handed him the album.

Dutch fetched a magnifying glass from his desk and peered at the pictures. Then he chuckled. "Yep, that's him all right. The short girl is Lucy and the one hanging on to him for dear life is Sara Claire." He scrutinized the pictures again. "Can't blame her, really. Carter was a handsome devil, wasn't he? Of course, she switched to that other feller—the Austrian whose name I can't remember—when Carter wasn't interested."

Katharine turned the page to the wedding pictures and put a finger on one face. "Is that you? You weren't too bad-looking yourself back then."

His face grew pink with pleasure. "I wasn't, was I?" He

bent to the picture again, and picked out two faces with a gnarled finger. "Your mama and daddy met at that wedding. Did you know that?"

Katharine was startled. "No. I thought they met nearly twenty years later."

"Nope, they met right there at Sara Claire and Walter's wedding. He was a classmate of Walter's from Yale. I wouldn't have called him a friend, exactly—Walter didn't make friends, even then, but he knew your daddy as well as anybody, so he invited him down to be a groomsman. That's where I met him, and we hit it off right away. He liked Atlanta, so he decided to come down and teach at Emory when he finished school. Taught there for years, until he moved down to Miami."

"But Sara Claire's wedding was 1939," she protested. "My folks got married in 1958."

"That's right." He nodded his big head and sipped his sherry. "They met again at Emory around 1952 and got married a couple of years after your daddy was widowed."

She sat up so quickly the springs creaked. "My daddy was widowed?"

"He sure was. He and—let me see—" He placed his thick finger beside a dark laughing girl. "—Mary Frances Wilson met at the wedding and got married the June before Pearl Harbor. She was a real sweetie. Pretty too, if you like brunettes. I dated her a few times myself." He stopped and looked wistfully at all those lovely young people who had not yet tasted war or death. "Funny," he added, "that your daddy would meet both his wives at the same wedding."

"What happened to Mary Frances?" Katharine felt like she was looking at her life through a kaleidoscope and Dutch had just turned the dial. Did she have a—what would Mary Frances be? A retroactive stepmother?—living somewhere in Buckhead?

Dutch's voice dropped. "Died of lung cancer. She smoked like a chimney. We all did, back then, but Mary Frances was the only one who got the Big C. She died in fifty-six."

Katharine was still trying to get her head around all that when Dutch rocked her on her heels. "Your mama had come back from Washington and gotten her divorce a few years before, and gone to work at Emory, too—"

"My mother got a divorce?" Her voice came out a strangled protest.

"Had to. She was married to a fellah named Frank Bell, who was a card-carrying Communist. Your mama always was a bit of a radical—maybe to balance out Sara Claire. She and Frank were real good friends of Carter's back then." Dutch stopped, and added as one both apologizing and explaining, "A lot of guys played around with Communism back before the war. Most gave it up afterwards, of course. But Frank never did. He went to Washington and edited a Communist rag up there until McCarthy started making things hot, then Frank decided to move to Latin America. Your mama had given up a lot for him, but she wouldn't go to Latin America, so she came back to Atlanta, divorced him, and got a job as a secretary at Emory Law School. Your daddy was teaching there and we all ran around together. He was the one who encouraged her to get her teaching certificate. After Mary Frances died, they started dating, and when he landed that job in Miami, they decided to get married and go down together. You were born a year later." He reached over and patted her hand. "You were the best thing that ever happened to either of them, Shug. Don't you ever forget it."

Katharine clutched her glass. The kaleidoscope was whirling. She had always pictured her parents as gently aging, each waiting for the perfect mate until they'd found each other. She had known that her daddy once taught at Emory, but had thought that was for a year or two between growing up in New York and moving to Miami. By the time she was born, all his New York relatives were dead, so it had seemed natural that all their family vacations should be spent in Buckhead or Cashiers, North Carolina, with her mother's friends and relatives. She had never imagined that they were his long-time friends, as well.

"Did Mary Frances have family here?" she asked, wondering if she wanted the answer.

Dutch chuckled. "Why, sure. Remember Ouida? She was Mary Frances's little sister."

"Aunt Ouida?" She had been another honorary aunt, a friend her parents always spent an afternoon with when they were in town. Aunt Ouida never forgot Katharine's birthday, sending small but delightful presents until the year she died. Now, Katharine was startled to realize that if the kaleidoscope had tuned another way, Ouida would have been her blood aunt.

Or she could have grown up in Cuba or something.

"Why did they keep all that a secret?" Katharine demanded, her voice harsh to her own ears. "Didn't they think I had a right to know?"

"I don't think they intended to keep secrets, honey. Everybody knew."

"Everybody but me."

She wondered what other secrets her family had kept, and vowed that as soon as she had solved the mystery of Carter Everanes, she would start researching her own family—if she dared. Who knew what she might find? "If I wanted to research my own genealogy, what books would I need to read?" she asked, hoping she sounded casual.

"Start on the Internet with www.ancestry.com," he advised. "That makes things so much simpler. Here let me show you."

sherry, and took the glass to the sink to rinse. "I'd better be going. Listen, why don't you have lunch at my house tomorrow?"

He pursed his lips to consider the invitation. "What were you thinking of having?"

"What would you like?" She'd been thinking along the lines of soup and sandwiches.

"Corn on the cob," he said promptly. "They never give it to us here. Probably think we can't chew it. And see if you can't get us some home-grown tomatoes—the red kind. Haven't seen anything but a pallid pink tomato this whole blessed summer."

The meal was turning into an old-fashioned midday dinner, but Autumn Village served its main meal at noon. She took a mental inventory of her fridge. She'd have to shop, anyway. "Do you want fried chicken? Oh—I forgot. You aren't allowed fried foods. How about baked fish?"

"Fry that chicken, Shug. If it kills me, I'll die smiling."

"You want mashed potatoes and gravy with that?"

"Spoil me that much and I'll be moving in with you. Don't worry about how much fat and salt I'll be eating. If I'd known I was eating right all these years so I could wind up sitting on my duff in a retirement home wondering what to do with myself all day, I'd have eaten what I wanted to. Then I'd be up in heaven with all my friends about to play a perfect round of golf with your daddy. Imagine, no balls in the water, none in the sand traps—"

"Don't talk like that," she said crossly.

He chuckled. "'Have I softened you up enough to invite me to move in? Actually, I like it here. I've got that bunch of guys I play poker with every morning, the place shows good movies several nights a week, and I get plenty of exercise running from the widows. If I get bored, why, I get in my car

Before she could protest that he didn't need to bother himself that evening, he had headed to his desk and was typing in commands. She went to stand behind him and watched, fascinated, as he pulled up the same census she had found at the history center. In just a minute he had located her grandparents' records, showing that her mother and Sarah Claire were both teenagers living in the house at the time. After her experience with Aunt Lucy's family, Katharine half-expected to find unexpected names listed there, but all she discovered was that her grandmother was two years older than her grandfather. She pointed to the figures.

"I never knew that, either."

Dutch chuckled. "You'll find all sorts of secrets in here. But don't hold it against them for not telling you everything, sweetie. You know that old saw—the best kept secret is something everybody knows."

Katharine headed back to the couch. "I guess everybody knew Aunt Lucy and Uncle Walter had a brother named Carter and that he got murdered. They just never saw fit to mention it." If she sounded like a ten-year-old working up to a tantrum, that's exactly how she felt.

"Now, that was different." Dutch held up a hand to still her temper. "The murder and the trial—well, they upset Walter and Lucy real bad. They never wanted to discuss Carter after that."

"But why?"

He sighed. "Some things are best left alone, Shug. No point stirring old pots."

"This from a man dedicated to family histories?"

"This isn't my family history and it isn't yours, either." She could tell that he wouldn't discuss it any further that evening. She'd have to try again later.

She reached over and picked up her glass, finished her

her driveway panting and shaking, pulled into a neighbor's driveway, and punched 911.

She was still giving her address when two police cars came screaming from opposite directions and turned in at her gates. "Never mind," she told the operator. "They're here." She started her engine and followed them in.

"That was fast," she called as she climbed down and hurried to the first cruiser. "I hadn't even finished talking to ..." She stopped in surprise. "I thought you worked evenings."

"That was last weekend. This week we're on days." Officer Howard climbed out of one cruiser, as stiff and poker-faced as he had been Friday evening.

"I just got home from the grocery store, and somebody has trashed my kitchen." She licked her lips and tried to catch her breath.

Officer Williams approached her from behind. "Your alarm company already called. That's why we're here. Have you looked at the rest of the house?"

"I didn't wait to check the rest. All I wanted was to get the heck out of there."

"Very wise. Please wait in your car for a moment, and lock your doors." The officers walked the perimeter of the house and then Officer Williams came back and motioned for her to roll down her window. "They smashed in the back door this time. Please wait until we make sure the house is secure. You might want to call your husband."

She looked at her watch. "At this moment, he's in an important meeting in Washington. I won't be able to reach him until after one."

Her teeth chattered in spite of the heat as she waited. Finally Officer Howard ran down the veranda steps at a loose-limbed trot, pulling sunglasses from his breast pocket and putting them on as he approached her car. They made him

look like a young Sylvester Stallone. She suspected he culti-
vated the impression. "They've gone, but the place is a
mess," he said. "We're getting a team out here, and we'll
want you to walk through with us."

In the front hall, Katharine felt she had been physically
assaulted. Living room cushions had been slashed and the
stuffing removed. Oriental rugs had been lifted and carried
away. Dining room drawers stood open, their contents flung
on the floor. Some oil paintings were missing. The rest had
been slit and tossed aside, including two they had commissioned of the children when they were four and two. She
moaned when she saw how those had been cut up through
the centers of their little faces. The sheets that she and Hollis
had so carefully taped to the music room shelves the night
before had been torn down and left in puddles of white on
the bare floor. Her new rug was gone.

Every feeling froze within her as she walked through the
house with the officers. Was this numbness what hurricane
victims felt, or victims of war? Moving on autopilot, she
pointed out where things were missing, but felt like she was
behind an invisible shield. Surely this hadn't happened to
her. Televisions and stereos were gone, as was all the silver.
China and crystal had been swept off shelves and left splin-
tered on the floor. Books lay in disorder all over Tom's library. His desk chair was slashed, the safe forced. All her
good jewelry had been taken from it.

Like a zombie she waded through bedrooms ankle-deep
in feathers and mattress stuffing, permeated with perfume
from smashed bottles. She peered into closets where clothes
lay in heaps on the floor. Jon's closet had been ravaged by a
snowstorm of down from his prized sleeping bag. The door
to the hideout stood open, the Jolly Roger flying in defiance
of more successful pirates.

Later, the thought that her jewelry, her grandmother's silver service, their computer and televisions were probably being sold to buy drugs would make her stomach heave for days to come, but at the time, she felt anesthetized. Dispassionately she told the officers about taking the necklace to the bank for safety. She even smiled faintly when Officer Howard unbent enough to joke, "Too bad you didn't leave a sign on the gatepost, if that's what they were looking for."

The word gatepost reminded her of the truck. She described it as best she could, and apologized that she hadn't been prescient enough to turn around and get its license number as it roared away. The first twinge of feeling she had was when Officer Williams remarked, "It's a mercy you didn't arrive sooner. They probably had a whole team in the back—almost had to, to cover the house between the time when the alarm went off downtown and we got here. They were probably watching the house until you left, knew what they were doing, and did it and got out. But they could have gotten rough if you'd walked in on them."

Katharine caught a ragged breath. Having seen the devastation of her house, she didn't care to imagine what they would have done to her if she had gotten in their way.

"Have you found Zach Andrews?" she asked. "He's been missing all weekend, and he was in a lot of trouble back in high school. He may have hired these men."

"We haven't found him yet," Office Williams admitted, "but we're looking. The Ivories want us to find him, too. Now, ma'am, I suggest you let us give you a ride back to your sister's. You'd better plan to stay a while."

"Sister-in-law's," Katharine corrected him automatically. "And I am fine. I can drive. But what if you have questions? We haven't listed everything that is missing."

"You'll go over all that with the insurance adjuster," he told her, "after we are done."

As she headed for her car, she heard him tell Officer Howard, "Remarkably calm. A strong woman."

As she climbed back into her SUV, the clock on her dashboard read eleven-ten. When she reached for her purse, she discovered that she held the remains of a clay duck Susan had made in fourth grade for Mother's Day and she used in her bathroom as a soap dish. She must have picked it up from her bathroom floor, but had no memory of doing so. Poor little duck, his head had been ground to dust and his tail chipped off. When she looked at what remained, she found herself wracked by great gasping sobs.

She cried for what seemed like an hour, but was only a few minutes. Finally, cried out and exhausted, she considered what to do next. She needed to call Dutch and tell him not to come. Had it been a century ago when she had invited him?

He didn't answer. She didn't want him driving all the way to her house for nothing and she still had Autumn Village on auto-dial, so she called the front desk. Leona, of the nasal twang, was on duty. "Dutch Landrum was coming to my house for dinner," Katharine said crisply, proud that her voice didn't tremble, "but I need to talk to him before he leaves and he's not answering. Could you go out and check to see if his car is still in the lot?"

"I'm sorry, Miz Murray, but we're real short-staffed today, on account of a bug that's goin' around, so Mr. Billingslea said I was not to leave this desk for any reason whatsoever. If there's anythang I kin do fer you from here—"

The organized part of Katharine's brain went into hyperdrive. She remembered that Posey's aerobics class on Monday was followed by a massage, so she never got home before one. "Never mind," she told Leona. "I might as well drive over there. I've had some trouble at my house, so we'll need to go somewhere else to eat, anyway."

She hung up and considered the groceries that she had flung in the passenger seat when she was fleeing. She and Dutch could eat the watermelon in his room. She would leave him the tomatoes, and take the corn and potatoes over to Posey. But the chicken would spoil in the heat before she had eaten with Dutch and gotten back to Posey's, and she could not bear to lose one more thing.

Saving that chicken became the most urgent item on her agenda.

She climbed back down from the SUV and ran with the bag toward the house. "Excuse me," she told two technicians in the hall, "but I need to put this in the freezer in the garage."

They stared at her like she had wandered in from another planet. She explained in a shaking voice, "I don't think the robbers went into the garage, and this chicken will spoil if I have to carry it around all day. It needs to go in my freezer!"

They exchanged looks. One finally said softly to the other. "Shock." He put out his hand. "We'll do that for you, ma'am." He carried it toward the kitchen.

"Would you like somebody to drive you somewhere?" the other asked.

"No, I'm fine." She turned and strode back to her car.

The door had barely slammed, however, when her hands started to shake so hard she couldn't grasp her keys. Her legs were trembling too much to trust her foot on the gas pedal. Her entire body turned to jelly. Tears again clogged her throat as one by one she pictured irreplaceable treasures that had been destroyed or stolen. It was not just the things themselves that broke her heart, but the memories that went with them.

"Grandmama always used that silver service when she entertained," she said between deep, ragged sobs, "and we'll never find more of the china we got in France on our honeymoon. And how could they walk all over my underwear? And take the pendant Tom bought for our anniversary? How could they? How could they?" She pounded the wheel with her fists. When she remembered the slashed portraits of her children, she laid her head on the steering wheel and bawled.

She finally felt calm enough to drive, but tears came again when she drove into Autumn Village. Driving up the tree-lined drive reminded her of her mother, Lucy, and even Sara Claire, and how much she missed them. She wished she could fling herself into their arms to cry out her loss.

She pulled into a shady parking space and noted that Dutch's Cadillac sat across the lot. Good. He hadn't left yet. She could sit a few minutes and recover.

Autumn Village was one of the best retirement communities in Atlanta. Only three stories high, it featured lovely paintings on the walls, fresh floral arrangements in the lobby, and level concrete paths outside that led to comfortable chairs in conversation groups under shady trees. Dinner was at noon, and supper at a civilized six-thirty, with snacks set out at nine in the lobby for any who wanted them. Live plants grew on wide, sunny windowsills. Bright tropical fish darted in tanks on each floor, and three parakeets entertained those who walked through the lobby. Residents popped in and out of each other's apartments, played cards, made crafts to sell in a shop that benefited a local literacy program, attended lectures and Bible studies, and volunteered in the lending library or a small store that sold basic foodstuffs and toiletries. Those who needed assistance with bathing, dressing, or medications could employ a helper or pay extra for discreet help from staff who came to their units. Only when residents needed total nursing care were they asked to move to another wing, where it was still convenient for their old friends to visit. Aunt Lucy used to joke, "Autumn Village is like a Vassar dorm without the hassle of exams."

Katharine sat in the parking lot until she felt composed. Then she entered the lobby, greeted Leona, and asked her not to let Dutch sneak past while she made a quick trip to the ladies' room to fix her face. "You got a cold?" Leona asked. "Your nose is mighty red."

"Just a little one." That was easier than explaining.

The elevator crept upward like it carried porcelain that needed to be lifted a centimeter at a time. When it finally reached the third floor, her sandals made a soft slap-slap as she padded down the long carpeted hall to Dutch's apartment. She knocked. He didn't answer.

"Dutch?" she called softly, knocking again.

He still didn't answer.

She checked a small wooden stoplight hanging beside his door. At night, the staff went around and pulled levers to turn all the lights red. Each morning, residents pulled levers to turn the lights green, to indicate they were up and about. If a light was still red by nine o'clock, somebody from the staff investigated.

Dutch's light was green, of course. He was always up by nine. So where was he? Probably playing poker with his cronies. He hadn't left yet, unless he had crossed the lobby while she was in the ladies' room. And surely even the phlegmatic Leona would have remembered to inform him Katharine was there.

She tried his door, but it was locked. She padded to the far end of the hall, to a sunny solarium where groups worked puzzles or played cards. It was empty.

If she had known who Dutch's friends were, she could have knocked on doors, but she didn't like to disturb strangers. With a huff of disgust, she headed back to the elevator.

"I'm too wobbly for all this walking," she muttered.

At the desk, Leona popped her gum and rang his apartment again, but nobody answered.

"Has he had any guests today?" Katharine asked, scanning down the visitor register she had already signed.

"Just the laundry branging shirts." Leona slung the gum from one side of her mouth to the other and pointed a sharp red nail at an illegible scrawl. The laundry man had signed in at 10:35 and out at 10:50.

Katharine sighed. "You don't know who he plays cards with, do you? We were supposed to have lunch together, and he may have forgotten."

Leona made a face. "Forgettin' is a fav'rite pastime around here." She chewed thoughtfully. "I don't know 'bout poker, but he eats with Jack Johnson. I could ring Jack."

Jack said, "I haven't seen Dutch all day. He called this morning and said he wasn't coming to our little game, he was going out to lunch and wanted to get a haircut first."

Katharine asked Leona to call the barber, who worked in the basement. He said Dutch got a haircut at nine-thirty and he hadn't seen him since.

Maybe it was what had happened at her house, but Katharine was beginning to feel anxious. She told herself it was silly to worry. But still— "Could you all open his door for me, just to be sure he's all right?" she asked.

"I cain't leave the desk," Leona reminded her, "so I cain't do a thang to help you myself. Mr. Billingslea is out at a meetin' in town, so he cain't help you, neither. But why don't I call Norman? He's fixin' a clogged toilet right now, but he'll get up there as soon as he kin. You wanna wait down here?"

"No, I'll wait in the hall up there." Katharine didn't want Leona lifting the weight of her mascara high enough to notice how red her eyes still were.

While the elevator crept back up to the third floor, she wished she had asked Jack who Dutch's other friends were. She was going to feel real silly if he came back from visiting somebody—or out of the bathroom—and found her and Norman, who doubled as handyman and daytime security, breaking into his apartment.

One nice feature of Autumn Village was a couple of comfortable chairs halfway down each hall. They were there for residents who found the long halls too much of a walk at one stretch, but Katharine availed herself of one and kept an eye on Dutch's door. Ten minutes passed before a lanky man in a brown uniform came upstairs jingling a big ring of keys.

"Hey, Norman," she greeted him. Norman and she had had a few run-ins in the past over the speed with which he didn't repair leaking toilets and faulty phones, but he seemed to hold no grudges.

"Hey, Miz Murray. What's the problem?" He played a tune on a fat ring of keys.

She stood. "I am supposed to be having lunch with Mr. Landrum but I can't find him. He's probably visiting somebody else, but since we had a date for lunch—"

"Probably just forgot," Norman said cheerfully. "Leona said you want me to let you in." When Katharine nodded, he pulled a wrinkled form from his pocket. "You'll have to sign here."

After she had made it official that she had requested permission to enter Mr. Landrum's unit uninvited, Norman found the right key and opened the door. "We can't let just anybody in, you know," he told her as he stood back to let her precede him. "We don't want our residents complaining." He raised his voice a pitch. "Mr. Landrum? You got company."

Dutch didn't answer. He sprawled facedown on the couch. And as soon as Katharine touched his hand, she knew he would never eat fried chicken again.

Chapter 21

Katharine started to turn him over, but Norman held her back. "I'm sorry, Miz Murray, but you'll need to wait in the hall. I believe Mr. Landrum has expired."

Katharine didn't know whether to burst into hysterical laughter or throw back her head and scream at Norman's asinine stupidity. Obviously Dutch had "expired." Nobody but a small infant can successfully mimic the stillness of death. Besides, when she bent over him, she could see that his face was purple and his tongue lolled out of his mouth. Had he had some kind of fit?

Poor dear, he must have been putting on his tie. It lay in a heap on the arm of the couch. She picked it up, rolled it idly, and stuffed it in her pocket as she left the room with tears streaming down her cheeks.

She slumped into the nearest chair in the hall, moving through a thick fog of grief. The morning's earlier events receded in importance before this blow. Losing Dutch was like losing her parents all over again. Dutch was the last remaining adult who had held her on his knee, attended her graduations and her wedding, and knew her family's private stories and jokes. When they buried Dutch, they would bury her entire childhood except what she carried with her.

In the next hour, she sat in a sodden lump while Autumn

Village dealt with violent death in its own discreet way. She considered calling Posey or Tom, but what could they do? She watched without seeing as a procession of people came and went. Mr. Billingslea himself appeared and stood guard, waving away curious residents with the bland, professional assurance, "Everything is under control."

Under control? In spite of a cup of strong, sweet tea brought to her by a woman with an equally strong, sweet face, Katharine wanted to laugh hysterically at the hackneyed phrase. Nothing in her life was under control at the moment, and Dutch had gone beyond control.

At some point Mr. Billingslea came to her chair and said, "Wait here, please, Mrs. Murray. They want to interview you in a little while." So she sat, threading Dutch's tie through her fingers, waiting. Once the initial tide of grief receded, she felt a curious sense of detachment. It was hard to believe she wasn't waiting to take Dutch to lunch. Or Aunt Lucy. Or her mother. She wished she had taken Dutch out more often—that he hadn't died so inconveniently *before* they'd had dinner.

She had cried out all her tears by the time they carried the heavy stretcher toward the freight elevator at the back.

When a policeman bent over her and asked, "You were the one to find him, ma'am?" she looked up at his uniform in surprise. She hadn't noticed who had been going in and out of the room. She had expected a doctor.

Before she could say more than, "Yes," she realized the interviewing officer wasn't listening. He was looking at what she was doing with her hands. "What is that, ma'am?"

She held it up. "Dutch's tie. He must have been putting it on when he had his fit. It was lying on the arm of his couch."

"Hey, Steve, come here!" he called to an officer down the

hall. When Steve arrived, the first officer pointed. "I think we've found your weapon."

Katharine dropped it in shock. "Dutch was killed?"

"Yes, ma'am. Can't choke yourself without a noose and something to stand on."

The man named Steve bent to retrieve the tie. "You been holding it?" he demanded.

"Running her hands all over it," the other officer answered for her.

"There went any fingerprints." Steve dropped it in a plastic bag. "Ma'am, haven't you watched enough television to know not to touch anything at a crime scene?"

"I didn't know it was a crime scene." She swayed and would have fainted if he hadn't caught her. Her ears roared.

Somebody pressed her head gently to her knees. "Stay like that for a minute, ma'am. Hey! Can I get a cup of something hot and sweet down here?"

In another minute, somebody thrust another cup of tea into her hands and held her shoulder while she drank it. As she obediently swallowed, Katharine decided to call Tom after all. She didn't care if he was in a meeting with the president. She needed him.

As soon as the world stopped spinning, she reached for her phone and called Tom's cell. After four rings it picked up automatically, and Tom's pleasant business voice came on the line. "This is Thomas Murray. I'm sorry I can't take your call right now, but if you leave a message, I'll get right back to you as soon as I possibly can."

"Tom? Katharine. Call me as soon as you get this, please? I have to talk to you at once."

Fiercely, she punched in his office number. "Louise, I need to talk to Tom as soon as possible. I've got an emergency down here. Two, in fact. I urgently need to speak to him."

"He's at a meeting right now, Mrs. Murray, but I'll be sure and give him the message. Is there anything I can do?"

"Yes. Try to get to him and tell him to call me. Then make him a plane reservation for this afternoon and clear his calendar for the rest of the week. I need him down here, real bad." She didn't even mind that her voice trembled on the last sentence.

After she hung up, though, she regretted the call. She didn't want Louise thinking she was a hysterical wimp. And what could Tom do that she couldn't besides hold her while she cried? The rest she could cope with. She always had.

Mr. Billingslea finally unbent enough to wander down the hall in her direction. "I wonder, Mrs. Murray, if you would call Mr. Landrum's son. You know the family so well."

"Oh, yes. I've known them all my life." She didn't add that Chapman Landrum was a prig who never approved of his father and had chosen to live in Schenectady rather than Atlanta, or that she had regularly knocked him down each time the families got together for holidays or summers up at Cashiers, when they were children.

When she agreed to make the call, Mr. Billingslea gave a small smile of relief. "You're practically part of our family here," he told her, patting her shoulder. Apparently he meant it for a compliment.

Katharine got Chap in his office and told him what had happened to his father. She listened to his rants about suing Autumn Village for negligence and countered by pointing out that Dutch must have let in whoever killed him, because the dead bolt on his door was open, but the night latch was on. She didn't know why she remembered that detail, but she did.

When Chap calmed down a bit, she gave him the name of the funeral home that had handled so many services for her in recent years. She even agreed to draft an obituary for him to edit when he arrived in town, but she refused to plan the service. "You can do that after you get here. Besides, there will have to be an autopsy, since it was a violent death." When Chap started to splutter, she said, "Just get here as fast as you can. We'll deal with the rest later."

Including the important issue of what Dutch wanted on his tombstone.

"Do me one more favor, Kat. Pick out something nice for him to be buried in. I couldn't stand to go into his closet."

She was touched. That was the first sign Chap had ever given of caring for his dad—until he added, "But you'd better wear sunglasses, his clothes are so bright."

Then she wanted to knock him down again. But she was sorry he wouldn't give himself the gift of time in Dutch's closet. Clothes carry a person's scent long after the person is gone. Katharine still had her mother's old bathrobe in tissue paper in the guest room closet. Sometimes she took it out and buried her face in its silken folds. The fact that Chap would not enter his father's closet was more his tragedy than Dutch's.

When she told Mr. Billingslea what Chap had asked her to do, he referred her to a policeman in the hall. "There will be time for that later," he told her. "The body won't be released for several days."

"Besides," Mr. Billingslea chimed in, "we don't permit anything to leave the unit until family arrives."

"I promised," Katharine pointed out, "and like you said, I'm practically family here. I was practically part of Dutch's family, too. I've known him all my life. And I'd like to choose the clothes before I leave, please. I don't want to have to come back. My house was broken into today, and completely trashed. I'll be dealing with that for days. All I want is one outfit. I will take it with me and give you a receipt." When the policeman started to speak, she repeated, "I don't want to have to come back here."

His eyes flickered.

She realized she had used the same tone she used to use with Jon, when she would call, "Don't make me come up there." Her social instinct was to apologize. Instead, she stood and waited.

He sighed. "Come with me, ma'am. And don't touch a thing. Just point to what you want."

Katharine stood in Dutch's closet for several seconds inhaling his scent and missing him. Then she began to look for clothes. He had far too many, and they were jammed together in a haphazard way that made her suspect his wife had organized his closet until she died. Several plastic bags of laundry and dry cleaning hadn't even been opened, just hung among the rest.

She spied the jacket to his best gray suit—the one he'd worn to Lucy's funeral such a short time ago—and pointed it out. She found the pants farther down the bar. She pointed to a red tie, certain Dutch would want a red tie, then she stopped, chagrined. How could she choose a shirt that would please both Dutch and Chap? Dutch had liked colorful clothes. For daily wear he preferred knit polo shirts from various golf matches where he had marshaled. With suits, he favored green, blue, yellow, violet, or pink dress shirts. Not exactly what the starched-white-shirt Chap would consider appropriate for a funeral.

Katharine finally spied a white shirt with blue stripes hanging in an unopened cleaner's bag with three yellow ones. She pointed. "That will do."

As the officer reached his gloved hands up to bring out the

shirt, she noted that the laundry was the same one she and Tom used.

"You all okay?" Norm called from the hall door.

"Fine," she called back. "We just have to get shoes, socks, and underwear."

"He won't need all those," Norman objected. She suspected he might be the clothing beneficiary for most of the men who died. It was hard to picture Mr. Billingslea wearing a former resident's suits to work. However, she refused to shortchange Dutch in order to increase Norman's legacy. Chap had left it up to her, so Dutch was going to be buried in full dress.

She accepted the top pair of shorts, the first undershirt, and the first pair of black socks she saw in the drawers. Then she nodded toward his best black shoes. "That's it," she said.

At the door to the bedroom she took one last look around. She had not been in Dutch's bedroom since she used to play hide-and-seek with Chap and their friends, but he still used the old mahogany suite he and his wife always shared and the pictures on the dresser were familiar. "Goodbye," she whispered softly before she followed the officer toward the hall.

Leona was waiting for them, holding a large carrier from Macy's. "Mr. Billingslea told me to brang you up somethin' to put 'em in. You don't want to carry them thangs loose through the buildin'." Katharine interpreted that to mean that Mr. Billingslea didn't want other residents reminded of their own mortality.

She folded each piece and put it in the carrier under Leona's critical eye. "Don't you thank he oughta be buried in a white shirt?" she demanded.

"He doesn't have any white ones," Katharine told her. "Besides, he liked this one."

"What about them the laundry brung today? They was white. I know, 'cuz the man had to lay 'em on the counter while he signed in, and I noticed, seein' as how I ain't never seen Mr. Landrum in a white shirt before."

"Maybe he was bringing them to somebody else."

"No, he weren't. He had to ask me for the room number. Said he'd just started with the company and hadn't been here before. Didn't even know to go around back and use the service entrance—just parked his little white van right in front of the door."

"What did he look like?" The dry cleaner was owned and run by a Vietnamese couple, and the only workers Katharine had ever seen there were members of their extended family.

"Sorta old, I thank, but he wore a Braves cap that covered all his hair but the sideburns. They were white. Had on dark glasses, too. Said he had a sinus infection that had spread to his eyes. Had a soft scratchy voice, not much more'n a whisper, and he was tallish and walked all stooped over and real slow, like this." Leona hunched her shoulders and tottered down the hall. She had a gift for mimicry Katharine had never suspected.

Katharine's breath caught in her throat. None of the Vietnamese she had ever seen at the laundry were old, and all were short, but she knew one man who had fooled a lot of people by impersonating an elderly street sweeper. The same man who got bad sinus infections from going underwater, and who knew she was visiting Dutch this morning.

"He brought Dutch white shirts?" she asked.

"Yes, ma'am, in a long plastic bag. Coupla white ones, at least. That's all I saw. They must be in there somewhere."

Leona peered into the living room as if expecting to see it festooned with shirts.

Katharine called to the policeman, "Could we look in the closet once more, please? There were a couple of white shirts delivered this morning we seem to have missed."

He reluctantly led her back to the closet and, at her request, checked all the plastic bags. They found no white shirts. "Maybe they are in with dry cleaning," she suggested.

He checked four suit bags, as well. "None of them have shirts, ma'am. Besides, all of these were promised at least two months ago. He had a lot of clothes."

She gave him a wan smile. "Yeah, he liked clothes. I wonder where those shirts are."

She asked him to reexamine the laundry bag the striped shirt had been in. It held only pale yellow shirts. "Maybe Leona thought they were white," she murmured.

The officer looked at the tag still attached at the top. "These were promised four weeks ago. You think they waited a month to deliver them?" He didn't expect an answer. "Looks like that laundryman is somebody we'll need to be talking to."

Chapter 22

"You haven't talked to Tom?" Posey sat with Katharine at the kitchen table drinking chilled white wine while Julia was over at the stove fixing her special grilled-cheese sandwiches with a slice of Vidalia onion and a big slice of one of Katharine's own red tomatoes. "And why you aren't bawling your head off, I cannot understand."

Katharine sighed. "I'm cried out. And I've tried to reach Tom twice, but can't."

"Eat up." Julia lifted the crisp brown sandwich onto a plate and added a slice of cold dill pickle and a few chips. "It's the best thing you can do right now."

"And while you do," Posey added, "I'm calling Tom myself and telling him to get his backside home before dark, if he has to sprout wings."

Suddenly she jumped up, her ear cocked toward the kitchen television, and dashed toward the den. "Wait a minute! Holly asked me to tape this if it came on."

The small kitchen television showed an antigay rally in front of the Georgia capitol. People on both sides of the issue faced off and shouted hate slogans at one another. Katharine couldn't help thinking of one of Jon's gay friends from college, a sweet, gentle boy who never hated anybody and who died in a car accident at twenty. She wasn't the only person with troubles in the world.

"What could Tom do if he did come home?" she asked as Posey came back. She smiled her thanks as Julia refilled her glass and set the wine bottle in easy reach.

Posey counted on plump pink fingertips. "Call the insurance company. Hassle the police to find the jerks who did this. Take you somewhere for a few days to get away from the mess. Hold you while you cry. But for now, eat up. You look like a drowned hamster."

"That makes me feel so much better." But Katharine did feel better, looking at food.

"You want some of this watermelon?" Julia asked, taking it out of its bag.

Katharine teared up again. "That was for Dutch."

"Then you oughta eat it in his memory. It looks too good to waste." She fetched two plates and divided it between Katharine and Posey.

Posey might look flighty, with her big blue eyes and flyaway hair, but she was a practical woman at heart. While they ate, she considered what Katharine needed to do immediately. "Call the insurance company as soon as you finish eating," she advised. "They need to see the house before you start putting anything back in place. Then call a cleaning company. Rosa won't be able to deal with all that."

"No, cleaning up is going to be awful. And I'll have to call Hollis's painter friends and put them off for a week or two, at least."

"They could clean." Posey fetched spoons for the watermelon. "From what she says, they've got nothing better to do. Just tell them what you want done."

"I can ask them." If Katharine sounded dubious, it was

because she hadn't met a friend of Jon or Susan yet who knew how to clean. Still, at the very least they could carry debris to the curb. "I don't know when they can start, though. The police have to finish checking everything out, then the insurance adjuster has to come." She slapped one cheek as another thought occurred to her. "I forgot to call the insurance people after Friday night's break-in! How could I be so stupid?"

"Or so overwhelmed?" Posey sprinkled her watermelon with salt. "Eat up. Watermelon stimulates brain cells. It's full of vitamin C." She chewed thoughtfully. "Do some adjusting of your own. Lump the jade with the stuff you lost today."

After lunch, Katharine called the insurance company, who said they would speak to the police and call her back to set up a time to come to her house.

"Now call Tom," Posey ordered.

She got Louise again. "I'm sorry, Mrs. Murray, but Mr. Murray didn't come back to the office after his meeting. He did call to say he was going to lunch, and I gave him your message."

"Call him on his cell phone," Posey ordered when Katharine reported back.

"And try to discuss all this while he sits in the middle of a power lunch?"

"He might not be at a power lunch."

"Don't be silly. All Tom's lunches are power lunches, unless he eats at his desk. Wonder what it would be like to eat elegant lunches all the time while discussing how to run the world."

Posey added more salt to her watermelon. "In one word? Fattening. Call him!"

She did, but again got voice mail.

Posey waved her toward the stairs. "Go stretch out a while. Molly has a robe in the closet that ought to fit you, if you want to take off your clothes. Get a little sleep and we'll talk about what else you need to do."

Katharine went upstairs feeling like her shoes were soled in lead. She got into Molly's robe—which was blue chenille and as soft as a mother's hug—climbed onto the bed and pulled the covers over her ears, but she knew at once she couldn't sleep. When she closed her eyes she saw her house with everything all over the floor. When she opened them and tried again, she saw Dutch lying on his couch with his face purple and his tongue sticking out. Those were not scenes she wanted to meet in her dreams.

She flung off the covers and headed to the chaise. Maybe lurid German prose would distract her. Her vocabulary for terms of passion had increased so much she probably wouldn't even miss her dictionary.

She flipped through the diary copy and pulled out a page at random. It was dated 15/8 and the first line read: *Morgen sprengen wir werden den Brücke.*

"*Morgen*" was tomorrow, and the verb was future tense. Was "*Brücke*" the word for brook? "*Sprengen*" was a verb she didn't know, but it looked like "spring." Were they going somewhere to spring over a brook?

"Context, context, context," her professor used to tell her. She scanned down the page. They were to meet very early the next morning and it must be a surprise, for the writer hoped that L^2 would not inform "my dearest love" of the plan. The following evening there was to be a party at the writer's home, and beer had already been delivered. Most of the other sentences could have been Greek. Katharine wished she had worked harder on memorizing vocabulary. She wished she had the dictionary she had left on the kitchen table that morning. Heaven only knew what shape the vandals had left the poor book in.

Her cell phone rang while she was trying to decipher another unfamiliar word. She grabbed it without looking at the number. "Tom?"

"No, Hasty. I've been thinking—"

"Wait a minute. What does '*emächtigen*' mean?"

"Empower," he said promptly.

"So *Emächtigen die Leute* means—"

"Empower the people. As in 'Power to the People.' "

"And '*sprengen*'?"

"Blow up."

"Blow up a brook?"

"Brook?"

"*Brücke*."

"That's bridge. I thought you said you knew German."

"I do, sort of. I just don't have much vocabulary."

He snorted. "That's like saying you speak English, you just don't know words. Are you planning to blow up a bridge?"

"No, but maybe our friend was. It says right here—wait a minute. Here it is. '*Morgen sprengen wir werden den Brücke.*' Are you sure '*sprengen*' means 'blow up'? It couldn't mean 'to spring across,' as in the carefree action of somebody in love?"

"No, but maybe it used to be slang for a stupendous romantic encounter."

"Or maybe it's like 'burning your bridges' in English— maybe they were getting married."

"Or something." He sounded impatient. "Listen, I've been thinking about that necklace."

"The necklace is fine," she snapped. "The diary is fine. It's just the rest of my life that is currently lying in pieces all over my floor." Her voice trembled so she laughed to cover it. "I think there's a curse on Aunt Lucy's things, given what's happened to me since I found them. Where were you this morning?"

"Is that related to the curse?" She could picture his black brows rising above his glasses, but he didn't sound like he was stalling for time. Would she be able to detect it if he were?

"It may be," she told him.

"Well, let's see. I got my teeth cleaned bright and early at eight-thirty. Then I had a fascinating department meeting until eleven. After that—"

"That's enough." She was surprised at the relief she felt. "Let me tell you about my morning."

When she had finished, he said, "I'm real sorry about Dutch."

She wondered if a police officer could detect confession in his voice. She heard only sympathy. "Me, too. He was a special friend."

"And one of the last ties with your parents."

She appreciated his understanding that so quickly. "Yes. The very last." She didn't mean to sound pitiful, but she did.

"Well, at least you know I wasn't robbing your house or killing poor Dutch, if that's what you were hinting at. Thanks for the vote of confidence."

"It was just—" She stopped. There is no sufficient apology for suspecting a friend of rampage and murder.

"Where are you now?" he demanded.

"Over at my sister-in-law's. I'll be staying here again for a few days until things get cleared up at the house."

"Why don't I come get you and take you out for coffee?"

She ought to refuse. It was entirely possible that he wanted to get her alone so he could force her to take him to the necklace—or to simply take him. But she also knew she wasn't going to sleep, and Hasty could read the diary a lot faster than she could.

"Let's meet somewhere," she said quickly. "You know what I really want? A Krispy Kreme fix. You know where the main store is on Ponce de Leon?"

"Who doesn't? I can be there in fifteen minutes."

"I'll be there in twenty."

"Bring the diary?"

"Of course."

Posey wasn't in the kitchen when she went downstairs, which made things simpler. She told Julia she'd be out for a while and left.

Hasty stood inside the store beside a long plate glass window watching soft dough form into circles that were put on shelves and carried up several levels inside a hot-air tunnel while they rose. "Watch this," he said as she came up beside him. "I've got my eye on that row right there." Together they watched the shelf of skinny doughnuts swell into plump ones and then fall simultaneously into a river of hot oil. Hasty put a hand at the small of her back and guided her down the window while the doughnuts bobbed and cooked. "Now they're going to turn over," he announced as if he had personally orchestrated the event.

When the rounds were cooked on both sides, they were carried by conveyor belt out of the oil to drain, then under a solid sheet of liquid sugar that coated them. "There's our batch done," he said with satisfaction. He tapped on the glass and pointed them out to the woman standing at the end of the conveyor, putting hot doughnuts into boxes.

"We don't need a dozen," Katharine objected.

"Did you eat lunch?"

"A sandwich and some watermelon I'd bought for Dutch." Tears filled her eyes. She blinked and looked away.

"We need a dozen." His hand at her waist steered her to the counter, where he handed her the warm box while he picked up two cups of coffee. She clutched the box to her chest and the heat melted some of the ice within her as she followed him to the farthest end of a long counter with an unprepossessing view of the parking lot and street. The only other person in the vicinity was a man who looked homeless, dozing over a cup of coffee.

The doughnuts were hot to touch and went down like greased sugar. Katharine felt her spirits rise as she reached for her second. Hasty grinned. "I've always thought the world can't be skidding to hell in a handbasket so long as Krispy Kremes are still being made. Remember how far we used to have to drive to get them back home?"

Miami's only shop was on a causeway to the beach at the far north end of town. Katharine blushed as she remembered some of their extended stays on the beach after those doughnut runs. "I brought the diary," she said to cover her confusion.

He put a hand on her arm. "We had some fun times, didn't we, Katie-bell?"

"Yeah, we did." For one wistful moment she wondered what would have happened if he hadn't gotten drunk, if she had forgiven him, if they had—

That road took her places she didn't plan to go. She drew her thoughts back to hear him saying, "And I was infernally stupid. I cannot imagine why I went off with Janie that night. I made her bring me right back—you need to know that. Nothing happened. If you had just let me tell you so at the time—"

"I know. I was a self-righteous little prig." She gave him a searching look. "But it's over now. You do know that, right? I have Tom, Susan, and Jon. And you have Kelly and Melissa. Have you talked to them about moving down?"

"Not yet." He looked away. "I'm thinking about it. I just haven't decided it's worth the hassles." He reached for the diary pages. "But I solemnly swear that my only interest in you at this moment is these pages. Where's that one about blowing up the brook?"

She found the page and he perused it and those that followed while she ate a third doughnut. She was reaching for a fourth when Hasty let out a surprised whistle, but before he could explain, her cell phone rang. She snatched it from her purse. "Hello?"

"What's going on, Katharine?" Tom sounded rushed. "I've got two messages from you on my cell, and just got back to the office and found two more. Louise says you want me to come home today, but that's not possible. I—"

"You have to. Somebody else broke into the house again and this time they completely trashed it. Then somebody—" Her voice wouldn't go on until she swallowed, and even then, it trembled. "Somebody murdered Dutch. I need you, Tom. I can't deal with all this alone."

He used up a minute while he digested all that. "Dutch was murdered?" His disbelief echoed her own. When she confirmed it, he asked, "How bad is the house?"

"Bad. They took all our silver including Grandmama's silver service and all my jewelry and some of the paintings and the televisions and stereos and the computer, and they slit our pictures and cushions and mattresses, and—"

Tom had always been able to go straight to the heart of a crisis. It was one of the things that made him good at what he did and one of the first things she had admired about him.

He interrupted her now. "Have you talked to the insurance adjuster?"

"Yes. He'll come when the police say we can walk through the house."

"Does Chapman know about his dad?"

"Yes. I called him. He's coming as soon as he can."

"Where are you?" She almost blurted "At the Krispy Kreme" before he added, "Staying at Posey's?"

"Yes, for the time being. I practically live there now."

"Stay there until I can get home. But it will be at least Wednesday night. I need to mop up a few things here first. If you want to, tell the adjuster to wait until Thursday morning to come, and I'll do the walk-through. And hang in there, honey. I'm coming as soon as I can."

She hung up, blinking back tears, and saw Hasty's eyes on her with an unreadable expression in them. "He's coming?"

"Wednesday night." She tried to sound casual about it, as if it didn't matter and she completely understood.

"Wednesday night? Not on the next plane?"

She shrugged. "He's got some stuff he has to mop up in D.C. first."

He gave a short sarcastic laugh. "You've got some stuff down here he needs to mop up, too. You need him, Kate. He ought to be here."

"He can't just drop everything—"

"I can't believe you're defending him! You need him now, and he isn't coming until Wednesday night?"

She glared back at him. "Your wife and daughter need you and you aren't going at all."

His face grew hard. "That's different. They're getting along okay."

"Does it ever occur to you absent husbands that maybe we

get tired of just getting along okay? Of always being strong? Making all the decisions? Does it never enter your pointed little heads that sometimes we'd like somebody around to share the load?" She covered her mouth and darted a look toward the man down the counter, who was watching them like they were better than TV. She lowered her voice and muttered, "I'm sorry. This has nothing to do with you. Did you find anything interesting in the diary?"

Hasty looked as if he were about to say one thing, but decided to say another. "Sure did. It's almost unbelievable. Listen to the next day's entry." He picked up a page and translated.

> *We met at dawn as planned and traveled to the bridge in three groups. L^2 had purchased plenty of explosives. Hans transported them in his car. D took longer than we had expected to set them and the train passed before we were done, so no lives were lost. Pity. That would have gotten more attention. However, the bridge is utterly destroyed. That ought to make Hitler supporters sit up and take notice that Austria is not unanimous in support of his policies. Power to the people!*

As he read, Katharine's eyes had grown wider and wider, until she felt the wrinkles in her forehead. "They blew up a real bridge? It wasn't a figure of speech?"

"No, and listen to what happened afterwards." He read:

> *We returned this afternoon, where all was in readiness for celebration, but my little love decided he must study for an exam. We quarreled and said hurtful things. I hoped to comfort myself with L^2 as in days*

gone by, but was rejected by him, as well. After such a
triumph, I must sleep alone.

"She slept with both of them?" Katharine spoke louder
than she intended. The old man down the counter lifted his
head again and looked at her through bleary eyes. "Both of
them?" She repeated in a whisper.

"Not only a vamp, but a tramp," Hasty agreed in an under-
tone. "Poor little love, studying for finals while his lover is
trying to make it with an old friend. Maybe we ought to
translate this and send it to Tom." He caught her expression
and held up both hands. "Hey, it was a joke. I told you, I'm
only interested in your diary and your necklace. And speaking of that necklace, I'm worried about it. If somebody is
after it and has failed to get it twice, the chances are real
good he'll come back."

"I took it to the bank," she admitted. "The police have already suggested I should put a sign on the gateposts: 'The
necklace is no longer here.' You reckon that would take care
of it?"

"No. I reckon he'd come after you, to make you tell him
where it was and get it for him."

"Thanks. That's a cheering thought." Especially since it
was exactly what she had been thinking about him.

"It's also a realistic one. Somebody wants that necklace,
Katie-bell. You have to have figured that out by now. What
I've been thinking is, you ought to donate it to Emory, in
memory of your dad. Make a public production of handing
it over to the history department. We can arrange for newspapers, television, the whole shebang. That gets you off the
hook but good. Then when the guy from Carlos gets back,
we can take care of having it authenticated. If it's a fake, it's

no skin off your nose—you gave it in good faith. And I'd sleep a lot better at night knowing you weren't being stalked to get it."

The intensity of his expression startled her, and the picture of Hasty lying awake worrying about her touched her soul. She felt herself leaning toward him. Who knows what might have happened if the old man down the counter hadn't had a phlegmy coughing spell?

Katharine straightened in her chair, feeling like she had just come back from a daze. "I'll think about it," she promised. "Did you find anything else in the diary while I was on the phone?"

"Yeah. A couple of days later the group was discussing whether to leave Austria and go help the freedom fighters in Spain. Our writer wonders whether her father will lend his Mercedes to the endeavor."

"Freedom fighters? I don't know much about Spanish history."

"Also known as Communists. They opposed General Franco, who appealed to Hitler and Mussolini for help."

In a sudden awareness of how much faster he could read and understand the diary than she could, she thrust the pages at him. "Take this home with you and translate the rest. I'm going to be real busy these next few days. And just let me have the high spots, okay? I've had all the death and destruction I want for a while."

He picked up the last doughnut and said in a somber voice, "I just hope you've had all you are going to get."

Chapter 23

Early Wednesday morning, a man from Atlanta's Midtown neighborhood took his Doberman for a walk along a stretch of old railroad line that surrounds central Atlanta.

The stretch he chose was at the bottom of a gentle embankment covered with kudzu, but the tracks continued through a number of in-town communities, brushing the edge of Emory to the northeast and Georgia Tech to the west. For decades they had not been used except for short scenic train rides for tourists and school children. Then a Gen-X Georgia Tech graduate student looked at the tracks with fresh eyes. He pointed out how easily those rails could form an in-town beltline that could circle the city and connect to existing transit lines. City mothers and fathers began taking a serious look at the tracks. Developers rushed to acquire land along the route for condos and townhouses. Environmentalists began to talk green space. New in-town residents girded their loins to put up inevitable protests against change—for it is the nature of pioneers to become the most vehement against newcomers after they secure their own private patch of ground.

The man with his dog was one of a cadre of interested

citizens who regularly monitored the tracks, although at that particular point there was little to monitor except beer cans and the growth rate of the kudzu.

The man whistled as his dog veered off the tracks toward the embankment. "Watch out for snakes," he called. Snakes love kudzu. The animal ignored him. He nosed the long green tendrils, backed off, stiffened his dainty legs, and howled.

Annoyed, the man strode toward him. When he neared the dog, he became aware of a sweet unpleasant odor floating up from the leafy ground cover. His first thought was a dead 'possum. Then he saw the hand.

He lost his morning yogurt and granola before he pulled out his cell phone. By the time sirens wailed to a stop on the street high above, he had clipped a leash on the dog and dragged him a short way down the tracks. That hand would haunt his dreams for years.

Police officers scrambled down the banks on faint paths worn by dogs, 'possums, raccoons, and neighborhood children, paths that the kudzu had not yet obliterated for the summer. The jogger's Doberman raised his hackles and bared his teeth, defending his prize. The man held the leash and pointed. "There. In a straight line from that pole up there."

The officers poked around in the kudzu for only a few seconds before they found the body. It had a bullet hole in the forehead.

About the time the officers in Midtown were calling for a forensics team, Katharine was meeting the insurance adjuster at her house. He was a short middle-aged man with a round belly, thinning gray hair, a soothing tone of voice and a perpetually worried expression. She had tried to stall him until Tom got home, but he'd said he'd like to go ahead and look the place over and take pictures, then he could talk with Tom after he had run some numbers.

She walked beside him with her senses raw and bleeding, not only seeing and smelling the devastation but feeling it with every nerve in her body. As he walked around making notes and snapping photos, she grieved the death of her home.

"I think that's all I need," he finally said. "I'll take a quick look around outside, then talk with your husband tomorrow or the day after."

That was the only comfort she could derive from the situation. By that afternoon, Tom would be there to shoulder this burden. After the adjuster left, she leaned against her kitchen cabinets drained and helpless. She couldn't even think where to begin.

Dane, whom she had brought over at Posey's urging, looked through the panes that remained of the French doors and whined to come in, but Katharine said, "Sorry, fellow, but there's glass on the floor. Your paws might get cut."

He gave her a reproachful look. "You could sweep," he seemed to say.

She fetched the broom and dustpan and began to clear the kitchen floor. She stacked metal mixing bowls, cutting boards, spice bottles, and other unbroken objects in an indiscriminate heap on the counter and collected larger pieces of broken dishes and crushed cartons into a garbage bag. Finally she swept up a large pile of flour, sugar, cornstarch, cereal, and oatmeal.

"If you added milk and eggth, you'd have a cake," joked a perky lisp at her doorway.

Katharine jumped, spilling a stream off her dustpan.

"Hey. I'm Misthty, Hollith'th friend," said the young

woman who went with the lisp. "Matt and Dave are in the front hall. The man outthide let uth in. We came to help, and it lookth like you thure need it." Misty stood about five-feet tall in her chunky sandals. Her hair was the vibrant green of emeralds and less than an inch long all over her head. She had lovely brown eyes, ringed by thick mascara on both upper and lower lashes. And she looked like she had been attacked in a piercing shop by a man with a long needle and an inexhaustible supply of silver studs. They sparkled from her lips, her nose, and her eyebrows, and ran up both earlobes. One pierced her navel, perching atop the jeans slung low on her hips. The one in her tongue was responsible for the lisp.

Katharine went with her to meet the others. Dave was short and chunky with soft dark hair and a scruffy goatee that made him look like a pudgy goat. Matt was a tall, gangly blond with almost as many piercings as Misty. Katharine wondered whether they realized that the initial impression they made might have something to do with their failure to find jobs, but maybe she was just being old-fashioned and provincial. Besides, if they'd found jobs, they wouldn't be there to help when she needed them. She gave them her genuine thanks and took them upstairs, where she set Misty to hanging clothes back in the closet and worked with the other two for a time filling garbage bags with debris to be hauled to a large red dumpster that was squatting in her driveway.

When she was sure they understood what to do, she returned downstairs. At the foot of the steps she stumbled over Beethoven, with a large piece missing from the back of his skull. She picked him up and held him for a moment of sad farewell, for even his scowls belonged to the era that had been destroyed. When Dave clomped down the stairs carrying two large bags, she thrust the broken bust under his elbow. "Put him in the dumpster, but gently. He's family."

She wandered into the music room, pleased that it had suffered so little. The invaders had ripped the makeshift drop cloths from the bookshelves and flung them in heaps on the floor, so the piles of cloth had cushioned the fall of the small items she had arranged in front of the books. She idly began to restock the shelves, taking special pleasure in each unbroken item. She had so few left.

As she was replacing some of Aunt Lucy's books on the bottom shelf, she noted one bound in blue with the word FAIRE on the front cover in gold. The spine read *The Conrad Faire Family*. She wrinkled her forehead. Faire. Where had she heard that name before?

She carried the book to the window, where the light was better, and turned the pages. It was a genealogical history, with a pullout family tree in the front. Each chapter dealt with one descendent of Conrad Faire and contained short paragraphs marked by odd numbers like I-5, I-11. Thank heavens for Lucy's compulsive historical nature, for she had penciled inside the front cover, "Page 178."

Katharine turned to page 178 and found the family of Eugene Claude Faire, one of the shorter branches on the family tree. Eugene and his wife, Emily Simpson, had five children, but only two survived: Simpson Claude and Delia Jean. Simpson Claude Faire had one daughter, Mildred, who married Clifford Charles Everanes. Of course! Mildred and Clifford had Walter Charles, Carter Simpson, and Emily Lucille. Katharine touched the names with sadness. Since none of those ever had children, that branch of the family was extinct. She had never before considered the fact that entire branches of a family tree could come to a screeching halt in one generation.

Curious about the rest of the family, she turned the page to see what had happened to Delia Jean. The answer was so surprising that she carried the book into the living room and sat down on the piano bench—the only intact seat in the room. Delia Jean had married Napoleon Ivorie. They had two children, Napoleon Jr. and Emily Faire, but Emily died at sixteen. Napoleon Jr. sired Napoleon III. Napoleon III had one daughter, Rowena Ivoric Slade, and she had two children, Brandon Ivorie and Amy Faire Slade.

Katharine stared at the page, trying to work out the connection. If their parents were first cousins, did that make Aunt Lucy and Napoleon Ivorie III second cousins, or first cousins once removed? Either way, that must be why he had slipped into her funeral. He had gone to Uncle Walter's, too, but Katharine had presumed they'd had business dealings. Aunt Lucy and Uncle Walter had certainly never mentioned the family connection.

"Okay if we take a break?" Misty stood at the door, a pretty little waif in spite of the funky makeup. Katharine checked her watch and realized that the three cohorts had worked for well over two hours, lugging heavy bags to the dumpster like Santa's elves.

She smiled. "Sure. Why don't I give you some money to go buy some lunch? I don't have a thing here to fix you."

"That'th cool." Misty and her friends trooped out to a red Audi convertible. Hollis's friends might be unemployed, but they weren't exactly destitute.

Katharine tucked Aunt Lucy's book on the shelf and resumed work on the kitchen. As she swept and restored order to her much-depleted pantry, she mulled over how much you can learn from genealogy, and how many ways it can be uncovered. In less than a week she had used microfilm, books, personal reminiscences, and newspapers to discover Aunt Lucy's brother Carter, their connection to the Ivories, and astonishing facets of her own parents' history. And she hadn't even begun to use the Internet yet. Who knew what she might find there?

But first, she wanted to complete the puzzle of the necklace and the diary. How had Carter gotten them? Who wrote the diary? To whom should the necklace belong? And who was trying to get it first?

Perhaps her two break-ins in three days had nothing to do with Aunt Lucy's box, but she didn't believe it. So who had hired the invaders?

Her prime suspect was still Zachary. Had he asked old Mr. Ivorie's bodyguards to recommend men willing to rob and trash a house? Was Zach hiding out, waiting for a chance to try for the necklace again? The thought made the hair prickle on the back of her neck, and sent her on a quick tour of the downstairs to make sure all the doors were locked.

But why should Zachary be so interested in the artifacts? Did he hope to sell them to Napoleon or Brandon Ivorie? Could they have put him up to it?

Brandon, perhaps, but not Mr. Ivorie. Brandon used demagoguery and force. His grandfather was a gentleman, even toward business associates he ruined. Besides, if Napoleon Ivorie was Lucy's only remaining family, chances were good that he had known that. Had Katharine told him she found the diary and necklace among Lucy's things? She was pretty sure she had. Why hadn't he mentioned then that they were cousins?

And did he know that Aunt Lucy had never written a will? She had just said in her offhand way, "You take my bits and pieces, Katharine. There's nobody else who wants them." That sly old billionaire was probably waiting for Katharine to go through the trouble of authenticating the necklace so he could bring in his lawyers to point out that as her closest living relative, he was her legal heir. That was the kind of stealthy acquisition for which he was famous.

"If I'd known he was related to her," Katharine told her dustpan, "I'd have had Mr. Billingslea ship him all those boxes of junk." But then she would have missed out on seeing the necklace.

She had gotten that far in her thinking when a shout at the front door disturbed her reverie. "Aunt Kat? Aunt Kat!"

She ran to the door and found Hollis, her eyes like black holes in a sheet-white face. She stumbled into the breakfast room and held on to the table for support. Her voice came in gasps and gulps. "The police have found Zach. He's dead!"

Chapter 24

Katharine snatched a dishtowel to drape over a ripped chair seat and shoved Hollis into the chair. Then she went to fill Susan's blue kettle, which had survived the onslaught with only a dent. Not until she turned from the sink did she ask, "How do you know?"

"When I got up, there was a message on my cell phone from Amy. She said the police had found Zach dead and Brandon had gone to identify him. I called her back and she said she couldn't talk right then, but she'd meet me here."

"Meet you here?" To hide her chagrin, Katharine busied herself finding three intact mugs and usable tea bags. She was sorry for Amy's grief, but she had enough to deal with at the moment without a hysterical young adult who wasn't even her own.

Behind her, Hollis had finally noticed the mess around her. "Boy, this is awful! When Amy comes, we'll go somewhere else, I promise." She jumped up and began to prowl. "Didn't Misty and the guys come to help?" she called from Tom's library. "They said they would."

Katharine noted that Hollis didn't offer her own help—or Princess Amy's, although work could take one's mind off grief. She'd been practicing that all morning.

"They've worked a couple of hours already, and gone to

lunch," she called back, "but the whole house is like this. Clearing it out will take days."

Recovering could take years. As Katharine turned, she saw pieces of the breakfast room china she had carefully chosen to match her new décor lying under the table. Suddenly the loss of everything in the house was too much. She swayed and clung to the counter to keep from joining the plates on the floor. Fortunately, Hollis was still roaming the downstairs, taking stock. When the doorbell rang, Katharine let Hollis answer it.

Amy came in sobbing like she had already cried a river and was working on a sea. "Oh, Mrs. Murray," she blubbered when she saw Katharine, "did Hollis tell you? Isn't it awful?" She flung herself into Katharine's arms and held her so tight, Katharine could hardly breathe. She disentangled herself, helped Amy into the draped chair, and pointed Hollis to another.

"Let me fix you a cup of tea," she suggested. The herbal tea was one of the first boxes she had rescued from the kitchen floor. "I don't have any honey, sugar, or milk," she added as she poured a mug of grass and herbs for Amy and Lipton's for Hollis and herself and joined them at the table.

"That's okay." Amy's voice was clogged with tears. She laid her head on her arms and began to whimper.

"So tell us what happened," Hollis demanded, her hand resting on Amy's shoulder.

"The police called Brandon," Amy said without lifting her head. "They said—they said—ohhh, I can't stand it!" The table shook with her sobs.

Hollis patted her until she grew calmer. "Tell us, Amy. We want to know what happened."

Amy sniffed, a drowned shadow with a very pink nose. "Brandon was over at our house talking to Mama, so he had forwarded his calls to his cell. I wasn't paying attention to what he was saying until he hung up, then he told Mama they had found Zach. Shot!" Her eyes filled again at the last word.

"Here. Blow." Hollis handed her a tissue from a stack Katharine had reconstructed from the floor. Their box had been destroyed. Katharine looked at her niece with new respect. Hollis and Posey might look very different, but in a crisis they had the same nurturing heart.

Amy coughed to clear her throat. "They wanted Brandon to identify him because his parents are on that stupid cruise." She peered at Hollis, her eyes drenched with sorrow. "I tried to call you, but your mama said you weren't awake yet and she didn't like to bother you. So I called and left a message on your cell."

Hollis uttered an expletive that Katharine took for a comment on mothers who can't distinguish important calls from trivial ones.

Katharine dipped her tea bag up and down to hurry the steeping process while Amy picked up her story. "I went up to my room so Mama wouldn't see me cry, but when the phone rang again, I tiptoed downstairs and saw her listening, and I could tell it was Brandon. When she hung up, she called Papa and told him Zach had been shot to death. Then they started figuring out how to keep his connection with the foundation out of the papers. That's all they think about, newspapers and politics! While Zach has laid there since Friday and nobody knew."

She threatened to break down again, but Katharine shoved the hot herbal tea closer to her and asked quickly, "How do you know he's been there since Friday?"

Amy sipped her tea and wrinkled her nose at the lack of honey. Poor Amy, so much of her life had been sweetness and light—at least on the surface. Zach's death would be harder to stomach than tea without honey.

"Mama told Papa that when Brandon told the police what kind of car Zach had, they looked around the neighborhood and found it in the parking lot of some scruffy apartment not far away. A woman told them it has been there since at least eleven Friday night, because she came in then and found it parked in front of her apartment. She had to park down the hill, and got soaking wet. She said she's been trying for two days to get the manager to have it towed, but he wouldn't because the spaces aren't reserved. Zach loved that car!" She laid her head down again and bawled.

Hollis rose and started to prowl the room. Amy looked up and accused, "When we couldn't find him Friday night, you said he was fine, that he'd just gone away for a little while. You said he'd be back."

"I thought he would!" Hollis's voice rose in anger and grief. "Aunt Kat's house had been robbed that night. I thought Zach might have taken her jade and was hiding out somewhere." She threw Katharine a desperate look. "The key to your house was missing from my ring. I'd just noticed when they gave me one to the theater that evening and I was adding it to the others. I was scared Zach might have taken it when I let him drive my car that afternoon—and that he had come after your jade."

Amy glared up at her and pushed damp hair off her face. "Zach wouldn't steal!"

"Zach liked that jade," Hollis countered. She spoke to Katharine. "After you told me about the robbery, I got really scared he was the one who had come in. So Amy and I drove around all night looking for him. " She sank back into her chair as if all the air had gone out of her balloon. "But now we know where he was. At least he didn't break in here."

Katharine could have pointed out that Zach's innocence wouldn't be proven until they knew exactly when he had died, but she didn't. Amy was too heartbroken and Hollis too frustrated by her inability to help Amy's dreams come true. Hollis was learning a nurturer's bitterest lesson: we cannot always protect the weak or grant the desires of their hearts.

"God help us," she murmured in almost silent prayer.

Hollis turned her wrath where she thought it belonged. "Why didn't God protect you from all this? And Zach? And Dutch?"

Katharine had no idea what had happened to Zach, but she would have been willing to wager that his death was the result of his own bad choices, somebody else's, or a combination of the two. She remembered Dutch, the night before he died, telling her how ready he was to die. Had God withdrawn protection to give Dutch his heart's desire? If there was golf in heaven, she hoped he and her daddy were enjoying a round. But Hollis wasn't looking for old men's fantasies about heaven.

Katharine sent up a quick plea for help. It was answered by a memory that curved her lips in a smile. "God did protect me. Monday morning I was furious because I started late, the bank was slow, and I got a clerk at Publix who was new and took forever to check me out. I wanted to hurry home to cook lunch for Dutch. Instead, I was delayed long enough so that the robbers were gone before I got here. In a very real sense, God saved my life."

"That's dumb." Hollis shoved back her chair and went to stand at the window, glowering at the lawn. But Katharine, who had claimed faith in divine protection for years, had finally recognized it. Thanksgiving rose like a winged thing in her heart.

Amy had been too lost in her own grief to pay them any attention. Now she took a ragged breath and gave Katharine a pleading look. "Would you do me a favor, Mrs. Murray?"

Katharine hesitated. When Amy's mama asked that question in a committee meeting, it usually turned into a lot of work for somebody. "If I can."

"Would you call Mama about the funeral?"

Katharine was bewildered. "What about the funeral?" First Chap Landrum and then Amy—did she look like a funeral planner? Had she missed a calling that was obvious to everybody else?

Amy swallowed. "I want to sit with his family. I was almost family. But Mama doesn't know that, so I wondered if maybe you could, you know, like tell her."

Katharine wondered if the Atlanta Aquarium had an opening for someone to swim with the sharks. She would far rather take that job than tell Rowena Slade that her daughter wanted to sit on the family pew for Zach's funeral because she considered herself engaged to him.

Chapter 25

Katharine was clearing her living room when Officer Williams called. She answered in the music room—my study, she mentally corrected herself—and was pleased that Hasty's telephone worked fine.

"Mrs. Murray? We've found your jade. It was in a car connected with a homicide. I checked it against the list you gave us, and it's all there. The diary wasn't, though."

That was puzzling, but she was delighted about the jade. "Was that the murder of Zachary Andrews?" When he hesitated, she added, "I heard about it from the Ivorie family."

The name worked its usual magic. "Yeah. The jade was in a bag behind his car seat."

"Will you bring it to me, or do I need to come get it?"

"We can't release it, since it's part of an ongoing murder investigation."

She started to argue, but why should she? The jade was Tom's, and Tom would be home that evening. He'd missed the break-in, he deserved the hassle of fighting the police to get it back. "I'll tell my husband. He'll be in touch. Thanks so much for calling."

She had finished in the living room and was working in the dining room, mourning her china and crystal, when the telephone rang again. "Katharine? It's Tom. You doing okay?"

She gave a short, unfunny laugh. "Sure. I'm having the time of my life. I've been picking up all the dishes we bought on our honeymoon, piece by tiny piece, thinking real happy thoughts."

"Leave all that. We can get somebody to do it when I get home. Go over to Posey's and relax until I get there. Go to a spa or something."

She knew then how far removed Tom was from the devastation of their home. If he were there, he would be in his library cradling each book in his hands as he set it back on the shelf, or swearing as he returned his clothes to the closet in the precise order he insisted on. She was tempted to do as he said—drop everything and leave it exactly as it was for him to see, but that would be like abandoning an injured child. She couldn't bear to do that.

Still, he deserved to know the good news. "They've found your jade."

"Really? Where did it turn up?"

"In the back of Zach Andrews's car. He was killed Friday night, so it's part of his murder investigation, but you can go down and talk to the police about it when you get here."

"That's fantastic! Did you talk to the insurance adjuster and set a time for me to meet with him?"

She bent and began to replace her books on the shelves. "Yes, he was here this morning. He said he will get back to you tomorrow, once he's had time to crunch some numbers."

"Good, but tell him to make it Friday afternoon, will you? I've had to change my flight. There's a Senate subcommittee hearing tomorrow afternoon I've got to cover. It may run over into Friday morning."

"Tom—" She didn't try to hide the irritation in her voice.

"I know, honey, I want to be there, too, but this is critical. I thought somebody else from our shop was handling it, but he's got a conflict."

"*He*'s got a conflict? What the hell do you think you've got? Our house is in ruins, I am running on adrenaline, there's somebody out there who did this thing who could come back any minute—"

"Steady," he said, in the same tone he used with a willful horse.

"Don't you 'steady' me. I'm not some irrational being having a tantrum. I am overwhelmed. What part of Please Come Home Right Now don't you understand?"

"I would if I could—"

"No, you could if you would. I'm used to covering for you, coping for you, pretending to understand why your work is more important than me, but that's wearing real thin. I'm warning you, Tom, if you aren't here for Dutch's funeral—"

"When is the funeral?"

"Friday morning at eleven."

"I'll be there, no matter what. And I've taken off all next week. I thought maybe we could fly down to the Bahamas or something, get away a bit."

Katharine looked around the house and thought of all the decisions they were going to have to make. She sighed. "You have no clue, do you? I am standing in the middle of a mess like you never saw before. Not one of our chairs or sofas has a cushion we can sit on. Every piece of porcelain is broken, every painting slashed—even the children's pictures—" her voice trembled, but fury steadied it. "You sit up there in your tidy office with Louise to fetch your coffee and file your papers and dare tell me we can go off for a week in the Ba-

hamas and leave all this mess behind? And then what? You
fly back to Washington to your tidy office and I come back
here to pick up everything after all?"

"You can hire—"

"I can hire?"

"We can hire."

"Who oversees anybody we hire? Can you do that from
Washington? Somebody has to stand here and tell them what
to save and what to trash."

He heaved the sigh of a misunderstood and beleaguered
man. "We'll talk about it when I get home, hon. I can't do
anything from up here."

"That is the first sensible thing you have said since you
called. If I don't see you before Dutch's funeral, don't bother
to come home at all." She hung up and leaned against the
wall, clutching her middle and sick to her stomach. What
was happening to her? She never used to fuss at Tom. He
was just like most of the men who ran the country—preoccupied with important things.

"But I'm important, too," she said, and for the first time in
a week, she believed it.

When the phone rang almost immediately, she thought he
was calling back. Instead, she heard, "Katharine? Chapman
Landrum here. I've been over at Daddy's today packing up
his junk—"

No "Hello, Katharine, how are you?" or other conversational lubricant. No acknowledgement of grief—his or her
own. And the term "packing up his junk" was the insufferable
sort of remark that always made Katharine want to knock
Chap down. She surfaced from memories of times she'd
decked him good to hear, "—thought you'd want to know."

"Want to know what? I'm sorry, I got distracted."

"About the note." Impatience poured through the receiver.

"There was a note on Daddy's desk, under his phone book, with your name on it and a long number. Do you have a pencil?"

"Wait a minute while I find a one." That took longer than it should have, for the pencil she usually kept by the kitchen phone and its companion pad had disappeared in the chaos. She found her purse and rummaged in its depths for a pen, then grabbed a cereal box from the trashcan and ripped off a flap to write on. "Was there anything else on the note?" Dutch had a habit of keeping all the notes and numbers from one project in the same place.

"Yeah, a 931 number and the name Maria. Here's the number. Ready?"

She copied it carefully. "There's nothing to indicate what it is?"

"No, but it looks like an international phone number, since it starts with 011. Listen, I have to go. There's a lot to do here, and I left my kids at a motel and promised them we'd check out the aquarium this afternoon."

What else do you do with your children the afternoon after you arrive to attend your father's funeral?

Katharine rebuked herself for that thought. Chap's children hadn't seen Dutch more than twice since their parents' divorce five years earlier. According to Dutch, Chap only saw his kids at Christmas and for a few weeks each summer. Dutch had claimed that was because Chap's new trophy wife wasn't fond of children. She wasn't fond of her father-in-law, either. They had never invited Dutch to share their holidays. But while Dutch used to complain about not seeing the boys, he had never invited them down since his wife died, so far as Katharine knew. Remembering the phrase in Genesis, 'it is not good that man should be alone,' she knew God hadn't been talking just about sex.

Some men could be such klutzes when it came to maintaining relationships.

She was surprised that the boys had even come, until she remembered they were out of school for the summer. She'd have been willing to bet that Chap had called his wife and asked her to take them back that week and she had refused, and that he had asked his trophy wife to keep them in New York and she had refused, too. It just went to prove that men got the kind of wives they deserved.

Then he surprised her. "I know you and Daddy were close. Is there anything of his you would like to keep, as a memento?"

She answered at once. "I'd like his genealogy books, if you don't want them." She could see the place on her shelves where they would go.

"I sure don't want them. I'll box up all his books for you. Keep what you want and get rid of the rest. And Katharine, thanks for picking out his clothes. I couldn't have done that." Was that a tremor in his voice?

She hung up feeling more charitable toward Chap than she had in her life.

Katharine looked at the long number for some time and then checked her phone book, which was still intact. She found that 931 was a Tennessee area code. Had Dutch managed to call Sewanee about Ludwig Ramsauer's relatives before he died?

She used her cell phone and dialed the long number, was rewarded after only two rings. "*Ja?*" It was a loud, forceful syllable, the voice decidedly female. Katharine pictured a large stout woman with grizzled braids wound around her head.

She hoped the virago spoke English. "Is this Maria?"

"*Ja.*" The voice was guarded now.

"My name is Katharine Murray. I am the friend of a man named Dutch Landrum from Atlanta. He seems to have gotten your phone number from his college—"

She got no further. A delighted laugh rippled over the wire. "Dutch? He is still alife? He is vell? Och, some of us old var horses go on longer dan de rest. Ve had such goot times ven he vas over here vun summer. Dat man loved gut beer and a gut laugh."

Katharine amended her picture to include a jolly pink face. "He sure did," she agreed. She explained as gently as she could that Dutch was now neither alive nor well. "But Sunday night, just before he died, we were talking about Ludwig—"

"About Ludvig? Did Dutch not know he died? It vas many years ago dat he vent."

"Yes, he knew, but he was puzzled. He had heard it was a climbing accident—"

Maria interrupted, and Katharine struggled to translate v's into w's and d's into th's as the woman spoke excitedly, "Dat's vat dey said, but Ludvig vas always careful. He had no accident. Myself, I alvays t'ink he vas pushed."

"By whom?" Katharine was so startled she blurted the words before she thought.

"I do not know, but Ludvig did not climb alone. Never! I tell dat to the police, but dey insist it vas an accident, dat he was alone." Her voice grew dark. "Or dat he vent up alone and it vas no accident. Dat vas impossible. Ludvig vould never kill himself!"

Katharine remembered the five question marks in the margin of the article she had found in Carter's box. "Dutch said he was a very careful climber. He said Ludwig fussed at him for even hiking alone. So you think he went up with somebody else?"

"I don't know. I just know Ludvig never vent up a mountain alone before, and ven he vent out that morning, he vas whistling, which meant he vas happy. He said before he left, 'I have a surprise for you tonight, Maria. Fix a special meal.'" Her voice grew dark again. "It vas a surprise, yes? Ludvig carried home on a stretcher."

"I am so sorry."

"It vas long ago." The voice was brusque, refusing sympathy from a stranger.

"Do you remember the summer when Dutch came over? Ludwig had other friends over from America, too, didn't he?"

"Ja. Lee and Donk. Lee, Donk, and Ludvig—t'ree of a kind. Alvays up to some prank. Donk died in the var, but for years after, ven Lee came across on business, he alvays looked me up. Ve liked to talk about happier times."

"How long were you and Ludwig married?" Katharine inquired.

"Married?" Her surprise rippled through the wires. "Ach, no, I am Ludvig's sister. Neither of us married, so ve lived together until his death." She sighed. "I hope Ludvig and Dutch are sharing a beer in heaven tonight. Dutch alvays made me laugh."

Katharine scarcely heard the last two sentences, her heart was pounding so loud. Had she found the Austrian woman who had written the passionate diary? "Did you know Carter Everanes?" She held her breath while she waited for the reply.

Maria's voice was guarded. "*Ja*. He vas here for a while. Until Hitler came."

The sudden chill in her tone puzzled Katharine. Was that the sound of a woman scorned? Had Maria expected Carter to write when he came back to the States and been disappointed? "Carter and Ludwig were good friends, too, right?" she hazarded.

"*Ja*." It was a grudging admission. Had Carter and Ludwig remained friends after Carter and Ludwig's sister were no longer lovers? Was there a tactful way to ask? But Maria had questions of her own. "How do you know Carter? Is he still alive?" She didn't sound like she was inquiring about someone she had loved—quite the opposite, in fact.

"His older brother married my mother's sister, but Carter died before I was born. I found a diary in a box with his name on it among his sister's things when she died recently. The diary was in German." What the heck—she wasn't likely to ever meet this woman. "Could it have been yours?"

"Mine?" Katharine could almost see the elderly Austrian woman leaning back from the phone in horror. "I never kept a diary. Nor vould I read dat of another. Burn it!"

Katharine added a staunch aura of Lutheran morality to the stout, pink-faced Amazon with grizzled braids. Unless Maria had changed greatly, she didn't sound the sort of woman to plan a seduction, much less describe it to an earlier lover and expect to sleep with him when the new lover didn't turn up. She was definitely not the sort to let any record of her own passions out of her own capable hands.

Katharine floundered, wondering what else to ask. She didn't know any more than she had before she called. She reminded herself again that she wasn't ever likely to meet Maria. That gave her the necessary audacity to inquire, "Did Carter have a special romance while he was over there, do you know?"

"Let de dead keep der secrets," Maria said gruffly. Then she seemed to remember her manners, for she added, "I am glad you called to tell me about Dutch. I did not see him for many years, but it makes me smile to t'ink of him now. I vill say a special Mass for him tomorrow."

Not Lutheran, then. Katharine would never make a detective. Ludwig's sister was probably a tiny woman with the bones of a bird and gray sausage curls. And if she knew about Carter's romance—which seemed likely—she wasn't going to gossip about it.

Katharine had only one more question to ask. "Are you related to Georg Ramsauer, who excavated Hallstatt back in 1846?"

A sharp intake of breath bounced up to a satellite and back down to earth, followed by eager words. "Did you find anyt'ing else in Carter's box? A circle of metal, perhaps? Green, vit little knobs on it?"

"Yes," Katharine admitted. "They were both in the box."

"Dat circle is mine! Carter stole it from dis house! You must send it back. It is very special to our family, and it curses dose who misuse it."

"How did it come to your family?" Katharine intended it for a test. She held her breath while she waited for the answer.

The accent grew strong with agitation. "My many times great-grandmudder vas a daughter of Georg Ramsauer. He gaf it to her for a vedding gift. It has been in our family for many generations. It does not belong in America!" Katharine heard a pounding sound, as if she were pounding the wall or a table with her fist.

"If you will give me your address and send me a letter, describing it and saying what you have just told me, I will return it to you," Katharine promised.

Maria gave her address readily. "I vill write you dis afternoon, and God vill reward you for an honest voman ven de necklace has been returned."

Katharine hung up feeling like she had been pummeled by large, heavy hands. Whatever Maria might look like, her spirit was not that of a bird-framed little female.

Katharine rummaged in the fridge again and found a carton of yogurt in the far corner. It was a couple of weeks out of date, but she carried it outside with a spoon and sat on the patio, her back to the disaster inside. It was good to know where the necklace had come from, but she felt a decided sense of anticlimax.

Carter Everanes was a thief. Perhaps Maria and Ludwig had regaled him with stories of their famous ancestor, showed him the necklace, and left him alone with it once too often. If he had stolen the necklace, he might have stolen the diary, too, thinking it was Ramsauer's accounts of the dig. Perhaps it was Maria's mother's diary, or maybe she and Ludwig had a sister who died in the war. Carter could even have stolen it from another house altogether. Did he make a practice of lifting items from his friends? Was that the dreadful secret that had come out during his trial? If so, had a providential balancing of the scales of justice decreed that he be killed by a thief? She hoped Dr. Flo's cousin would provide a few answers.

Chapter 26

Thursday, June 15

"I don't know what to tell you about Cleetie except Alfred Simms was her brother and she's willing to talk to you about what happened to him."

Dr. Flo had suggested that she pick Katharine up and drive her to Cleetie's house, which was in the same quadrant of Atlanta as Buckhead, but out what used to be called the Bankhead Highway—a term synonymous with drugs and death until the city dealt with that problem in typical bureaucratic fashion: they changed the name of the street to Hollowell Parkway.

Katharine had not been in that part of Atlanta for several years, since she had tutored in an elementary school. While Dr. Flo continued talking, Katharine found herself surreptitiously checking her car door lock. She felt ashamed—until she saw Dr. Flo reach over to punch the button to make sure all four doors were locked.

"Cleetie was a nurse," Dr. Flo continued, "and a choir soloist back when Daddy King and Martin were preaching at Ebenezer Baptist. She doesn't get out much any more, though. Her legs are so bad, she can hardly maneuver from her chair to the bathroom or her bed."

"But she lives alone?" Looking at the poverty of the neighborhood, Katharine couldn't help comparing the plight of her own elderly relatives with the plight of the elderly poor.

"Not exactly. Her three daughters, their children, and even their grandchildren take turns staying with her, so there's somebody over there all the time. One granddaughter is a doctor and checks her out at least once a week, one is a nutritionist and plans her meals, and one grandson owns a lawn service and keeps up her yard. It helps to have family in town. But they would all move her out of here in a second if Cleetie would go. She flat-out refuses to give up her house." Katharine detected exasperation in Dr. Flo's voice as she pulled her Volvo up to the curb. "She says, 'I been livin' in this house for more than fifty years, and I might as well stay here 'til the end.' " Dr. Flo's voice changed to a deep boom, then resumed its normal pitch. "Watch your step on that sidewalk."

Katharine opened her door and stepped onto a patch of grassless red clay littered with cans and shards of glass. The sidewalk it bordered was cracked and uneven. Beyond it, a short, smooth walk led to a small house with two concrete steps leading up to a wide screened porch. The house was dazzling white, its concrete steps fresh green, its gray roof neat and whole. Bars on the windows were green to match the steps. Pink and white begonias bloomed on each side of the steps, and a handkerchief-sized plot of grass lay on each side of the walk.

In that neighborhood, the house looked like a fresh pillow case thrown on a dung heap. Other houses in the block seemed in competition to see which would fall down first, and several had a good chance at winning. Porches sagged. Steps crumbled. What little paint there was curled and flaked.

Most roofs sported several shades of shingles, while others had bits of metal nailed over leaks. The yards—lawns would be too kind a word for those plots of tall weeds—were filled with debris and discarded appliances in various stages of rusting out. The air was heavy with a smell she could not identify, but associated with rancid meat and decay.

The specimens of humanity that Katharine could see lounged on porches or steps looking as if they, like their houses, had been inadequately cared for and patched up so often they had given up on life. A shirtless young man sat with his back propped against a discarded washing machine on the porch next door. He raised a hand in languid greeting. "Hiya." Dreadlocks hung past his shoulders and his eyes were slits in his face, half-covered by lids too heavy to rise.

Dr. Flo grabbed a green thermal cooler from her back seat, then took Katharine's elbow and led her briskly up the walk. "Don't say a word and don't look at him, or he'll be over here wanting money. Spends every penny he gets on drugs and there's not a thing you or I can do about it. Let's get inside before he rouses himself enough to stand." She hustled Katharine up the steps and used a key to open the first deadbolt Katharine had ever seen on a screened door.

She had time to notice three white rockers—one of them gigantic and rump-sprung—on the screened porch while Dr. Flo used her key to lock the deadbolt behind them and unlock another on the front door, which led straight into a small room. "Cleetie," she called in. "It's Florence. I've brought my friend."

"Tha's nice. Tha's real nice." The deep voice came from the corner. Katharine was fully inside before she saw who was speaking.

The old woman was a mound of flesh in a huge recliner over in the corner. She filled the recliner and spread out on

both sides, and her enormous calves were elevated and en-
cased in white support stockings. Katharine used to put
stockings like that on her mother each morning, and they
were so hard to pull up on her mother's dainty legs that they
used to joke that they needed two people and a hydraulic
jack to get them on. Who on earth pulled Cleetie's stockings
up each morning—sumo wrestlers?

Whoever it was had also helped her into a black crepe
dress with a white linen-and-lace collar. Katharine wished
she had put on something dressier than black slacks and a
bright green shirt. It was some comfort that Dr. Flo wore
another bright cotton skirt and top, but she was family.
Katharine realized that Cleetie considered her visit a mo-
mentous event.

The woman must have been past seventy but her face was
plump, unlined, and ageless, surrounded by gray hair neatly
combed and waved around her face. "How do you do?" She
put out a hand the size of a salad plate. "I am Cleetie Webb."
Her voice was low and well modulated. Katharine wished
she had been able to hear Cleetie sing.

Katharine gave Cleetie her hand and murmured a greeting.
Cleetie waved her toward a nearby chair. "Have a seat, and
pardon me that I don't get up. My legs aren't what they used
to be. Florence said you want to talk to me about Alfred."

Dr. Flo, who had trotted through the small living room to
the adjoining kitchen, came back with several Krispy Kreme
doughnuts on a large plate and three smaller plates. "I'm
making coffee. It will be ready in a minute. But go ahead
and start on these. I picked them up on my way, and they
were piping hot when I got them." She distributed plates and
napkins and then passed the doughnuts. Katharine took one.

Cleetie took three and munched the first with strong
greedy teeth. "Don't tell Vicki and Latisha I ate these things,"

she warned Dr. Flo. She turned to Katharine to explain, "My granddaughters feed me the most gosh-awful things. If it wasn't for my girls and Florence, here, I'd have died of boredom years ago. Only pleasure I get anymore is eating—and talking. So ask me whatever it is you want to know."

Katharine chewed her lip. How frank could she be?

Cleetie seemed to understand her dilemma. "Anything at all." She waved a sugar-spotted hand. "Alfred has gone where nothing can ever hurt him again."

Dr. Flo rose. "I think the coffee ought to be finished. I'll be right back."

Katharine leaned forward in her chair. "I am trying to learn all I can about Carter Everanes. Do you believe that Alfred killed him?"

Cleetie shook her head without hesitation. "He couldn't have. For one thing, Alfred had an airtight alibi. He was at our aunt's for dinner that night. He picked me up and we rode the bus together, and we got there by seven. Mr. Everanes's sister testified she talked to him later than that. The jury thought we were all lying, of course, to save Alfred's skin, but it was gospel truth. And there's another reason I know Alfred didn't do it. He was terrified of guns. Our stepfather used to threaten him—" She heaved a sigh that made her enormous shelf of a bosom rise and fall. "Maybe I ought to just tell you about Alfred, and you can pick out what you want or need to know." She raised her voice. "Florence, I don't know how much of this you want to hear. Close your ears if you want to."

She settled back against her recliner and brushed specks of sugar icing off her black skirt. "When I was six and Alfred eight, Mama married a man named Ty Wilson. Ty started molesting Alfred almost as soon as he moved into the house, while Mama worked nights. I didn't know a thing about that at the time, of course. All I knew was that Ty made Alfred sleep with him and it made Alfred cry. When I begged him to let Alfred sleep with me like he always had, Ty said boys and girls shouldn't sleep together, it wasn't right." She worked her lips in distress at the memory.

"Sometimes Alfred used to beg to sleep on the couch. Ty would get out his gun and wave it around and he'd say, 'You do what I tell you, boy, or I'll give you what-for. And if you ever open your mouth about my private business, I'll blow your head off. You hear me?' I felt real left out, because Alfred knew Ty's private business and I didn't. Lordy, Lordy, how that sweet child suffered. Ty finally died when Alfred was fifteen, but Alfred never said a word about what had happened between them. Mama and I never suspected a thing until Alfred's trial. Then he told the court that he was a homosexual, and that he had become that way because our stepfather molested him for years when he was a child."

Cleetie stopped. For several minutes she stared out the window at the wreck of her neighborhood—or was it at the wreck of her brother's life? "Mama sat there with tears streaming down her cheeks, whispering, 'Oh, God, and I never knew. I never knew.' Until she died, she carried a broken heart at how that boy had suffered." She lifted a dark hand and shaded her eyes. It was several minutes before she spoke again.

"Of course, Alfred cooked his bacon in court by telling them what he was."

Dr. Flo spoke from the doorway, where she stood holding a tray of steaming mugs. "So why would he have said such a thing, then?"

"To explain why Mr. Everanes gave him a ring he was wearing—the one folks claimed he stole after he shot Mr. Everanes. Alfred's defense was that he and Mr. Everanes were lovers, and Mr. Everanes gave him the ring. Any fool would have known that defense wouldn't work. Homosexuality was a disgrace in both the black and the white communities in those days. People didn't talk about it, or admit it. Why his attorney let him testify that way, we'll never know. He could have said Mr. Everanes gave him the ring for Christmas or something and left it at that. Once he had accused Mr. Everanes of being homosexual, not one member of the jury or the judge, either, heard another word in his defense. They couldn't wait to get rid of a yard nigger who'd dare say things like that about a rich Atlanta lawyer." Her lips curved in a humorless smile. "Poor Alfred had the distinction of getting the fastest execution in Georgia history. Mama always said if they could have lynched him then and there, a lot of folks would have been pleased."

"He claimed Carter Everanes was homosexual?" Katharine tried to fit that piece into her puzzle. No wonder she had never heard Lucy or Walter mention him. That wasn't the sort of thing either of them would have discussed around a niece. She remembered a time when Jon had been writing a paper on gay rights in high school and his granddad had warned him in a mild voice, "Don't mention that subject around your grandmother's relatives, okay?" Katharine had presumed that was because they wouldn't be comfortable discussing sex in any form.

"Oh, yes," Cleetie said, reaching for her fifth doughnut. "Alfred claimed at the trial that he loved Mr. Everanes and Mr. Everanes loved him—that that was why Mr. Everanes had hired him in the first place. But if Alfred thought claiming to have been in love with his white boss was going to get him off, he was sorely disappointed." Her teeth bit into the doughnut like she would have preferred to crush jurors between those strong teeth.

A key turned in the lock and a fresh-faced boy of about nineteen looked in the door. "Hey, Granny, where'd you get that doughnut?" He noticed her visitors and turned to Dr. Flo in indignation. "You know Mama said she's not to have sugar."

"What's it gonna do, kill me?" his grandmother asked, reaching for a sixth. "I'm here to tell you, boy, I'd rather die eating a doughnut than linger several years eating healthy."

"Well, don't hog them," he told her. "Save some for me." He reached over and took one, perched on the couch and ate it, dripping sugar all over the rug.

"You got everything you needed to know?" Dr. Flo asked Katharine.

Katharine nodded. She had gotten far more than she needed to know.

Neither woman spoke for a long time on their drive back to Katharine's house. Dr. Flo broke the silence. "When I think how many years I wasted, moping around thinking the love of my life had died in the electric chair—and all the time, he wasn't interested in me at all." Her voice was so sad that Katharine looked out the window to give her privacy for her grief. Dr. Flo was silent again for several blocks, then spoke as if she was making a discovery while speaking. "Some good came out of it, though. I never had any interest in any other man until Maurice came along. I guess Alfred saved me for Maurice."

Katharine scarcely knew what she replied. Her thoughts were going around and around. If Carter was gay, he couldn't have been the little love of the Austrian woman. He must have stolen the diary as well as the necklace.

All she had to show for a difficult week was the name of the person to whom the necklace belonged and a house that had nearly been destroyed.

She wouldn't have minded never hearing Carter Everanes's name again. No wonder Aunt Lucy and Uncle Walter had stricken him from their lives.

Chapter 27

Misty greeted Katharine at the front door as she returned. "We finithed the upstairth. Do you want uth to clean up the attic?" That tongue stud could become annoying, Katharine thought as she followed Misty upstairs to take a look at the attic.

Once they stood in the dusty space, she had to confess, "The robbers didn't get this far—this is the way it always looks. I keep meaning to clean up here, but I never get around to it."

Misty wandered over to peer beneath old sheets at dresses they swathed. "Cool! You've got thum neat vintage dretheth up here." Katharine refrained from mentioning that most of them were her own prom dresses and formals. She didn't want to be classified as an antique.

While Misty examined dresses, Katharine wandered over and looked down at Dutch's boxes. She felt she ought to get them to Chap, although she doubted he'd want his father's old yearbooks. Yearbooks?

She knelt on the dusty floor and pulled open the first box.

She found what she wanted in the second: four Sewanee annuals. Dutch had already had the social instinct to keep track of people he knew, because he had bought one every year and collected signatures from every class. Katharine's dad used to claim that Dutch never forgot a person and was a world champion at networking. He'd parlayed those skills and connections into a successful investment firm.

She looked up as Misty said, "I geth I'll get back to work, then. What thould we do netht?"

"Shelve the books in the library," Katharine suggested.

"Okay. But if you ever want to thell any of theeth dretheth—"

"I'll call you first," Katharine promised. After all, you never knew when Tom might lose all his stocks and need a few dollars.

She carried the yearbook for '36–'37—Dutch's sophomore year—over to Tom's father's chair and wiped the dusty covers before she opened the book. Both inside covers, all the ads, and most of the activities pages were covered with scrawled messages. Many of the remarks were light and some were irreverent, but none were cruel. Dutch seemed to have been a favorite with all classes.

Two messages caught her eye. One was written in the lovely European script she was coming to know as well as her own. It read, "Come see me in Austria, Dutch. We will party all night long." It was signed "L¹." The other, written in a tall, skinny hand with compressed capitals, declared, "Gone but not forgotten. We're passing the torch, Dutch. Don't drop it!" That one was signed "L²."

L-one and L-two, not L-squared. Two men whose names both began with L.

Ludwig and . . . ?

Lee. Dutch and Maria had both mentioned him.

The diary had been Ludwig's, then. Not an Austrian woman, an Austrian man who liked men. No wonder Maria had been guarded when asked about Carter's friendship with him. Was it Carter he had seduced and then persuaded to love him? Was that why Carter had kept the diary, as a memory of his first love? Or had Carter stolen it as he had the necklace?

She looked through the junior class pictures and found Ludwig Ramsauer. He sported no beard, but the high forehead and humorous eyes were the same as in the newspaper clipping that Carter had slipped in the diary. Carter looked young in his picture, a bit ethereal. If he had been one of Jon's friends, she would have suspected he was gay. Had Ludwig merely awakened something that was already latent?

She also found Donk—Don K. Western—but didn't see his brother, Lee.

She flipped through all the classes. Lee Western did not appear.

Was he Donk's brother? She had presumed he was because Dutch and Maria had lumped them together as "Lee and Donk Western," but perhaps that was another tape from the past—two names spoken together so often they became one, like Kat-'n'-Hasty. She flipped through the entire junior class and came across several other names she remembered from Dutch's friends and acquaintances. She also saw Mr. Ivorie, already handsome but a lot less formidable than he would become. It took her two trips through the junior class to discover Leland Bradford.

Leland, shortened to Lee by his buddies. She studied the picture intently. This was the man who had convinced Ludwig's "little love" to come to Austria and be seduced? Who had bought supplies to blow up a bridge? Who had slept with Ludwig before the big love affair, but turned him down after the bridge exploded? That shy smile and the thick glasses were deceptive, good camouflage for the rake he had been.

Maybe it was because all those boys were younger than Jon, but to Katharine, Leland looked unfinished and callow, timid enough to run from a mouse. What had become of him? Had he died like the others? Or was he the sole survivor of their unholy band?

She stood to go downstairs and caught sight of her reflection in the mirror of an old oak dresser. In that light she again saw the woman with long dark hair and pale, thin face. Now she wore a worried expression. She looked like she wanted something from Katharine, but when Katharine moved closer to examine the image, her own face appeared. She had a smudge of dust on her chin.

She scrubbed her chin with her palm as she headed downstairs to call Hasty. She wanted to tell him what she had learned.

She tracked him down at his office.

"Tom get home last night?" he asked immediately.

"No, he's coming in tonight or first thing tomorrow."

"Tomorrow?" He swore.

She might berate Tom, but nobody else got that privilege. "He had important business to finish. I don't suppose you called your wife."

"Not yet. I've been busy."

"Yeah, well, I have, too. I have solved all our mysteries." She filled him in on what she had learned about Carter from Cleetie and what she had found in Dutch's old college yearbook. "So Carter may have been Ludwig's 'little love,'" she concluded.

"He was. I finished the diary late last night, and it's real clear about that at the end. I tried to call you this morning, but I guess you were at Cleetie's. I didn't like to leave a message, in case—"

He broke off, but she could finish the sentence. "In case Tom got it." With a pang, she realized their relaxed friendship was almost at an end. Once Tom got home—

Before she could fully explore that thought, he started talking again. "On the last page, there's a quote. The night before he left Austria, the 'little love' said, 'Ludwig, Hitler has come between us, but you will always be my heart and my life.' Then Ludwig wrote that he had decided to tuck the diary and 'a precious family heirloom Carter has often admired' into his luggage before he left."

"He mentioned Carter by name?"

"Absolutely. And quoted Carter using *his* name."

"So that's how Carter got the things. He didn't steal the necklace—it was a gift."

She was glad of that, but Hasty had other things on his mind. "That diary turned out to be dynamite in more ways than one."

"You mean the part about blowing up the bridge?"

"Not just that. Our friends were active little boys that fall. They started an avalanche, stopped a train, and set off a bomb in a village square late one night, all in the name of calling for revolution. Each of them seems to have had a specialty."

"Even Carter?" Katharine didn't know why she cared, but she did.

"No, Carter seems to have been fully preoccupied with his books. But as for the others, Ludwig scouted out the terrain and decided where to attack, Lee bought the explosives, Hans arranged transport, and Donk set the bombs. They apparently hoped to rouse Austria to side with Russia against Hitler. By late autumn, they tired of that and went to Spain to join the Communist forces there. Ludwig kept detailed reports of their daily activities for the rest of the year."

"Was Carter fighting in Spain?"

"No, though Ludwig spent weeks deploring the fact that he would not come, and agonizing that he himself would die alone on a Spanish plain far from the one he loved. It makes for torrid reading. But Ludwig also recorded every detail of their daily lives and battles. That makes fascinating reading. And he finally persuaded Carter to join him once the term was over."

"Poor Carter. Imagine surviving both the Spanish civil war and World War II, only to get shot in your own house. I wonder if there's any way to figure out what happened to him."

"You've got the mystery bug, Katie-bell. It was probably a good old home invasion, just like yours."

"But what about Dutch? Somebody murdered him."

"And I know you think his death is connected to the necklace, but it's probably nothing more than coincidence. Leave it to the police."

"I don't believe in coincidence. Daddy always said that what looks like coincidence is usually part of a plan we cannot see. These things are linked. I know it. And I'm getting convinced the key could be Lee. He has come up several times in conversation, and Dutch said he was going to try to get a hold of Lee and see what he might know. I wonder if he did."

"Did you run his name through a search engine?"

"On what? My computer is history."

"What's his full name again?"

"Leland Bradford."

"Wait a minute." She heard him typing, then pause. "The name is too common. There are almost forty thousand references, including some bigwig educator from the last century. Any idea how to narrow down the field?"

"No, but I've just had another idea about how to track him down. Napoleon Ivorie was in his class at college. Maybe he'd remember him."

"Good luck getting through. I've heard he's an absolute recluse by now. And if you do get through, are you going to tell him why you want to know?"

"I'll play that by ear. He may not remember them. Dutch said that Lee and Donk were kicked out after their junior year. But it's worth a try, don't you think? And I'm glad the diary turned out to be interesting after all."

"It's a terrific personal account of what was going on at that time in history."

"You may have it as a gift. I know Maria won't want it. But I'll copy the last page and send it to her with the necklace, to clear Carter's reputation."

"Who's Maria?"

Katharine had forgotten she hadn't told him about that call. "Ludwig's sister. Dutch tracked her down just before he died, through the Sewanee alumni office. I spoke with her yesterday, and she says Georg Ramsauer gave the necklace to one of his daughters—her 'many-times great-grandmudder'—as a wedding present. It's been handed down in their family for generations, and she thought Carter had stolen it. I told her I'd send it back—"

His voice was sharp. "It shouldn't be in private hands. It belongs in a museum."

"It belongs where it started out. We can't keep her necklace."

"It's not her necklace. Georg Ramsauer had no right to give it to his daughter."

"That's for the Austrians to decide, not you."

"Don't you mail it back to some old Austrian woman before I've spoken to the university lawyers."

"Emory has no claim on that necklace whatsoever. If any university is involved, it ought to be an Austrian one."

"Don't you mail it back. I'm warning you."

After all she'd been through that week, Hasty's threats didn't scare her.

Chapter 28

Another summer storm was brewing. The sky to the west was dark and thick with clouds.

She headed back to the kitchen phone and gathered her courage to call the Ivories. They intimidated her more than she liked to admit, but she owed it to them to tell them she had found the rightful owner of the necklace, and she had promised Amy to talk to Rowena about Zach's funeral. She would begin there.

She found Rowena's number in a club directory and told the secretary who answered that it was important that she speak to Rowena Slade on a matter of personal importance. She was both disgusted and amused at how gratified she felt when Rowena came on the line at once. "You rate, girl," she crowed silently.

"Is it about the necklace?" Rowena asked immediately.

"Only partly," Katharine admitted. "I have some information about it, but I mostly want to talk about Amy. She was over here yesterday and asked me to speak to you, but I'd rather do it in person. Would you mind if I ran over for a few minutes? This is terribly important to her."

"Amy?" Rowena sounded like she was trying to remember who Amy was or how Amy fit into her current schedule.

"Well, if you feel it's important, I'll be here the rest of the afternoon. Do you want to come over now?"

"Perfect. Thanks. I won't take up much time. But I need to ask one more favor, if I may. I need about five minutes with your father, to ask him a question relating to his college days. Do you think—?"

"Dad never sees anyone," Rowena's voice was brusque and final. "If you'll tell me what the question is, though, I will ask him and have an answer for you."

"Very well. I am trying to track down a man named Leland Bradford. I believe he may be connected with the history of that necklace, and I would very much like to talk to him. If your dad doesn't know how to get in touch with him, perhaps he could ask the Sewanee alumni office for a number. They are more likely to give it to him than to me."

Only a few minutes later, Rowena called her back. "Dad asks if you will stop by his house on your way to mine. He says he can give you an address and phone number for Leland Bradford." Her voice was puzzled. "I told him I'd give them to you, but he said he'd prefer to speak with you personally. You seem to have made a hit with him the other night."

Katharine was delighted. Once she got the address and phone number, she would turn them plus everything she knew and suspected over to the police who were investigating Dutch's death. That old laundryman might have even been Leland, who had gotten wind of her investigation and decided to eliminate Dutch, who might have known more than he had realized.

Before she went to the Hill, she decided to send Maria the necklace immediately, and mail the diary's final page later to clear Carter's name. It would be a lot easier to tell Rowena about Maria's claim to the necklace knowing it was already out of reach, so she couldn't pressure Katharine to change her mind. She would give Rowena Maria's address if she wanted to try and persuade her to sell. Picturing negotiations between those two, Katharine smiled. How sparks would fly!

She would not mention to Mr. Ivorie that Ludwig had given the necklace to Carter, though. Ivorie lawyers might argue that that gave Mr. Ivorie, the Everanes's closest living relative, a better claim to it than Maria—particularly if Carter had not willed it to Lucy but merely left it in the family home. Then it might not legally be part of Lucy's "bits and pieces," as she had called them. Katharine hadn't the foggiest notion how to find Carter's will, but she had no doubt that Ivorie lawyers could.

She retrieved the necklace from the bank and took it to a UPS store. In the parking lot she took it from its bag and held it to her neck once more. In the small rearview mirror, it looked more like a chain of slavery than something a lover would give a woman. She pitied any woman who had to wear it long. She held it a few minutes, though, trying to absorb its age and some sense of all those who had owned it since it was first forged. In the past week it had come to seem a part of her. Sending it away felt like sending Jon to China, except more permanent.

She carried it into the store and watched it being wrapped in several layers of bubble wrap and placed in an ordinary box. She told the man behind the counter that it was a piece of jewelry she had commissioned for a friend and casually insured it for two hundred dollars. When he tossed it into a bin with other boxes, she sent up a prayer that it would arrive safely.

As she left the store, she turned back in indecision. Had she been too impulsive? Too casual? Should she have insured it for thousands? Asked a museum to ship it for her? Waited to ask Tom what he thought she should do?

In the plate glass window she saw her reflection, peering in. At her shoulder stood a slender woman with long dark hair. She smiled and raised one hand.

Katharine turned, but there was no one there. When she looked back at the window again, only her own face peered back.

Entering the Hill was not for the fainthearted. A high brick wall and an equally tall metal gate obscured any view of what lay inside. A uniformed guard asked for her name, business, and picture ID and then walked around to peer into her car on both sides and at the back. Satisfied she was not carrying bombs, firearms, contagious plants, terrorists, homosexuals, illegal immigrants, or whatever else he was currently guarding the Ivories against, he pressed a button to open the gates and waved her through. When they closed behind her, Katharine considered turning around and heading home, but she had come this far. She might as well complete her errands.

Her hands began to sweat and her heart to drum as she drove down a short incline and around a bend. Then she was too enchanted to be nervous. Ahead of her the drive crossed the narrow end of a silver pond that gleamed and glittered to her left, lit by one ray of slanting light that pierced the lowering clouds. The drive then crossed a grassy meadow full of wild flowers and ran alongside a small orchard to the right, where a white van was parked and a man was spraying the trees. Beyond the orchard, the driveway climbed upward and curved toward three houses perched on a hill. The first was built of gray stone and stucco, with steep slate roofs and arched windows, and looked like a chateau airlifted from the Loire Valley of France. The one beyond it was Greek revival style, slightly smaller, but impressive nevertheless. The third was contemporary, all wood and glass. Massive trees framed all three houses.

As Katharine slowed, delighted by the view, thunder boomed overhead. A rabbit hopped alongside her car and across the meadow, and a bluebird darted toward a small birdhouse nailed to one of the peach trees, heading for cover ahead of the storm. They could have been out in middle Georgia somewhere. How many acres were inside these gates? Twenty?

Her nervousness returned as she pulled under the porte cochere of the first house and a uniformed man came to open her door. "Mr. Ivorie is expecting you. I will park your car."

Katharine wished she had changed into something dressier than the black pants and green shirt she had put on for Cleetie. For the second time that day, she felt like a Cinderella who had come to the ball underdressed. A burly man whom she presumed was the butler met her at the door, wearing a dark suit and white shirt. As he escorted her across a marble-tiled foyer, she saw Amy sitting with a book in a room to the right—a living room half as large as Katharine's whole downstairs. Katharine would have liked to inform Amy that she was heading to Rowena's later to present her request, but Amy didn't look up.

The butler ushered Katharine through wide double doors into a library Tom would covet, where long shelves of books rose twelve feet to a ceiling decorated with an ornate plaster medallion. Before Katharine could do more than glance around, the butler led her across thick red carpet to two black leather chairs placed to face long windows overlooking the meadow. Lightning flickered. Mr. Ivorie turned his head in the nearer chair. "Ah, Mrs. Murray. I am weary today, so I will not rise. Please excuse me." He looked hearty enough in a red silk dressing gown over a white shirt and black slacks, but his hand was dry and limp in hers. "I am so pleased you could come. Would you like coffee?"

Thunder rumbled while she hesitated, wondering what he would prefer. She didn't want to intrude too long on his time. He motioned to the butler. "Coffee for two, Styles." When the butler had moved out on soundless feet, the old man gave her his charming smile. "Welcome to the Hill."

"Your grounds are gorgeous," she told him, indicating the view. "I had no idea there was this much undeveloped land in the heart of Buckhead."

He chuckled. "The developers do—and drool."

While they waited for coffee, he spoke of his love of plants, of how he had planted the peach orchard with his own hands and tended the trees, trying to develop a new variety with deep pink meat. She told him about finding the book about Conrad Faire and his descendents and how surprised she had been to discover that he and Aunt Lucy had been cousins.

"Oh, yes, I grew up with Walter and Carter." He touched his fingertips to one another in a arch and looked far over the grounds as if he were looking down the years. "Walter and I grew apart after Carter's death, but we boys used to have some wonderful times down yonder in the meadow. We would set up our tents and pretend to be Billy the Kid and his cohorts, camping out to avoid the sheriff, or we'd swim and race canoes on the pond. I have always been sorry that Brandon didn't have cousins. There is a special bond that develops with those of your own blood." He looked up as Styles set a tray of coffee and assorted cookies on a table between them. When they each had a steaming cup, he murmured, "That will be all for now. Mrs. Murray and I want to speak privately." He turned to her. "Now, what was it you wanted to ask me? Oh, yes, about Leland Bradford. I called the college alumni office and got an address for him. He's in a nursing home up near Nashville. I have written it down for you." He took a folded piece of paper from a drawer in a table beside his chair and handed it to her. She slid it into her pocket to read later, and wondered how quickly she should drink her coffee and depart.

He forestalled her by asking, "Why do you want to speak to him?"

Those piercing silver-blue eyes compelled her to be frank. "Dutch Landrum told me Sunday night he would try to get in touch with Leland. I have been translating the diary I found with the necklace, and while I know you aren't interested in old books—"

He arrested her midsentence with a gesture of one hand. "I did not say I am not interested in old books." He waved toward the well-filled shelves around them. "As you see, I have a few. I just don't collect them seriously. But if this was the diary you found, the one Georg Ramsauer kept of his archeological excavations, I understood from Amy that it had been stolen."

"The diary was stolen, but fortunately I had made a copy."

"Ah, yes." He sipped his coffee. "I believe Amy mentioned that, as well. She has been full of stories about you and your family this week." He gave her a charming, frosty smile and his eyes twinkled.

Katharine was surprised Amy had had time to notice or hear anything at her house, considering how full her mind had been of Zach. She did not say that, however. Instead, she explained, "The diary turned out not to be the one from Hallstatt, as I first thought, but it may still be of some importance. It was the journal of Ludwig Ramsauer, a descendent of Georg. You may have known Ludwig—he studied at Sewanee for a year."

"Journaling seems to have to run in their family." His lifted his cup to his lips again, holding it in both hands because of tremors. "Were you able to translate this diary?"

"With the help of a friend. And as incredible as it may seem, Ludwig, several Austrian friends, and two of your classmates—Leland Bradford and Donk Western—were Communists and conducted a campaign of terror, protesting Hitler's influence in Austria. They spent several months in the summer and fall of 1937 blowing up things. According to Ludwig, Leland financed their enterprises, Donk set the explosives, and he chose the targets."

"Remarkable!" Mr. Ivorie paused in the process of lifting a delicate lemon cookie to his mouth. "Are you absolutely certain you translated that correctly? I knew Donk. He died in the war."

She smiled. "That's what Dutch kept saying about him, too."

"You tend to remember friends you have lost in combat. You are certain that Donk was part of this?"

"Pretty sure. Ludwig called him 'D' throughout, and Dutch ran into Donk and Leland over in Vienna that summer, with Carter and Ludwig. The diary says that they stayed all fall and eventually went to Spain for a time, to join the communist forces in the civil war."

"Fascinating." He again raised his cup to his lips with shaking hands. She looked away to give him privacy. He took a sip and returned the cup to its saucer with a delicate clicking like castanets. "But why should you care about that, especially after all these years? Are you a historian?"

"No, but my friend is. He teaches history at Emory and

actually did most of the translation. My German is poor and rusty."

He brushed a crumb from his leg. "Ludwig mentioned Leland Bradford by name?"

"No, he called him L^2. Apparently it was a nickname between them. It was Dutch who referred to 'Lee and Donk,' and in Dutch's Sewanee yearbook, I found messages from L^1 and L^2. The handwriting for L^1 was the same as Ludwig's in his diary."

"Fascinating," he repeated. He turned and looked over the lawn, where the first thick drops of rain were falling. "It sounds like you have been doing some pretty detective work this week, Mrs. Murray. This is one of the most interesting—and disturbing—stories I have heard in a long time. It is hard to believe about people I once knew. And now, you think if you can speak with Leland—what? He will fill in more details for your friend to write a book? Confess to what they did? What help do you expect him to give you, if he can?"

She hesitated. "I don't know how much news you keep up with—"

"Very little, any more, except what my family brings me. They are carrying on things these days. I sit here and enjoy the wildflowers and the butterflies, putter a bit in my orchard, hit a few golf balls—"

A loud clap of thunder interrupted him and he chuckled. "Although, before I am struck by lightning, I'll confess I no longer am able to play. There is little I am able to do anymore. My life is very restricted, and almost over." One hand stroked the arm of his chair.

She felt a twinge of pity. His mind seemed as vibrant as ever. What a shame that his body had let him down.

"But you were going to tell me some news?" he asked.

"Dutch Landrum was murdered Monday morning," she said as gently as she knew how.

He grew very still. "Oh, my! You are certain it was murder?"

She nodded. "Somebody impersonating a laundryman went to his apartment and strangled him with his own tie. But the evening before, Dutch had told me he was going to try and get in touch with Leland. I want to know if he did, and if Leland has any information that might help the police solve Dutch's murder."

His white brows rose an inch. "Surely you don't suspect Leland of murdering Dutch? It would be rather difficult, don't you think, from a nursing home in Nashville? And aren't you a little concerned that if Dutch got killed after asking questions, you yourself might be in danger?"

She gave him a rueful nod. "I'm being very careful—especially since I've had a couple of break-ins that may be connected to the necklace. Zachary Andrews—" She paused, wondering how much he already knew and how much risk she ran of upsetting him too much by what she was about to say. "Zach broke into my house Friday evening and took the diary. At least, I presume he did, although the police didn't find it, because he also took a jade collection they recovered from his car."

"How infuriating!" he exclaimed. "Amy said something about hoodlums destroying your home."

"That was Monday morning, after Zach was dead. It may have been a random home invasion."

"Did they get the necklace?" His voice was anxious.

"No, I had taken it to my safe-deposit box."

"Very wise. Now, back to Leland. When you see him—"

"I don't plan to see him. All I want is to give the police information about how to reach him. I really appreciate your getting that for me. And I'd better be going. Rowena is expecting me." She started to stand, but he waved her back to her seat.

"Not so fast. In exchange for the number, I want to know about the necklace. Have you had any success in learning where it came from and whether it is genuine? And are you ready to sell?"

"Yes, yes, and no. It did come from Hallstatt and was given by Georg Ramsauer to one of his daughters as a wedding present. It has been passed down in their family ever since, so I think its authenticity would not be hard to establish. But I have spoken with Ludwig's sister. She told me Carter lived with them one winter, and she thought he had stolen it from them. She was delighted to know it had turned up. I have promised to send it to her. You will need to contact her to see if it's for sale, but I failed to bring her address with me. I'll send it to you."

His hand reached out and stroked hers with a whisper of dry skin. His felt as delicate as fine china. "My dear, when you have lived as long as I have, you will learn not to be so trusting of people. I knew Carter well. He was no thief.

Katharine opened her mouth to explain that Ludwig had given Carter the necklace, but he gave her no chance.

"Before you do anything rash, let me give you the name of somebody who can take a look at the necklace and authenticate it, then we can discuss the ramifications of this story of hers."

He opened the drawer again, to take out a pad of paper and a pen. He wrote a name, and handed it to her. He had written "Dr. Donald Donns." All three capitals were long and compressed, exactly like the "*D*" in the greeting in Dutch's yearbook from L^2.

She stared, puzzled. Then she began to tremble. Was her

heart beating loudly enough for him to hear? She wasn't sure her legs would hold her, but she stood and said in a party voice not unlike Amy's a few days before. "Thank you so much, but I've already arranged to return the necklace to Ludwig's family. I really appreciate your getting me Leland Bradford's address. Now I need to be going. Rowena is expecting me."

She had been taking small baby steps away from him. As she turned, he called her back, his voice like silk. "Stay, Mrs. Murray." When she looked around, he was piercing her with those frosty eyes. "You have seen my handwriting before?"

Again he compelled frankness. She nodded.

He reached into the drawer and took out a small book bound in caramel leather. "And you recognize this, I presume?" He didn't give her time to reply. "I should have realized that Ludwig would put everything down in those daily scribbles of his. It is unfortunate you made a copy—and shared it with that history professor. Which one was it, again?"

His voice was so persuasive, she almost answered before she knew it. At the last second, she bit her tongue.

"It doesn't matter. Amy has prattled about you and that history professor for days. She will remember his name. Please be seated while we consider what to do about this situation."

Katharine was glad to sit. Her knees had turned to sponge and her mind whirled as she tried to put these last senseless pieces into the puzzle.

Napoleon Ivorie leaned toward her in his chair. "Tell me again how you arrived at the conclusion that it was Leland Bradford who was involved in the Austrian activities. Did Dutch tell you that?"

The silver eyes were mesmerizing. Katharine could no more refuse to answer than she could will her own heart to stop. "No, but Dutch talked about 'Lee' as part of the group. I looked for a Lee in Dutch's yearbook after he died, and Leland seemed to be the only one who—" Her voice betrayed her. It would not go on.

"The same yearbook where you read greetings to Dutch from L^1 and L^2?"

She was surprised she could nod. Every cell in her body felt paralyzed.

"Pity. Boys can be so very foolish when they are young. Make up pet names, write things, keep things—" His eyes did not leave hers, but in her peripheral vision she saw him reach into the drawer again and bring out something that glinted as he slid it down beside him in his chair. "Old men can be foolish, too. I have found it necessary to do some things for myself these past few days, and it became a habit. I should have let Styles write down that address for me. Now you have concluded that perhaps Leland Bradford was not the only Lee in our class."

She nodded.

He gave a slight shrug. "When you are something-the-third, the family has to stretch for a name to call you. My grandfather was called Napoleon, my father, Leon. My mother balked at Nap, so I became Lee. After my father died, during the war, when I took over the business, I became Napoleon. Nobody nowadays remembers me as Lee except a few old high school and college chums. Almost none of them are left."

So many things ought to have alerted her. Dutch had spoken of "Lee" in a familiar voice, as if it were a name she would recognize. Her mother would have, perhaps, and Walter, Sara Claire, and Lucy. Would she have as well, if she had paid closer attention to the conversations of grownups around her?

She'd been right about Zach, too—but she had thought he was working for Brandon, seeking the necklace for his grandfather. She had focused on the necklace when it was the diary that was more important. It had the power to damn.

The old man turned and stared out the window while tapping one slender finger against his lips. "I was a wild, unruly youth, willing to try almost any forbidden fruit. I came to my senses during the war and returned to the convictions of my parents and grandparents, and I have lived a life worthy of them for nearly seventy years. However, if word of my youthful—ah—indiscretions were to get out, they would give the press levers it could use to smear not only me but also the fine work of our foundation. And Brandon—" He paused. "Brandon has always admired me and modeled himself after me. I would hate for him to learn that his grandfather had been guilty of—you know of what I speak."

Katharine gave him a reluctant nod.

"So the question is," he said in a gentle, conversational tone, "what to do with you. Even if you were to promise to keep all his to yourself, I dare not trust your word. And I certainly cannot trust that of a history professor whom I have not met. You have put me in an awkward position. I hope you can see that."

"No more awkward than mine," she retorted, surprised at her own daring.

He smiled. "Spirited to the end."

She didn't like the sound of that. She started to rise again, but from beside him in the chair he brought a small silver pistol. "Please stay where you are."

Katharine had heard that little guns seldom killed people, simply injured them, but she didn't feel like testing that theory. She resumed her seat. Dear God, how was she going to get out of there? How had she walked into this without seeing it coming?

She dragged her attention back to Mr. Ivorie, who was looking at her like he was waiting for her to come up with a solution to their dilemma.

"I have no interest in washing your dirty linen in public," she informed him coldly. "What you did seventy years ago is between you and your Maker."

"Since you aren't likely to spread the word, I can confess to you that I don't believe in a maker. The only almighty I believe in is the almighty dollar. That faith has served me well."

"I had guessed as much." She was surprised how calm she sounded when her whole being was screaming, "God! Where are you? Help!"

His eyebrows rose in surprise. "How did I give myself away? The Ivories have always been strong supporters of the church."

"While serving its greatest enemy, the Prince of hatred and lies."

"Surely you don't refer to the Devil? I don't believe in fairy tales."

"Some fairy tales are ancient truths in fancy trappings. And truths in which we don't believe can be our downfall."

He gave her another frosty smile. "I congratulate you! You spar like your father. I always did enjoy a conversation with him. I regret that we must bring this one to an end. However, it is not only what happened seventy years ago that concerns me. You have stirred up a lot of trouble these past few days, my dear, and you know too much. I cannot let you go. You are an intelligent woman. I am certain you can understand why."

"Dutch?" The word rose from her lips unbidden, but he

was not listening. He had inclined his head to the two men who came through a small door that had swung out from the shelves in the far wall. Katharine had not seen him summon them and he had certainly given them no instructions, but as they advanced on her, she saw that one carried a length of nylon rope and the other a gun that looked far more business-like than Mr. Ivorie's silver toy.

Mr. Ivorie spoke to them in a pleasant tone. "You know what to do. But remember, no pain. I respected her father." He laid the little silver pistol beside him on the table and turned to the window. She had the same feeling she had had at the club. Their interview was over and his attention had moved on to other things.

"Come," barked the man with the rope. He reached for her. Katharine pressed back into the chair. "Come," he said again. He jerked her up, pulled both hands behind her, and tied them. She cried out as the rope cut into her skin.

"No pain," Mr. Ivorie said again, almost absently. "I told you, no pain."

The man loosened the knots slightly, then took her elbow and marched her toward the little door.

Her options were few, but she had one. She opened her mouth and screamed.

Chapter 29

The man who held her covered her mouth with a broad, salty hand and clutched so hard his fingers dug into her cheek. She opened her jaws and bit his palm, hard. That gained her just enough time to shriek, "Amy, help!" before he grabbed her in a hammerlock that cut off her air.

Thunder crashed beyond the windows. Lightning lit up the room.

"She's a feisty one," he told Mr. Ivorie as Katharine struggled to breathe.

"No pain," Mr. Ivorie repeated—but automatically, as if his mind was far away.

"Papa?" Amy burst in from the hall. "Are you all right?"

Katharine twisted in her captor's arms, for she could not get enough air to scream again. Her movement attracted Amy's attention. "What's going on? Papa!" When he didn't reply, she ran toward the bodyguards. "Let her go, Clark! At once! Let her go." She pounded his arm with her fists.

He let his arm fall from Katharine's neck and she gulped in huge swallows of air. The man with the gun stepped back and held it behind him, out of Amy's sight but where Katharine could see it. Mr. Ivorie spoke sternly. "This does not concern you, Amy."

"They're going to kill me," Katharine gasped. "Please, they will kill me."

"Why should they kill you?" Amy's voice contained the curiosity of a child's.

As she moved toward Katharine, her grandfather repeated, "This does not concern you." Amy wavered and took a step back.

"He killed Zach." Katharine said urgently. "I can prove it."

"Zach?" Amy turned whiter than the plaster medallion and her eyes darted from Katharine to the two bodyguards to her grandfather. "Papa, did they kill Zach?"

"On your grandfather's orders," Katharine added.

"That's enough out of you," the bodyguard growled to Katharine. "Come on, time to go." He started to march her toward the small door in the shelves. She struggled, but his grip was tight.

"No!" Amy dashed to the table and picked up the little gun. She waved it toward the bodyguards. "Let her go! She's my friend! Tell them, Papa. She's my friend."

Katharine had not improved her position. She now stood between Amy and her targets and Amy trembled from head to toe.

The man holding Katharine spoke in the gentle tone of a friend. "Put the gun down, Amy. You can't hit anybody from there. And this is your granddaddy's business."

Amy aimed the gun at her grandfather. "Papa? You didn't tell them to kill Zach, did you? Did you?"

"Put down the gun." His voice was stern and did not tremble.

Hers grew wild. "I will kill you if you did, and kill myself! If you killed Zach, I don't want to live." Tears streamed down her cheeks. "You didn't, did you, Papa? Tell me you didn't!" She waved the gun in his face.

The man with the gun started toward her in a purposeful stride. Amy could not see his gun, but Katharine could, and his finger was tense on the trigger. Katharine gave a little moan of protest.

Amy whirled and saw him advancing. "Don't come any closer, Brick!" she shrieked, "and make Clark let Mrs. Murray go!" He kept walking. Amy squeezed the trigger.

Brick fell to the floor grabbing his knee. The acrid smell of gunpowder filled the room. Clark released Katharine and lunged toward Amy. She fired again. He clutched his shoulder, but bent to snatch up Brick's dropped gun.

"No!" Mr. Ivorie roared "Clark, no!"

"What on earth is going on in here?" Rowena Slade stood in the double doors. "Amy! What are you doing? Put that gun down at once."

"No!" Amy waved it between her grandfather and her mother. "Papa killed Zach, Mrs. Murray says. Did you know, Mama? Did you find out about us and tell Papa to kill him? Tell me!" She stamped her foot. "If you did, I'm going to shoot all of us!" Tears streamed down her cheeks and she waved the gun wildly. Her grandfather reached for it, but she aimed it straight for his forehead. "Don't you touch me, Papa. I warn you. And don't hurt Mrs. Murray. She's my friend. Mama, don't let them hurt her!"

"Put down the gun. Nobody is going to hurt anybody." Rowena spoke with authority. Amy lowered the gun and stepped beyond her grandfather's reach. Rowena frowned at the bodyguards. "You all are dripping blood all over the carpet." She went to the desk and pressed a button. "Mrs. Goodwill, please come see to Brick and Clark. They have had an accident."

Nobody spoke until an elderly woman in a gray uniform and white apron bustled in. "Oh, dear, oh, dear. Come with me, boys, and we'll fix you up. Oh, dear." She bustled through the small door in the bookshelves, shooing the burly bodyguard named Clark before her like a chick. Brick paused long enough to retrieve his gun, then limped after them.

Katharine started for the main door but Rowena held up her hand. "Please don't go until you tell me what all this is about." She motioned Katharine toward a chair across the room, but Katharine could not walk. Her knees buckled and she would have fallen if Rowena had not caught her and helped her into the seat.

"Now," Rowena said, frowning at her father. "Whatever is going on, let us talk about it like civilized people."

"The time to talk like civilized people is past, my dear." He turned and looked out the window, as if the others were actors on a television show that no longer held his interest. He paid no attention even to Amy, who still clutched the little silver gun. It wobbled dangerously in her hands, and her face frightened Katharine.

Rowena said sharply, "Amy, put down that gun. You are making me nervous." She spoke as if her daughter was five, not twenty-two, and held nothing more dangerous than a water pistol. Amy made a sulky mouth and went to sit on the other side of the library, but kept the gun in her lap.

"Now, what is this all about?" Rowena paced between the three of them and waited for answers.

Katharine felt wearier than she had ever felt in her life, but when nobody else answered, she spoke. "The necklace and the diary. Terrorism and seduction. Secrets long buried, now come to light. Murder, and deceit."

Rowena zeroed in on the thing that interested her most. "Is the necklace authenticated? Is it for sale?"

"It's authenticated but it's not for sale. It belongs to a family in Austria. They want it back."

Rowena was, first and foremost, her father's daughter. "Can they prove their claim?" When Katharine nodded, she asked, "So what do you want?"

Katharine sat there enjoying the simple act of breathing. Was there anything more precious? What else could she possibly want?

To leave that house alive topped the list. No matter what the social register might say, these were not nice people. But she wanted something more.

"Justice," she said slowly, "for at least two people who have been murdered. Perhaps four. And an end to hypocrisy."

"Hypocrisy?" Rowena raised her perfect brows.

"I was robbed Friday night," Katharine said in answer. "Zachary Andrews did it."

"No!" Amy cried. "He wouldn't!"

"I'm afraid so," Katharine told her. "They found our jade in his car, and he took the diary, as well. I thought it was the necklace he was after, but it was the diary."

"The diary was worth more than the necklace?" Rowena clearly didn't believe it.

"Ask him." Katharine nodded toward Mr. Ivorie. "Ask why he sent Zach to steal the diary. It's there, on his table. Ask why he killed Zach, or had him killed, afterwards. Ask why he sent a truckload of goons to my house to destroy it in the process of looking for the necklace and copies Amy knew I had made of the diary. Ask why he killed his old friend, Dutch Landrum," she had to pause to steady her voice, "if not to prevent Dutch talking to me about all this."

"Daddy?" Rowena asked, clearly thinking Katharine had lost her mind.

Amy watched with wide, terrified eyes.

"She has no proof whatsoever," he said abruptly. "Comes in here making accusations without one shred of proof. "

"Do you read German?" Katharine asked Rowena. When Rowena nodded, she said, "Pick up that diary and open it at random. Read the entry for August 15—dated 15/8."

Mr. Ivorie put out his hand but Rowena snatched the diary first and opened it.

"Tomorrow we blow up the bridge," she read, then paused and bent her head. She turned the page, scanned it, and looked back at Katharine. "It sounds like a gang of terrorists."

Katharine nodded. "Do you see the name L^2 on the page?" When Rowena nodded, she said, "I can prove that your father was L^2 and that the diary was written by a man named Ludwig Ramsauer. Now read the next day's entry—the one about the party." Rowena scanned the page and her eyes widened. "Daddy?"

He said nothing, but what she read in his eyes enraged her. "You did these things? Blew up bridges?"

He waved her away like a troublesome fly. "We were fighting Hitler."

"One man's terrorist is another man's patriot," Katharine murmured.

Rowena waved the diary in his face. "You slept with men?"

"And lured his cousin Carter to Vienna to be seduced by Ludwig," Katharine added in a flat, weary voice.

"Daddy?" Rowena's voice was harsh and raw.

He turned away. "It's a long time ago. I was young and foolish."

Her eyes flashed like lightning. "I was once young, too. But did I get to be foolish? Could I even marry the man I loved and live with him? Oh, no. Married today, divorced tomorrow, with good old Daddy in control. Daddy the Righteous, god on my Olympus, arranging my life so I could grow up to be just like him. And poor Joe," her voice trembled with passion, "paid off and sent packing like poor white trash. While you—you—"

"It was for your own good," he said. "You would never have been happy. He'd have bored you in a year."

"But that would have been my decision, wouldn't it? You got to make your mistakes. The rest of us never got a chance. You make me sick!" She flung the diary away from her and stalked to the far end of the room.

"Did you really kill Zach?" Amy crept over to her grandfather and peered down at him. "I loved him, you know. I was going to marry him."

"Don't be ridiculous," her mother snapped, diverted from her rage. "You are far too young to be thinking of marriage—especially to somebody like Zach." She continued to pace.

Amy stared down at her grandfather. Then deliberately she lifted the gun, pressed it to his forehead, and squeezed the trigger.

"No!" Katharine leaped from her seat. But nothing happened. The gun made only a small click.

Mr. Ivorie put out his hand. "It had only two bullets in it. Now give it to me, Amy, and run along. And send in your brother."

"I hate you." Her voice was calm. She laid down the gun, turned, and walked from the room.

"You wanted me?" Brandon asked at the door a few minutes later.

"Come in and sit down," his grandfather said. "Mrs. Murray has something to say to us all. Tell your story, Katharine. That's what you came to do, isn't it?"

As Katharine recalled, she had come to get a number for Leland Bradford. That seemed at least a week ago.

"I'll tell the story." Rowena's color was high and her eyes glittered. "This man—this man who has set himself up all these years as a pillar of righteousness, a hero for the rest of us to emulate, the be-all and end-all of morality—this man, the epitome of values in this family and many others, was, in his youth, a terrorist, a homosexual, and a panderer."

Brandon made a strangled protest. Rowena picked up the book and gestured with it. "This diary gives chapter and verse of his depravity. He hired Zach to steal it last Friday while we were at the dinner meeting—which is why Zach never came with your speech. He apparently met Zach afterwards or had Brick meet him to get the diary, then someone shot Zach so he tumbled down that embankment where he was found. Katharine claims that he also sent goons to vandalize her home and try to get copies of the diary, and—what else, Katharine?"

"Someone went to Dutch Landrum's Monday morning in a white van pretending to be from his laundry, and they choked him with a tie he kept on the door."

"Which might explain," Rowena said to Brandon in a voice like crystal, "why the gardener's van wasn't available to carry your picket signs and materials down to the protest march and why Daddy was 'indisposed' all morning." She threw her father a look of contempt.

"Did you also kill Carter?" Katharine asked Napoleon. "I would like to know. Did you let Alfred Simms go to the electric chair for a murder you committed?"

"Carter was supposed to have the necklace and the diary," Mr. Ivorie explained, as if they were discussing the weather. "That's what Ludwig said. He gave them to Carter."

"When did you speak with Ludwig? Was it when you

went to Austria to stage that climbing accident? The fall of the man who never went on the mountains alone, but who could ruin you if he chose? Did you then send Carter that clipping about his death?" She nodded toward the diary.

His only acknowledgment was a slight movement of one hand. Katharine pressed on. "Did Carter then call to ask if you knew anything about that? Maybe suggest a drink together to grieve an old friend?"

"The necklace and diary were not in his house." Napoleon spoke to himself, gazing out across his lovely lawn toward the lake. "Ludwig said he gave them to Carter, but they were not there." His voice sounded distant, as if coming from far down the tunnel of time.

"Maybe because Carter had given them to Lucy," Katharine suggested, "or stored them in the attic of their family home. Maybe Lucy found them when she cleared out her house, and took them with her to Autumn Village because they were all she had of Carter." She stopped.

He said nothing.

"Mrs. Murray!" Brandon leaned forward in his chair with his hands clasped in front of him. "These are some real serious accusations you are making. I want to remind you that there are severe penalties in this state for slander. My grandfather has led an exemplary life. Many people will attest to that. If any of what you have said or implied is ever spoken beyond this room, I want you to know that I personally will prosecute you to the fullest extent of the law. And you, Mama, give me that book. It's filthy, and deserves to be burned. I don't ever want to hear those lies you were telling again. You hear me? Not one word."

Rowena stared down at him. "You're a chip off the old block, aren't you, boy? The trouble is, the block is cracked, flawed to the core. What is it the Bible says?" She turned to

Katharine. "We don't really believe in it, honey, but we can sure quote it. 'The sins of the fathers will be visited on the children to the third generation.' Isn't that how it goes? Well, Daddy, you had your fun and did your sinning. The rest of us are paying for it."

"Mama!" Brandon said urgently.

She looked down at him with a sad smile. "Your daddy was a wonderful man. I wish you had known him. Oh, I wish—" Her voice broke. The diary fell to the floor as she turned away, covering her face with her hands. Tears flowed between her fingers.

Katharine stood and walked from the room. Just beyond the doors she took a quick look around the foyer to be sure the bodyguards were not around. The butler was nowhere to be seen, either, so she walked alone toward the door. If she got out of the grounds alive, she would go to the police. She would take them what she knew and show them the proofs she had. And no matter how long it took, she and Dr. Flo would clear Alfred Simms's name.

As she reached the front door, she heard a voice behind her. "Goodbye, Mrs. Murray." She turned in time to see Amy slip back into the library. As the door closed behind her, Katharine heard shots. She did not turn back.

Chapter 30

Friday, June 16

"Mr. Ivorie wants to see you." The voice on the phone was cool, professional, belonging to a woman who dealt with pain and death every day.

Katharine froze. Then she recalled that Napoleon Ivorie was no longer a threat to her. He lay, critically wounded, in intensive care at Piedmont Hospital with guards at his door, accused of attempted abduction and murder. The police had all her proofs and the complete story, including one copy of the diary and photographs of the rope burns on her wrists and bruises on her cheek where Clark had held her. Leona, the receptionist at Autumn Village, had positively picked out Napoleon's picture from a photographic lineup. "I'd know them eyebrows anywhere," she had exclaimed. As Katharine had suspected, killing Dutch was one of the things the old man had done for himself. Whether his lawyers could get him off was moot. Nobody expected him to live long enough to stand trial.

The press had reported Rowena Slade's version of how Napoleon had been wounded. "My daughter Amy accidentally shot my father and herself with his bodyguard's gun, which the bodyguard had laid aside while being bandaged for a self-inflicted wound. Amy did not realize the gun was loaded."

Poor Amy, Katharine thought—as inept at shooting people as she was at everything else, and still being wrapped in cotton wool and money. Her grand gesture would ultimately kill her grandfather, but having only a vague understanding of anatomy, she had managed to shoot herself only through the shoulder, not the heart, and would soon be released from the hospital to face whatever charges the D. A. decided to bring.

Rowena had stuck by her story even when Brandon tried to insist it was Katharine who shot his grandfather and Amy and then dashed to her car and got through the gates before they could order the guard to stop her. But Rowena visited her father daily. Brandon had not yet come. He was too busy fending off reporters who were having a field day with rumors about Napoleon Ivorie's past—rumors that must have leaked from Katharine's statement to the police, but which Brandon laid at her door every chance he got to speak. "That godless liberal," he raved, "spreading lies about our family." She wore the title proudly, considering the source.

She drove to the hospital and found the room. The guard at the door checked her ID and told her, "Five minutes. Doctor's orders." He added in a tone too low to be overheard, "Good thing the kid's hand trembled, or he'd be dead already. Still not likely to make it, you know."

With a bandage covering most of his chest and tubes sprouting from his cavities, Napoleon looked so old and vulnerable that Katharine felt a pang of pity. He reminded her of her father, and Dutch, and Uncle Walter. What were they called? The greatest generation?

Then he opened his eyes and his frosty gaze glittered. He gasped for air between snatches of words. "So, Mrs. Murray—you have—won. Satisfied?"

"Satisfied?" She shook her head. "No. Not satisfied. And I'm very sorry for Rowena and Amy."

"Amy is—weak." His graceful fingers played with his top sheet, clutching and unclutching. After a lifetime of gathering power, all he had left to cling to was a sheet. His voice was bitter as he went on, "—spineless—like her dad." He paused to take several shallow breaths. "What more—do you want?" *Gasp.* "Confession?" *Gasp.* "Repentance?" He attempted a chuckle, but achieved only a series of faint coughs.

She considered. "Repentance is always good. But what I'd really like to see would be a little compassion—compassion for Dutch, Alfred, Zachary, Carter, and Ludwig. For Amy, and your bodyguards. For poor Rowena. And a little— at least a little—for yourself."

His lips curved in a sardonic smile. "None—for Brandon?"

Her mouth twisted. "I've never cared for Brandon very much."

His hands continued to play with his sheet. "Take—more." His head jerked slightly toward a bedside table. "Drawer." He struggled for air while she opened it and lifted out the caramel leather diary. "Give—to your—professor." *Gasp.* "Won't matter—soon." *Gasp.* "Sign paper."

She saw a paper folded inside, and took it out. It was a promise that she would not permit the contents of the diary to be published for twenty-five years. She found a pen and signed, then put the document back in the drawer and balanced the diary in one hand. The leather was cool and impersonal in her palm. "Five lives for a bit of history," she mused sadly. "Not a very fair exchange."

"All I—have left."

"You have one more thing—the Ivorie Foundation. Give it

to Rowena. She'd run it well, and fairly. And people like her."

"She's—a woman."

"She's the best thing you ever did. Is it a deal?"

He turned his head away.

She waited, in case he had more to say, but he did not. She had been dismissed.

"God have mercy on your soul," she murmured as she prepared to leave.

"Never—cared about—God." His breath was labored.

She bent and kissed the top of his white hair. It was as soft as her father's had been at the end. "That doesn't matter," she told him, smoothing down a strand where she had mussed it. "God cares about you."

She reached the door before he spoke again, one breathy word. "Deal."

She carried the diary to her car and called Hasty's cell phone. "Where are you?" he demanded. "And what's going on? I didn't like to call you—"

In case Tom answered. He didn't have to say it.

"At Piedmont Hospital," she replied. "I've just had an audience with his majesty. He asked to see me."

"How's he doing? I read in the paper he got shot."

"Not well. They don't think he's going to make it. More important, he doesn't think he's going to make it. Old people often know these things."

"So, did Tom ever get back to town?" He was casual. Too casual.

"Last night." On the first plane he could catch after they had talked—having arranged for somebody else to handle his important meeting. He had been at Posey's when she had gotten back from the Ivories' and Katharine had never been so glad to see him in her life.

"I suppose you welcomed him with open arms and forgave everything?"

"I was glad to see him," she agreed without going into details. "He's over at the house as we speak, seeing to things, talking with the adjuster and making him recalculate everything. He's going to meet me at Dutch's funeral, so I can't talk long. Did you ever call your wife and daughter about coming down?"

"Not yet."

"Well, when they get to town, give me a call. You all can come over for supper and a swim, and I'll give you Ludwig's diary. The real diary."

"The real diary?" His voice was shrill with excitement. "Not a copy?"

"Nope. Mr. Ivorie wants you to have it. He was Lee, Hasty. Napoleon Ivorie was Lee."

He took several seconds to digest that. "Son of a gun," he finally murmured. "Why don't I meet you somewhere and you can tell all and hand it over?"

"Because for the next two hours I'll be at Dutch's funeral and the cemetery. Then I'll be packing. After that Tom and I are going up to our house at the lake. I plan to spend next week sitting on the porch drinking gin and tonics and watching ducks while he commutes back home to deal with the mess. We'll come back next Friday, and after that, come anytime. Bring one wife and daughter, and the diary is yours. There's just one catch—you can't publish anything from it for twenty-five years. I figure that'll give you something to look forward to in retirement."

He was silent, but the silence on the line felt familiar. She

and Hasty used to commune silently on the phone for minutes on end, just listening to each other breathe and feeling
each other there. Finally he asked, "What about the necklace? If Mr. Ivorie can't buy it—"

"The necklace is on its way back to its lawful owner as we
speak. I sent it yesterday."

She ignored all the nasty things he said about her just
then. Having failed to forgive Hasty once, she had no intention of making the same mistake twice.

Finally he said thoughtfully, "It might be good for my
wife to meet you. Might set her mind at ease."

"Not the most complimentary thing you've ever said," she
chided him.

"I didn't mean it like that. I just meant that she'd see you
aren't competition—"

"Dig that hole a little deeper and you won't ever get out."

"Oh, hell, she'll see you aren't the least bit interested in
me. Do I have to say it straight out?"

"I'm very interested in you—as a friend." She said it
firmly. She needed to believe that as much as he did.